ALSEA RISING

GATHERING STORM

FLETCHER DELANCEY

HEARTSOME PUBLISHING

To the readers, those honorary citizens of Alsea.

CONTENTS

PREFACE

As an English literature major, I was compelled to read various poems, most of which I found taxing exercises in patience. There were exceptions, of course: I am forever fond of Emily Dickinson for her brevity. At the other extreme was T.S. Eliot, who never saw a direct path that couldn't be replaced with a thousand words of tortuous meanderings. Yet from those piles of words, one could occasionally excavate a shining jewel. This one, from "Little Gidding," has stayed with me ever since.

> *We shall not cease from exploration*
> *And the end of all our exploring*
> *Will be to arrive where we started*
> *And know the place for the first time.*

The Chronicles of Alsea have been an exploration. With *Alsea Rising*, we are arriving where we started, at the beginning of the end.

If those words alarm you, remember the first line: we shall not cease. Alsea still has many tales to tell, and I already have the next series (or two) planned. We will see these characters again, even as we meet new ones and explore different parts of Alsea and the universe it inhabits. This is not good-bye.

What is it, then?

It is answers to questions that have been asked throughout the series. Resolutions to long-standing story arcs. Further growth of characters we have watched learn and change since their first appearances. It is an exploration of faith versus science, or perhaps faith *and* science, because Alseans know better than most that the two are not mutually exclusive.

It is the closing of a circle that opened with the crash of a ship—and the beginning of a new era.

Perhaps, then, it is not the beginning of the end but the end of the beginning.

Alsea Rising would not have been possible without my Prime Beta, Karyn Aho, and her in-depth analyses of the chapters I sent across one ocean and one continent. We met because of my stories. Eleven years later, I am proud to call her my best friend.

Rick Taylor lent his eye to the narrative structure and caused me a great deal of work when he pointed out a few shortcomings. For an accuracy check when it came to navy-based hierarchies, expectations, and terminology, I turned to the life experience of Ree McSween, Veteran, Gunner's Mate Second Class, USCG.

There is also quite a lot of flying in *Alsea Rising*, and while I do have experience piloting a two-seater Cessna, that only helped with basic physics. Putting readers into a military jet required the input of Maj. Chris Butler, USAF, Retired. Thanks to him, I can now label the parts of an F-16 control stick, including the pickle button—a name I *really* wanted to use but could find no justification for. Alseans don't eat pickles, as far as I know.

I also owe thanks to my proofreader Alma Tiwe, who caught the errors that always sneak past me; Saskia Goedhart, my advisor in hand-to-hand combat; Dane Low of Ebook Launch for the glorious cover art; and Mary Gray, whose creative mind gave me the main title of these books.

Special thanks go to Dr. Carol Blenning, because if there's one field I know nothing about, it's medicine. Dr. Wells would have my hide if I made her look anything less than thoroughly competent.

My tyree stood by me through a year of writing widowhood while offering a sounding board and many well-mixed gin and tonics. To Maria João Valente I say: Fahla never gives the gift without reason.

Finally, to the readers who have joined these characters on their journey of exploration: this is the Alsea you dreamed of, stepping into the stars at last. Come with me to the end of the beginning.

Fletcher DeLancey
July 2020

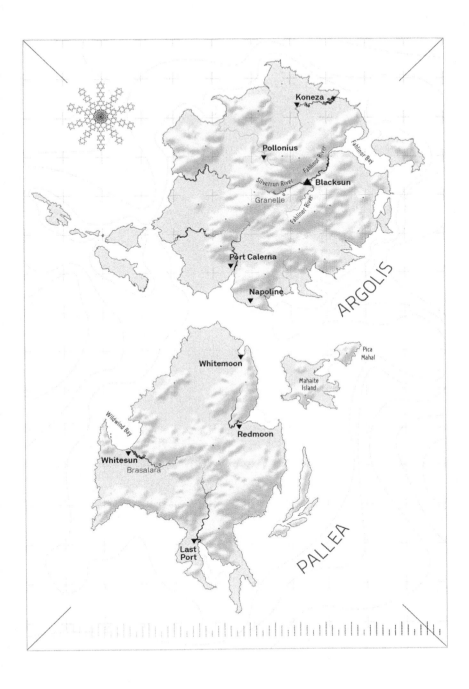

1

FLIGHT PLAN

"*Shuttle Ops to Captain Serrado. Dr. Wells just filed her flight plan.*"

"Thank you." Ekatya Serrado closed the report she had been reading, blanked her transparent terminal, and gratefully rose from the chair she had occupied for too long. The hanger behind her was supposed to hold her jacket when she wasn't using it, but she had never gotten in the habit, preferring to drape it over the back of her chair. Now she tugged it free and pulled it on as she crossed the room. Just outside the door's sensor range, she paused to be sure that a regulation length of cuff showed below the sleeves.

These days, she couldn't afford the tiniest crack in her image of the perfect Fleet captain.

Satisfied, she stepped out of her office and onto the bridge.

With the floor display inactive, the expansive bridge seemed smaller. Only the hemispherical upper display manifested their movement as they kept station above the small blue-and-green planet of Alsea.

Atop the three-tiered command dais at the center of the circular room, Commander Lokomorra occupied her chair. Now fully settled into the role of executive officer, he was comfortable enough to set the displays the way he liked, rather than leaving both top and bottom active as she preferred.

She glanced at the opaque deck beneath her feet and missed the sensation of standing among the stars. But Lokomorra held the bridge; it was his call.

"Commander Lokomorra," she murmured, letting her internal com route the call as she walked across the inactive display. "I'm headed for the shuttle bay."

"Acknowledged. Tell Dr. Wells I said good luck. And tell her that if she yells at an Alsean healer by thirteen hundred tomorrow, I win the betting pool."

Her smile drew the attention of a young ensign at the science station nearest the lift doors. "If I tell her that, she might wait until thirteen thirty just to spite you."

"I know. That's why I didn't give you the real time I bet on."

～

Some crew found the shuttle bay to be intimidating. Reaching six decks in height and housing eight shuttles of various sizes, it did have a cavernous feel. Ekatya liked it all the more for that sense of space and possibility.

Six of the shuttles bore the silver hullskin characteristic of all Protectorate ships. The other two, gleaming black beneath the bright lights, were the only Alsea-capable shuttles in Fleet. Lacking the semiorganic hullskin that made travel through base space possible, they were limited to the slower speeds of normal space. But they could fly through Alsea's nanoscrubber-infested atmosphere, safe from the microscopic machines that attacked hullskin due to the foreign radiation it produced. Another ship attempting that flight might land safely, but it would never get into orbit again—a fact Ekatya had learned in a memorable fashion.

She ducked under the nose of her favorite shuttle, trailing her fingertips across its smooth, black hull. Fleet called it "nanoscrubber-proof hull plating" and had refused to equip any of her fighters with it, despite the requirements of her mission.

If weaponized, Alsean nanoscrubber technology could change the balance of power in the galaxy. It had to be protected at all costs. A tiny, backwater planet at the edge of Protectorate space would not normally be assigned a warship to protect it, much less an entire battle group, but Alsea was different.

In every way, Ekatya thought as she neared the smallest shuttle.

Her chief surgeon had just lowered the ramp. Glancing over at the sound of bootsteps, she smiled in recognition.

"Ekatya. Come to see me off?"

"Did you know there's a betting pool on how long you'll last before yelling at an Alsean healer?"

The smile grew sharp. "No, but I'm not surprised. Are you in?"

"I would never take part in betting for or against my own crew members," Ekatya said primly. "But I think you can make it three days."

Alejandra Wells laughed, drawing startled looks from around the bay. Though slight in bone structure and average in height, she exuded an impatient energy that made others nervous, especially when combined with her legendary temper. That she also had a sense of humor was not widely known.

"Such faith you have in me, thanks. I don't plan on yelling at any of them. Not this time, at least." Tilting her head toward the ramp, she added, "I need to do the preflight. I appreciate your coming, though. It's nice to see a friendly face before I go."

"You'll be fine down there."

"I know. It's just intimidating. Rahel is one thing; I've adapted to her knowing what I feel. A whole group of high empath healers is something else. And I'll be in close proximity for a week."

"Just remember, they have their own rules of courtesy. It's rude to say what they feel from you unless it's relevant to the work. Or you bring it up first."

"And they're brutally honest," Alejandra said with a sigh. "All the times I've wished my patients couldn't lie to me . . . I have a feeling I'm about to see the other side of that."

"It'll be good for you." Having been through this adaptation herself, Ekatya was enjoying watching someone else take the first steps. "Besides, one of the things they'll be honest about is how much they respect you. You solved a thousand-cycle-old mystery."

"Sure, no pressure there. Nothing like having to live up to your own advertising."

She flapped her hands in the direction of the ramp. "Get out of here. And fly safely."

"I thought you'd say 'may Fahla fly with you.'"

"No, I need to get out of the Alsean frame of mind. It's almost time for my check-in."

Alejandra stiffened. "It's criminal, what they're doing to you."

"Don't start—"

"Don't start? I never finished. How can you do this, day after day?"

"This is not the place to discuss it," Ekatya said shortly. They were as public as they could be; she had already seen two nearby crew members turn their heads.

"Fine." Alejandra seized her wrist and pulled.

Startled, Ekatya let herself be drawn up the ramp into the shuttle. In the quiet interior, Alejandra released her grip and turned, all spikes and ire. "You're the best captain in Fleet and they're treating you like a criminal on parole. And Admiral Greve of all people! Pompous asshead. I'm just waiting for him to get sick and end up in my medbay. I've got an enema with his name on it."

Ekatya couldn't help the snort of laughter. "Ordinarily, I'd say 'let me watch,' but in this case . . ."

"It's not funny. They're trying to break you!"

"Do you think I don't know that?"

"Then why are you letting them?"

"Because I don't have a choice!" Ekatya snapped.

They stopped, staring at each other in surprise.

Alejandra drew back first. "Shit, I'm sorry. You came to see me off and I—dammit. I didn't mean to bring that up. It's just so *infuriating*."

Ekatya sat in the nearest seat. "Tell me about it. You think I'm not angry? It's all I can do not to plant my fist in his smug, superior mouth. But I have to play the game."

"Why?" Alejandra sat in the opposite seat. "I don't want you to resign. I'm not sure I'd last another week after you, given what I've seen these last few years. But if your only other option is to let them humiliate you, why not go?"

"Game it out. What happens if I resign? They assign another captain to this duty. Someone as far from me as they can get. Someone who's in no danger of ending up with a tyree bond. Someone who thinks the Defenders of the Protectorate have a good point."

Alejandra looked horrified. "The DOP is smashed. Completely discredited. You can't think—"

"I do think. I think Andira embarrassed both Fleet and the Protectorate. The leader of a backward planet blackmailing a galactic power into doing what she wanted? They hate her because she beat them at their own game. But they need her. And she needs me, so here I am. If I leave, they can bring in anyone they want, and they sure as Hades won't want another Alsea sympathizer. Do you know what my primary mission objective is?"

"To protect Alsea." She frowned when Ekatya shook her head.

"No. To prevent the nanoscrubbers from falling into Voloth hands. Protecting Alsea is secondary to that. The Voloth could destroy Alsea and I'd still fulfill my primary mission objective as long as I made sure they never got out of orbit with the nanoscrubber technology."

Alejandra melted into her seat, her normally upright posture dissolving. "Sainted Shippers. I had no idea."

"Alsea needs me right where I am," Ekatya said heavily. "Andira needs me here. So I'm doing what I have to."

Alejandra studied her, then straightened as some of her earlier spark returned. "And here I thought the Fleet brass were incompetent. Turns out they've got one thing right. You really are loyal to Alsea first."

Ekatya opened her mouth, ready to deny it. She had lied to an investigative panel packed with admirals and government ministers, perjuring herself repeatedly without the slightest remorse.

Those words, so easy then, would not come now. She couldn't lie to her friend.

"It's all right," Alejandra said in an uncharacteristically soft tone. "You're prioritizing a unique civilization over political maneuvering. You think I'd report you for that? I think they should give you a damned medal."

CHECK-IN

"Admiral Greve will see you now."

Ekatya didn't bother to thank the adjutant, a lieutenant commander whose rank had not come from what she considered real service. Until now, he had managed never to be posted aboard a ship. He made no secret of his distaste for the compromises of space travel: smaller offices and quarters, amateur cultural events, limited access to fresh foods. But the worst, she suspected, was the lack of backs he could trample to advance his career. Command Dome was a target-rich area for a ruthless climber like him. The *Phoenix* was not. It was hers, despite the admiral waiting behind that purposely closed door, and she had built a crew that worked together.

Greve and his adjutant were interlopers, treated with the required respect and not one iota more. It galled them to see the crew respond so differently to her. They would never understand that institutional respect bore no resemblance to respect that was earned.

She entered the office and stopped in front of Greve's desk. "Admiral."

"Captain." He leaned back in his chair and offered an insincere smile. "I thought you might actually be late this time. Heard you were in the shuttle bay, giving last-minute instructions to Dr. Wells."

"I was wishing her good fortune. She doesn't need my help to do her job."

"Her job." The smile twisted, marring his handsome features. "Fleet sure has changed since I was a captain. Back then, a chief surgeon's job was to care for her crew, not aliens."

"I believe a chief surgeon's duties have always included learning about new and useful procedures. Alsean medtech has already changed how we heal bones and treat burns. Who knows what else Dr. Wells might find?"

She could play this game all day long. Greve was forever trying to get a rise out of her, hoping to lead her into a statement he could use.

He was an amateur. Sholokhov would eat him for breakfast and use those admiral bars to pick his teeth. Though she rarely had occasion to be grateful for her tour of duty serving under the Director of Protectorate Security, it did have benefits. She had learned to defend against the best.

You aren't even close, she thought, keeping her expression bland.

He glowered. "Captain Serrado, have you received instructions from Lancer Tal or any member of the Alsean government?"

"I have not."

"Has your command been mentally or emotionally influenced through your tyree bond?" He pronounced *tyree* with extra emphasis on the first syllable, making it sound like a profanity.

"It has not."

"If you receive an order in conflict with anything you've promised Lancer Tal or your wife—"

"Dr. Rivers is my bondmate, not my wife. It was an Alsean ceremony. We prefer the Alsean term."

"Your *wife*," he repeated, "how will you respond?"

"I will uphold my oath to the Protectorate."

He opened a file on his pad, tapped it several times, then threw the pad on his desk with a clatter. "And we're done for another day. What a load of useless crap. I ask, you deny, and you're probably lying through your teeth. But I'm supposed to take you at your word."

She refused to show the anger that coiled through her stomach. "The value of my word has been established through a lifetime of service to Fleet."

Disdain dripped from his voice. "Right up until you disobeyed orders, sided with a foreign government, and then got yourself some jacked-up alien brain bug. You're a liability, Captain. But somehow you keep climbing to the top of a shit mountain without getting a speck of it on

7

your boots. You may have fooled half the brass at Command Dome, but you don't fool me." He leaned forward. "Don't get complacent. Sholokhov won't always protect you."

She stared at him, shocked, and a genuine smile lit his face.

"You didn't know. Interesting." Resting against the chair back, he steepled his fingers and studied her. "I was being literal when I said you fooled half the brass. The panel was divided until Director Sholokhov came in and tilted the scale in your favor. You're here because he wants you here. I thought you were a favorite, but if he didn't tell you . . ." He chuckled. "Then you're nothing more than a game piece he's moving around. He's not protecting you, he's using you. When he's done, he'll move you right off the board."

In all the times she had stood here for this farce of a check-in, Greve had never been able to rattle her. Now she stood speechless.

Sholokhov had interceded on her behalf and kept it quiet. Not only was it a favor unasked, but he had passed up the chance to hold it over her head.

He wanted something from her. Worse, he was biding his time, waiting to demand it.

Greve was speaking, exuding satisfaction at this perceived win. She paid no attention. Let him think he'd struck terror into her heart; it would get him off her back for a few days. She could use the time to think.

What did Sholokhov want?

COLONEL GRAND SHIT

The fourteenth floor of the State House was always quiet.

Beneath it were the gears of government, churning and whirring, powered by a thousand dedicated Alseans from all six castes. Those corridors were never empty, even at night.

Few State House staff ever set foot above the thirteenth floor, having no authority to pass the biolocks on the lifts and stairwell doors. But for those with the security clearance, the fourteenth was a world of hushed corridors and rich tapestries, inhabited by the most powerful people on Alsea. The Lancer's office was here, as well as those of her closest advisors and support staff. Here also was the famous Unification Chamber, where the original High Council had come together to work out a power sharing system that brought a millennium of peace. The caste Primes had met there ever since.

On the other side of the great dome were the equally famous guest suites, each a museum in its own right, yet seen by very few. Staying in a State House guest suite was the pinnacle of achievement for Alsean political society.

Colonel Corozen Micah would never sleep in one of those rooms—his quarters were several floors down—but as the Lancer's Chief Guardian, he had an office on the fourteenth. For the son of low-ranking warriors with more love than prestige to offer, such an achievement felt unreal even after eight cycles.

Duty had kept him in his office well past evenmeal this night, and he emerged into a corridor so quiet that he might have been the only one here. An illusion, of course, but one he embraced. These glorious artworks, this ancient bench pieced together and carved by a crafter when Blacksun Temple's molwyn tree was still young—in this moment, they were his to enjoy.

He strolled down the hall, hands behind his back, bootsteps muffled by a handwoven rug still resistant to traffic after three hundred cycles. Lhyn Rivers had once told him that in most Protectorate cultures, this rug would be behind protective glass in a museum.

"What a waste," he muttered, his gaze on the intricate patterns beneath his feet. How strange, to lock away things that were meant to be used.

The rug curved gracefully around a corner, and he saw a small boot and bare calf just before a body collided with his. Instinctively he reached out, his hands settling on the slim shoulders of a woman.

A Gaian woman, in a formal dress and jacket that smelled of hyacot. She had been to an expensive restaurant, then. Hyacot twigs were generally used in ceremonies or as atmospheric enhancers in the type of restaurant he tried to avoid.

He steadied her while she found her feet. "Dr. Wells. Are you all right?"

"Hm? Yes, yes, I'm fine." She straightened her jacket with the deliberate movements of one who has overindulged. "Can't find my room, though. This place is a damned ant nest. Passages going every which way, and half of them dead ends."

He kept his amusement off his face. "You're on the other side of the dome from your suite."

"What? No, that—" She lifted her head and looked around in confusion. "Oh. Are these the offices? How did I end up here?"

"With the help of several bottles of spirits, I suspect."

Her gaze snapped back to him, remarkably sharp despite her inebriation. "I can hold my spirits, Colonel."

"Since you're still walking upright, I agree."

She frowned. "Why does that feel like a disagreement?"

"I have no idea. May I escort you back to your suite?" He held out a hand, indicating the direction from which she had come.

"I suppose you'll have to," she grumbled, turning in place. "Ant nest." After a tick of silent walking, she spoke more quietly. "But Shippers, what a beautiful ant nest."

"It is, isn't it? Sometimes I wish the State House tours could come to this floor, so more people could see it." He put a hand on her elbow, gently nudging her through a doorway.

"No wonder Ekatya and Lhyn love living here. I don't know how Ekatya goes back to the *Phoenix* after a few nights in this place. I have one of the biggest suites on the ship, and it'll feel like a shannel cup after this."

In his few interactions with Dr. Wells, she had been edgy and sharp-tongued, forcefully sharing her professional opinions while keeping anything personal behind stone walls. This was a different view of her.

"I can imagine," he said.

She glanced over. "Imagine? You don't have a suite here? Aren't you the grand shit of security?"

"The grand what?" It was an effort to hold back his laugh, especially when she put a hand to her mouth with an expression of genuine surprise.

"It's possible," she said, enunciating carefully, "that I've had a bit too much to drink."

"A bit, yes. Does 'grand shit' mean anything more than what it sounds like?"

She chuckled, then let out an open laugh that melted her reserve. "It does, and I'm just drunk enough to tell you. It's Fleet slang, dating back to the days when our ships were a lot smaller and the, hm, facilities were much less reliable. And by facilities, I mean sewage plumbing."

"I assumed." She looked so elegant, standing there in her fine clothes and the formal hairstyle that bared her neck. Gemstones flashed at her throat and sparkled from her ears, she smelled divine, and she was talking about sewage.

"In those days, if someone produced . . ." Her hands lifted, slender fingers curving to indicate a sizable object. ". . . a fecal output that was larger than normal, or more solid, it would block the plumbing. When you block a ship's plumbing, everything else is secondary. Unless you're in the middle of a battle, of course."

"Of course," he agreed, losing control of his smile.

She grinned at him, a flash of teeth and satisfaction that warmed his skin. "So a grand shit is important enough to bring everything to a stop. You are, aren't you?"

"I can't say I ever thought of myself in those terms. But yes, I'm the Lancer's Chief Guardian, which does indeed make me the grand shit of security." He offered a short bow. "And therefore the most important escort you could have back to your suite."

"I'm honored." She matched his bow, looking up briefly with an impish gleam in her green eyes. When she straightened, the gleam was lost behind a familiar wall of reserve. "You're different from the healers. I'd think it was because of your caste, but you're different from Rahel, too. Is it your job, or just you?"

"I'm not sure I can answer that without knowing what you see as different." He resumed their journey, noting that she walked closer now, her movements less guarded.

This was dangerous territory, and he should put a stop to it.

He wouldn't. That look in her eyes, the flash of teeth—they had done something to his insides that he hadn't felt in too long. He wanted to see them again.

"On my home planet, we say we have three faces. One we present to the world, one we show our friends and family, and one we keep for ourselves. I've just finished seven days in the company of a whole herd of healers. They don't have three faces. I'm not sure they have two." She paused when he touched her elbow, guiding her around a corner. "Rahel *should* have three faces, and sometimes she does. Other times, it's all there for anyone to see if they know how to look. But you, Colonel. You have at least two faces."

They walked the length of a corridor while Micah considered how to answer.

"Have I offended you?"

"No. Intrigued me, perhaps. Not offended." He opened a door and motioned her through.

She stopped, gazing around with a furrow in her smooth brow. "All right, I know where I am now. But I don't know how we got here."

"The main corridor follows the dome." He drew a circle in the air. "In theory, you could have kept walking and returned to this point eventually. But that would take you past the Lancer's office; you wouldn't have gotten much farther before my Guards stopped you." Making a straight line through his imaginary circle, he added, "We took a route that crossed the dome. And here you are."

"Here I am." She looked down the hall to her suite, three doors away, then back at him. "And you've managed not to answer either of my questions. Would you like to come in, Colonel? I won't offer you a drink, but if you're in the mood for a cup of shannel . . ."

He ignored the practical voice informing him that this was an extremely bad idea. "It would be my pleasure."

Her suite was half the size of the one given to Lhyn and Ekatya, but every bit as splendid with its tapestries, historically significant furniture, and priceless art. On a table near the tall windows, a vase the size of his thigh held an enormous bouquet of flowers. Such bouquets were a standard courtesy for guests, assembled from park plantings by State House producers. They were also a subtle indication of the guest's importance or favor with whomever had issued the invitation.

"Make yourself comfortable." Dr. Wells slipped off her jacket, exposing bare shoulders and the insubstantial straps of her dress, and vanished into the small kitchen space.

In that brief glimpse, he had seen only smooth skin where an Alsean's chest ridges would be. His fingers itched to touch it, to feel that difference, and he hurriedly crossed to the bouquet to give himself something else to focus on. Inhaling the delicate scent of tintinatalus blossoms helped only a little, a small distraction of one sense while his entire body seemed attuned to clinking cups and the whoosh of a shannel dispenser. When her footsteps returned, he moved to wait by the sofa.

She appeared with a cup in each hand, walking with less care and more grace than he expected.

"You're not drunk any longer," he said, accepting his cup.

"Good eye, Colonel. I brought a few doses of kastrophenol with me. It neutralizes most of the negative effects of spirits."

"Yet I'm still here."

"Yes, you are." She took a seat facing the window and smiled when he chose a chair opposite. "Definitely a warrior. Every soldier I know sits facing the door."

He lifted the cup in a salute. "You see more than you allow others to know."

"Three faces." She matched his gesture and sipped her drink, the motion drawing his eyes to that smooth expanse of skin and the shadowed valley between her breasts.

Dragging his gaze away, he pointed across the room. "Do you know the significance of this bouquet?"

"I didn't know there was any."

"All guests receive them. The bigger they are, the more status they convey. Yours is as big as they come, and it's not made with flowers that put out new blooms every nineday. Those branches are tintinatalus. A tree, not a shrub. It'll take a cycle for the tree to regrow them."

She studied the bouquet with new appreciation. "They came from Prime Scholar Yaserka. He's the one who authorized this collaboration."

"He holds you in high esteem. The producers who made that bouquet know it, the staff who prepared this suite know it. It's surely common knowledge in the State House by now."

"Did you know?"

"Yes, but I get my gossip through a different route."

"Top down instead of bottom up, hm? Fleet works like that, too." She kicked off her boots and pulled up her legs, sitting sideways with knees bent and one arm resting on the back of the sofa. "I believe you owe me a few answers, Colonel. Is it your job or you?"

He hadn't forgotten. "If we're in your suite talking about faces, call me Micah."

"Your family name?"

"It's what I'm most comfortable with. A warrior tradition for those of us in the protective forces. The eldest uses the family name as long as they're serving."

"Rahel doesn't go by Sayana."

"Rahel is unique. She never served in a normal Guard unit, and her oath holder styled himself a parental figure. He always used her first name."

"I don't think Shantu styled himself a parental figure. I think he *was* her father. If he hadn't been, she wouldn't have obeyed those orders."

"You're protective of her," he observed.

"Yes, I am." Simple and firm. "I've read her file. I know what she did to you. I don't know how you handle being her commanding officer after that, but I'll tell you right now: don't say a word against her to me."

A tendril of tension rose between them, poised for explosive growth.

"What an advantage she has, with someone like you as her shield." He watched the slight drop of her shoulders, a result of her relaxing spine, and added, "Rahel has paid her debts. I made my peace with her some time ago."

"That's a story I'd like to hear someday."

There were quite a few stories he suddenly wanted to hear.

"I don't think I can answer your question," he said. "I can't remember a time when there was a me separate from my job. Can you separate from yours?"

This laugh was not the uninhibited one from earlier. "Do you know what I was doing tonight?"

"I know you were in a very nice restaurant." At her visible surprise, he tapped his nose. "Your clothes. They're infused with the scent of hyacot twigs."

"Oh. Those are wonderful, aren't they? I'd like to bring some back with me." She sipped her shannel, then slid cup and saucer onto the side table. "I was celebrating the success of our first medical collaboration. Ten of us went out to do what healers do best, regardless of species. We self-medicated."

"Is that how you separate from your job?"

"That's how I forget enough of my job to remember who I am without it."

"But you're sober now."

"I'm not bringing a man into my quarters if I'm too drunk to handle him."

"Has that been a problem before?" He forced himself to stay still, but his blood thrummed at the mere thought of it.

"I learned that lesson the hard way, yes." She pinned him with a glare that said pity was not welcome. "But I'm told that's very unusual on Alsea. Only one of the healers I worked with had ever treated a victim. I still can't quite believe it."

"Unusual and swiftly punished," he said tightly.

"Oh, he was punished. Just not by the Fleet judicial system." She retrieved her cup and took a sip.

He shouldn't ask, but . . .

"What did you do?"

She cradled the cup between her hands, her gaze on the bouquet. "He was an officer, which meant he had a personal matter printer. About a moon after my experience, I treated an ensign from data systems with familiar symptoms and a very familiar story. She wrote a self-deleting program that delivered a toxin to his next food order, and I found a medical code to authorize the installation. He's not in Fleet anymore," she added offhandedly. "Medical discharge. Not fit for active duty."

"Great Mother," he blurted. "You're not like any healer I know."

He caught a glimpse of wide, startled eyes before she dropped her head and rubbed the back of her neck.

"I don't think the kastrophenol neutralized everything," she muttered. "Dammit. Must be the difference in Alsean spirits."

She had not meant to tell him that much. He had taken advantage of the vulnerability she had tried to eliminate.

"It won't leave this room." When she looked up, distrust written across her face, he added, "I swear on my honor as a warrior. I hope Rahel has taught you what that means."

Her expression cleared. "She has."

But she was still skittish, and the only way forward was through.

He rested his forearms on his knees, hands clasped together. "May I ask why you didn't appeal to your judicial system?"

She assessed him and made her decision with a defiant lift of her chin.

"It doesn't work like yours. There's no empathic scanning to determine guilt and innocence. The only physical evidence wouldn't have proved coercion. He would have said it was consensual. I had no proof to the contrary, and he had witnesses to my behavior in the bar before I took him to my quarters."

While he tried to wrap his mind around that, she added, "Not to mention that he was two ranks above me."

"What difference does that make?"

She stared at him, then made a soft sound of amazement. "Shippers, I love Alsea."

"Do you mean—" He stopped. If they had no empathic scans to determine the truth, then rank probably did matter.

"It wouldn't have impacted his career," she said, confirming his guess. "But it would have ruined mine. It was my first posting; I was still an apprentice."

Which meant she had been very young. "And you stayed in Fleet after that."

"I wasn't going to let him keep me from my goals."

"I doubt you let anything keep you from your goals."

"We might have that in common, Colonel Grand Shit."

The sheer surprise of it after such a dark story left him unable to stop the bark of laughter. She watched with a spark of humor in her eyes, and no, pity was not necessary.

"Not only did he lack both honor and decency, he was a grainbird on top of it. I only needed two ticks to know I didn't want you angry with me. You threatened to stick me with something sharp."

It was her turn to laugh, the real, open one that made him want to do whatever it took to hear it again.

"I'd forgotten. You *were* being an overbearing ass."

"I was not."

"We may have to agree to disagree." But she was smiling, and her posture had softened. "You still have a question to answer. Why don't you have one of these suites?"

"I didn't want one. Tal offered it when she won the election, but it was difficult enough to spend my days surrounded by politicians and people with agendas. I didn't want to spend my nights with them, too. I'd rather be with my warriors." He pointed at the floor. "I'm a few floors down."

She needed a moment to find her voice. "You're not what I expected."

"Is that a good thing?"

"It's a very good thing." She set her cup on the table and took a more defensive position: shoulders forward, feet on the floor. "It's been a long time since I've done this. And I was never good at it to begin with."

"I don't quite know what it is we're doing," he said truthfully. "But I'm happy to stay and talk, if that's all you want. I'm enjoying getting to know you, Dr. Wells."

There: shoulders back, spine loose once more, small tilt of the lips. "Alejandra. Whatever happens tonight, it's not going to happen with you calling me Dr. Wells."

"Agreed, as long as you don't call me Colonel Grand Shit."

He could get addicted to that laugh.

"Sorry, I can't guarantee that. But I promise to do it sparingly." Her eyes were dancing, and she pulled her legs back up in the pose he now recognized as being one of mental ease. "Nothing much will happen tonight. At the very least, I'd have to study some anatomical charts first. And ask Rahel for advice." She chuckled at his silent reaction. "Well, who else do I have up there? Besides, I hear she knows her way around Alsean sexual responses."

"You make it sound like a clinical study." But her matter-of-fact attitude allowed him to admit, "I'd need a few charts, too. Goddess above, I'd have to ask Lhyn." He buried his face in his hands, then dragged them down to his jaw. "Do you have *any* idea how long she would lecture me?"

This time she laughed so hard that her body curled with it, arms around her torso as if her ribs were in danger of flying apart. "Oh, stars. Yes, I can imagine it." She laughed again, then wiped her eyes. "Micah, thank you. You're making this easy, and that—I can't tell you how much that's worth."

There was an unspoken history beneath those words. He suspected that not much in her life had been easy.

This, he vowed, would be a different story.

4

MENTORING

"Well done," Tal said when Lead Guard Vellmar finished her report. "I remember the first time you did this. You were so nervous I thought you might vibrate right out of that chair."

Vellmar flashed the brilliant smile that had helped make her one of the most public faces of the warrior caste. "Anyone who's not nervous the first time they're reporting to you is either foolish or foolhardy. Or both."

"Salomen wasn't."

"I won't call you a liar, but Salomen says different."

Chuckling, Tal rose from her desk chair and led her guest to the comfortable armchairs overlooking a spectacular view of the State Park. "Fair enough. Though it was only that first time, and if she'd had her perfect front then, I would never have known. Shannel?"

"Please."

"Have a seat. I mean it this time." She stood, hands on hips, until Vellmar relented and sat stiffly on the edge of a seat cushion. "Oh, for the love of Fahla. It's taken me three moons to get you to sit before I do. Will it take three more before you'll relax?"

"At least."

With a grumbled sigh that was mostly for show, she crossed to the antique sideboard in the corner and pulled out two cups. In truth, she understood Vellmar's reticence. Observation of rank and hierarchy was trained into warriors from the beginning; to act against that training was difficult even with permission. But if she were to mentor her chosen successor, she needed to chip away some of the institutional walls between them.

Vellmar bounced up when she returned with the full cups balanced on their delicate saucers. Taking one from Tal's hands, she carefully set it on the low table between their chairs. It was a choreographed delay, allowing her to sit a moment after Tal did.

This time, Tal chose not to notice. "I have a new toy for you. Actually, I have them for both the Lancer's and Bondlancer's units, but you get the first one." She picked up the box that sat on the table and held it out.

"New tech?" With an excited grin, Vellmar opened it and admired the sleek new wristcom and earcuff nestled within. "Hands-free activation and muting, speedy!"

"Speedier than you know. It has translation capabilities."

"Really?" She pulled out the wristcom and studied it from all angles. "How does that work?"

"The builders figured out how to port Lhyn's translation program to our hardware. The wristcom sends the results to the earcuff if it's translating Common to High Alsean. If it's doing the opposite, it sends the results to either the external speaker or the screen, whichever you choose. I've been testing the prototype. When you beat your birthmother at the Global Games last moon, I understood exactly what Captain Serrado was shouting."

Vellmar looked up with interest. "She was shouting in Common?"

"She reverts to it when she swears. We made a friendly bet on who would win."

The smile reappeared. "She was betting on age and experience."

"Her mistake," Tal said sleekly. "After last cycle's Games, I knew you'd win these. Salomen and I enjoyed an excellent meal at Meadowgreen last nineday as a result. Not having to pay for it made it taste even better."

"Victory is an excellent spice," Vellmar agreed. "I'm glad my blade handling earned you a fine meal. It earned me more than one."

"I should hope so." Tal pointed at the earcuff. "In terms of understanding Common, that works nearly as seamlessly as a lingual implant."

"But without the brain surgery."

"Exactly. It's not quite as seamless when it comes to speaking Common, but it will be invaluable if you end up boarding a Voloth ship."

Vellmar pursed her lips as she returned the wristcom to its cushioned bed. "May I speak freely?"

"You haven't figured it out yet?" She indicated their overstuffed chairs. "We're over here by the windows, with shannel cups in hand. You're not in the guest chair on the other side of my desk. If I bring you here, that means we're not interacting solely as Lancer and Lead Guard."

"What are we interacting as?"

"Two warriors of slightly different ranks, having drinks and a discussion."

At the *slightly*, Vellmar made a sound that was close to a laugh. "Then this is something like our runs?"

"Something like. Speak freely."

"All right. Ah . . ." She cleared her throat. "We're doing a lot of prep and training for a possible Voloth attack. Not only the Lancer and Bondlancer's units, but the whole warrior caste." She held up the box. "And the builder caste, too. The new fighters, new tech . . ."

Tal nodded encouragingly.

"But today you said you have no solid intelligence that they're planning anything."

"Nothing solid, no. And that does not leave this room."

Vellmar hesitated, then forged ahead. "Why are we committing to a course of action with no evidence to support it? I never thought I'd see ground pounders off base unless it was an emergency, and you've got them deployed around every major city. Fighter construction isn't cheap. And training the pilots and gunners—those are entirely new units. Not to mention taking warriors away from their normal duties to practice for resistance or evacuations. I mean, the fighters—those have to happen eventually, to protect the space elevator. But you've got it running on an accelerated schedule. Why?"

"Why do you think?"

"I don't know! I thought you knew something we didn't, until you said otherwise. Now it doesn't make any sense."

"It makes perfect sense. Tell me, what was the overall attitude of the warrior caste five and a half moons ago?"

It took her less than a piptick to find the connection. "This is about the uprising?"

"Not entirely. Making decisions with only one thing in mind is a luxury I don't often have. But if I play my tiles right, I can make decisions that pay off on multiple fronts." She held out one hand, palm upward. "I had a volatile political situation that had already turned lethal and had the potential for more. The Council vote for Salomen's caste reform silenced the loudest objectors, but it made the quiet ones even more dangerous." Lifting her other hand, she continued, "Then I had a military situation which, while unknown, also had lethal potential. But if I combined the two . . ." She brought her hands together.

Vellmar frowned at them before rising brows and wide eyes telegraphed her realization. "You used the Voloth threat to give our caste a purpose."

There were times when Tal was positively smug about her choice. Vellmar was so good at putting pieces together that the merest nudge was usually sufficient to send her down the right path.

"Exactly. Purpose leads to self-respect," she said, expanding on the lesson. "What made the reform so contentious was the threat it presented to our collective image. If we could see ourselves as publicly acknowledged protectors against a powerful external enemy, we could remember who we are as a caste. How long has it been since the last act of warrior violence against a producer?"

"Three moons," Vellmar said immediately. "And the threat assessment for Salomen is back to normal levels."

"In the meantime, we're increasing our military readiness in leaps and bounds. If the Voloth do come, we'll be a much more difficult target than the last time they dropped by."

"It brought in the scholar caste, too." Vellmar was already thinking ahead. "And the builders, which means the merchants as well, since they're providing the materials. You mobilized the castes with the biggest objections to the reform and got them working with the castes who were most involved in the uprising." She looked up with admiration written on her face. "And got full Council support for the expense of military preparations."

Tal was not above enjoying a little well-earned pride. "As a side benefit, Alseans are getting used to seeing our Voloth Empire settlers working with the ground pounders. We finally found a way to start their social integration on a visible level."

"It helps that they publicly refused to operate the weapons."

"Yes, that was a rare case of getting what I wanted without having to ask." She could wish their refusal weren't rooted in trauma, but the result was ideal.

"Does the Council know? The real reason for doing all this, I mean?"

"The High Council does. The Primes smoothed the path in the full Council." She reached for her shannel cup. "A Lancer can't lead effectively without the support of her Primes. I've had times of fighting against them, or trying to push them into making the right decision, but I would far rather work with them. Except for Ehron, they know their castes better than I do. I can draw the map and point to where we need to go, but they know the best alleys and shortcuts." The hot shannel soothed her throat, dry from too much talking in too many meetings, and it wasn't even midday.

Vellmar watched with sharp eyes, missing nothing. "Your voice is rough."

"The price I pay for two days off with Salomen. I have to make up the lost time." She sipped again, smiling as she remembered Salomen's extreme reluctance to let her leave this morning. "The roughness might not be entirely from talking. About business," she amended.

"Uh-huh." Vellmar hid a grin behind her own cup. "You do seem more relaxed than when I went off duty yesterday."

"As do you. Tell me, how much oil did you burn in the temple last night?"

Vellmar coughed, then dabbed a sleeve to her mouth. "Was that a euphemism?"

"I don't usually bother with those." These were the moments that delighted her, when she could tease her Lead Guard without rank getting in the way. The first few attempts had fallen flat, but Vellmar was gradually loosening her rigid expectations.

"There was oil," Vellmar allowed. "We didn't burn it."

"Ah, massage. So that's what Lanaril meant. She mentioned that you had magic fingers to go with your magic tongue."

"She did not say that!"

Tal set her shannel down, laughing too hard to hold it. "You've been courting her for a cycle and you still don't know how sensual she is? Lanaril works with minds all day long. It's a relief for her to focus on the simplicity of bodies instead."

"There's nothing simple about her," Vellmar mumbled. "Fahla, I can't believe she told you that."

"Don't worry, it only made me respect you more."

Though Vellmar's front was perfect as always, that did nothing for the flush in her cheeks. "How did you get the Primes to cooperate with each other so soon after the uprising?" she asked in a blatant subject change.

"We'll have to work on your subtlety. The short answer? I didn't. Salomen did. Her marches brought the Prime Producer, Builder, Merchant, and Crafter together in a way they haven't been in . . . well, never in my administration. Or the three before that. You'd have to go back to Lancer Julsine to find such unity."

"But that's only four. Stasinal hates Yaserka."

"True, but she respects Ehron. It's not the merchant-scholar link we need right now, it's the merchant-warrior link."

The flush had receded as Vellmar contemplated the political ramifications. "Salomen got four Primes to work as a unified force, and you leveraged that plus warrior unrest into a planetary mobilization for an attack that might never come."

"You make it sound manipulative."

"I guess that depends on the likelihood of the attack." She pointed at the new wristcom and earcuff. "You're equipping me and my team for an unfriendly boarding. That seems rather specific to be mere manipulation."

Tal hesitated. "I'm worried," she admitted. "So is Captain Serrado. There's no hard intelligence, nothing coming through diplomatic channels, but she has connections inside Protectorate Security. Word is that the Voloth are planning something, but no one knows what or where. If they mean to harm us, they won't be sending engraved invitations first."

"So you're planning for the worst and hoping for the best, while using the worst to get the best out of our castes."

Tal lifted her cup in a silent acknowledgment.

Vellmar matched the gesture and eyed her over the rim as she drank. "Well," she said, setting the cup back in its saucer, "I'm glad you're the one in charge."

5

POLITICAL HEADACHE

"How did it go with Vellmar?" Micah asked, settling into his ready position.

Tal swung her sword in a double loop pattern, loosening her wrists. "Good. She figured out the other reason for our mobilization." She bent her knees and assumed her opening stance. "Ready?"

"Begin." He struck out immediately, hoping to catch her by surprise. She parried with a comical look of indignation.

"Whatever happened to the warmup?" she demanded as they circled each other.

"My best opportunities come early."

"If we're in competition! I thought this was a friendly practice."

"When it comes to sparring, nothing with you is friendly."

"That is an outrageous lie. I cannot count the number of times I've passed up the chance to humiliate you."

He pointed at her with his blade. "You see? That was an unfriendly aspersion on my skill."

She attacked, removing all possibility of conversation as their blades clanged together in a timeless dance. He loved these sessions, when they had the training room to themselves. Tal left her title on the mat then, becoming a looser, easier version of herself.

When they had tired themselves sufficiently, they broke apart and resumed circling.

"Vellmar is a sharp blade," he said, watching her warily. "You chose well. Did she ask about the divine tyrees?"

"That was the only thing she didn't ask about. Speaking of which, we're ready for our first test."

He straightened, startled into dropping his guard. "You're joking. Already? Shek!" His hastily raised forearm barely blocked the fist that had been aimed for his face.

"Spar or talk, Micah." She had let her momentum take her past him, infuriatingly energetic despite her claim of exhaustion from too many meetings. He blamed it on her relative youth and small stature. It took less power to move a body so much lighter than his.

"How are they ready so soon?" He didn't wait for an answer before attacking.

She caught his blade on a circle parry, threw it aside, and riposted with a thrust that went through air as he twisted away. "Salomen," she answered, settling into her stance. "She worked with the low empath and weaker mid empaths. Brought them up to the level of the others."

He feinted, drawing her blade into a defensive position, but withdrew when no opening presented itself. "Well done. Then we're at fifteen fully trained pairs?"

The sudden grin warned him before she attacked. Their blades sang together in a furious harmony before she stepped back, still smiling. "Sixteen. Don't forget Salomen and me."

"What's your first target?"

"Rahel Sayana."

They locked eyes for a breath before dissolving into laughter.

"Fahla, what an irony." Micah wiped his forehead with his sleeve.

"It's never stopped being an irony. If you had told me a cycle ago that I'd be using a group Sharing of divine tyrees to help Salomen project onto Rahel—"

"And not for the purpose of killing her," he interjected.

"—I'd have laughed in your face."

"After punching me."

"Micah," she said in a wounded tone. "I'd never punch you."

"You punched me yesterday. And tried again not five ticks ago."

"Sparring doesn't count! Besides, yesterday you dropped your elbow. You deserved it. Never drop your elbow."

"I taught you that, you ungrateful little dokker."

Her light eyes crinkled with amusement, but he couldn't help remembering the day she had struck him with true intent, blinded by Rahel's attack on Salomen. The impact had knocked him down three stairs, an impressive accomplishment given their size difference.

"I know what you're thinking." She retracted her sword into its grip and walked toward the water flasks they had left beside the mat. "It was a cycle ago last nineday."

He followed. "The temples have burned a lake of oil since then. When is the test?"

"Tomorrow morning. We're fortunate that Rahel always accompanies Ekatya on leave. Admiral Greve won't think anything's amiss." She picked up both flasks and handed one to him.

"Seems to me he ought to be the first target," he grumbled, twisting off the cap.

"Not for Salomen. She's too gentle. But for me?" Her jaw tightened. "I have a few fantasies."

He didn't ask for details. "How is Ekatya holding up?"

"She says she's fine, but she's not. I don't know why she tries to lie." Tal shook her head, a few blonde wisps escaping from her short braid. "That's not true, I do know. I just don't know why she thinks we can't see it."

"Has something changed?"

"No, it's the same questions, the same idiotic game, day after day after day. But it's building up." She swirled her flask, making its contents gurgle. "I think it's the Fleet equivalent of water wheel torture."

In the ancient days of the warring kingdoms, a favorite method of torture had been to cut a flexible switch from nearby rushes and fasten it to a water wheel so it jutted out horizontally. The victim was tied to a plank and positioned next to the wheel. With each rotation, the switch would slap the victim's body and then slide away as the wheel carried it down, rewetted it, carried it back up, and slapped it again on the same point.

Water wheel torture was renowned for the way it built from minor irritant to excruciating pain. The first slaps only reddened the skin, but eventually it would part, layer by layer, until the muscle was exposed. Left in place long enough, the switch would cut all the way to the bone: slowly, inexorably, with precisely the same interval between each impact.

Every day, at exactly the same time, Ekatya reported to Admiral Greve and answered the same questions. At first she had dismissed it with a bitter laugh, relieved at surviving her inquisition with her career intact, if under much closer scrutiny.

She wasn't laughing any longer.

"How deep has the switch gone?" Micah asked.

"Well into the muscle layer." Tal looked haunted. "And I can't do anything about it. I want her out of there, but she knows we need her."

"She's a warrior. She'll serve as long as she's able."

"Service shouldn't be like this." She tilted her head from one side to the other, stretching her neck and inhaling deeply. "Ready?"

They returned to the center of the mat and extended their swords.

"Begin," Micah said.

In their usual fits and starts, between the metallic song of clashing blades, they discussed the upcoming divine tyree test, the schedule for future tests depending on its outcome, and the point at which they would convene the war council to unveil the existence of a new defensive weapon. It was a well-kept secret for now, Tal's private strategy that she would not reveal until she had solid results. That the divine tyrees were training together was common knowledge. What they were training for was not.

When a rare opening appeared, he disarmed her with a sweep of his sword and brought it up, level with her throat. "Do you yield?"

"I yield. But that was a lucky move."

He stepped back, retracting his blade. "You could simply admit that I won."

"Or I could truthfully say I'm tired." She scooped her sword off the mat.

"Young and tired should still be equal to old and well rested."

"You're not old, Micah, stop trying."

No, he thought as they gulped water, he didn't feel old. Especially not after last night.

"I have something to ask you," he said.

She recapped her flask with a nod, her sudden focus proof that she had sensed his trepidation.

Which made it more difficult. He cast about for the right phrasing, found none, and gave up. "How much of a political headache would it be if I joined with Dr. Wells?"

He had rarely seen her eyes go that wide.

"Shekking Mother! When did—how—Dr. Wells?" Her voice went up on the last word. "The woman with more thorns than a hornstalk?"

"Interesting that you're more concerned with her personality than her species."

"I'm concerned about you! For the love of Fahla, you could have anyone you want. And you want Dr. Wells?"

"Yes," he said simply.

She snapped her jaw shut on whatever she had been about to say. After a moment of wordless staring, she dropped gracefully into a cross-legged position on the mat. Patting the space in front of her, she said, "Sit down and tell me."

He sat with less grace, folding his legs only after settling down, and took another pull from his flask. Then he spoke of a conversation that had lasted half the night and a goodnight kiss that robbed him of sleep for the other half.

"I haven't seen you this interested in someone since before my election," she said when he finished.

"Longer. I don't know what happened. We've met several times before, spoken to each other, it's all been professional. But last night . . ."

"Last night she had spirits instead of blood in her veins."

"She neutralized them as soon as we entered her suite."

With a noncommittal hum, Tal unfolded one leg and bent over it in a stretch. "As far as the politics go, her species isn't the issue. The issue is that she's the chief surgeon of a ship currently under the control of an unfriendly admiral. She's also Ekatya's friend. Both of those could be a problem if this fruit turns sour."

"And if it ripens?"

"It could put her in a bad position with Greve."

Micah thought back to the story Alejandra had not meant to tell. "She's not the type to let a higher-ranked officer get in the way of her goals."

"Are you one of her goals?"

He remembered lips against his jaw and a heated whisper. "Er . . ."

She sat up straight and pointed an accusing finger. "You're blushing!"

"I'm hot. We just finished sparring."

"It's as if you forget I'm a high empath." She switched legs and resumed her stretch. "You really didn't sleep after that kiss?"

He shook his head.

"That was some kiss."

He nodded, unable to keep his own smile from growing embarrassingly wide.

"Great Mother," she said with a laugh. "Remind me to have a maintenance team check the fire suppression system next time she's here."

6

TEST

First Guard Rahel Sayana watched the walls of the exit tunnel slide by and thought she would never tire of this view no matter how routine it became.

She loved flying past the large window of the control room and seeing the shuttle operations staff inside. She loved the green guidance lights flashing down the tunnel to mark their way out. Most of all, she loved that square of black at the end, delineating the magical moment between the safety of the *Phoenix* and the vastness of space.

Beside her, Captain Serrado spoke quietly to shuttle ops as she made tiny adjustments with her control stick, keeping them in the center of the tunnel. There was little room for error. Most shuttle pilots opted for the automatic navigation, taking over the controls once they emerged into space, but Serrado refused. "If I'm going to fly, I'm flying from start to finish," she had explained. Rahel thought that described more than just her piloting philosophy.

They passed through the bay doors and into an infinite wonderment of stars. She sank into her seat, breathing it in. It was a double impact every time she flew out of the *Phoenix*: the visceral joy of being in space and the exquisite release from emotional pressure.

More than twelve hundred Gaians crewed the ship behind her. Every one of them was sonsales, unable to sense emotions or keep from broadcasting their own. Though her blocks had grown stronger in her time aboard the *Phoenix*, they would never be proof against that relentless river of emotion. Her first two weeks of service had been a nightmare of increasing pressure and pain, culminating in a breakdown that still embarrassed her when she thought about it. Yet it had also been the catalyst for Dr. Wells finding solutions. Now she had touch treatments that reduced her stress hormones and medical dispensation to accompany the captain every time she went down to Alsea—which, given that Serrado's bondmate and divine tyree lived there, was as often as she could manage.

Captain Serrado worked unusual shifts, refusing to take normal days off during their patrols. When they returned to Alsea, she would collect her banked days and spend them dirtside, as they said in Fleet. While they were in orbit between patrols, she would do much the same, working longer shifts in order to earn larger blocks of leave.

Each time Serrado flew down on leave, Rahel accompanied her for what Dr. Wells called an emotional reset. Being away from the ship was a physical relief, yet she missed it while she was gone. When she was back on board, she missed Alsea.

"Transit completed," said the guidance officer on their com. *"Exit tunnel clear; bay doors closing."*

"Acknowledged. Commencing external inspection." Captain Serrado turned them in a tight loop, taking them up and over the enormous engine cradle with its dual exhaust ports, each large enough to house several shuttles. It was her personal indulgence disguised as duty, and the traditional start to their leave.

"Tail to tip," Rahel murmured.

Captain Serrado glanced over. "What did you say?"

"I was thinking about the dock inspectors at Whitesun, and how they'd spot-check fish landings. For some species, it's illegal to catch fish old enough to breed. The inspectors measure the length of the fish and check it for the swellings that mean it's sexually mature. They call it 'checking from tail to tip.'" She waved a hand at the sleek silver hull passing beneath them. "That's what you do, every time we leave. Check the ship from tail to tip."

Serrado chuckled. "I like it. Though if I find signs of sexual maturity, we're all in trouble."

"I thought that was where shuttles came from," Rahel said innocently, smiling when Serrado burst into laughter.

"Don't tell shuttle ops. They're not supposed to know."

The captain's emotions were already lighter, their spiky edges smoothing out. Rahel didn't know what was happening, but she suspected it had something to do with Admiral Greve. Ever since the rear admiral had arrived with the two destroyers and support ships that made up Alsea's battle group, Captain Serrado had gradually changed. Outwardly she remained the same, but her emotions had hardened and grown more brittle, underlaid by a hot base of anger and crystalline shards of grief. Though she never showed it in word or deed, clearing the exit tunnel was as much of a relief to her as it was to Rahel—except her relief was emotional, not physical, and always paired with bitter guilt. She didn't *want* to be happy about leaving.

Checking the ship's hull soothed the anger and softened the brittleness. It was, Rahel thought, the equivalent of her touch therapy.

The silver hullskin gave way to the transparent hull over Deck Zero, and they looked down on the landscaped park that comprised the ship's top deck.

"This is my favorite part," Rahel said.

"Mine, too. Well, after the engine cradle." Serrado banked to one side, then the other, a ritual farewell to her crew. She called it waggling her wings, which made no sense when the shuttle's wings were kept flush against the hull while in space flight.

"Did you know the state transport does the same thing when it flies into Blacksun? It's a tradition to let Blacksun residents know the Lancer has returned."

Serrado didn't take her gaze off the view, but a prickle of interest floated through the air. "No, Andira never told me that. I'll have to ask her about the history." She shifted the control stick forward, skimming down the elevated portion of the hull, and leveled out over its skirt. Ahead were the enormous black markings that spelled out the ship's name and identification. From this angle, Rahel couldn't read them, but she knew what was coming.

They soared over the markings and past the bow of the ship, an abrupt visual shift that put pleasant squirms in Rahel's stomach as her brain reacted to the sudden loss of a perceived floor.

A flick of the control stick and they were looping up and around; another flick and they stopped, hanging upside down above the ship. It loomed before them, now visible in its entirety, a great silver jewel against the endless black.

Serrado did not speak, but her emotions were shouting. Rahel raised her blocks, both to protect herself and respect her captain. It happened every time. And every time, the complicated, twisted mass of emotions grew darker.

"Captain Serrado to *Phoenix*," she said at last.

The com screen activated, showing the ferocious visage of Commander Lokomorra. His dark eyes were outlined with a black tattoo, his thick beard was forked and tied off with decorative beads, and his short, black hair was marked with two decorative stripes running from one temple to the other. When Rahel first met him, she had assumed the stripes were shaved. In truth, they were created by permanently destroying the follicles.

"Are we still in one piece?" Lokomorra asked cheerfully.

"External inspection shows no hull damage on the dorsal side." Serrado was more formal. "I'll check the ventral when we come back."

"Very good. I'll let Commander Zeppy know he won't have to schedule any hull walks."

"Not today, anyway. See you dirtside, Commander." She cut the communication and tapped her control board, turning them in place as the engines thrummed. They accelerated quickly, leaving the *Phoenix* behind and racing across space toward Alsea.

Intellectually, Rahel knew they were traveling at outrageous speeds. Visually, it seemed like a crawl. She could never get used to the distances involved in space travel, even within the relatively short range of orbit, but it made for enjoyable contemplation as they approached the beautiful blue-and-white vision she never tired of seeing.

A loud *pop* and flash startled her into a leap, cut short by her harness.

"It's all right," Captain Serrado said calmly. Too calmly, Rahel realized as she tried to slow her racing heart. Serrado had *expected* that flash.

"What was it?"

The captain checked her board, gave a satisfied nod, and turned in her seat. "An unfortunate electrical short that took out the security cams." Triumph wound tightly around her. "I'll have to report it before too long.

An easy fix once we get back, and no one will get in trouble. It's already arranged."

Rahel stared at her in bafflement. "Why?"

"Because Salomen has a request for you, and she can't ask it with Fleet listening in. This is Alsean business." She turned back to her board and activated the quantum com.

Bondlancer Salomen Opah appeared on the screen, her dark hair up in an elegant formal twist at odds with her casual shirt and unlaced collar. "It worked, then?"

"Like oiled gears. Did you have any doubts?"

"None at all." Her gaze shifted to Rahel, deep brown eyes warming with affection. "I apologize for the subterfuge. Things are happening that we couldn't share with you for your own protection. I'll tell you more once you land, but before that, I have a favor to ask."

"Name it." Salomen never needed to ask, but she always would. That was who she was.

"We're working on a method of long-range empathic projection. I'd like your permission to replay our old training sessions." The dimple in her chin deepened when she smiled. "At a slightly greater distance than across the table."

"You're going to project on me from there?" Shekking Mother, how strong had her powers become?

"Not until you get closer in. But I wanted to give you as much time to prepare as we could. Will you consent?"

"Yes, of course. Comfort?"

"Comfort," Salomen agreed. "I won't be able to warn you before the attempt, but it'll be during your descent. It might be more intense than you're used to."

"You mean like our first time?" Those were fond memories.

"Possibly." She glanced at the harness holding Rahel in place and added, "At least this time, you won't fall out of the chair."

"I'm sure it won't be for lack of trying."

"You have no idea. But you will soon. Thank you, Rahel." Her attention returned to the captain. "We appreciate the maneuvering this must have taken."

"Not much, really. Besides, I'm getting something out of this as well."

"What is that?"

"A few extra minutes of privacy."

Salomen watched her with a solemn expression. "Come home, Ekatya."

"We'll be there soon." Serrado closed the call, then contacted shuttle ops to report the electrical short.

They began their descent through the atmosphere, soon reaching a high layer of clouds that cut their visibility to zero. Rahel let her head rest against the seat and closed her eyes, no longer interested in what was outside. Better to focus on what was coming.

She waited for what seemed like an eternity before a familiar and beloved sensation flowed through her body. Contented lassitude turned her muscles to water and suffused her brain with the comfort of being home on a rainy night, of enjoying touch therapy from Dr. Wells, of giving taboo warmrons to her mother and Sharro.

"Approaching Blacksun Basin," Captain Serrado said from somewhere far away.

Dimly, Rahel understood that she had a reason for making that announcement but couldn't be bothered to figure it out. She basked in the warmth and tranquility until its sudden, shocking absence jerked her back to full awareness.

"Gah." She pulled herself upright, having slid down in her seat, and rubbed her eyes. "It's done."

"I can see that. You looked like a puddle of goo. I might have ask Salomen to practice that on me."

"Not if you want to keep flying."

Serrado chuckled. "We're not too far away. There are the mountains."

Familiar snowy peaks stood stark and austere against the now-blue sky. It was spring in the northern hemisphere, and the mountains ringing Blacksun Basin were laden with their winter snowpack. The sight never failed to gladden Rahel's heart. They always landed in Blacksun first, where she would visit friends and report to Colonel Micah. Tomorrow she would catch a flight to Whitesun to see her mother, Sharro, and Little Mouse, her tiny new brother.

These mountains meant home was only a few hanticks away—and Salomen was mere ticks away, waiting to see her.

They soared over the highest peaks and continued their descent into the Basin, now flashing beneath them in a vibrant patchwork of forest, grasslands, and cultivated fields dotted by compact villages. They were low enough for their groundspeed to be visually obvious, though at this point, Captain Serrado wasn't flying any faster than an Alsean transport.

A shining ribbon in the distance resolved itself into the Silverrun River, roaring through the Basin with snowmelt pushing it over its banks in the annual rejuvenation of the floodplain. And there was Blacksun, rushing up to them in all its breathtaking beauty.

When Rahel had first come to this city a lifetime ago, she had not appreciated its landlocked position or the grandeur of its architecture. Now her stomach tightened in anticipation as she searched for her first glimpse of the famous domes of Blacksun Temple and the State House. It took only a moment to find them, occupying the center of the forested State Park and ringed by the six great caste houses with their colored roofs.

"Welcome home, First Guard," Serrado said as they flew over the city outskirts. She dropped their speed yet again and flipped on the quantum com. "Captain Serrado to Lancer Tal, requesting permission to land."

Lancer Tal looked flushed, her light blue eyes sparkling with triumph. "Your usual pad is open. See you in two ticks."

"I look forward to it."

Rahel had her nose pressed to the window, recognizing individual streets she had walked down. There was the corner cafe with the best rajalta outside Whitesun, and the bright yellow restaurant famous for its meltingly tender fanten in exquisite sauces. There were the expensive houses in the triangle of land where the Silverrun ran up to the Fahlinor River. There was Serenity Bridge, and now they were flying over the beautifully landscaped meadows of the State Park.

They circled around Blacksun Temple, giving her a glimpse into the interior courtyard with its massive molwyn tree, and came to a hover behind the soaring domes of the State House.

Who were all those people? At least forty stood waiting by the landing pad, and only a few of them were Guards. The rest seemed to be in mostly casual attire, an oddity on the grounds of Alsea's center of government.

Captain Serrado brought them to a smooth rest on the bricks of the landing pad. As the engines spun down, she notified the *Phoenix* of their safe arrival, then shut down her boards and detached her harness. "Would you get my bag, please?"

Rahel scrambled to comply, throwing off her harness and hurrying to the lockers in back. By the time she reached the top of the ramp, the captain's bag in one hand and her own on the opposite shoulder, Serrado was already standing in front of Lancer Tal. They had met in a double palm touch and were resting their foreheads together, a greeting reserved for close friends and family members.

They looked like reverse images of each other, similar in build but shaded with hues of day and night: on one side, Lancer Tal's bright blonde hair and ice-blue eyes, on the other, Serrado's midnight hair and eyes the deep blue of the twilight sky. They were the same height, a head shorter than Salomen and deceptively slight of body for women who wielded such power. Yet Serrado seemed suddenly smaller, her emotional exhaustion flowing from her in waves. Beside them, Salomen watched with a frown.

Captain Serrado looked up at Salomen, then took one step to the side to repeat the familial gesture with her. Now it was Lancer Tal frowning while she watched.

As a mid empath, Rahel had no hope of seeing through the fronts of either Salomen or Lancer Tal. But their expressions told a worrisome story. They were deeply concerned with Serrado's emotional signature, yet unsurprised by it.

Something was wrong, and it originated on the *Phoenix*. Down here, Serrado felt safe enough to let go.

And she had just coordinated with members of her crew to black out the data recorders on a Fleet shuttle.

With a start, Rahel realized she had witnessed her captain running a covert operation—but for Alsea, not her own government.

She walked slowly down the ramp, unsure of her place.

Lancer Tal met her eyes. "First Guard Sayana. It's time for you to join us."

7

WEAPON

Tal waited by the fireplace, Salomen at her side, and watched thirty divine tyrees file into the room. On her other side was Ekatya, once again in control of her emotions after her brief release on the landing pad.

Rahel stood beside Salomen, worried and wildly curious. She was nearly Salomen's height but broader in the shoulders, with auburn hair and an exotic slant to her amber eyes. Her balanced resting stance, ready to move in any direction, bespoke cycles of training. Even in this protected place, her gaze was alert and constantly roving.

They had chosen this salon for their practices because it was large enough to handle the crowd, yet cozy enough to not intimidate. A committee meeting room would have been more practical, but Salomen had advised against it. Too official, too uncomfortable, she had said.

The salon was quite the opposite. Designed for social gatherings, it featured cozy armchairs and sofas grouped into conversational areas and no obvious point of focus other than the enormous fireplace at one end. Its sides and mantle were built from large stones arranged to appear as a natural outcrop, while the rest of the wall was taken up by an intricate tile mosaic depicting a forest around the stones. There were dark tree trunks encircled by brilliant green vines, thick vegetation hiding glimpses of colorful birds and more cryptic mammals, and a treecat watching the room with golden eyes as it perched just beneath the ceiling.

It was a good choice. In their first practice, the divine tyrees were so intimidated by Tal's presence that they hadn't been capable of the necessary concentration. Putting them in official surroundings would have made the problem worse.

Now they murmured excitedly amongst themselves as they settled into their usual places, with one man choosing to sit cross-legged on the floor. He was only twenty, barely past his Rite of Ascension, and during their second training had confessed his fear of breaking something expensive if he sat in any of the chairs. Salomen promptly informed him that Tal had once shattered a priceless vase and fatally damaged a historic table while joining with her in a different salon.

That story had ended the group's collective awe of her title while simultaneously elevating a different aspect of her reputation. Tal had no complaints about either.

Across the room, Lead Guard Vellmar gave a nod as she stepped in and closed the door. They were all here.

"Let's begin," Tal called.

The buzz of conversation fell to an expectant silence.

"We didn't tell you who we were targeting with this first test. There was a purpose to that. We won't always know who we're searching for, so it was important to learn whether we could do this without everyone having that information. The answer to that question is now a resounding yes."

In the ensuing noise of triumphant celebration, a retired, white-haired Guard named Jorsil watched from the nearest seat. He had the experience to guess her real motive and was waiting for the confirmation.

"I'm proud of you," she continued. "You've worked hard and exceeded even my most optimistic timeline. When I told Colonel Micah that we were ready for our first test, he thought I was joking. He couldn't believe you had all learned this quickly."

Even Jorsil smiled at that.

"Since you have, let me make two introductions and bring you to the next phase of our training. Some of you may recognize Captain Ekatya Serrado—" She stopped at the enthusiastic applause, appropriate in a formal setting but unexpected here.

Jorsil rose to his feet and thumped a fist against his chest while bowing his head. His merchant bondmate stood up beside him, and that was enough to set off the room. In a wave of movement, every tyree stood and applauded more loudly, most with wide grins while others were awed or even tearful.

Ekatya's control slipped. She brushed a knuckle beneath one eye, her smile tremulous, and Tal knew she was on the edge of a display that she would hate to make in public.

When the applause died down and seats were retaken, Tal turned and said casually, "It seems they know you."

Amid the laughter, one tyree spoke up. "The Savior of Blacksun? Of course we know her!"

"And one of the Gaian divine tyrees," said another.

"Is Dr. Rivers here, too?" a third asked.

Ekatya let out a short chuckle made rough by her emotion. "Yes, she's upstairs. I haven't had the chance to see her yet."

"How do you tolerate it?" asked Pilannon, the young man sitting on the floor. "I can't be away from Savisi for more than a day before my brain starts to itch."

"That's not because you're a divine tyree," Jorsil commented. "It's because you're twenty."

Amid the general amusement at Pilannon's expense, Ekatya brought herself back under control. "She comes on patrol with me sometimes. The rest of the time . . . we do what we must, don't we?"

Thirty divine tyrees, who had all been obliged to adapt to their bonds in sometimes inconvenient ways, made loud noises of agreement.

"Before we go too far off the beacon," Tal interjected, "let me also introduce First Guard Rahel Sayana."

They applauded once more, and Jorsil repeated his salute. Savisi, who was a few cycles older than Pilannon and normally quite shy, exuded excitement as she called, "Can you show us your stave?"

Rahel looked to Salomen for permission.

"Just don't break anything," Salomen said.

"I never break anything unless I mean to."

"Not even a vase?" Pilannon asked, sending the tyrees into raucous laughter.

"Don't mind them," Salomen advised. "Go ahead."

Rahel drew her stave grip from its holster and extended it in one smooth motion, then twirled it from one hand to the other and back again, thumped it on the floor twice, spun it once more, and somehow collapsed it midspin. She had it back in her holster and was standing in a casual pose before anyone registered what had happened.

After a moment of stunned silence, Savisi whooped and the tyrees burst into another round of applause.

"If that's what we get for a successful test, I can't wait to do another one," Savisi said. "That was speedy!"

"Show-off," Salomen muttered. "She only asked to see it."

"She did see it." Though Rahel's expression was stoic, her amusement was plain to sense.

Their antics had the desired result: Ekatya was now relaxed, her previously turbulent emotions smoothed on the surface. Tal gave Salomen's hand a grateful squeeze.

"First Guard Sayana was our target today," she said. "Since she and Salomen have previously worked together on projection training, it was a familiar connection. Captain Serrado facilitated the test and will continue to do so as we expand our range. Captain, how far from Blacksun were you when Salomen connected?"

"We were coming over the western mountains, at an altitude of just under eleven thousand strides."

Astonished murmurs swept the room.

"Eleven vertical lengths!" Jorsil said. "Are you certain?"

"That was when First Guard Sayana almost slid out of her seat despite wearing a harness. I'm fairly certain."

"Salomen's comfort projections are the equivalent of a full-body massage," Rahel said. "I was grateful for the harness."

Salomen bumped her with a shoulder.

"This is only the beginning," Tal said. "We'll be working to expand our range, with the next test taking place when Captain Serrado returns to the *Phoenix* in five days. First Guard Sayana has already agreed to be the subject."

Rahel crossed her arms. "I could use another massage."

Though the other divine tyrees were smiling, Jorsil looked thoughtful. "Lancer Tal, am I correct in thinking this is more about vertical distance than horizontal?"

"Yes. Our hope is that we'll eventually be able to push Salomen's range into orbit."

The smiles vanished under varying expressions of disbelief or confusion. Jorsil simply nodded.

"Captain Serrado's job is to protect Alsea, and she will do that to the best of her ability. I trust her. But I don't trust fate. We cannot afford to depend on her and her officers to be our only defense against those who wish us harm."

"Wait." Savisi's alarm sparked. "We're training to—to fight? Like the Battle of Alsea? I can't do that!"

"No, not like the Battle of Alsea." Tal kept her voice low and calm, cutting across the rising emotion in the room. "Fahla willing, we will never have to ask such sacrifice from our people again. And strategically speaking, it's very unlikely."

"You didn't just defeat the Voloth," Ekatya interjected. "You set them back by several cycles. You destroyed the assets of an entire invasion fleet. Thousands of trained soldiers, hundreds of ground pounders and fighters —they still need time to finish replacing the equipment and people. Even when they do, they won't try another ground invasion. You terrified them. They have no defense against empathic force."

"If they come back," Tal said, "they'll most likely plan an aerial attack with fighters modified for our nanoscrubbers. In that case, they'll run into our fighters and one hundred and eighty of their own ground pounders."

"And you still have the *Caphenon*," Ekatya added. "Blacksun is well protected."

"We believe they're most likely to target our space elevator. It's lower risk with a high payoff. Destroying the elevator would do more than delay our efforts to get into space. It would demoralize us and notch up a victory against the Protectorate."

The tyrees murmured amongst themselves, heads nodding across the room.

Jorsil caught her eye. "If we set them back, then setting us back in turn would boost their pride, no? They'd knock us down when we're trying to stand up. Keep us caged, in a way."

"Exactly. But the attacking ships will have commanding officers, like the *Phoenix* has Captain Serrado. If we can empathically project on a ship's commander, we could end a fight from the inside."

"Great Goddess. That wasn't what I was thinking at all! But it's brilliant."

43

"But you're still talking about what the high empaths did during the Battle of Alsea," Pilannon said. "Even if we're only supplying the power like we did today, we're there. We feel it. You're asking us—"

"To use a nonviolent means of defense," Salomen said. "Do you think I'd be involved in this otherwise? I'm a producer, not a warrior. It would make me sick to use violent empathic force."

If the tyrees knew the truth of that, Tal thought, they would talk of nothing else for a moon.

"There are other ways," she said. "I promise, on my honor, we are not training you to be an offensive weapon. I would not ask that of Salomen and I won't ask it of you. But if we can learn to reach into orbit and convince a Voloth commander to cease fire—"

"It would be worth five warships like the *Phoenix*." Ekatya's sharp tone attracted the attention of everyone in the room. "I've fought my share of battles. It only takes one mistake, one bit of bad luck, and the tide turns the other way. Yes, I took down an invasion fleet before it could hit Alsea, but I lost my ship in the process." She let that sink in before adding, "The Voloth know I'm in charge of Alsea's protection. They'll have studied my tactical history. If they come back, it'll be with a specific strategy to counter me and the assets in my battle group." Her smile was vicious. "But they won't know about you."

8

COMING HOME RITUAL

The divine tyrees had fewer questions than Ekatya had expected. Rahel had none at all, calling it a sensible strategy and offering herself as a test subject whenever necessary.

"We'll work with you as long as we can," Salomen said after the tyrees had filed out. "But if this goes as far as we hope it will, there will come a time when I'll need to work with a Gaian mind." She shook her head as Rahel glanced at Ekatya. "No, I know her too well. Much too well."

Ekatya had to smile at that. "It'll need to be someone new to her. I haven't decided who to ask. It's . . . delicate."

"You can't let this get out," Rahel translated. "Alseans able to affect Gaians in orbit? The DOP would hit the farthest moon."

"They aren't the only ones," Ekatya muttered.

"Ask Commander Lokomorra."

In fact, he had been Ekatya's first thought. But his position as executive officer meant he was in Admiral Greve's target scope. She would not risk his career by asking more of him than she already had.

"I'll take it under advisement," she said. "You have a report to make."

"That means 'go away now,'" Vellmar observed. "And I'm under orders from Lanaril to bring you over for midmeal after you see Colonel Micah. Shall we hit two targets with the same throw?"

The two warriors went one way, already in animated conversation, while Ekatya followed her friends deeper into the maze of the State House. She appreciated their easy silence and didn't even mind that it came from awareness of her emotions. The time when she had resented having a transparent head seemed long past; now she welcomed the freedom from having to play a part for the sake of appearances.

They walked down corridors she didn't recognize and through an airy room full of arched doorways, each topped by paintings depicting a different scene from Alsean history. Ekatya was lost until Andira led them through one of the doorways and down another hall to stop in front of a familiar lift.

"Oh," she said as she turned in place. "That's where that hall goes."

"Another piece of the mental map?" Andira asked.

"One more piece in place, twelve thousand to go."

Salomen chuckled. "I know what you mean. I still have at least eight thousand left."

"That puts you four thousand ahead of me." Ekatya watched the lift doors open. "It always seems incongruous to have such modern lifts in this building."

"Modern but disguised." Andira waited until they were in before tapping the control pad.

The doors closed smoothly, etched and colored metal coming together to complete a map of Blacksun Basin. This was Ekatya's favorite lift, though the one where the doors showed a lifelike winden leaping from one mountain ledge to another was a close second. Alsean artistry never failed to impress her, both with its skill and the way it was incorporated everywhere she looked. Even something as utilitarian as a pair of metal lift doors was turned into a canvas for creativity.

The map split down the middle and parted again, opening onto the quiet elegance of the fourteenth floor. She led the way out, knowing this section as well as her own bridge.

As always, Andira and Salomen followed her into the suite.

"Finally!" Lhyn strode out of the kitchen, her face wreathed in a welcoming smile. "You landed ages ago."

"It was a short meeting," Andira protested.

"It was still a delay." She reached for Ekatya's hands and looked her over with eyes that saw too much. "I'm not used to having to wait. Come on, let's get you out of that uniform."

For most of her life, Ekatya had stripped off her uniform at the end of a shift and never thought a thing about it. That changed when Lhyn introduced her coming home ritual.

While Andira and Salomen drifted into the living area to wait, she followed Lhyn into the bedroom and shut the door behind them. Cocooned in their ritual space, she stood still while Lhyn detached the captain's bars from her collar and set them on the bedside table.

On her ship, she left the bars in place except on laundry day, but Lhyn had been right: removing them each time weighted them with meaning. When she saw them come off, something in her chest began to unwind.

Next, Lhyn methodically opened each tab on the uniform jacket and slipped it from her shoulders, hanging it in the closet while Ekatya shrugged off the overshirt. This was plucked from her hands and hung next to the jacket.

The cushioned bench beside the closet was perfect for sitting on while removing boots and socks. Next to go were the trousers, which Lhyn efficiently folded over another hanger while Ekatya peeled off the undershirt. By the time she returned from dropping her underclothes in the hamper, Lhyn was holding out the Alsean trousers, made of a soft and stretchy material that still managed to look elegant.

She pulled them on and stood erect, waiting.

"My favorite part," Lhyn said, pressing against her front and reaching around. A sudden sense of release, a flash of arm, and the bra went flying to land atop the hamper.

Ekatya chuckled. "So meticulous with the rest, and then you fling the bra."

"Bras should always be flung." Lhyn stepped back, her hands sliding around Ekatya's waist and then up.

Ekatya let out a purr as her newly freed breasts were massaged. "This is my favorite part."

"I know." Lhyn glanced up, wide green eyes alight before she refocused on her massage. "It's a sign of a good relationship when you both enjoy the same thing."

"I don't think this particular thing makes us unique."

She bent to drop a soft kiss on each nipple. "Bye, sweeties. I'll see you later. And don't listen to her, you're completely unique."

Ignoring Ekatya's snort, she held open a short-sleeved shirt. Ekatya slipped it on and pulled the sides together, running her finger up the front pressure seam to seal it. Out of habit, she closed it all the way to the top, then remembered that this was not a duty shirt and she could be as comfortable as she wished.

"Much better," Lhyn said when she reopened the top quarter.

"It takes me a while to get out of the mindset. But I always get there, thanks to your ritual." She had been stripped of her uniform and clothed head to toe in Alsean materials. It was time for the final piece.

"Welcome home, tyrina," Lhyn murmured, wrapping her in a hug.

Ekatya slid her arms around the lean torso and tucked her face into Lhyn's throat. Here were safety and comfort, the things a warship captain was not supposed to need. But she wasn't a warship captain now.

She was just Ekatya, and she was home.

9

THE SEVENTH STAR

"There she goes," Tal said quietly.

Standing beside her at the large window overlooking the State Park, Salomen nodded. "She was wound up tight as a coil of baling wire."

"Amazing how Lhyn can unwind her so quickly."

"It's the ritual." Salomen turned toward a pile of cushions in the corner and pulled the first off the stack. "She created a physical demarkation. It does the same thing that flying over the Silverrun River does for me. As soon as we cross it, I breathe easier because I'm on Opah land." She tossed the cushion at Tal and reached for another.

"You think this is her Hol-Opah?" Tal dropped the cushion at her feet.

"This suite? Somewhat. Lhyn in this suite, definitely." She tossed another cushion and watched Tal set it at right angles to the first. "In a way, I think Alsea is her Hol-Opah. She gave up so much for it, even before she knew us." She spun the third cushion into its place on the floor, then dropped the fourth and sat on it cross-legged.

Tal tidied the placement of the third, which had landed slightly crooked.

Salomen's amusement fizzed through their link. "How do you get anything done when you worry about tiny details like that?"

"I delegate them. To very professional people." With the cushion now properly aligned, Tal sat across from her.

"And then terrify them into making sure they meet your standards."

"My title terrifies them, not me." At the audible sound of disbelief, she added, "Unlike the person in this room who is famous for her sharp tongue."

"Yes, but not over a *cushion*."

They were chuckling when the bedroom door opened.

"They're laughing already," Lhyn commented.

"Always a bad sign." Ekatya followed her out, transformed both in appearance and emotional signature.

"I beg to differ." Salomen patted the two empty cushions. "There's no better way to start a Sharing than with laughter."

"With you, I don't think there's any bad way to start a Sharing." Lhyn's long legs easily cleared the two cushions, putting her in her favored spot nearest the windows.

She and Ekatya settled in unison, their bodies a study in contrasts. Lhyn was even taller than Salomen and slender enough that the State House kitchen staff were forever trying to "pad her bones," as one had put it. Ekatya was the same height as Tal, but her compact body was well-muscled for a Gaian, and she knew how to use it. A winden and a treecat, Salomen called them, and now Tal thought of it every time she saw them together.

Ekatya hadn't sealed her shirt all the way, leaving her upper chest exposed. Tal did not resist the downward drift of her gaze, instead appreciating the hint of beauty there and the fact that she was no longer bound by honor to turn away from it.

From adolescence onward, Alseans negotiated their varying abilities to conceal and detect sexual attraction. Mid empaths could rarely hide their desires; for low empaths, it was an impossibility. But if they chose not to speak of it, the subject was closed. It was the height of rudeness to speak of another's unacknowledged attraction, though good friends and family had more leeway in the social nuances.

As a high empath, Tal never had to worry about being unable to hide an attraction. Her experience was all on the other side: that of politely ignoring what she sensed. She could not count the number of times she had blocked her perception of another's desire for her, but they had certainly increased with her rank.

Her desire for Ekatya tilted the world on its side. She had thought herself successful in hiding it until Lhyn, unaware of the unspoken rules, said she knew.

That had been the first shock. The second was when Lhyn advised her to tell Ekatya.

Nothing in her life had prepared her for the emotional nakedness of admitting what she had failed to conceal. She had no idea how mid and low empaths lived with such exposure. The only consolation was that her friends took their knowledge with them when they left Alsea.

She had not expected them to return. She had certainly not expected that when they did, it would be for her bonding ceremony. And she had never imagined that foursome Sharings would become a constant in her life.

In the Sharings, there was no concealing her attraction, the fact that it was reciprocated, or the tyree bond she had accidentally created with Ekatya. It became an issue at one point, when Salomen lost faith in her own place within their complex web of connections. But Salomen had been right from the very beginning: whatever they did, they would all decide together.

Five and a half moons ago, events around the uprising made it clear that they were building something new. Tal had sat the others down to share their thoughts about the changes. To her surprise, each had come to the same conclusion: their emotions could not be confined to two bonds. Salomen and Lhyn had formed a unique relationship, new and fragile with desire that had only begun to germinate, while that between Tal and Ekatya remained static only through their mutual honor. The remaining two connections lacked a physical draw but grew emotionally deeper each time they Shared. Unknowing and unintended, they had created a six-pointed bond.

Six, Lhyn had said. *The most important number on Alsea.*

They chose to accept the truth and follow where it led. Ekatya asked only that they keep the physical aspects unexplored for now. With the uncertainty and stress of her Fleet service, she needed stability at home.

Before the next moon passed, it became apparent that Tal and Ekatya were not alone in having two tyrees. Salomen's connection with Lhyn flared up to a new level, ushered into existence by the power shared between the four of them.

It made sense, they agreed. It balanced them.

Ekatya said they were two pairs of binary stars orbiting each other. Lhyn said there was precedent in several cultures she had studied. Salomen said nothing in her life had ever fit social expectations, so why should this be different?

Tal, the master of choosing words to affect outcomes, could not find words for this. After a lifetime of constricting herself in pursuit of her title —and then in service to the demands of that title—her joy at this freedom was beyond her ability to express.

But she could show them. And so she did, in every Sharing.

"Are you ready?" she asked.

Lhyn smiled at her. "It's sweet that you still ask."

"Consent is never not necessary," she said, trying to sound stern.

"I for one am glad you always ask." Ekatya ran a finger down the front seam of her shirt, separating it entirely. "And yes, I'm ready. I've been ready since my last leave."

Lhyn opened her shirt as well, then scooted forward to a more comfortable position on her cushion.

They were in a square, with Tal facing Salomen and Ekatya facing Lhyn. Tal braced her elbows on her knees and rested one hand on the swell of Ekatya's left breast. Salomen did the same for Lhyn, carefully finding the correct placement. Her other hand settled atop Tal's, pressing it into the warm skin, while Tal mirrored the gesture, doubling up on Salomen's connection with Lhyn. In the beginning, they had taken turns being the primary skin contact, but found that this worked better.

Completing the four-way circuit snapped a multiplying lens on their empathic senses, rocketing Tal and Salomen up to a point where they could perceive the life energy of every Alsean in Blacksun Basin. Though they had tried, they could never contain this initial burst. It was as if they had to use up the excess power before they could retake control.

As the power leveled out, they dove back to the combined mind created by their Sharing and found a familiar imbalance. Though greatly reduced by the coming home ritual, Ekatya's anger and grief were still weighing her down.

Working together, the four of them lifted the weight and sent it outward to dissipate in the vastness of the mindscape—for that was how Tal visualized it. Ekatya saw it as knots tied in colored threads, which they worked to untie and straighten. Salomen saw diseased leaves on a great, noble tree with its roots in bare rock and its branches reaching to the stars. To her view, they were carefully pruning away the unhealthy leaves and discarding them, allowing the tree to pour its energy into proper growth.

Lhyn saw abstract patterns she could never adequately describe, other than to say that it was blindingly obvious where the patterns were disrupted. She saw them rubbing out the sections that didn't belong and redrawing them to perfection, or as close as they could get.

Ekatya always needed this rebalancing, a fact she detested despite the obvious cause. But she was never the only one. Tal sometimes arrived at a Sharing with a feeling of diving into cold water on a sweltering day, seeking relief after dealing with intransigence, idiocy, or simple small-mindedness. Lhyn, the most even-tempered of the four, was surprisingly harsh in her self-expectations and judgment. She did not give herself the benefits she so freely gave to others, and her apparent ease often hid anger or disappointment that was viciously directed inward.

Of them all, it was Salomen who required the least rebalancing. Her tendency for quick bursts of anger and scorching words, which she often rued, had the effect of burning off her frustration. She also credited her work, which kept her hands in the soil and her mind centered.

Once the balance had been restored, in whichever way each of them viewed it, they settled into the comfort of their bond. They could wander at will among the emotions, soaking up the best of them. They could float in the embrace of this unity, reveling in the depth of peace it offered. Or they could listen to the harmonies they all heard regardless of individual visualizations, a symphony Ekatya called the music of the spheres.

Today, Tal listened. She would never grow tired of this beauty, or of trying to discern the melodic progression. The symphony was a living thing and wonderfully unpredictable, but she often guessed correctly. Hearing the expected notes filled her with a joy she could not explain. It wasn't about being right, but rather a sense that these particular notes were proof of her belonging. She was exactly where she should be.

When the symphony faded, it was time. She let go, returning to her individuality with only a slight jar, and opened her eyes.

"I had a thought," Lhyn said immediately.

"When do you not have thoughts?" Salomen teased.

"When she's sleeping." Ekatya rubbed her eyes. "Stars and Shippers, I needed that. Thank you."

Tal laid a hand on her knee in quiet acknowledgment. "What was the thought?" she asked.

"Hold on." Lhyn scrambled up, tossed her cushion into the corner, and strode across the room, resealing her shirt along the way. At her desk, an extra-wide affair with few drawers but a great deal of surface area, she shuffled through stacks of old books that were no doubt borrowed from either Blacksun Temple or one of the caste houses.

Finding what she sought, she returned with her gaze fixed on the pages. "Ah! Here we go," she said, settling into a cross-legged position. "I was thinking about the fact that we have six bonds between us, and every one of them is different. But we forgot one thing. The seventh star. The single entity we create when we're Sharing."

She turned the book and set it on the floor, her finger marking a specific point on the image shown.

"Great Goddess," Salomen breathed.

The book was open to a beautifully hand-colored Shield of Alsea, an image that adorned every temple and government building on the planet. Tal saw it nearly every day, carved and inlaid in the doors of her office.

In the shield was the molwyn tree, sacred to Fahla, creating a perfect circle with its roots, branches, and leaves. Above it shone six stars, representing the six castes, which were also seen in the six main branches. In the fork of the top two branches, sheltered beneath the tree's crown, was a seventh star, larger than the rest.

The star representing Fahla.

"Normally, I'd call this an interesting coincidence with no correlation," Lhyn said. "But what we make when we Share—what *all* Alseans make when they Share—it's a piece of the divine, isn't it? If we define that as being something existing outside of us yet rooted within us."

"Well, I know what you'll be discussing with Lanaril tomorrow," Ekatya said. "She'll love to dive into that philosophical question."

"True words." Tal could easily picture it. "Can you wait until the midmeal you've planned, or will you be running across the park after mornmeal?"

"I'm not *that* impatient." But Lhyn's eyes were bright, and she cradled the book against her chest.

"Of course not." Ekatya rolled forward, landing on all fours, and leaned over to kiss her. Then she pushed her cushion an arm's length away, in perfect position for her head, and collapsed onto her back with a groan. Her open shirt fell to the sides, exposing her torso.

Lhyn set down her book. "Ekatya?"

"Hm?"

"If you're not ready to explore the physical aspect of Bond Number Three, maybe you should close your shirt."

"Too tired."

"Andira's eyeballs are about to fall out of her head."

"It's good for her. Gets the blood pumping."

Salomen glanced from Ekatya's supine form to Tal. "I think I see it. Right there." She leaned forward to brush a finger over Tal's throat and let out a startled squeak when her wrist was caught and pulled. Off balance, she braced herself against Ekatya's leg with her other hand.

"Are you volunteering your medical assistance?" Tal pulled her closer.

"If she does, could you take it somewhere that's not right on top of me?" Ekatya grumbled.

"She has a point," Salomen said with a wicked smile. "We wouldn't want to break any vases."

Ekatya's eyes popped open. "Wait. Wait, wait, wait. That's what that young man said to Rahel." She sat up, pushing Tal and Salomen apart, and sealed her shirt. "What was he talking about?"

"Remember the day of the uprising?" Salomen said. "When we caused a slight bit of damage during our reunion?"

"Yes . . . ?" She drew out the word in a suspicious tone.

"I told Pilannon about it. He was too stiff and uncomfortable in that salon, and the other divine tyrees weren't much better. Especially once they saw Andira. So I told them that story to loosen their spines."

She looked as if Salomen had admitted to dancing naked down Fahlinor Way in midday traffic. "You told all of them?"

"It wouldn't have done much good to tell just one." Salomen glanced over with a *why is she asking* expression. Tal shrugged.

"You shared details of your sex life with thirty strangers."

"We were training for a group Sharing. They wouldn't be strangers for long. It was an easy way to break down barriers."

"With stories of your *sex life?*" Ekatya pointed at Tal. "For the love of flight, she's the Lancer!"

Lhyn, whose amusement had been growing by the piptick, gave up and laughed. "I told you the Alseans have an open culture when it comes to sex. I told you that the day we crashed. Did you forget?"

"No, but I didn't think—stars and Shippers, I can't imagine telling any of my crew why I had to requisition that new computer display. I can't think of a faster way to destroy my credibility."

Intrigued, Tal asked, "You broke a display? In your quarters or your office?"

"Quarters," Lhyn answered. "Your star will go nova before Ekatya joins in her office."

"How . . . limiting," Salomen said. "Andira's office is wonderful for that. Even better than mine."

"Fucking Hades." Ekatya fell onto her back and covered her eyes. "I need a brain wipe."

Her embarrassment was hot, flavored with an interest that Tal chose to leave unremarked. "Lhyn isn't this juvenile about joining. Why are you?"

Scowling, she uncovered her eyes. "Juvenile?"

"You're acting like Jaros," Salomen said. "Sometimes we kiss in front of him just to hear the horrified sounds he makes."

"Come to think of it, Nikin isn't much better," Tal commented. "Perhaps you and he should talk."

Lhyn put up a hand and gave a slight shake of her head.

Tal's senses had told her the same thing: Ekatya had abruptly reached her limit. Tilting off her cushion, she kicked it away and stretched out beside her friend, head propped on her fist. "I'm sorry. We only tease because you give such good reactions."

"Could you not? I can't—this is hard." Ekatya stared up at the ceiling. "I'm walking a tightrope every damned day. They've taken so much away from me. But I know that I can come here and let it all go, and that keeps me sane. Then I get a reminder like this that I'm still an outsider here, too. I'm an outsider everywhere."

Shocked both by the admission and the surge of grief, Tal reached for her hand. "That is not true."

Salomen shifted closer to Ekatya and rested a hand on her stomach. "It's not within ten lengths of being true."

"I am . . ." Ekatya hesitated, squeezing Tal's hand. "I'm so envious, sometimes." She rolled her head to focus on Lhyn, now beside Salomen. "Of you. You fit in here like you slipped on a comfortable old shoe. You know the culture. Nothing surprises you. Every time I come home, you know something else I don't. You're a citizen and in the scholar caste. And I know you've paid a horrible price for it and I would never, ever want anything less for you. I'm so glad you're here and so grateful, but I—" She clenched her jaw and refocused on the ceiling.

Tal looked to Lhyn for permission and received a nod. Carefully, she scooted forward to press herself against Ekatya's side, paying close attention to her emotional signature. There was no discomfort, only grief and shame.

Lhyn had moved at the same time, going around to sit at Ekatya's head. "You grainbird," she murmured, brushing back her hair. "Why didn't you tell me?"

"I didn't want you to feel bad about it."

"One of these days, you'll learn that I'm strong enough to carry you when you need it." Lhyn dropped a kiss on her forehead. "I want you to notice one thing. You said 'every time I come home.' You don't come home to a place where you're an outsider."

"Words for Fahla." Tal looked into the dark blue eyes that met hers and added, "You are not an outsider. I'd make you a citizen in a heartbeat, you know that."

"You can't. It would end my career. They'd say I can't serve two governments."

Tal swallowed the regret at pushing her to this point and focused on fixing the damage. "But someday that won't matter. When that day comes, I'll sign the declaration that's been sitting in my desk drawer since Lhyn received hers."

"You did mine at the same time?"

"I'm efficient. And nothing would give me greater pleasure than to sponsor you into the warrior caste."

"I'd offer to sponsor you into my caste," Salomen said. "But I've heard that you can kill a Filessian orchid."

The laugh that burst from Ekatya disintegrated much of her grief. She let go of Tal's hand and reached for Salomen's instead, holding it against her stomach. "There's a reason I give the botany staff access to my quarters. Lhyn isn't any better."

"I object to that. I know how to take care of a Filessian orchid. I just get . . . distracted."

"Same end result."

"You're both disqualified," Salomen announced. "On behalf of all plant life everywhere."

Ekatya shook her head with a watery smile. "Thank you. All of you. This helps, so much. I'm sorry I ruined our Sharing."

"Ekatya Lucia Serrado. You cannot think you could ruin our time together by showing us your true emotions. What is a Sharing about if not that?"

"Three names," Tal said in a stage whisper. "I'd pay attention if I were you."

"I'm paying attention. I never stop paying attention."

Stopped mid-scold by a few strained words, Salomen gentled her voice. "That's not what we want. Not all the time. Home is a place you go to be yourself. To relax and know that you're loved for who you are, not who you try to be. Fahla knows it's taken me a lifetime to learn that lesson." She lifted their clasped hands. "You are loved. Because we see you."

Ekatya took in a quick breath, her eyes brimming. Her emotional signature shivered with urgency as she released Salomen's hand and draped her forearm over her eyes.

Tal understood. Tears were a step too far for a warrior like her, even in trusted company. But if they were to push past this sense of exclusion, it had to start here.

She brushed her knuckles down Ekatya's jaw, the only part of her face she could reach. "We do see you."

"All of us." Lhyn rested a hand on her bondmate's shoulder and squeezed.

"Whether you want us to or not," Salomen added.

At that, Ekatya let out a gasping laugh and abruptly rolled, burying her face in Tal's shirt and tucking her arms between them.

Tal embraced her rigid form and looked up at Lhyn, unsure what to do next.

Silently, Lhyn held a finger to her lips, gave a nod, and stood up. Salomen rose as well, tossing her cushion into the corner before following Lhyn into the kitchen.

Their quiet voices blended with the creak of cupboards opening, glasses tapping on the counter, and the pop of a bottle of spirits being opened. The normalcy had a calming effect on Ekatya, though she did not move.

Tal caressed her hair, an indulgence she had not allowed herself before now. It was such a deep black that it shone beneath the lights, and the strands slipped easily between her fingers.

Ekatya settled under the touch, her body gradually releasing its tension.

From the dining room came the scrape of chairs sliding against wood: Salomen and Lhyn were sitting at the table. It seemed to be the final key, allowing Ekatya to relax completely.

"That was good of them," she mumbled.

"They do know how to handle us."

The chuckle was muffled in her shirt. "All too well." She remained still for another half tick, then pulled back and wiped her cheeks. "I hate doing this."

"You and me both. I also hate admitting that it helps."

This time, Ekatya's laugh was unencumbered by tears.

10

LECTURE

His timing was good; Lhyn was just turning onto the main path leading from Blacksun Temple when he reached the junction. The first warm day of spring had brought out residents and tourists in droves, filling paths that had been quiet a nineday ago. Lhyn stood out from the crowd like a winden on a city street: graceful, exotic, clearly out of her natural habitat.

She hadn't seen him and was moving in a leisurely stride, her arms full of books. Given the length of her legs, even her unhurried pace meant he needed to hustle to catch up.

"Lhyn!" he called from a few steps behind.

She stopped and turned, her face lighting up at the sight of him. "Micah, well met! Can you believe these crowds? It's like the sun came out and suddenly everyone remembered there's a park here."

They were family through their ties to Tal and Salomen, their connection sanctified by the rituals of the bonding break. She had the right to call him Corozen. But once she learned of the warrior naming conventions and his preference for Micah, she had given up her right in favor of his comfort. Ekatya followed her lead. Only Salomen and her family called him by his first name now, though from them it somehow fit.

He indicated the books in her arms. "May I offer my assistance?"

"Only if you want the responsibility. They're from Lanaril's personal library." She laughed when he jerked his hands away. "That's what I thought. This one on the bottom? It's two hundred and eighty cycles old. That's why I'm holding onto it with both hands."

"Why didn't she give you a bag?" he asked as they resumed their walk.

"She didn't have one handy, and we used up our time. There was a patient waiting at her door when I left."

"Don't tell me you got distracted by philosophy."

"You know, I don't need empathic senses to detect sarcasm."

"Good. I won't have to try very hard."

Her sideways look indicated only partial amusement. "She said she trusted me to take care of them. Which is the heaviest weight she could possibly put on me. Now I'd rather break a leg than let anything happen to one of these."

He had to admire the tactic. "Lanaril knows what she's doing."

"I know, believe me. We should all be grateful that she only uses her powers for good. What brings you into the heaving sea of people today?"

"I wanted to talk to you."

When she didn't answer right away, he knew her mind was working through the possibilities. He pushed up his shirt sleeves, letting the sun soak into his skin. The last ninedays of winter were always the worst, giving everyone a collective case of weather-induced despondence. It was why they all ran outdoors at the first sight of warmth and sunshine.

He wondered if high empaths could sense the universal lifting of spirits.

"It would have been easier to see me in my suite," Lhyn said. "But Ekatya's there, so you want privacy. Does this have to do with her?"

"No. Well, in an indirect way, possibly. But I hope not."

She tilted her head toward a side path angling off to the right. "Shall we?"

For all the teeming masses in the State Park, tranquility was easy to find. Most people stayed on the main paths, which were popular for good reason: they featured the most jaw-dropping views of the great buildings and passed through the most extravagantly landscaped areas.

But there were smaller paths winding all through the park, lingering in little copses and clearings which were no less carefully landscaped. Offering privacy in place of sweeping vistas, these spaces were sought by

61

lovers and bondmates, readers seeking quiet, crafters looking for inspiration, and politicians pursuing deals outside the usual channels.

Lhyn walked with the assurance of one who had explored them all.

"There's a lovely water feature over here," she said, stepping onto an even narrower path. It meandered downhill to a dense grove of trees, where they passed from brilliant sunlight into dappled shade fragrant with the scent of shade-loving winterbloom.

At the heart of the grove was a single bench facing a scene Micah had seen in images but never in person. Three massive stone slabs were set horizontally at different heights, each carved with multiple curving channels. The water moved quietly and with nary a ripple, sliding through its channels and dropping from the top slab to the next and the next. At the bottom edge of the lowest slab, it plashed onto pebbles and vanished.

Lhyn settled on the bench, protectively cradling the books atop her legs. "Privacy and beauty, what more could you ask for?"

"Answers." He sat beside her and rubbed his hands nervously on his thighs. "Lhyn, I need to ask for your discretion."

The way she examined him was reminiscent of Alejandra. Their eye color was quite similar, he realized, though the shape was not. Alejandra's eyes reminded him of a complacent feline. Lhyn had a perpetual look of wide-eyed interest.

"You mean you don't want me to tell Ekatya."

"For now. It's personal."

That reassured her. "I promise."

"Good. The situation is—" He broke off, realizing he was about to give the equivalent of a security report. What was the point of couching this in any language other than the most straightforward? "I'm interested in courting Alejandra Wells."

Her eyes grew even wider. "You—fucking stars! How long has that been going on? I can tell you Ekatya has no clue."

"It's very recent. Right now, she's probably asking Rahel Sayana for advice on joining with an Alsean. I'm asking the same thing. Not the same thing," he corrected himself. "In reverse. I mean—"

She was laughing. "It's not as if you can look it up in a book, can you?"

"No." He exhaled, relieved at her easy understanding. "I wish I could."

"Oh, I'm happy for her. And you. I'd never have imagined you together, but if any two people deserved joy . . . and that you're asking for help? If my first lovers had done that, my early sexual life would have been a lot different."

"Don't your instructors teach you in school?"

"It varies from one culture to another. Mine valued procreation but not pleasure. We only learned about the biology and the acts necessary to produce children. For Gaians, that's possible without any pleasure for the female. In fact, it's possible with pain for the female, and I don't mean the good kind. I started joining at seventeen and didn't know it could feel good until I was twenty-two."

Had it been anyone but Lhyn, he wouldn't have believed this for a moment. No Alsean could procreate without pleasure. Gamete production depended on it. A creation ceremony spread pleasure over five days, the time required to mature the gametes and ready the body for implantation. He could not imagine a biology so different, much less a culture that exacerbated the lack.

"That's an impressive scowl," she said. "Don't worry, not all Gaian cultures are that backward. Some have wonderful rituals to ease their young people into sexual matur—oh! That's what you need! A sexual maturity rite."

His heart sank. "Lhyn, I hardly think—"

"Do you want my advice?"

"Yes, but I would ask that you keep our ages in mind. Please don't suggest something embarrassing."

She turned to face him more directly, earnestness written in every line of her body. "I want this to be good for both of you. I owe Alejandra my health and my sanity. She was there for me in my worst times. And you're my chosen family."

He relaxed. Of course Lhyn would want that; she was one of the kindest people he knew. "I'm listening."

"Right, here's what I'm thinking. I could lecture you for a hantick on Gaian female sexuality and how it differs from Alsean. I could show you books and diagrams and vids, but it would still be abstract. How much of that would you retain when it counted? I think you need something different."

She wasn't going to lecture him? That was a surprise. "What do I need, then?"

"You need *her* to tell you what feels good." She held up a hand, stopping him before he could protest. "You said you were listening."

"I am."

"One of the cultures I studied has no written language. They don't have books or instruction manuals. Their history and wisdom are handed down in oral tales. They have a beautiful sexual maturity rite that uses—hm. That might be a little hard to find here. They use a bioluminescent fungus."

"A what?"

"A mushroom that glows in the dark."

"Lhyn, really—"

"Keep listening! I promise there's a point to this. The young couple meet in a hut made for the purpose. It has a floor and ceiling to protect them from rain, but no walls. That way, the elders of the tribe can attend and make sure nothing goes wrong."

"I hope it's a tropical climate."

"Oh. Yes, it is. I forgot that detail. Anyway, the floor is heaped with pillows and soft sheets, and there's water and plates of food to keep them going. The setup is important," she said, raising a finger. "You shouldn't have to leave the room for anything. It would break the ritual."

"And the mood, I suppose."

She nodded. "The elders know that. They don't tell the youngsters. They tell them it's all about the ritual, because that gives it importance and meaning. Otherwise, you'd have two young people giggling about getting in the mood. Or stressing themselves to the point of killing any arousal because they're not in the mood and they think they should be."

He thought back to his first time. There had indeed been stress, the kind he devoutly wanted to avoid with Alejandra.

"They start the ceremony by lighting candles around the edges of the room. For the youngsters, this would be a familiar tradition, because they do it for all their feasts and special occasions. One candle for the sun, one for each of their four moons, one for the ancestors, one for the children of the future, and so on. You could do whatever you wanted with it."

"Like lighting oil bowls in the temples," he said. "On days of remembrance, we light one for each person we're remembering. It brings them closer."

"Yes! A tradition that eases both people into a calmer frame of mind."

He crossed his arms. "I'm liking it so far."

"You'll like the next step, too. They undress each other."

"That seems somewhat necessary."

"Getting naked is necessary," she corrected. "But that can happen any number of ways. The method has meaning. Alejandra always wears her hair up in a twist with two ornamental hair sticks. The first thing you do is take out the sticks and unwind her hair. Then you undo her jacket and slide it off. Then her shirt or dress. It's step by step. A process done with reverence."

She had lost him at "unwind her hair," her words setting off a vivid memory. Alejandra had done just that during their long night of conversation, when she was comfortable enough to relax more fully. He had watched with a dry mouth, wishing it were his hands performing the task. She had done it distractedly, a thoughtless act that held no importance for her. But it had held great importance for him.

"I think you see my point," Lhyn was saying.

He shook himself back to awareness. "Yes. Reverence."

"And she'll do the same for you. Remember, this is as new to her as it is to you. You're not undressing each other. You're *unwrapping* each other."

In this shady grove, cooled further by the falling water, he should not be this warm. He opened his shirt at the throat and laid one arm along the back of the bench, trying to ignore her knowing smile. "It's getting interesting," he allowed.

"Mm-hm. Back to our youngsters. On a special table at one end of the hut, there are two bowls. One holds an oil that has been blessed by the elders. The other has the mushroom, crushed to a paste. They start with the oil, taking turns rubbing it into every part of the other's body. It has a spiritual basis, but—"

"It's really meant to relax them."

"Yes."

"Those elders are devious."

She laughed. "Aren't they all?"

"It makes sense. Every detail so far is meant to calm the youngsters and ease them into the proper mental space. Almost like centering. The massage puts them at the point of physical touch, but it still isn't sexual."

She looked proud. "You see it."

"I like it. What about the mushroom?"

"That's the best part. They decide who goes first, and that person lies down. The other begins to touch them. Light brushes with the fingers, licking, kisses, whatever they want, as long as it's gentle. But it's done in a specific pattern, from top to bottom and back to front. First the scalp, then the back of the neck and around the ears, then every part of the back, then the arms, then the buttocks and legs and feet. And then the person being touched rolls over and they start from the top again. Face, throat, chest . . ."

He was lost in another vivid image, this one from his imagination: Alejandra, lying warm and naked on a bed, her skin glowing from the oil he had rubbed into it. Every part of her open to his touch, waiting—

"And when something feels particularly good, the one being touched says *shala mai rihilar*, which means 'blessed by the gods.' Then the person touching takes a dab of mushroom paste and marks the spot."

"Oh," he murmured. "I think I understand."

"Isn't it a beautiful ritual? They call it the Rite of Knowing. By the time they're done, each of them is marked head to toe in the places that bring them pleasure. They literally glow with it. When they finally begin their joining, they know exactly where to touch. They've drawn maps on each other. Then there's the other benefit."

"What's that?"

"The mushroom is an aphrodisiac."

The vision dissipated. "Naturally," he said with a chuckle. "And they lick it off each other."

"Right! A night of pleasure, mapped specifically to each of them." She pressed her lips together and gave a firm nod. "That's what you need. Even if I gave you that lecture you were expecting—yes, I know you were —I could only tell you in general terms what Alejandra might like. Or I could tell you what works for me, or what works for Ekatya. But that doesn't mean it would work for her. Everyone is different. I know that's true for Alseans as well as Gaians."

"It is," he agreed.

"I'll send you a file with the anatomical details. We can go over it together, so you know what to look for and what the differences are. But this ritual allows her to tell you exactly what she wants. And it allows you to tell her what you want."

His brain stopped. For some reason, he hadn't thought of that side of it. He had assumed that Alejandra would return, flush with knowledge from Rahel, and they would go from there. But like Lhyn, Rahel could only give general knowledge. She wouldn't know about that spot behind his ear—

"Of course, you'd have to modify it," Lhyn said, interrupting his increasingly compelling thought process. "The massage oil won't be a problem, but I don't know what you could use for the mushroom."

He grinned at her. "I'll think of something."

11

LIAISON

After four and a half lovely days off, it was time to be the captain again. Ekatya had left her Alsean clothing in the closet and was back in uniform, waiting in Andira's office with Ambassador Solvassen. She had one political task before flying back to the *Phoenix*: meeting the new Gaian liaison officer who would coordinate training between Fleet and Alsean fighter pilots. She had arrived at the *Phoenix* on a personnel ship and was being flown down right now.

"How many fighters are you up to, Lancer Tal?" Solvassen asked.

"We finished our one hundredth Serrado fighter last nineday." Andira watched with an amused look as he blew across the top of his shannel cup. "Too hot?"

"I know, I know," he said good-naturedly. "I'm a limp flower who can't handle proper shannel."

"Who called you that?"

"I'd rather not say. It might cause an interplanetary incident." Solvassen blew again, took a cautious sip, and winced. "Nope, not quite."

Ekatya didn't hide her amusement. She liked Solvassen, with his ample stomach and genial nature. He was more scholar than politician, a trait that had dead-ended his career in the Protectorate Diplomacy Corps but which earned him the respect of the Alseans.

"You could pour it into the saucer," she suggested. "It would cool faster."

Andira looked over with an expression of such horror that Ekatya nearly spit out the sip she had just taken.

Solvassen chuckled. "Practical advice, but I do unfortunately have to keep up appearances. At least in the Lancer's office." He tried another sip and swallowed. "Ah, there we go. One hundred Serrados total? Or one hundred plus the thirty you started with?"

"The latter, and seventy-two Candini fighters. We were able to build faster once we established the facilities and workflows."

"And when you didn't have to strip hullskin and rebuild existing construction," Ekatya added. "It's always faster to build from scratch."

"True words."

"The builder caste has been phenomenal these past two and a half cycles," Solvassen said, demonstrating one of the characteristics that made Alseans like him. "Repairing the damage from the Battle of Alsea, constructing the space elevator, building a fleet of fighters, and I hear the first shuttles are ready for test flights? The Protectorate wishes you could export that kind of efficiency."

"The builders have an excellent Prime," Andira said. "Eroles inspires and motivates them. She's the best we've had in three generations."

"Have you told her that?" Ekatya asked curiously. She remembered a time when relations between Andira and the Prime Builder had not been quite so smooth.

"Of course. It's easier to motivate your people if you feel motivated yourself."

Ekatya lifted her cup in a salute. "Words for Fahla. They should teach that in command training. I was a captain for several cycles before I figured it out."

"They could teach it in the Diplomacy Corps, too." Solvassen gulped the rest of his drink, as was his wont once it cooled. He set the cup and saucer aside and checked his wristcom. "She should be here in a tick."

"Should I ask why this happened so suddenly? All these moons and there was never a candidate who satisfied everyone's expectations. Then I go on leave and when I come back, boom, there's a new liaison arriving."

Andira shrugged. "You said it yourself. We never had the right candidate before. Once she was available, though, everyone agreed within a hantick."

"That must have set a record."

"You have no idea. Ah, she's here."

With rising suspicion, Ekatya watched her cross the room. Andira didn't let people into her office; her aide showed them in.

She swung open the left-hand door and said happily, "At last. Well met!"

"Well met, Lancer Tal. It's great to be back," said a familiar voice. It was so out of place on Alsea that Ekatya couldn't make the connection.

Not until a woman with short, spiky red hair and an impish grin stepped into the room. "Captain. How the Hades are you?"

"Stars and Shippers! Candini! What are you doing here?" Throwing all dignity out the window, Ekatya bounded across the office to meet her friend and former officer in a laughing hug. "It's so good to see you!"

Candini squeezed her to the point of breathlessness. "Likewise. I've missed you so much." She pulled back but didn't let go. "I went through three different captains before giving up. It was never the same without you."

"You gave up? What does—you left Fleet?" Ekatya took a step back. "Great galaxies, of course you did. You're the liaison." She paused. "*You're* the liaison?"

Candini's laugh was infectious as always. "You used to be faster than this."

"First Pilot," Andira said with a smirk. "I'd advise you to be more respectful of the captain you'll be working with."

"Why should she start now? I can't believe this. 'Not available,' no wonder. Were you waiting for her to take early retirement?"

"They were waiting for me to finish my last cruise. I'd barely started when Ambassador Solvassen contacted me, and then I was locked in."

"But you were in line for an instructor position at Command Dome. Complete with promotion. You threw away a lieutenant commander's bars?"

Candini shrugged. "First Pilot is better." She turned to Solvassen, who had joined them in the center of the room. "Hi, Ambassador. It's good to meet you face to face."

"Indeed it is." Solvassen shook her hand. "You're a popular choice, I don't mind telling you. The Protectorate is pleased that a Gaian is in the position, and the Alseans never wanted anyone but you."

"Well, I couldn't pass up the chance to teach pilots how to fly a fighter named after me." Her grin reappeared. "Chief Kameha tells me I need to prepare for being worshipped. I told him I've always known how to handle that."

Ekatya raised her eyebrows at Andira. "And that's what you've brought on yourself. I hope you know what you're doing."

"I'm not her supervisor. She'll be reporting to Colonel Alportel at Blacksun Base."

"Have you warned the colonel?"

"What was that about respect?" Candini asked. "I'll remind you that you're not talking to a lieutenant anymore. I'm a First Pilot now."

"And the first Gaian officer in the Alsean Defense Force. You're a pioneer, Candini." Andira was suddenly serious. "You're representing your species and setting the standards you expect your pilots to follow. I assume those standards will be every bit as high in personal comportment as in flying skills."

Candini stood straighter. "They will, Lancer Tal. I know how to separate on duty from off."

"Very good. Then I think it's time to celebrate your arrival. We've been waiting a long time for you to be free. As I recall, I offered you an inducement to sign on with us."

"Yes, but you didn't have to—" She stared openmouthed in the direction Andira was pointing. On the floor, tucked against the wall, was a wooden crate with a distinctive logo stamped on the side. "You really did?"

"I promised you a case of Valkinon. I keep my promises. But I won't ask you to break into it now." She walked over to her sideboard and pulled a bottle from beneath. "Captain Serrado, would you get the glasses?"

"Certainly. I'm afraid I'll have to stick to shannel," Ekatya said apologetically, opening the cabinet door. "I'm flying back to the *Phoenix* this afternoon."

"Twelve hours from bottle to throttle," Candini said in Common. With a flourish, she produced an injector and switched back to High

Alsean. "Except Dr. Wells foresaw certain celebrations tonight and gave me a few doses of kastrophenol. I'm willing to share."

Ekatya had rarely spent a more enjoyable half hantick. She couldn't drink more than one glass, even with the kastrophenol, but she could revel in the company of a friend she hadn't seen in person for nearly four years. Candini was one of the first officers to be scooped up when the crew of the *Caphenon* returned to Protectorate space. Sixteen months later, Ekatya took command of the *Phoenix* and was looking for a pilot, but Candini was unavailable. The position was long filled when she did become available, and she wasn't interested in anything but the top spot.

She certainly had it now. Commander of a growing planetary fleet of fighters? And coordinating joint training with pilots from two cultures? It was a Hades of a jump from piloting a warship and being responsible for no one but herself. Had this been Candini from four years ago, Ekatya would not have thought her ready for the job. But her duties since then had included a stint as squadron commander and then flight ops commander, giving her a great deal of supervisory experience. She honestly could not think of anyone better suited to this unique position.

When their informal party ended with Andira's next appointment, Ekatya bid farewell to Solvassen and offered to walk Candini to the landing pad. She had only stopped here as a courtesy; her true destination was Blacksun Base.

As soon as they exited the State House, Candini spoke in Common. "How are you, really? Is the shit as deep as I think? No way they let you keep your command without some sort of leash."

Ekatya nearly stumbled as the new reality set in: Candini was no longer in Fleet. She did not need protection from the truth, nor a carefully drawn line between friend and superior officer.

The freedom left her unable to speak for several steps.

"It's deep," she said at last. "Daily check-ins to reaffirm my loyalty to the Protectorate. Weekly security reports on my movements so they can be spot-checked for irregularities. Admiral Greve has blanket access to any security cam footage he asks for, no probable cause necessary as long as I'm in it. And I found spy cams in my quarters."

Candini stopped walking and turned with a thunderous expression. "Are you fucking kidding me?"

"I wish I were."

"They're treating you like a traitor!"

"Not quite. They're treating me like someone they expect to become a traitor. Since I haven't done anything, they can't throw me out. But they're waiting for it."

"Spy cams in your quarters? That's not even legal!"

"No, it's not." Ekatya felt the heat in her face; even the memory of finding those cams made her angry. "Which is exactly what I said into the cams I removed, right before I destroyed them."

"Did they get the message?"

"Haven't found any since. But I hate that I have to check every day, just in case. And that they're listening to my interactions with the crew. It's not only my privacy being invaded. It's everyone I talk to."

Candini shook her head, the tips of her ears as red as her hair. "What a bunch of flat-assed desk pilots. Why haven't you left yet? If the Alseans made me a First Pilot, they'd probably make you the right hand to Fahla."

Laughing despite herself, Ekatya put a hand on her shoulder. "I can't tell you how good it is to see you. And to be able to talk to someone who understands."

Candini tugged her back into an embrace, this one a gentle counterpoint to her earlier exuberance. "I really, really missed you. It was so hard when someone else got your pilot's chair."

"It was. But it worked out. You're exactly where you should be." She pulled back and grinned. "I can't wait to see the fancy new uniform."

"Yeah, that'll take some getting used to. Along with a few other things." Candini tilted her head toward the landing pad and resumed their walk. "So? Why are you putting up with this shit? There has to be a good reason."

"Why did you take this position?"

"It's a once-in-a-lifetime opportunity. And no one can do it like me."

Ekatya lifted her hands in a *there you are* gesture.

"Well, fuck," Candini said quietly.

12

MENTOR

R ahel stood at the glass wall that separated shuttle operations from the bay. Beside her, Captain Serrado exuded a rare, uncomplicated happiness as she watched the guidance lights activate. They pulsed through the exit tunnel, a green wave bringing their guest from the outer doors to the bay.

The first Gaian to serve in the Alsean Defense Force was arriving, and Captain Serrado wanted Rahel to meet her. "She has a lot to learn," Serrado had said. "I think she'll find your counsel invaluable."

Rahel's protest that she was not a pilot and had never served in a Guard unit was met with the observation that they were counterparts. As the first Alsean to serve in Fleet, Rahel's experience was the mirror image to what First Pilot Candini was about to go through.

First Pilot. What an odd thing, to stand here waiting for a Gaian with the equivalent rank to her own. Rahel wasn't sure what she thought about it.

Then the nose of the Serrado fighter came into view, followed by the rest of its gleaming body, and her breath caught.

Fleet fighters had the same silver hullskin as its shuttles and ships, a semiorganic and cybernetic material that allowed them to withstand the high radiation levels in base space. It was practical, necessary, and visually dull. Two of the *Phoenix*'s shuttles had been designed without hullskin, specifically for use in the Alsean atmosphere, but their black hulls were no more interesting than the silver.

The white fighter emerging from the exit tunnel shone like a beacon in contrast to the drab shuttles parked below. Curved black and gold patterns marked its wings, while its side was emblazoned with a shield in the same colors. Centered in the shield was the unmistakable outline of the State House. Rahel needed no further confirmation of its home base, but the Alsean script spelling BLACKSUN beneath the shield made her heart beat faster.

This was a piece of home, come to the *Phoenix* under its own power. It brought her two worlds together in a way she hadn't anticipated, and she could not stop smiling.

"Gorgeous, isn't it?" Serrado said as they watched the fighter gracefully descend to the deck. "I remember the first time I saw one of these. I told Lancer Tal that none of my own fighters made me want to run my hands over it. But I wanted to pet that one."

"What did she say?"

"She said I couldn't have it."

That sounded about right.

"Then she let me fly it. It was—" She exhaled, her emotional signature expanding with an aching blend of joy and melancholy. "A moment of perfect freedom."

"She gave you a gift," Rahel said.

The captain looked startled, then offered a wry smile. "I don't know why it keeps surprising me when you understand. Yes, she did. Shall we?"

By the time they made it from shuttle ops to the floor of the bay, the fighter was fully settled and the all clear had been given. A maintenance crew hustled past them to lock down the fighter and begin checking it over. The pilot finished her own check and opened the hatch on her side, offering a jaunty wave to Serrado while waiting for the ladder. It smoothly extended from the belly of the fighter and had barely touched the deck before she was climbing down.

She jumped the last step and strode over, radiating confidence and a happiness that increased as she neared. "Captain. It's been a long time."

"A whole day, yes. Nice uniform."

"Sharp, isn't it? We're the only ones in the Defense Force who get them. Our fleet may be under ADF oversight now, but they're already planning to break us out into our own military branch."

"Don't hold your breath," Serrado said. "It'll be a few cycles. There's a little matter of building ships first."

"I know, but I'm going to be in on this from birth! And these uniforms . . ." She slid her hands down her sides in a blatantly provocative gesture, satisfaction coiling off her skin. "How can anyone resist this?"

Serrado crossed her arms. "The uniform, or you?"

"Well, both. Obviously."

Rahel looked back and forth between them, startled by the unprofessional behavior on one side and the tolerant amusement on the other.

"This bit shows my natural habitat." Candini pointed at the swirl of light blue triangles breaking up the black background on her torso. "I'm told they represent shards of sky against the darkness of space. Alseans really like triangles."

"They're a foundational aspect of Alsean art, architecture, and conceptual thinking, yes," Serrado said dryly. "If that's what you mean by 'really like.'"

With some effort, Rahel held back her laugh.

Undeterred, Candini pointed at the matching blue chevrons on her sleeve. "And these show my rank. Same as yours, I see," she said, looking up at Rahel.

"I'm not sure which of you took a more unusual path to that rank." Serrado gestured between the two of them. "First Pilot Candini, may I present First Guard Sayana."

"Pleased to meet you," Rahel said politely, holding out a hand for the inevitable shake.

"Stuff that. You're Alsean." Candini held up her hand, palm outward. "Well met, First Guard Sayana."

Startled but pleased, Rahel met her touch. "Well met. Call me Rahel."

"Good, that's fewer syllables. Call me Candini. Captain Serrado says I can learn a lot from you. I've already got questions."

"This will be easy," Serrado remarked. "I thought I might have to guide the conversation, but it looks like I can just throw you in a room together."

"As long as there's food," Candini said.

"And shannel," Rahel added.

"You have shannel here?"

"Captain Serrado does."

"But I don't share," Serrado said. "Except with the truly deserving. Come on." She wheeled around.

"Are you saying I'm not deserving?" Candini demanded, following close on her heels.

Rahel listened to them banter all the way out of the bay and up three decks to the meeting room, leaving her wildly curious about their history. In her experience, Captain Serrado didn't allow such familiarity with anyone other than Dr. Wells and Commander Lokomorra.

"Oh, we go way back," Candini said when she asked. "We met when I was a lieutenant junior grade and she was a lieutenant commander. Who was very much out of uniform."

"And off duty," Serrado added. "Wearing a uniform in that bar would have been asking for trouble."

They were clustered around one end of a conference table, enjoying the view of the shuttle bay offered by the large window. Serrado couldn't seem to keep her eyes off the white fighter.

"You asked for it anyway." Candini tapped Rahel's shoulder. "Something you should know about the captain. She's a rescuer at heart. She can't turn her back on something she thinks needs fixing."

"What happened?"

"It was a rough bar. In the part of the station where officers shouldn't go. Especially high-ranking officers."

"I heard the food was good," Serrado said easily.

"The food was fantastic. So was the gambling. I won a few games too many, and one of the other players took exception to it."

"She's forgetting to mention that the other player was twice her size." Candini waved a hand. "I could have taken her."

"Arms like this." Serrado indicated a shape the size of a large tree branch. "And scarred knuckles."

"A fighter," Rahel translated.

"She was looking for an excuse," Serrado agreed. "Candini gave it to her."

"Did you cheat?"

"Only a little bit."

"Don't try that on Alsea."

Candini shook her head. "With a bunch of empaths? Besides, those days are behind me."

"Good to hear," Serrado said with emphasis.

"Anyway, she laid me out across the table with one punch. Before I could get up and pay her back for it—which I would have—this one was standing in front of her." Candini jerked her thumb in Serrado's direction. "It was like a vallcat kitten facing off against a mountzar."

Rahel appreciated her use of Alsean comparators. Mountzars were massive beasts, apex predators of higher altitudes.

"I take offense to that description," Serrado said. "I'm not a kitten."

"No, you're a Fleet officer who can't stand an unfair fight no matter where it happens." Candini turned back to Rahel. "She lectured that woman on ethics and suggested she fight someone her own size. The mountzar didn't take kindly to the suggestion and tried to lay her out next to me. Next thing I know, there's a huge crash and that woman was out for the night."

Serrado smiled. "The bigger they are, the harder they fall. I used her size against her."

"Caught her arm and redirected?" Rahel could picture it.

"And stuck out my foot for good measure. She tripped and went headfirst into the table. Candini had just managed to roll off it."

"Thank the Seeders for that, or I'd have been out for the night, too. Though that might have been an improvement over the lecture I got on cheating in a bar where the patrons were less than forgiving."

"You lectured a stranger?"

"She's like that," Candini said.

Serrado practically glowed with smug enjoyment. "No, I'm only like that with officers under my command."

"But you didn't know until I introduced myself—" Candini stopped, a tendril of suspicion rising. "Wait a minute."

"I had just been transferred to a new ship. I was on the station waiting to be picked up. While I waited, I naturally memorized the files of the officers in my section—"

"Naturally," Candini muttered.

"—and learned we had a pilot with too much ego and too little respect for authority. My section chief said he didn't know what to do with her, but he couldn't let her go because she was our best."

It was Candini's turn to be smug.

"So I decided that if she wouldn't respect rank, maybe I could earn her respect another way."

"You set me up?!"

"Of course not. How was I supposed to make you cheat at kasmet? I only planned for our first meeting to be outside Fleet boundaries. Somewhere we could get to know each other before rank got in the way. Then you got yourself in trouble and handed me the perfect solution."

"Why didn't you ever tell me?"

Serrado leaned forward, suddenly all business. "You wouldn't have seen it for what it was. Not until now, when you're in the same place I was then. You've got a reputation to earn, and this time it can't be based solely on your flying skills. Though that's a good place to start. Find out what they respect and show them *why* they should respect you. Don't depend on your rank."

Candini's emotional signature flickered through surprise, annoyance, and a brief hint of hurt before settling on rueful admiration.

"Good advice, thanks. It doesn't change what you did, though. I may have been your subordinate, but we were off duty. You weren't responsible for me. You could have let her turn out my lights and then come to my rescue, without risking yourself. And called it a lesson learned."

"Then I'd have had to drag your unconscious carcass out of there. It's easier when they can walk."

Rahel watched them laugh together and wondered if Candini realized what Serrado had done. It was such a seamless shift from friend to mentor and back again that she thought it might have gone unnoticed.

An unexpected longing pierced her, carrying the sting of envy in its tail. Candini's relationship with Captain Serrado was reminiscent of her own with Shantu, but with the warmth of friendship in place of parental authority. How different her life could have been . . .

"How did you earn your respect?" Candini asked, interrupting her dark thoughts. "I mean, as an Alsean on a Gaian crew."

"I beat up seven security officers."

Candini stared slack-jawed. "At the same time?"

"In about twenty seconds," Serrado confirmed. "Saved me weeks of calculation and effort."

"You never told me that." Rahel was stunned by the pride hitting her senses. That had certainly not been apparent when Serrado punished her.

"It wouldn't have been appropriate then. Yes, I needed you to prove yourself. I didn't expect it to take that form, but it was effective."

"Huh." Candini looked at the captain thoughtfully. "I'm seeing a theme here. Didn't you earn Lancer Tal's respect by meeting her in an honor challenge?"

"You did?" Rahel barely managed to keep her own jaw shut.

"On second thought, it might be dangerous to leave you two in a room together," Serrado muttered.

"Ha! You haven't told her that story?" Candini turned to Rahel. "I read Lhyn's book. She had a lot to say about warrior honor, and a whole section on the way honor challenges can resolve disagreements that would otherwise infect a unit. Or cause political consequences," she added, tilting her head toward the captain. "Gave me a new appreciation for what Captain Serrado did. It was genius, really."

"It was idiotic, and I don't recommend it for your purposes," Serrado said flatly. Her expression morphed into a smirk. "But if you do, don't hit them on the cheekbones."

13

GUNNER

Serrado did eventually leave them alone together, and Rahel spent a pleasant half hour answering questions. After all those months as the trainee, it was a nice change to be the instructor. Candini had a quick mind, grasping concepts with an ease that reminded her of Lhyn. But where Lhyn would dive into a topic and make ever-deeper connections within it, Candini skated on the surface, darting from one subject to the next. It was a different flavor of communication than she was used to, but she liked the energy of it and was disappointed when they had to stop for the presentation to the fighter crews.

"Captain Serrado made me your duty assignment this morning, right?" Candini asked.

"For as long as you need me, yes."

"Good. Come with me and see what I'm doing."

In the auditorium, Rahel sat near the back wall and was startled by the number of crew members taking their seats. Given that the *Phoenix* carried thirty each of single-seat and two-seater fighters, she expected sixty pilots and thirty gunners to attend. By the time Candini began to speak, there were close to one hundred and forty filled seats.

Not everyone was mission ready, she learned. There were pilots and gunners still in training, instructors, and nonflying crew who oversaw operations. Even the mission-ready pilots had different responsibilities.

When two fighters flew together, one pilot was in charge. Flight leads commanded a group of two to four fighters, and flight commanders were in charge of missions involving six or more.

It was a fascinating world of its own, very different from that of the specialists who handled the defensive and offensive weapons built into the *Phoenix*. Rahel watched raptly, now understanding the true significance of Candini's position. If there were this many crew for sixty fighters, then the Alsean contingent must number more than four hundred.

When Candini outlined her plans for a competition to test the flight skills of both Alsean and Fleet fighters, she set off a rumble among the attendees.

"Are you going to give them a starting advantage?" one called.

"Twenty points might be enough," added another.

"I did think about offering something like that," Candini said. "To you."

They roared with good-natured disbelief and quite a few ritual insults.

"Don't make assumptions," Candini called over the noise. "I haven't had a chance to assess them yet, but the last time I was here, I saw some impressive flying. And they've had four years to practice since then."

"On our equipment," someone shouted.

"On our equipment that they rebuilt from the landing gear up," Candini answered. "And over a hundred more they've built since then. Don't you know better than to underestimate your opponents?"

She was good, Rahel thought. Not so far removed from them that she couldn't communicate on their level, yet still in command.

The crew members settled down for the rest of the presentation, some taking notes, others sitting back with arms crossed, all of them attentive. When Candini called an end to it, many went up to shake her hand or clap her on the back before filing out.

Rahel waited until the last one departed before walking down to the stage.

"What did you think?" Candini asked.

"I think they're looking forward to beating us in the competition."

"Who is *us*, Fleeter?" She grinned and ran a hand through her spiky red hair, making it stand up even more. "Say, Captain Serrado mentioned that you go with her on every leave just to get off the ship. Because of the emotional pressure."

Rahel nodded.

"Want to get off the ship?"

It took a moment to understand the question. "You're offering me a ride in your fighter?"

Candini sighed expressively. "A ride, Seeders, no. You don't go for a ride in a fighter. You go for a flight. And yes, I'm offering. I need to see how this Alsean build responds in all conditions, so I've arranged for some target practice. I was planning to ask one of the gunners here, but I don't actually need one. There's a seat if you want it."

With a grin she couldn't control, Rahel said, "I want it."

Until now, Rahel had viewed flying in a shuttle as the height of adventure. It combined all of her favorite things about working in space: the freedom, the speed, the glorious vistas, the fact that she was soaring among millions of stars with nothing but a thin hull protecting her.

As Candini hurtled through a series of maneuvers, the stars spinning madly around them, she revised her opinion. Flying in a shuttle was never going to be the same. She should have realized it from the start, when Candini helped her with the specialized harness and informed her that "you don't get into a fighter, you strap it on."

It did feel like that. This wasn't a vehicle she was traveling in; it was an extension of her body. It was *glorious*.

To top it off, there was only one mind broadcasting emotions within her range, and that mind did not have a single negative emotion at the moment. Candini loved flying with an intensity that permeated her emotional signature. Happiness, satisfaction, bright bursts of glee during certain maneuvers—all of them blended into a depth of focused pleasure that Rahel would have paid for.

They turned away from the two destroyers in the distance and sped back toward the *Phoenix*, which grew larger at a startling rate. Nor did Candini slow when the warship's engine cradle filled their entire front view. Instead, she shot straight up and over, then raced along the dorsal surface at a dizzying speed. They rocketed over Deck Zero and were past the nose of the ship before Rahel could blink.

"Shekking Mother! Captain Serrado never did that."

Candini laughed. "Not in a shuttle, she wouldn't. She could in a fighter."

"Does she ever fly a fighter?"

"Every now and again, to keep in practice. She's a good pilot. She's just not a fighter pilot."

"But you said—"

"I mean, she can fly this. But in combat? She wouldn't last. It's not her skill. Or maybe I should say it's not the skill she's chosen to hone. She's a strategist. We need her on the bridge, not out here." The stars suddenly shot downward.

Rahel's seat curved around her, flowing into a new shape to protect her head and neck from the acceleration forces. When the stars stopped moving altogether, the seat retreated and she had full range of motion once more. Straight ahead of them was the *Phoenix*, hanging upside down relative to their position. Candini had flipped them end over end and brought them to a standstill.

"If that didn't make you vomit, you're never going to," she declared. "Good job."

Though Rahel didn't see how she could take credit for her biology, the praise warmed her. "Exit transition doesn't bother me, either. I don't have to take the foramine."

"Really? Damn, that would be nice."

"This is amazing." She indicated the malleable seat. "I don't know how it moves so quickly. It's like part of my body."

"That's the idea. Pressure seats revolutionized fighter technology. No more helmets, no more clunky suits to keep your blood pressure from crashing. It makes an even bigger difference in atmospheric flight."

"I can understand that. I also understand why you told me to take out my braid." She patted the bun atop her head, a style she rarely wore. But it kept the hair away from her neck and allowed the pressure seat to do its job. It also stayed out from under the Alsean crash collar both she and Candini wore.

"You'd have had a Hades of a headache otherwise. Or neck ache. Some pilots put their hair up like yours, but most cut it short. It's easier."

Rahel nodded, examining Candini's red hair more closely. "What purpose do the spikes serve?"

Candini gave a great shout of laughter, then covered her mouth and laughed harder. "None," she finally managed. "My hair doesn't behave when it's short. It needs length to weigh it down, otherwise it's everywhere. I figured out a long time ago that it was better to work with it than fight it."

"A good warrior attitude," Rahel said approvingly.

Candini pointed both forefingers at her. "I like you. Now, are you ready for some target practice?"

"Me? I thought you were doing it."

"Sure, after you. Don't you want to try?"

"Yes! What do I do?"

Candini tapped her board, bringing up twin virtual targeting screens in front of their seats. "Okay, I've transferred weapons to your side. That means your control stick is now mapped solely to the weapons systems. Any movement you make here won't affect flight inputs. This is for the laser cannon," she said, pointing to a trigger on the forward side of the control stick. "And this button here is for firing missiles, which we're not doing."

"So don't touch it?"

"You can, but it won't do anything. We're not carrying live missiles today. Here." She wrapped Rahel's hand around the control stick and positioned her fingers. "See how the trigger falls naturally under your first finger?"

Rahel flexed her finger slightly. "Yes."

"Go ahead and pull it. Nothing will fire yet. Get a feel for it."

She pulled the trigger, first slowly and then with more confidence. There was very little travel distance. Halfway down, a physical click told her exactly where the action point was.

"Got it?"

"Yes."

"Good. Your job is to watch this screen. I do the flying, you do the watching. You'll see the target moving all over the place. My job is to get it here, in the target window." She pointed at an outlined square, then dipped her finger down to indicate a cross in its center. "That's what you're in charge of. You'll be fine-tuning the target solution."

Rahel experimented with the control stick, watching the cross move within the square. "It's sensitive."

"Yeah, it takes a light touch. You don't want to grip it like a—" She stopped. "Never mind, you won't get that reference. Anyway, keep it gentle. I'll get the target in here, then you kill it."

Rahel pulled the trigger once, feeling the click. "Prepared to kill on your command, First Pilot."

Candini barked a laugh. "Did I mention I like you?" She turned to the quantum com and called the *Phoenix*, surprise zinging off her skin when Captain Serrado appeared. "Captain! I wasn't expecting you."

Serrado looked unamused. "I wanted to have a talk with the idiot who just did a flyby of my ship a meter off the hull. Next time you try that, I'm sending you out to polish our ID number by hand."

"Yes, Captain. I'm sorry." Whatever contrition Candini managed to drum up vanished as she added, "There wasn't any risk, though."

"Was there any risk of First Guard Sayana getting sick?"

"I'm fine, Captain. She said if I didn't vomit after that last maneuver, I never would."

"You had to tell her that?"

"She's honest." Serrado raised her eyebrows. "Something you might want to emulate."

"Alseans respect honesty," Rahel said helpfully.

"I take it back about liking you," Candini muttered. "Captain, we're ready to begin target practice if you have the drones loaded."

"Which threat level?"

"Let's start with three."

"Three? Are you that out of practice? Oh—First Guard, did she talk you into being her gunner?"

"There wasn't much talking involved," Candini said. "I asked and she leaped."

"I'm watching history repeat itself." Serrado glanced offscreen. "Lieutenant, threat level three, please. Activate shields. Get going, Candini."

The com went dark, and Candini swung them around to face away from the ship.

Rahel gripped the control stick, then remembered and lightened her touch. She had no idea what to look for, but it became obvious when a green dot appeared on her screen, moving in a sinuous motion. The pressure seat shot up to protect her head as Candini gave chase, throwing the fighter into a high-speed turn.

When Candini had said the target would move all over, she hadn't exaggerated. Rahel paid no attention to the wild motions of the stars around them, focusing solely on her targeting screen and the gyrations of that green dot. It danced all around the edges of the central square but wouldn't go inside. Then it did go inside, only to zip back out as a beam of light flashed in Rahel's peripheral vision.

"It's armed?" she asked.

"It's just a light show. We won't die if it hits us, but my reputation will. Ah, there you are, you little shit."

The green dot dropped into the central square, right below the top edge. Rahel tracked it and managed to intersect its trailing curve for a fraction of a piptick, but held her fire in an instinctive response to the anticipation Candini was broadcasting. It wasn't time yet.

She kept trying, getting used to the way the dot moved and her own reaction time. The target danced along the upper edge, and Candini was fiercely focused, her emotional signature radiating expectation, anticipation—and then a blinding burst of triumph.

"Now!" she shouted, but Rahel had already fired. A brilliant white beam lanced out from their fighter, impacting the drone and blowing it to atoms.

Rahel whooped and Candini swore, bringing them to an easy stop.

"How the fuck did you do that?" Her tone was demanding, but she was genuinely astonished. "You fired the *exact* moment the firing solution came together. Before I said anything. No way a first-time gunner does that. You've done this before."

"I haven't," Rahel protested. "I've never been in a fighter until now."

"Then how did you know? That was—it looked like you've put in two hundred hours of training."

"I felt you." She wasn't sure how to explain it. "You weren't ready, and then you were."

Candini gaped at her. "You weren't watching the targeting screen?"

"Yes, of course, but I fired when you stopped anticipating and felt . . ." She searched for the right word. "Victorious? Like it was already done. It was instinct."

She waited nervously. Candini was still looking at her as if she were a mythical beast, disbelief vying with shock.

Then came a wave of elation. "Is that why you've built more two-seaters? Because of that kind of empathic teamwork? Holy Seeders, you could be—we have to test this." Bursting with enthusiasm, Candini called the *Phoenix*. "We've got a prodigy on our hands," she announced when Captain Serrado appeared. "I want to try level six."

Serrado smiled. "Why does that not surprise me?"

A level-six drone, it turned out, was twice as hard to catch as a level-three. Rahel still hit it on her first attempt.

It ceased flying immediately, emitting a brilliant burst of red light that could surely be seen for a hundred kilometers.

"What happened?" Rahel asked in confusion.

"You killed it." Candini caught up to the drone and stopped beside it. "On your first shot, damn!"

"Why didn't it—?" She mimed an explosion with her hands.

"Yeah, I should have mentioned that, sorry. The pad pushers back at Command Dome decided us pilots and gunners were having too much fun blowing shit up. They said it cost too much to replace single-use drones, so they made them reusable with a little light show. Red is a kill shot. If I hadn't set our laser cannon to training mode, you really would have atomized it. Orange is a mobility kill, a disabling strike. Puts it out of the fight. Yellow means damaged but still flying, still a threat. We call a yellow strike a getta."

Rahel's language chip had no translation for that. "A getta?"

"It's an acronym. GETA. Short for Good Effort, Try Again."

"Isn't it easier just to say yellow?"

Candini scoffed. "Boring. Besides, this is Fleet. We live for acronyms."

"You're not in Fleet."

"Yeah, but it's a hard habit to break. Do you know what we used to call gunners? Tactical officers, which we shortened to tac officers, which then got shortened to tacos, which is a food from Captain Serrado's home planet." She grinned. "It would be like me asking if you wanted to come on this flight as my pastry."

"I can see why that didn't catch on."

"Oh, it did—for the pilots."

Candini's high spirits suffused the fighter, making Rahel wish she could bottle this feeling and take it back to the ship with her. It would be a fantastic treatment for the days when she was feeling overloaded with her shipmates' unshielded emotions.

"Wait. Why did the first one blow up?" She had a sudden suspicion. "Did you 'forget' to set the laser cannon to training mode?"

"Are you kidding? Captain Serrado would have my head if I blew up a reusable. The simple drones are cheap enough to produce that we still get to make them go boom. Levels one through three. Besides, it's important to have that in training. To see what it looks like, both here—" She pointed at her eyes, then at the targeting screen. "And here."

"I want to shoot another level three," Rahel announced.

Laughing, Candini pointed both forefingers again, which seemed to be her gesture of approval. "Let me figure out your limits first. Then we'll wrap it up with a multiple. I'll ask Serrado to give us two level threes to go after."

"At the same time?"

"Yep."

"I'm ready."

Apparently, Candini subscribed to the "test to failure" philosophy of training. She jumped them to a level-nine drone, which flung itself around the targeting screen like a dartfly on stims. Rahel missed her first shot but got an orange hit on the second.

Candini's glee was so great that she might have leaped out of her seat had the harness not held her down. "We're going straight to twelve," she said breathlessly. "That's as hard as it gets. The only way to increase the difficulty from there is to add multiple drones."

It took four shots.

Pounding her fists on her thighs, Candini let out a long howl of triumph. Rahel could not help laughing, both at the display and the joyous excitement that inundated her senses. The last time she had made someone feel this good was during a joining at Blacksun's warrior caste house, and even that hadn't included this sense of victory.

It was the best thing she had felt in a long time.

"I want you to be my gunner," Candini said.

"I'm in security, not weapons—"

"Stuff that. It doesn't matter. This is a fucking breakthrough. This could turn a battle. I need to find out if Alsean gunners consciously train for this, or if they even realize that's what they're doing. But if they do what you do—it's like our brains are connected." She motioned between their heads. "Like you're my trigger finger. It's an incredible advantage. I want to study this, and I want to do it with you."

"I don't see how that will work. You're in the ADF, I'm in Fleet."

"And I'm the liaison. In a way, you're a liaison, too. Who better to work together?" Candini's excitement grew. "Seeders, it's like it was ordained. I'll be up here a lot anyway, and you have a medical need to get off the ship. I can train you as a gunner, and you can train me as an Alsean commander."

Her confidence began to seep into Rahel's pores. "You'll have to get permission from Commander Cox. He's my section chief."

Candini waved a hand. "Leave that to me."

14

PRIVATE TOUR

Micah tugged on the hem of his dress uniform jacket, straightening out nonexistent wrinkles and trying not to feel like he was twenty. He checked one more time to make sure all buttons were properly shined and that the ceremonial braid on his left shoulder was looped just so. With a deep breath that did nothing to quell the shivers in his stomach, he tapped the entry chime.

After ten agonizing pipticks of silence, he wondered if Alejandra had changed her mind. Then he heard quick footsteps, followed by the sound of the lever turning, and had time for one more inhale before the door swung open.

All air immediately left his lungs.

"Damn." Alejandra leaned against the door jamb with an appreciative smile. "You look like you conquered the galaxy. Fleet can only wish we had such gorgeous dress uniforms."

Micah stared at her, unable to find words. It wasn't that she looked greatly different from the last time he had seen her. She wore a new dress and jacket with the same short boots, the same upswept hairstyle held in place with two sticks, and jewelry in her ears and at her throat, just as before.

The difference was that she had dressed like this for him.

And now that he was seeing more than the overall impact, he realized that her hair was done in a more complicated fashion, with small wisps left to dangle artfully over her forehead and ears. The jewelry was a different color, matching both her eyes and her dress, and her hair sticks were not bare wood but adorned at the ends with golden beads etched in complex patterns.

"Magnificent," he said, then shook his head. "I mean, you look—"

She was laughing. "Micah, you've already made my night. I can't remember the last time someone looked at me like that. Or lost the power of speech for nonmedical reasons."

"There's a medical reason," he muttered.

She stepped forward and kissed his cheek, freezing him in place. "Thank you for that. Now, I'd like to dine, but you're blocking my door."

He hurriedly backed up and thanked Fahla that he hadn't fallen over his own feet, a considerable accomplishment at this point.

Moving in a more leisurely fashion, she exited her suite and closed the door behind her. "Did you make reservations in the name of Colonel Grand Shit?" she inquired.

The laughter vaporized his tension. "In fact, I did." He offered a deep bow and continued, "Dr. Wells, if you would please accompany me, I've arranged a demonstration of how grand a shit I can be."

"Wonderful. I can't wait."

He couldn't help glancing at her as they strolled to the lift, marveling that this was his reality tonight. She truly was here. He had not imagined their rapport or made a tree from a blade of grass.

In the lift, he surreptitiously blocked the control panel and enjoyed her surprise when they stepped out on the second floor.

"I thought we were going to a restaurant," she said.

"I can do better than a restaurant."

She looked intrigued. "Do I get any clues?"

"One, but it won't help. I'm taking you stargazing."

"On the second floor?"

"Yes."

"You're right. That didn't help."

He led the way down the corridor, noting how she tried to see all the art on the walls, and made a snap decision to take the scenic route. They passed through the Hall of Triumph, with its wraparound murals depicting the first Battle of Blacksun and the subsequent surrender of the invading army. The next stop was the Whispering Vault, where he pointed to the door on the opposite side and asked her to stand there. She crossed the empty space and turned, gazing up at the fresco on the high, arched ceiling.

"Beautiful," she murmured, sounding as if she were right next to him.

"Yes, it is," he said softly.

"Oh! I've heard of places like this." With a delighted smile, she spoke in a whisper. "I didn't realize I'd get the private tour."

"You came down from orbit just for evenmeal," he answered at the same volume. "I had to make it worth your while."

"It's already worth it." She watched him every step of the way as he walked across the room, her gaze intent and her lips tilted upward.

"This is an improvement," he said as he rejoined her.

"Over what?"

"I felt twenty cycles old at your door. Now I'm up to thirty."

The smile turned into a smirk. "I remember thirty. That was right around the time I rediscovered joining."

He led her into the next corridor. "Rediscovered? Had you lost it?"

"More accurate to say I lost interest in it." Before he could formulate the right question, she added, "It's an apt comparison. I've discovered a whole new level of interest lately."

"So have I."

From there, they visited the Glass Gallery, where she made him promise to bring her back in the daytime so she could fully appreciate the thirty-six stained glass windows. Next was the Room of Remembrance, where he stopped to light an oil bowl and invited her to do the same. Soberly, she lit the bowl next to his, bent her head, and closed her eyes.

She had claimed to worship no gods, but he recognized a prayer when he saw one. In this intimate space, lit only by eternal flames and the few bowls currently burning, she looked both more alien and more beautiful than before.

Her expression was thoughtful when she raised her head. He silently offered his hand and watched the decision play out on her face before she accepted.

The sorrow that flowed through their skin contact bore none of the jagged edges of new grief, but was smooth with the passage of time. Her loss was an old one.

"Can you feel me?" she asked.

"Yes." He tilted his head toward the two flames. "We have something in common."

She stared at the bowls, then gave a single nod. "I suppose at our age, it would be a surprise not to have that in common."

"When you're ready, I would like to hear your story."

She squeezed his hand and let go. "When we're both ready."

They did not speak again until they arrived at their destination.

Outside the doors, Micah stopped and turned. "I considered taking you to a restaurant that Tal and Salomen recommended. Tal said it serves the best fanten in marmello sauce she's ever had. Except for Salomen's, of course."

"Tal sounds like a wise woman," she said, her humor returning.

"She can be. I gave it serious thought, but there was one problem."

"Which was?"

"This is a special night. I don't want to share it with anyone else." He opened the doors and watched her walk through.

Three steps in, she stopped and turned in a slow circle. "My sainted Shippers. This is stunning." Tilting her head back, she saw the ceiling and gave a delighted laugh. "We're stargazing!"

"It's the Celestial Salon," he said, closing the doors behind him.

"I can see how it got the name."

It wasn't the largest of salons in the State House, but it was one of the most beautiful. All four walls were covered in a mural that made it seem as if they were high up in the mountains, seeing multiple peaks and the clear, starry sky above them. The stars went up the walls and onto the vaulted ceiling, each one a glowing crystal.

"The constellations are accurate," he said. "If we went outside at the right time and looked up, this is what we would see."

"Is that a natural glow?"

"No. The original crafters chose this crystal because of its reflective properties. It's the best at catching candlelight. But this is on the State House tour. Candles and crowds aren't a good combination."

"No, I'd imagine not." She examined the ceiling, exposing a length of throat he had to consciously look away from.

"They use artificial light now," he said. "Installed behind the crystals. I like to think the original crafters would have done that if they'd had the technology. It does make the stars shine more brightly."

"And consistently," she agreed. After one more turn, she lowered her head and registered their true destination.

Taking pride of place in the center of the room was a long table made from the black wood of a molwyn. A long-ago crafter had created a starscape in its surface, carving out tiny plugs and replacing them with the silver wood of tintinatalus in recognizable constellations. It looked like a pool of water at night, reflecting the stars overhead.

Though it seated fourteen, it was bare but for two place settings at one end. Arranged around them were a bottle of spirits, an uncut loaf of bread, a bowl of grainstem powder, and a second, smaller bowl holding a hyacot twig.

"Who sits at the head?" Alejandra asked.

"You're the guest." As they crossed the room and pulled out their chairs, he added, "I originally planned for us to sit across from each other, so there could be no question of rank or position. But then I came to inspect the room and realized how wide this table is. I didn't want us to be that far apart."

She paused in the act of sitting, then leaned over and dropped a kiss on his cheek. "You are a rare man," she said, taking her seat. "First, that you would even think about avoiding issues of perceived power. Second, that you would inspect the room."

"I didn't get where I am by leaving things to chance." He picked up the hyacot twig and snapped it in half, then dropped the pieces into the bowl. "There. We're officially on a date."

"We started our date when you came to my door. I never expected a private tour. But now that you've established the precedent, I'm looking forward to the next one." She reached for the serrated knife and pointed at the bread.

"Yes, please." He held out his plate and accepted the first slice. As she cut a second, he sprinkled his with the sweet grainstem powder, then handed her the bowl and reached for the spirits. After filling both glasses, he raised his and said, "To new beginnings."

"To new beginnings." She tapped their glasses together.

They spoke of his work and hers, then told stories of their pasts, sliding into the ease of conversation they had reached on what he now thought of as their first date. State House kitchen staff ghosted in and out with perfect precision, whisking plates away as they finished and sliding new ones in before they could register the empty space. When dessert arrived and he knew there would be no more interruptions, he said, "I had an interesting talk with Lhyn last nineday."

She set down her fork. "I spoke with Rahel. Very educational, I have to say. How was your lecture?"

"It was much better than a lecture."

She listened raptly as he described the Rite of Knowing, her eyes alight and a smile taking over her face. "Did you find a substitute for the mushroom?"

"Yes and no. I found a nontoxic plant that glowed, but the flavor left much to be desired."

"What did it taste like?"

"Have you ever smelled something so far along in decomposition that you could taste the smell?"

Her laughter was musical. "Yes, and that would qualify as an anti-aphrodisiac."

"That was what I thought. For the real aphrodisiacs, I'm not aware of any that wouldn't also compromise our thinking. I want a clear head for this."

"Not to mention that I'd have to test any aphrodisiac for its effects on Gaian body chemistry."

"I didn't think of that," he said in dismay.

"It's all right, Micah. You didn't choose one, so it doesn't matter. What did you choose?"

He withdrew a small box from his jacket pocket, took off the lid, and offered it to her.

"Berries?" she asked, peering inside.

"Dala berries. A traditional dessert. Try one."

She popped one of the dark blue berries in her mouth, stopped with a surprised look, and swallowed. "Mm. That takes me back. Reminds me of a crop we grew on my home planet. Delicious."

That was a better reaction than he could have hoped for. "They stain the skin, too. It won't come off until we wash it off with soap."

"You experimented?" At his nod, she dropped her fork and threw her napkin on the table. "I'm done. Let's go."

"But you didn't finish your dessert," he said, and immediately wanted to kick himself.

"An extraordinary man just told me that he went to considerable trouble to create a ceremony for us to explore each other. Dessert is the last thing on my mind right now." She pointed at the plate. "That dessert, anyway. This one, on the other hand . . ." She plucked another berry from the box, held it between forefinger and thumb, and slowly placed it between her lips.

An explosion going off in the next room could not have made him look away as she closed her lips around her fingers, then pulled them out and smiled. Her eyes danced with humor and a promise that left him breathless.

He didn't remember getting out of the chair. But he would never forget the taste of dala berry on her mouth.

15

RITE OF KNOWING

Alejandra stepped out on the fourteenth floor and looked back quizzically. "We're not going to your quarters?"

Moving up beside her, Micah gestured in the direction of the suite he had reserved. "Lhyn said they used a place made for the purpose. It makes sense, doesn't it? A place that's not familiar to either of us. A place we go into together."

Her answer was to clasp his hand as they walked. Bright approval sank into his skin, richly blended with warm anticipation. She wanted this as much as he did.

"I'm finding it difficult not to break into a run," he said.

She swung their hands. "Those elders knew what they were doing. It's not just the young who need to be slowed down."

At the door of the suite, he laid a palm on the pad and followed her inside with a tingling stomach. Her expression as she examined the layout made all the preparations worthwhile.

"The bedroom isn't large enough," he said. "I rearranged."

"I hope you had help." She ran a hand along the heavy bed frame centered in the spacious living area, then rubbed the fabric covering the mattress. "This is soft. What is it?"

"Winden wool. In the summer, they climb up to higher elevations and gather in groves of a tree with spiky bark. I've seen footage of them rubbing against the trees. It looks . . ."

"Orgasmic?" That alluring spark was in her eyes again.

"Very. When they're done, we collect the wool and spin it into this."

"I'm guessing this is not a common material."

"Fit for a Lancer," he agreed. "And you."

The spark vanished. With a serious set to her mouth, she walked up and wrapped one hand behind his neck. "And us," she corrected, before kissing him with a passion that exceeded what they had shared in the Celestial Salon. Both were breathing hard when she pulled away and rested their foreheads together. "I'm sorry that I can't do what an Alsean would," she said softly. "You've made this so wonderful. I wish—"

He cut her off with a gentler kiss, mourning the thread of doubt in her emotions. "A joining can be beautiful without a Sharing. Besides, you've already given me more than almost any Alsean could."

"I have?"

He held up their hands between them. "It's in your touch."

They had discussed this on their first date. She was fascinated by the differences between high, mid, and low empaths, and found his inability to sense without touch a positive trait. He had never seen anyone react that way to his handicap.

"We're careful about touching. So much can be read through skin contact, but for most of us, it's not necessary if we're physically close enough to a person we care about. It's more of . . ." He didn't know how to describe something no Alsean needed to learn. "A confirmation. Or a gift. Something in addition to what is already known. I'm not explaining this well."

"Others sense without it, so it's an extra layer for them," she said. "But for you, it's the only layer there is."

"Yes. That's it exactly." He rested their clasped hands against his chest. "You touch without thought. You freely share yourself with me. And your touch is potent."

Her eyebrows rose.

"Not like that. Well," he amended, "perhaps it will be. I look forward to finding out."

The thread of doubt dissipated. "So do I. But you're talking about the way I broadcast?"

"When you touch me," he said slowly, choosing his words, "I feel like a mid empath. Or even a high one. I sense you as I've never sensed anyone. It's like projection in its power." He gave a nod, satisfied with that word. "You make me feel more powerful than I am. All my life, I've lived with a handicap. You take it away. It's a gift."

A fierce joy burned through her skin, reflected in eyes that seemed a darker green than before. She started forward, stopped herself, and spoke in a tight voice. "We need to begin this ritual, or I won't be slowed down."

With great reluctance, he released her hands and took a step back. "Let's light the candles."

He had placed them all around the living area, on the windowsills, tables, even atop a sculpture, yet still lacked the appropriate prayer.

"I visit the temple regularly," he said, lighting a taper. "To burn oil bowls for Fahla. But those are personal prayers. I don't have any that will work here."

She held out a hand. "I do."

He gave her the taper and watched her walk to the farthest candle. One by one, she lit each candle in the room, speaking first in her own tongue and then in High Alsean before moving to the next.

"We honor those who came before us."

"We honor their sacrifices."

"Made for us, their children."

"To bequeath us a better world."

"We promise not to shy from."

"The sacrifices asked of us."

"Made for our children."

"To bequeath them a better world."

She hesitated on the next candle, then said something with one word he recognized.

"We offer thanks to Fahla."

"For watching over us."

"And strive to be worthy."

"Of her regard."

"This we swear."

"Hear us."

She blew out the taper and set it next to the last candle, head bowed. "I haven't said that prayer in a lifetime."

He rested a hand between her shoulders. "Who did you pray to?"

"The Seeders. We said that before every midmeal." She gave a short laugh. "It worked. I'm definitely slowed down."

"It's a beautiful prayer. I could hear the rhythm in your language. Lhyn would love it."

Her head lifted, and she looked at him with a wondering smile. "She would. I'll have to tell her. In the meantime . . ." She reached for the first button of his jacket. "Since I said the prayer, I think that entitles me to the first touch."

He wasn't going to argue.

She undid each button and slid the jacket off his shoulders, then stepped behind him to pull it off completely. With a precision that surprised him, she folded it and set it carefully atop a side table.

He reminded himself that she was in a military organization despite not being a warrior. She had a dress uniform of her own and a lifetime of experience caring for it.

The thought heated his skin as much as her finger sliding down the front seal of his shirt. She stopped halfway down, realizing it was tucked in, and tugged it free. Then she unsealed the remainder and pulled it apart, sucking in a breath as she examined his torso.

He missed her touch and the knowledge it would have given him. Did she like what she saw? Was he too different? She wasn't showing anything on her face, and he did not want to ask.

Once again, she went behind him to pull the shirt free of his arms. It was folded with equal care and set atop the jacket. At last she turned and stared, her mouth tilting up with that small smile he so enjoyed.

"Lucky me," she said quietly.

"Oh, thank Fahla. You had me concerned."

"Really? I don't see why." She stepped forward, running her fingertips from his chest ridges to his stomach. "You must know how attractive you are. This is not the body of a man who's unaware."

The pride threatened to burst through his chest. "It's not the body I used to have," he admitted. But he was still active, having never wanted the sedentary life of many higher ranking warriors.

"Neither is mine." Her fingers trailed back up to his chest ridges, then out to his shoulders and down his arms. "But when I had that body, I wasn't a happy person. I'll take what I have now over what I had then, no question."

He had never thought of it that way. While he considered it, she stepped back and gestured to his boots. "Can we depart from tradition long enough for you to do those? Lhyn's ritual takes place in a tropical location. They were either barefoot or in sandals."

"Good point." He stepped to the bed and sat on its edge to swiftly remove both boots.

She did the same for hers, hopping on one foot and then the other. When he stood up, she moved close to examine the fastening of his trousers. "Simple enough," she said, and undid it with nimble fingers. Then she hooked her fingers in his underwear and pushed down, kneeling as she followed the trousers to the floor. A hand at his ankle guided him out of one leg, then the other, and he was naked before her.

She didn't look, instead focusing on folding the trousers and even the underwear, setting them neatly on the table next to the jacket and shirt. Only then did she turn, an expression of fascinated wonder taking over her face. "Images aren't the same."

He caught her wrists when she tried to touch his pelvic ridges. "My turn."

"Fine," she grumbled, amusement skittering along her skin. "You really aren't Gaian."

"Why? What would a Gaian man do?"

"He wouldn't stop me from touching him, that's for sure."

"Next time, I won't." He gestured toward her hair. "May I?"

She stood straight, watching him with hooded eyes, and nodded.

"I've fantasized about this," he said, reaching for her hair sticks. They slid out smoothly, and her hair fell from its intricate twist. She gave her head a shake, just as she had on their first date, and reached up to straighten the last loops that hadn't yet fallen into place. In a piptick, her hair was a curtain that fell to her shoulder blades.

"That is magic," he informed her.

She laughed. "If you say so."

"I do." He ran his fingers through the thick tresses, wanting to satisfy his fantasy. To his surprise, her head fell back and she made a sound like a purr.

"That explains," she mumbled.

"Explains what?"

"Why this makes Rahel turn into a puddle. Shippers, that feels good."

"This is one of the places I should mark with the dala berry paste?"

"I'd rather not have blue hair. Maybe you could just remember."

As if he was likely to forget.

He didn't know how to take out her ear jewelry. They weren't the cuffs he was used to, but hooks that went through actual holes in her ears.

"Doesn't that hurt?" he asked as she removed the jewelry. "Making those holes?"

"A little. It was a long time ago. Once they heal, it's fine."

"That's an odd practice."

She set the jewelry in his hand. "Remind me to tell you about the other places Gaians get pierced. I look forward to seeing your face." She cast a quick look down, her meaning clear, and he cringed at the thought.

"I don't want to know right now."

"Tattoos hurt more than most piercings," she said as he placed the jewelry on a table. "I've seen them here. We're not the only ones who mark our bodies."

"That's not the same thing." He examined her necklace.

"In the back." She lifted her hair.

"Ah." He went around behind, found the clasp easy to undo, and dropped a kiss where the chain had been.

"Oh," she murmured. "That's a spot you should mark."

He kissed her again to be certain. Watching her shiver was entirely secondary to the purpose.

With the necklace safely on the table, he turned his attention to her jacket.

To his disappointment, its removal revealed a dress that was short-sleeved rather than leaving her shoulders bare. But when he moved behind her to pull the jacket from her arms, he stopped dead, his eyes glued to the expanse of naked back.

Slowly, he folded the jacket, set it on the table, and returned to slide his fingertips down her spine.

This time, her shiver was more pronounced. "You didn't let me touch you. Stop taking advantage. You're the one who set these rules."

"I'm beginning to regret that."

"Micah."

He couldn't resist a final kiss to the top of her spine before undoing the catch of the dress. It pulled apart in his hands and pooled at her feet.

She stepped out and turned, clad only in underwear. Her breasts showed little sign of aging, and her upper chest was as smooth as he remembered. His hands itched to touch.

"Wait," she said as he hooked his thumbs in the underwear. "Lhyn told you about Gaian body hair, right?"

"She didn't need to. I've seen both her and Ekatya naked."

"What? When did that happen?"

"Tal and Salomen's bonding break. We spent a great deal of time swimming and sunbathing. I know what Gaian women look like, but—" He stopped, letting his gaze rake down her body. "I never had the right to look until now."

Arousal sparked through their skin contact. She was heating up from mere visual appreciation, and he thanked Fahla that this gift to him was also a gift to her.

He nearly choked when she put her hands atop his and pushed.

Taking the hint, he pulled the last scrap of clothing to her ankles and helped her step out of it. Soon it was folded next to the jacket, and he retrieved the dress from the floor.

He hadn't planned for this detail. There were hangers in the bedroom closet, but that would require leaving her here while he went to a different room.

"Just drape it over a chair," she said.

That worked. He hung it over an armchair and picked up the bottle of massage oil on his way back. "Lhyn said they do this part standing up. Otherwise they get too relaxed."

"No falling asleep during the anointing?"

"Ideally, no." He pressed his thumb against the bottom of the bottle, activating the heating element, and gave it a vigorous shake. "Please let me go first. I need to touch you."

"As if you haven't already. Remember, this part is supposed to be nonsexual."

"I might fail this test. It's a good thing there are no elders watching."

Her eyes crinkled. "Didn't you know? We're the elders."

"I've never felt less like one." He could hardly believe he was about to put his hands on her. "I don't know what a Gaian elder is supposed to look like, but you . . . Alejandra, you're beautiful."

She stepped close, planting both hands on his chest and leaning in to run her nose along his neck. "So are you," she murmured. "And so different." She kissed his throat, his jaw, and hovered over his mouth, not quite making contact. When she lightly swiped her tongue over his upper lip, he nearly dropped the oil.

"Nonsexual," he gasped.

Her deep chuckle was nearly enough to bring out his throat ridges. "Did Lhyn say what the elders did if the youngsters went ahead of schedule?" She nuzzled the skin beneath his ear.

"Threw a bucket of cold water on them," he managed.

She stopped, then stepped back and laughed uproariously, wrapping her arms around her torso as she bent over in her mirth. "Those poor young people! We'd be soaking wet right now if we were there."

He didn't think he'd ever seen anything more striking than a naked Alejandra lost in laughter. It was arousing and endearing at the same time, and his body didn't know how to react.

She straightened, still smiling widely, and shook her head. "The way you look at me, Micah. I don't know what I did to deserve this, but if lighting oil bowls will keep it coming, I'll go to Blacksun Temple first thing tomorrow."

"Lanaril would be delighted to see you." He gave the bottle another shake, satisfied that it had heated through, and squirted a good amount in his palm. "Now stand still, you tempting woman. Let me do this."

She stood motionless as he rubbed his hands together, releasing the scent of cinnoralis, and laid them on either side of her neck.

The next tentick was a blur of skin and sensation, both physical and emotional. Having a purpose helped. He could focus on rubbing gentle circles into the smooth skin of her forehead, with its curious lack of ridges, and following the sharp cheekbones that were nearly Alsean in their prominence. Then it was down her jaw and onto her throat and shoulders, and from there to an arm, all the way down to her fingertips.

She relaxed, trusting, letting his touch bring her pleasure. His mental checklist was the only thing that kept his brain from overloading.

Once both arms shone with oil, he worked on her back and then her buttocks, which he suspected would be marked with dala berry before the night was over. Then he rubbed down each of her legs before rising from his knees and returning to her front.

By the time he massaged the oil into her breasts, they had both sunk far enough into the ritual to avoid breaking it. She hummed happily, her arousal obvious through the abundant skin contact, but made no move to escalate.

He squirted more oil onto his hands and moved to the last part of her body. Her stomach was softly rounded, a pleasure to touch, and—

He bent to look more closely. The striations were silvery white, rather than the darker stripes he was used to, but they surely meant the same thing.

"You bear the Child Sign," he said.

Confusion rose through her skin, followed by sharp realization and spiky discomfort. "Are you talking about my stretch marks?"

"Is that what you call them? These." He laid a hand atop the Sign.

She nodded, still uncomfortable.

"They're beautiful."

Disbelief prickled. "No, they're not."

"Is this a cultural difference? We revere the Child Sign. These marks are a testament. You brought—"

He stopped, his arousal-saturated brain finally putting the clues together. She had borne a child, but never spoke of one. She had lit an oil bowl in the Room of Remembrance for an ancient sorrow. And she was uncomfortable with him calling attention to the memorial her child had left on her body.

He set aside the bottle and took her hands in his. She was wary, dreading his next words, and he hoped his choice was correct.

"When you're ready, I would like to hear your story." A deliberate repeat of his earlier offer.

Her eyes narrowed, grief rising to the surface and warring with frustration. "You see too damn much," she said harshly.

He made no response other than to tighten his grip.

After a moment, she squeezed her eyes shut and sighed. "I'm sorry. I didn't expect that. Most men don't notice." The frustration ebbed, and she gave a chuckle that held no amusement. "They certainly don't read me like there's a shekking text written on my stomach."

"They don't notice?" Where were Gaian men looking?

When she pulled her hands away, he worried that he had said the wrong thing. But she merely retrieved the bottle.

"My turn," she said.

Warm, oil-smooth hands landed on his neck. She was silent, focused on her task, and there was no arousal in her touch.

"You revere it?" she asked, her hands sliding to his shoulders.

"Bringing life into the world is a blessing and a miracle. We revere the physical testament to that."

She poured more oil in her palm and rubbed her hands together, then set them on his chest. "Right now, this is my favorite part of your body." A tiny spark of sexual interest reignited as she traced his chest ridges. "I reserve the right to change my mind later, because these"—her hands moved lower, rubbing his pectoral muscles—"are a close second. I've seen men half your age who don't look this good here. Alsean musculature has definite advantages."

He didn't know what to say. Her compliment was genuine; that much was in her touch. But her vibrant presence had dimmed. She was not entirely with him.

She moved around to his back and set to work on one arm. When she reached his wrist, she began to speak.

"On my home planet, a woman's worth is measured by her child-bearing ability. But once we have a child, our desirability diminishes. If we want men to *see* us again, we have to somehow snap our bodies back to how they were before the pregnancy. Which is physically impossible."

"Of course it is. Why would they expect a miracle to leave no mark?"

She stopped, then uttered a quiet oath in her language and rested her forehead against his shoulder. "You're astonishing."

"I'm Alsean."

This time, her chuckle was genuinely amused. "You're all astonishing." She poured more oil and resumed her massage on his other arm. "One of the things we can't change is our stretch marks."

"That's a terrible name."

Her humor grew. "Would you believe I never realized that until now? 'Child Sign,' for the love of flight. What a beautiful term. Anyway, since we can't change it, men tend to blind themselves to it. Most consider it unattractive."

"You're joking." But he knew she wasn't.

"I haven't been with that many lovers. At the age when most women are enjoying their youth and desirability, I was already a failed bondmate and the mother of a dead child. I threw everything I had into learning medicine and getting into Fleet. Finding a lover was the last thing on my mind."

She finished working his fingers, added more oil, and moved to his back.

His mind was racing, remembering her inadvertent admission from their first date. The timing of it, oh, Fahla . . .

For the first time, he was glad she couldn't sense him.

"No man has ever paid attention to my—my Child Sign," she said. "Much less called it beautiful."

"It is. I wouldn't have said it if I didn't mean it."

"I know. And despite my, hm, poor reaction . . ." She slid her arms around his chest, embracing him from behind. "It means more than I can say."

He barely had time to cover her hands before she pulled away.

"Can I do that? Give you a warmron? We haven't joined yet."

His laugh was unstoppable. "Alejandra, we're naked and covered in oil. I don't think the taboo applies at this point."

A throaty laugh burst from her in response, dancing along his nerve endings and heating him from the inside out.

"Good." She dropped to one knee and began rubbing oil into his buttocks. "For the record, this is my third favorite spot, but it might move up to second. We'll see."

By the time she came around front to finish, her arousal had attained a comfortable simmer. They were in no danger of having a bucket of cold water thrown on them, but he had also let go of his fear that she might give up altogether.

Five ticks later, he happily abandoned his second fear: that she would be put off by his differences. On the contrary, she was transfixed by his pelvic ridges and the way they dipped to meet in the sensitive curve of his molwine. Her fingertips traced the ridges on each side simultaneously, sliding down almost to the molwine before retreating. She began again, this time rubbing in the oil.

He watched, mesmerized by the sight of those slender fingers making rhythmic circles as they moved closer and closer to the junction of his thighs. According to the rules, she should not be venturing onto the molwine, but she lacked the experience to recognize where the pelvic ridges ended and the exquisitely erogenous molwine began. It was up to him to tell her.

That, he discovered, required more strength of will than he possessed.

Her movements became more careful, the circles growing smaller as she neared his molwine. Then she reached it, sparking a response so intense that he shuddered.

She did not comment on his reaction, though her enjoyment was clear. Slowly, she traced the curved ridge with a fingertip, then slid down to tease his entrance.

"That's not nonsexual," he finally managed in a hoarse voice.

Her wicked smile reappeared. "Oh. I didn't realize."

Not only was she unashamed of her blatant lie, it somehow reignited her passion. Though he was pained by the loss as her hands dropped away, the return of her full, vital presence more than made up for it.

When she asked to be the first to mark him with the dala berry paste, he agreed without hesitation.

She led him to the bed, where he lay face down and enjoyed the contrast of relaxed muscles and tense expectation. Then she straddled his hips, and he nearly flew off the mattress.

"Shh," she murmured, brushing her lips over the back of his neck. "Calm down."

"Wait." He turned his head to the side. "What will we say? When we find those places? Lhyn said it was something like 'blessed by the gods.' I could say 'blessed by Fahla,' but that wouldn't work for you."

She sat up, idly rubbing circles on his back. "How about something simpler? Just 'blessed.' I feel blessed tonight."

He glowed with happy pride. "Blessed it is. And so do I."

She found the spot behind his ear right away, satisfaction sinking into his skin as she marked it with the paste.

"Is it bilateral?" she asked, and nuzzled her nose behind his other ear.

When he gasped out a "blessed," she laughed in delight.

"This is the best ritual I've ever heard of." She marked it, then moved her lips across his upper shoulders.

He soon discovered that high arousal made it difficult to separate truly sensitive locations from overall receptivity. After the undressing, the mutual massage, and most of all, her conscious return of trust, his entire body was an erogenous zone. But she was patient, testing places multiple times until he could decide.

By the time she turned him over, she had marked sixteen locations.

She found twenty-three more on the front, though he argued that the molwine should only count as one, not the three she claimed it to be.

"You're wrong," she said, painting a mark on his right ankle. "You reacted differently in those places. The spot just left of center—you jumped so high that I thought you might damage your spine. One finger-width away and you only jumped half as high." She set the bowl on the bedside table and sucked her finger clean. "You're done. Thirty-nine locations, I'm impressed. That gives me a lot to work with."

He sat up and scooted to one side. "Lie down and let me map you."

"Impatient?" she teased, sliding forward onto her stomach in a graceful motion that made his mouth go dry.

"Disbelieving." She was there, in the position he had fantasized about during his talk with Lhyn. But this was real, and he could hardly believe his luck.

He skated his fingers through her hair and across her scalp, inspiring an immediate groan.

"We already established that one," she mumbled. "But you don't need to stop."

"Do you know the greatest benefit of not being a youngster?"

"What?"

"Much better stamina. I don't plan to stop for hanticks yet."

The back of her neck was a given. He tested its full length with lips and tongue, finding it beautifully sensitive at the nape yet dulled to his touch where it met her shoulders. Retrieving the bowl, he dipped a finger and drew a blue line down the top two-thirds of her neck.

She didn't share his sensitivity behind the ears, but when he moved across her upper back, he discovered an area around her shoulder blades that she didn't know about.

Her spine was soon blue along the entire length of her back, a journey he drew out as long as he could. Eventually, it was joined in its decoration by two rings encompassing her buttocks. He hadn't needed to test those, but did a thorough job of it in the interests of satisfying the ritual.

She approved of his dedication to gathering data.

The crease where thigh met buttock, the backs and sides of her knees, and the soles of her feet were added to the list.

"That's how I know I'm aroused." Her head was resting on crossed arms, and her leg was bent at the knee while he held her small foot in his hand. "If I'm not, it tickles and I won't let you touch them. If I am . . ."

"I can do this?" He ran his tongue from toe to heel.

A guttural series of syllables came out of her mouth, sounding like a particularly fervent oath. "Yes," she said breathlessly. "Blessed."

He painted a blue line to match the one adorning her other foot. "Much as I hate to lose this view, we're done on this side."

She drew her foot from his hand and rolled over, presenting a whole new view as she reached for a pillow and pulled it beneath her head. "Then you'd better start gathering data on this side."

He sat on his haunches and admired her unmapped skin, broken only by the exotic patch of hair where an Alsean's central pelvic ridges and molwine would be. Then he picked up the bowl of dala berry paste, moved back to her head, and began the second half of his explorations.

It was immediately apparent that, while she lacked his sensitivity behind her ears, she had it and then some in front. He brushed his nose there, intending to kiss it, but she was already groaning out a "blessed."

He marked one side, then the other, then kissed her mouth, which was not part of the ritual.

She didn't point that out.

One side of her jaw was sensitive, while the other was not. Her biceps, inner elbows, and palms were soon marked. When he took one of her fingers into his mouth and laved his tongue along its length, she looked at him with the wide eyes of one undergoing an epiphany.

"Shekking—oh, blessed. I can't even describe how that feels. Incredibly erotic." Her lips were parted, and her opposite hand curled into the bedcover.

He slowly pulled back, finding her focused stare nearly as stimulating as the emotions coming through her skin. "Has no one ever done this for you?"

She shook her head.

Her previous lovers were fools, but there was no need to say so. Instead, he took her second finger into his mouth, never breaking their gaze.

By the time he had sucked all ten fingers, she was short of breath. He marked the base of each, fiercely proud that she was learning her own body through his touch.

Then he caressed the smooth skin that had so fascinated him, marveling at the lack of chest ridges and losing himself in the softness of it. She had no particular sensitivity there, but her nipples and the underside of each breast were left with a dab of paste. He set the bowl on the table and returned to pull a newly blue nipple into his mouth, delighted when she arched her back in response.

"You already marked that," she managed.

Slowly, very slowly, he allowed the nipple to slip free. "I wasn't certain the mark would remain."

"Ah. That was a test."

"Yes, but an incomplete one."

"I applaud—" She gasped when he switched sides. "Your attention to detail." An incredulous laugh escaped. "My sainted Shippers, you're good at that."

That she was incapable of further speech for the next several ticks was, he felt, a greater compliment than any words she could have said. There were many ways to touch this particular area, and he tried them all. When her hand came up to hold his head in place, he knew he had found the best one.

Leaving was difficult, especially when she voiced her objection with a wordless murmur that was the very definition of erotic.

He explored her sides, loving the curve of her waist but finding nothing to mark there. Her stomach he left for last.

The fronts of her legs were not as sensitive as the backs, but her toes were soon dabbed with blue dots. She had already known about those, leaving him to wonder why her past lovers were unaware that her fingers were twice as responsive.

Deciding that was a question for later, he moved back to her stomach and sensed her surprise. She hadn't noticed the omission, he realized. Which meant she was not accustomed to being touched there.

A shiver ran through her when he brushed his lips along the first silvery stripe.

"Oh, stars," she whispered. "Blessed. I can't believe it."

He painted it blue, then moved to the next one.

"Blessed." Her voice was choked.

Carefully, he marked that one as well. She was trembling, a complicated mixture of arousal, shock, joy, and sorrow rising through her skin.

When he kissed the third, she covered her eyes with her forearm. "Blessed," she said hoarsely.

There were two more on the opposite side. By the time he ran his tongue down the second, she was chanting.

"Blessed, blessed, blessed . . ."

He heard the tears in her voice, though grief was not her ascendant emotion. Something had been triggered, and she was lost in an emotional storm that burned his palms as he pressed them to her stomach.

"Micah." She raised her head, tears streaming down her face. "Please."

When she held out a hand, he moved over her and slid his arms around her back, then rolled them to their sides.

She clung to him, her face tucked into his throat, and shook. "It's not you," she managed.

"I know. It's all right." He stroked her back, hoping the touch would calm her, but she could not stop whatever had taken hold. She trembled and shivered, her breath coming in short gasps, until a violent shudder racked her body and she inhaled deeply. On the exhale, she went limp.

He kissed the side of her head and moved his hand into her hair, lightly scratching her scalp.

"Astonishing," she murmured. "It still works even after that. Please don't stop."

"I have no intention of it."

She relaxed in his arms, her breathing returning to normal, and he was startled by the ferocity of his emotions. He had not felt this protective of a lover since Realta.

All too soon, tension returned to her muscles. He loosened his hold, unsurprised when she pushed herself back.

Her eyes were wet but clear. "I think I owe you an explanation."

"Can you? From what I sensed, you're not certain what that was."

"I'm not. But I can make a guess." She wiped her cheeks and gave him a tremulous smile. "What we're doing here tonight—this isn't just a joining. I'm not alone in thinking that, am I?"

He shook his head.

"Does this feel as spiritual to you as it does to me?"

"Yes. But I wouldn't have had the courage to say it."

She put a hand to his cheek, tenderness soaking into his skin. "You would have. Eventually." Her hand slipped to his throat, then traced his chest ridge before dropping to the blanket. "Part of me has been dead for a very long time. I know you understand why."

He nodded.

"I never imagined it could live again. Eleven moons ago, Rahel woke it up." Seeing his surprise, she added, "That's a long story, and I'll tell you, but not now."

"I look forward to it."

"Mm-hm. I realize now that I've made the classic mistake of a healer. I've misunderstood my own healing process. I thought what I went through with Rahel put something back that was missing, but what really happened is that I *began* to heal."

He reached for her hand, missing that connection.

"And then you touched my—"

"Child Sign," he said firmly.

She chuckled. "Yes. That. And it felt incredibly good. But I didn't know I was sensitive there. I didn't know, Micah. No one has ever touched me the way you just did. It felt like a true blessing. And while you were doing that, I was trying to understand. Have I been dead there all this time and I'm only now waking up? Or was I always sensitive there, but never knew it until now? Did I waste half a lifetime in ignorance of this part of myself?"

She paused, having no answers to give. He knew she expected none from him, but perhaps he could help.

"There is a passage in the Truth and the Path that might apply. The philosophy that guides honorable warriors." Encouraged by her curiosity, he continued. "It says a system in precarious balance is one breath from failure. In the right circumstances, even a pebble may start an avalanche."

Her smooth forehead crinkled. "That's a war philosophy?"

"It's a philosophy that can be applied to war. But also to governance and politics. To relationships. To ourselves."

"To medicine," she said wonderingly. "To every biological system in the body. To our minds."

He rested a hand between her breasts. "To our hearts."

"Damn," she whispered. "That's what happened. It was everything at once, and all on top of the beautiful spirituality of this ritual and the prayer I haven't said since I was twenty-one. I felt something come back to me." Her chest rose as she inhaled. "Will you take me to the temple tomorrow?"

"It would be my pleasure." He would call Lanaril first thing in the morning to make certain she was available.

"Thank you." She lifted his hand and kissed the knuckles, then pushed him onto his back. A moment later she was astride him, her hair hanging over one shoulder and her face sharply beautiful in the candle-light. "I've set us back, but you did say something about stamina. Are you willing to work back to where we were?"

"It won't take long," he said, and reached for her.

16

TEMPLE

Lanaril Satran sat comfortably on a padded bench within sight of the great outer doors. She had chosen a vantage point off to the side and quite some distance away, not wanting to disturb Micah and his new lover. Her distinctive tunic was laid across her legs, its silver molwyn design hidden in the folds. Without it, she was as anonymous as she could be in the temple.

The glass dome overhead showed a cloudless blue sky, but she would have known the weather even with her eyes shut. On days like this, so much light poured into the temple that it might have had no walls at all. The ancient molwyn tree bathed in it, its leaves seeming to lift and swell with happiness. When she was in a particularly fanciful mood, she swore she could hear it humming as it transformed sunlight into life.

Few worshipers stood beneath it, and the crowds scattered around the rest of the temple were thin compared to the early rush that had passed or the midmeal rush to come. She had suggested this time to Micah for the sake of her schedule and because it would offer more privacy.

A third, unspoken benefit was that she saw them as soon as they walked through the doors.

Colonel Corozen Micah was distinctive, with his powerful build, military bearing, and short-cropped silver hair. Beside his bulk, Alejandra Wells looked small.

It was an illusion, one that had shattered the first time Lanaril met her at Ekatya and Lhyn's bonding feast. Alejandra's forceful personality could barely be contained in her slender body. She only seemed small until she spoke.

The new couple walked toward the molwyn tree and stopped at the first available oil rack. When Micah pulled out a credit chip rather than cinteks, Lanaril knew this would be a substantial offering.

He picked up the wand of eternal flame and offered it to Alejandra, who lit the ten bowls in the top row. She returned it to Micah, who lit the second row and handed it back. Taking turns, they proceeded to light all one hundred bowls, creating a glorious display of dancing flames in the translucent rack.

Substantial indeed. Micah had not indicated their relationship during his early morning call, but she had listened to the words between the words and made an educated guess. This confirmed it. They had lit the rack together, an offering of gratitude for the gift of each other.

She hardly needed the additional proof of Alejandra slipping an arm around his waist as they bowed their heads and prayed. It was a public statement, even if she didn't realize it. But he did, and his only reaction was to lay his hand atop hers.

"Fahla's blessings upon you," Lanaril murmured. She rose from her seat and walked a leisurely path across the temple, waiting until she was closer before donning her tunic. When she was ten paces away, Alejandra lifted her head, saw her immediately, and offered a hesitant smile.

"Well met, Alejandra." She held up a palm.

"Lanaril, well met. Thank you for seeing me." As with all Gaians, her touch was a blast of emotions, adding to those already saturating the air around her.

"I'm honored that you've come to my temple. And that Micah chose me," she added, turning to him. "What a surprising morning! I'm so very happy for you both."

His grin transformed him from formidable warrior to lovestruck man, and she thought no one deserved it more. "Thank you. This is all rather sudden, as you know. But nothing has ever felt so right."

"Wait," Alejandra said. "I heard his side of the call. He didn't tell you anything. Can you feel it from us?"

"Yes, but I knew before I came in range." She gestured toward the flaming rack. "That's as good as a printed sign, and when you put your arm around him, you made an announcement."

Alejandra covered her face. "Dammit. I forgot."

"I didn't." Micah nudged her. "Don't worry, there are no Fleeters here to see."

She raised her head. "I don't care if anyone in Fleet knows. I just don't want to cause trouble for you."

"You won't. Are you sure about Fleet? What about Admiral Greve?"

"Admiral Greve can take his opinions and shove them in the dark place he keeps his brains," she snapped. Her spark of anger, quick to rise, was equally quick to sink beneath embarrassment as she glanced at Lanaril. "Sorry. I shouldn't say things like that around you."

"Have I become a different person since the party at Hol-Opah?"

"We weren't in a temple then. And you weren't wearing that." She indicated Lanaril's tunic.

"I can take it off, if you prefer."

"No," she said with a thoughtful frown. "No, I'd rather you keep it on. It reminds me that you're different." She gazed up at the morning light streaming through the dome. "This is different. I need that."

"Very well. Then if you're ready, I have a shannel dispenser in my study and two cups waiting for us. Join me?"

She nodded, her nervousness returning.

There was little Lanaril could do about it here, so she nudged them through their good-byes and held back a smile as Micah promised his timely return. If the infamous Admiral Greve caused any issues and survived Alejandra's ire, he might not survive Micah's.

Alejandra walked silently beside her as Lanaril led the way out of the temple and through the inner corridors to her study. She declined an invitation to sit, preferring to stand at the windows until the shannel had been served and Lanaril was taking her own seat.

"It's been a long time since I spoke with a minister," she said, sitting straight-backed in the opposite armchair. "I lost my faith at the age of twenty-one and haven't seen a shred of it since. Until recently."

"Can you tell me what led to your loss of faith?"

She nodded, one side of her mouth twitching upward. "Some habits really do die hard. You sit there wearing a tunic that says you speak for a deity and I'm already thinking it will be easier to tell this story to you than it was with Micah."

Lanaril held up a hand. "Please, let me say this first. I cannot speak for Fahla. I can speak for my belief in her, for her teachings, for what I believe she wishes for us. But I'm not a translator. I'm an interpreter."

Alejandra tilted her head, examining her with keen intelligence. "You're the Lead Templar."

"Yes."

"Of Blacksun. The capital city of Alsea."

"Yes."

"Which makes you the equivalent of the High Prelate on my planet. He spoke for the Seeders. His word was their word, and he passed it to his ministers. To doubt any of them was to doubt the Seeders themselves."

This was shaky ground. She had never trod a path like this before.

"I'm not familiar with the religion you grew up with. I can only speak for my own. This tunic merely says that I have accepted the responsibility that comes with wearing it." She hesitated, looking for a bridge. "When you put on your uniform, does it mean you know everything there is to know about healing?"

"No, of course . . . not," Alejandra finished, her eyes narrowing. "I see where this is going. It's not the same thing."

"Isn't it?"

"I got where I am by studying until my eyes fell out of my head and then learning on the job. Making mistakes, losing people. Learning how to save them. Plain hard work."

"So did I."

She planted an elbow on the armrest and dropped her forehead into her hand. "Then how am I supposed to talk to you? If you're nothing more than a woman in a fancy tunic who makes the same mistakes I do?"

"You're looking for infallibility?"

"I'm looking for someone who knows!"

"Did that work for you before?"

She stiffened, her surprise chased by a wave of realization. "No."

Lanaril leaned forward. "I've only met you a few times, but you don't strike me as the kind of person who lets people tell her what to do or how to think. Is that truly what you want from me?"

Alejandra stared at her, the conflict showing on her expressive face. "I don't know what I want," she said at last. "Maybe I just wanted you to say something I could believe. Something that would make it right. But I'm not twenty-one anymore."

"And I'm not a Seeder minister," Lanaril said. "You said you needed me to be different."

"Oh, you are. You made that clear in the first two sentences."

"Then let me be that for you. Loss of faith is a spiritual wound. You're a healer in need of healing. This is the kind of healing I know about."

Alejandra propped her head against her fingers, a slumped pose far removed from her straight back of mere ticks ago. "Healing," she mused. "That's what I told Micah I was starting to do."

Lanaril waited. The next step could not be hers.

"I lost my child. A beautiful boy named Josue. He died of a fever."

For the next thirty ticks, Alejandra outlined a heartbreaking story, her short, clipped sentences gradually gaining strength and detail. By the time she finished, she had one of Lanaril's kerchiefs clutched in one hand and a refilled shannel cup in the other, but her posture was relaxed and she was speaking freely.

"The thing I've never been able to understand is why. Why take a tiny, innocent child? Why try to take me with him when I'd already offered my life for his? What did I do to deserve the pain of outliving my child? I lived my whole life in observance of the Seeders' laws. I went to services, paid the assessments, prayed every day, never questioned their benevolence. I never even asked them for anything. My friends would pray for things like good weather for some special occasion, and I'd think, 'Save your prayers for something that matters.' But when I made the most desperate prayer of my life, Josue and I mattered as much as rain on a picnic." She fixed Lanaril with a glare. "If you say something ridiculous like 'we can't fathom the wisdom of the Seeders' or 'we have to trust in their plan,' I'm done here."

Lanaril sipped her shannel, giving herself time to consider a response. *Why* was an impossible question with no good answer. But Alejandra's pain had more than one source.

"You didn't ask whether you deserved that pain," she said at last. "You asked what you did to deserve it. Does your religion teach that you're responsible?"

"Not in so many words, but the message is there. We're taught that the Seeders are omnipotent and perfectly just. They can't be wrong. It's circular reasoning—whatever they do is right by definition, so if it hurts us, we must have done something to deserve it. If we don't deserve it, then it wasn't right, which isn't possible." Her emotions hardened. "But that isn't what my minister said. He said the Seeders wouldn't give me a burden I couldn't bear. As if losing the only child I will ever have was some sort of test to prove my worthiness. I failed that one in record time."

Lanaril was glad her guest could not sense the effort it took to keep her voice level. "Do you believe this teaching?"

She rocked her hand from side to side. "Yes and no. Intellectually, I know it's dokshin. But faith isn't intellectual, is it? Not the part that goes into your heart. I did go to fewer services after Josue was born. Life was so much busier. I probably did pray less. I loved my son more than I loved my gods. So they took him."

It was spiritual malpractice. Lanaril spent a savage moment wishing these ministers were in her jurisdiction so she could personally strip them of their tunics. Alejandra's dismay at her unwillingness to speak for Fahla now made perfect sense. She was searching for a new authority to counter the old one.

"When we began," she said, "I told you I was an interpreter of Fahla, not a translator. That may have been too simplistic. There are times when I'm certain enough of her teachings to feel confident speaking in her voice. This is such a time."

The sudden tension in Alejandra's posture accompanied a fragile blossom of hope.

"You ask what you did to deserve this. The answer is nothing. You did *nothing* to deserve such a tragedy. Even if you never did any of the things you were taught would show your faith—even if you never had faith to begin with—none of that would mean you deserved to have your child taken from you. Josue was innocent. So were you."

Alejandra inhaled sharply, her eyes brimming. She tried to speak, then clenched her jaw and shook her head. "Thank you," she whispered.

Lanaril's heart ached for this woman who had carried such an unnecessary burden for so long. Had no one helped her in all these cycles?

"If you were a Seeder minister," Alejandra said thickly, "you'd give me absolution. You'd tell me I need to have more faith, not that I didn't need any at all."

"You don't require absolution. But I do think you need more faith." She lifted a hand, forestalling the angry response. "Not because your lack is an insult to your gods or mine. Because it's hurting you not to have it."

Alejandra coughed out a bitter laugh. "Did you need your empathy to see that?"

"Just my eyes."

She nodded, swallowing hard as she wrestled herself under control.

"It's all right. Take your time."

Half a tick passed before Alejandra spoke again.

"I miss it," she admitted. "What I went through with Micah last night —it was so beautiful, so spiritual, but it hurt."

"The beautiful pain," Lanaril said. "That's what one of our oldest writers called it. The beautiful pain of remembrance and longing. A pain that only exists when we have loved, when we know what we're missing."

"Yes, that's it. That's it exactly. It made me remember what I loved about believing. The rituals, the community, the sense of being part of something larger. I've lost that, and I don't know how to get it back. I can never believe in the Seeders again. I'm too far away from them." Her gaze grew steely. "You called them my gods. They're not."

Lanaril's attention had been caught by one phrase in particular. "Did you join Fleet to be part of something larger?"

"No. I joined it because I wanted to be the person who led a team out of a shuttle and stopped a plague in its tracks. I wanted to be the one who saved people instead of watching them die while offering nothing but helpless *prayer*." There was pure poison in her voice.

"That makes perfect sense. I was merely wondering if there might have been a secondary purpose. Perhaps one you weren't aware of at the time."

Alejandra drained her cup and set it aside. "I suppose it's possible. I never thought of it that way, but it did give me a new community. A bigger purpose." Her quiet huff of amusement was not reflected in her emotions. "If I was trying to substitute Fleet for the Seeders, I put my faith in the wrong place. Fleet took the exact skill set I developed to help people and tried to weaponize it. They lied to me. They told me I was creating an antidote for a virus when that virus was their own bioweapon. I nearly walked away after that."

"Why didn't you?"

"I accepted a deep space mission to give myself time to think about it. When that ended, Ekatya personally recruited me. I wanted to serve under the captain who stood up for what was right and saved a planet. We got off to a rocky start—" She stopped, glancing down with a smile and a deep surge of affection. "A very rocky start. But at least in her, my faith hasn't been misplaced."

Two uses of such a charged word could not be a coincidence.

"It seems to me," Lanaril began, feeling her way through, "that when you lost your faith in the Seeders, you didn't lose it altogether. You kept it in your heart while trying to find the right vessel for it. Fleet was that vessel until it betrayed your trust. Then Ekatya became that vessel. Two cycles later, you're talking to a templar for the first time since you were twenty-one. This is a significant step. It tells me that a great deal of healing has gone on in those two cycles. What you shared with Micah last night appears to have been a trigger, but I think the ground was prepared before that."

Alejandra's eyes were on her, but her thoughts were clearly elsewhere. "Lhyn," she said. "It started when Lhyn was tortured."

"What changed for you then?"

"Ekatya told me the most ridiculous story I'd ever heard and asked me to perform a medically risky procedure on her, all based on what sounded like a fantasy. I almost refused. I almost left Lhyn there to die."

"But you didn't. Why?"

"Because the strongest woman I knew was falling apart in front of me, begging me to believe her, and I . . . had to. I had to believe her. The alternative was too awful. I told her then that she was asking me to take a leap of faith."

"And you did." Lanaril had not heard this side of the story. Lhyn was a dear and close friend; she knew everything about her experience and a great deal about Ekatya's. But she hadn't known their lives hung on the thread of a healer's lost faith.

"I did, and it worked. It *worked*. That qualified as a genuine medical miracle. I remember telling Lhyn that, on Tlahana Station. That she and Ekatya had made me believe in miracles again. Damn," she murmured. "I didn't think about that until now. And that was only the first miracle."

"Lhyn's brain healing," Lanaril guessed.

"She told you about that?"

"She's a good friend, and she doesn't like to carry secrets."

This time, the amused huff was genuine. "No, she doesn't. And a few days after that, I watched her and Ekatya light up the molwyn tree out there. Now that you've got me thinking about it, maybe the surprise isn't that I'm here now. Maybe it's that it took me this long."

Her emotional signature was so far removed from what it had been at the start of their session that Lanaril could hardly believe it was the same woman. The healer was healing herself, asking only for guidance on the path she had already chosen.

"Micah will be here soon," Lanaril said. "I want you to think about something when you go. Think about the memorial you've created for Josue."

"What memorial?"

"You gave his life a profound meaning. You went out and learned how to help others. You stepped in front of death and said no. I can only imagine how many lives you've helped or saved over the course of your career, but I know for a fact that Lhyn would not be here without you. Ekatya is a divine tyree; she would never have been the same after that loss. And Rahel tells me that no one else could have gotten to her when she was injured on your ship."

Alejandra was listening with intense concentration, her heart fertile ground for the seed now being planted.

"Josue's life was tragically short," Lanaril said gently. "But his legacy has been extraordinary, because his mother kept her faith."

17

WAR GAME

Ekatya flipped her command chair onto its back, wanting to see the action directly overhead. Both the top and bottom displays were active, offering an immersive view of the space around them and the battle raging through it.

A combat grid overlaid the displays, showing optimum targeting solutions for the weapons rooms that ringed the *Phoenix*. Each was crewed by a four-person team handling rail guns for defensive and offensive use, two launch tubes for firing shield breakers and missiles, and a Delfin launch tube for the expensive, high-yield torpedoes that could end a battle.

At the moment, half of her weapons rooms were hurling projectiles at the two enemy destroyers and Alsea's space elevator.

"The *Victory* is trying to flank us," she said. "Lieutenant Scarp, get us to the other side of the space elevator."

She brought the chair back to level and glanced at the two rings of stations below her. Lieutenant Scarp was fiercely focused on his control panel, piloting the ship through the blizzard of weaponry being flung at them by the destroyers. Beside him was Commander Lokomorra; navigation and main weapons completed the ring. Level with the deck, the third ring held eight more stations.

The central dais was a brilliant design plan, minimizing physical obstructions to the otherwise perfect display imagery. Sitting at its top, she had the best view of the displays and her crew. All other stations lined the walls of the circular room, their operators largely hidden by the vertical panels that bridged the imagery from the bottom display to the top.

She ignored the figure standing by the lift. Admiral Greve had no place on her bridge during a war game. His authority was over the battle group as a whole, but that group was not whole at the moment. The three ships assigned to Alsea were fighting each other with dummy missiles and disarmed laser cannons, testing offenses and defenses in a simulated Voloth attack. Greve should have been in a personnel ship outside the battle, observing and analyzing, but had predictably chosen to watch her instead. With nowhere to sit and no battle harness holding him in place, he could only hold on to a grab bar near the lift. She was disappointed that her opening gambit, a fast ship rotation to enable almost instantaneous port and starboard broadsides, had failed to dislodge him and crack his skull.

At least it had severely disabled the *Thea*, which had lost maneuvering ability but was still firing when it could.

"Fighter losses at forty percent," her weapons officer reported.

Frowning, Ekatya looked down.

Beneath their feet, the blue-and-white beauty of Alsea rotated in peaceful ignorance of the battle, swinging the nearly complete elevator through space with it. Up and down its length, the elevator was swarmed by white fighters defending and silver ones attacking.

They had begun with equal numbers of fighters, but white now outnumbered silver by a two-to-one margin. Two dozen silver fighters floated on the outskirts, their battle over.

That was going to hurt morale. Her fighters had already lost their first competition with the Alseans a moon ago. They had been drilling relentlessly since then, determined to prove their supremacy. Unfortunately for them, so had their opponents.

Ekatya did not intend to lose.

"We knew we couldn't finish this with our fighters," she said. "But they've done their jobs. Tactical, find me a target on that elevator."

"Acknowledged."

From the bottom ring, her engineering officer spoke up. "Shields nearing red line in four sectors."

"Show me."

The report appeared on her console two seconds later, an outline of her ship with four red lights clustered at the stern. They were trying to take out the shields over her engine cradle. Good for them.

Too bad they wouldn't have enough time.

"Lieutenant Scarp, keep our bow facing them. We've got a soft spot in the stern."

"Acknowledged."

"Target acquired," said her tactical officer. "Marking."

A green circle appeared on the space elevator, overlaid with targeting data. In that area, their fighters had weakened enough of the elevator's shielding to enable a strike.

"Excellent. Recall our fighters, tell them to cover our stern. Weapons, concentrate fire on the elevator."

The silver fighters scattered, many followed by white Alsean fighters that did not want to let them go. Temporarily abandoning their attempts to disable the *Victory*, every *Phoenix* weapons team with a targeting solution now fired at the space elevator.

The destroyers reacted quickly, sending a flurry of laser cannon fire in an attempt to shoot down the missiles before they could impact.

It was not enough. A flare of light indicated their success: the space elevator had been severed.

The *Victory* immediately activated its tractor beam, capturing the lower part of the elevator and holding it in place.

"That was a mistake," Ekatya muttered under her breath. "Weapons, load up for a double spin maneuver, breakers first, missiles second. Lieutenant Scarp, take us back around and get us broadside to the *Victory*." It was a direct countermand of her previous order. Their stern would now be exposed.

Her fighters swooped in to protect it, but the Alseans gave them no peace. Forced to divide their attention between defending themselves and shooting down missiles targeting the *Phoenix*, they were doing an inadequate job of both.

Ekatya kept one eye on her console and one on the display, watching as Scarp brought the *Phoenix* around.

"Port weapons, ready," she said. "Fire!"

Fifty shield breakers launched across space toward the *Victory*, which had nowhere to go. Having tied itself to the severed space elevator, it could take no evasive maneuvers and had halved the number of weapon ports available to respond to the threat.

"Rotate!"

Alsea slid from beneath her feet, up the side, and ended overhead as Lieutenant Scarp flipped the *Phoenix* in place.

"Starboard weapons, fire!"

Fifty more shield breakers hurtled toward their target, which was now frantically trying to shoot down the first set.

"Rotate!"

She hadn't invented this tactic, but she had perfected it, drilling her teams over and over again until they had it down to an art form. No other warship in Fleet could perform even a single spin so swiftly, let alone the second spin she had added as a modification the Voloth would not be prepared for. Ekatya was exceedingly proud that she had taken a new crew of weapons specialists and made them even better than the last.

By the time Alsea slid back beneath her feet, the port weapons teams had reloaded their launch tubes, this time with missiles.

"Port weapons, fire!"

Fifty streaks of light arced across space, hard on the heels of the second set of shield breakers.

"Rotate!"

Credit went to Lieutenant Scarp as well: flipping a warship the size of the *Phoenix* was no easy task. But he was a worthy successor to Candini, flawlessly performing the maneuver for the fourth time in this battle.

"Starboard weapons, fire!"

In some corners of Fleet, she'd heard, they were calling the original maneuver the Serrado Spin. She couldn't deny the pleasure that gave her, nor the thrill she felt watching her modified version work now. As expected, the *Victory* failed to block the barrage of weaponry that breached its shields. The missiles impacted, creating a brilliant flash of light that briefly blanked out the display.

The *Victory* was destroyed—and with it, any chance the Alseans had of saving their space elevator or preventing loss of life as it fell.

For the first time since the exercise had begun, she looked across the bridge at Admiral Greve. "Shall we game it out?"

Though the *Thea* was still functional, its fighting ability was limited.

Everyone knew how this would end. Continuing the exercise would only humiliate a captain and crew.

As expected, the only captain Greve was interested in humiliating was her.

"No," he said crisply. "Send out the ceasefire. Postgame analysis in one hour." He turned and entered the lift.

Ekatya took a deep breath, sure that the air on the bridge was fresher now, and nodded to her comm officer.

The Alsean fighters peeled away, all but one heading back to the planet. The last joined her own fighters in returning to the *Phoenix*.

With a tap to open the all-call, she said, "This is Captain Serrado. Stand down from your battle stations. I want to congratulate all of you for a stellar performance that won the war game. You've got bragging rights over the crews of the *Victory* and *Thea*, but I'd suggest going easy on them. They're probably still smarting from the spanking we just gave them."

Her bridge crew cheered raucously, a microcosm of what was probably happening all over the ship. Even when playing the role of the enemy, winning felt good.

"Does Greve have glue on his feet?" At his station on the second ring, Commander Lokomorra had released his harness and now stood upright, bringing his head close to hers. "I thought for sure that a double Serrado Spin would send him soaring."

Ekatya barely kept a straight face. "I can't condone your disrespect for a superior officer, Commander."

"That's not disrespect. I was expressing my extreme admiration for his ability to stay upright."

She pressed her lips together and nodded. "I feel exactly the same way."

⁓

The next hour flew by amidst a flurry of reports and conversations as Ekatya gathered the impressions of her staff. She entered the bridge briefing room armed with data and wishing she could conduct the postgame analysis herself.

Greve was waiting for her, though she was exactly on time, and did not offer so much as a greeting before initiating the video link. Before she had quite managed to pull in her chair, the captains of the *Victory* and *Thea* appeared on the display taking up one wall of the room. They, at least, were accorded the basic courtesies before Greve waded in.

"Captain Kabbai," he said. "What was your fatal mistake?"

Kabbai pressed his lips into a thin line, the motion shifting his long beard. It wasn't as impressive as Lokomorra's forked beard, but Ekatya gave him points for the elaborate beadwork woven through it.

"I know using the tractor beam put me at a disadvantage," he said. "But what else could I do? Let it fall?"

"Captain Teriyong? Any ideas?"

The *Thea*'s captain looked just as irritated. "Yes, Admiral." With a nod toward Ekatya, she added, "I had some time to think about it after being sidelined in the first thirty seconds of the battle."

"I'd apologize, but . . ."

"Don't bother. They don't call that the Serrado Spin for nothing. Credit where it's due; I've never seen anything that fast. You should be training every warship crew in Fleet."

Ekatya thought Alsean empathy might be rubbing off on her. She could almost feel Greve's annoyance rolling across the table.

"Thank you. But I have to give credit to Lieutenant Scarp and my weapons teams. They're the ones who managed not to mutiny when I put them through the same damn drill week after week."

"It paid off." Teriyong scrubbed a hand through her short, graying hair. "I was thinking we should have planned for this. Our first mistake was in believing we had the advantage at two-to-one odds, even with the size difference. The tractor beam was our Plan B. We needed a Plan C."

Greve nodded. "What would you suggest?"

"A shuttle. We've all got shuttles with grappling capability. We only need to hold the cable long enough for the Alseans to repair it. But we'd need to have a shuttle prepped and ready to launch into battle."

"That could be a suicide mission," Kabbai said gravely.

"Depending on where the cable is severed, a shuttle might be more than we'd need," Ekatya said. "A fighter could have enough power to hold it, at least temporarily. It would also have weapons and greater maneuverability than a shuttle."

"Plans C and D?" Teriyong asked. "Each of us trains a shuttle crew, and you train half a dozen fighters?"

"Along with the Alseans, yes." She faced Greve across the table. "We should also work with the fighters to provide protection if a shuttle is needed."

He gave a crisp nod. "So ordered."

"Speaking of fighters," Kabbai said with a twinkle in his eye, "yours have nothing to write home about."

Ekatya had to smile. "I'm dreading that. Being beaten by the Alseans once was bad enough. Twice? I'll have to go back to Tlahana Station just to load up on alcohol."

They laughed, three peers enjoying a moment of mutual understanding, until Greve pointedly cleared his throat.

Like a teacher admonishing the students, Ekatya thought. No, worse: like a bully admonishing his minions for laughing with the wrong person.

She spent the next forty-five minutes ignoring him whenever possible, an easy task given the expertise of Kabbai and Teriyong combined with her own. They dove into their analysis, trading commentary and ideas. Every now and again, Greve would interject, but his battle experience was minimal and they all knew it. His long-ago ship assignments had been in the calmest parts of the Protectorate, far from hostilities, and his rank didn't hide the truth: he had little to offer here.

Ekatya soaked up the camaraderie and the sheer enjoyment of doing her job with competent peers. It was a welcome reprieve until the captains signed off, leaving her alone with an admiral stewing over his irrelevance.

"Captain," he said with an unpleasant smile, "congratulations on your victory. I have to say, I was surprised to see you being so effective attacking the Alseans."

She thought she deserved more congratulations for not leaping across the table and flattening his smug face. "It was a critical training exercise. Did you honestly expect me to do less than my best?"

"I don't always know what to expect from you. Sometimes you surprise me. Other times, you do exactly what your reputation suggests." He stretched his arms overhead and blew out a gusty exhale. "Well, it's been a busy afternoon. I think we're done here. Except . . . we do need to do our check-in, don't we?"

In that moment, she loathed him. Having been sidelined by more experienced captains, he would reestablish his importance by putting her in her place.

Again.

"Captain Serrado," he began.

She drew one hand off the table, resting it on her thigh to clench it where he couldn't see.

"Have you received instructions from Lancer Tal or any member of the Alsean government?"

"No," she snapped.

He looked pleased, and she cursed herself for letting him see her anger.

"Has your command been mentally or emotionally influenced through your tyree bond?"

"No."

"If you receive an order in conflict with anything you've promised Lancer Tal or your wife, how will you respond?"

"I will uphold my oath to the Protectorate."

He made a production out of recording the day's check-in on his pad. "Then we're done."

"It must gall you," she said, unable to stop herself. "Being stuck here in such a dead-end post. Babysitting me isn't a step up the ladder for a rear admiral. Are they punishing you for something? Did you step on the wrong toes?"

He abandoned all pretense. "It won't be a dead end if I get the proof they're waiting for."

"What proof? What is it that you think I'll do?" She pointed in the direction of Alsea, a gesture likely to be lost on a desk pilot who had no feel for how the ship was oriented. "Has it escaped your notice that we're allies? We signed a treaty. Our goals are aligned. What do you think I could possibly do that would betray Fleet or the Protectorate?"

"Oh, I don't know. Crash your ship on the planet?"

She stared at him in disbelief. "You can't be serious."

"You did it once. Gave them a top-of-the-line warship to play with. Don't think we don't know the Alseans are planning to put the *Caphenon* back into orbit. A free Pulsar-class warship to seed their fleet, that's quite a deal. What's to keep you from doing it again?"

"Besides my responsibility to my ship and crew? How can you think *any* captain would put them at risk?"

She wasn't surprised that Fleet knew of the Alsean plan. It was too big a project to keep secret. But she could not believe they actually suspected her of this. Losing the *Caphenon* had been one of the worst nights of her life, and they thought she'd done it on purpose?

"You're not any captain. You're the captain who disobeyed orders and gambled the future of the Protectorate on the toss of a coin. By the luck of the Seeders, you came out of that smelling like a perfumed courtesan. It could just as easily have gone the other way. We already knew you were reckless and arrogant. Now we know you're reckless, arrogant, *and* you've got an alien influence embedded in your brain."

"And if I had obeyed my orders," she snarled, "the Voloth Empire would have Alsea's nanoscrubbers. They'd be doing what we're doing right now, developing them into a weapon. But they wouldn't use it as a deterrent. They'd use it offensively, and in a few years the Protectorate would be confined to the core worlds. So you tell me, who was right? The politicians who sold Alsea for a profit, or the people on the ground who saw what was really happening?"

"It was not your decision to make, Captain! If I can stop you from doing it again, then yes, this shitpile of an assignment will be worth it." He shoved his pad into his sleeve pocket. "You're dismissed."

"You can't dismiss me from my own briefing room. Next time you want to pull rank, make sure you're in your office. The one place on my ship where you actually have power."

He looked as if he might choke on his tongue, a wave of red moving up from his neck to the top of his head. Without another word, he shoved back his chair and stormed out the door.

She stared at the chair, sitting out by itself while all the others were neatly stowed beneath the table. It seemed a perfect metaphor for his presence on her ship: disruptive and a potential threat. In a battle, that loose chair would become a danger.

Her fingers twitched with the sudden need to throw it into the bulkhead. But every move she made, every word she said, was subject to spot checks of the security vids. Unless she went to her quarters, she didn't even have the privacy to vent her anger.

Hades, she missed Admiral Tsao. Her former supervisor had richly deserved the promotion to Fleet Admiral, but replacing her with Greve was akin to trading a warship for a used shuttle. A rusting one, with ancient seats whose springs jabbed her in the ass.

The visual image cheered her somewhat. Calmer now, she pushed away from the table.

"Captain." Lokomorra's voice on her internal com stopped her. *"You have a call on the priority blue channel."*

She dropped back into her seat. "Thank you, Commander. I'll take it here."

The display came alive with the distinctive priority blue emblem and a prompt for her com code. She activated the deskpad embedded in the table, entered her code, and waited for the system to corroborate it with her fingerprints.

Onscreen, the emblem shrank and was replaced by the last com ID she wanted to see and the first one she should have expected.

"Shipper shit," she said wearily. "That man has galaxy-class timing."

At least she no longer had to worry about Admiral Greve checking the security cams. Priority blue automatically encrypted all security data at both ends for the length of the call. Greve would need a writ from Fleet Justice to access it now, and the name on her display guaranteed he would never receive it.

She tapped the deskpad, accepting the call. "Director Sholokhov. What can I do for you?"

The director of Protectorate Security raised his shaggy eyebrows, observing her with interest. As always, his blue eyes were unsettlingly vibrant against his black skin. "Captain Serrado. You've looked better."

"We just finished a war game and the first postgame analysis. It's been a long day."

"Ah. Did you lose?"

Her expression was probably as friendly as she felt. "What do you think?"

"I think you look tired for a victorious captain. But perhaps your victory feels hollow, given that you played the role of the Voloth."

"Is there a purpose to this call?" she asked pointedly.

"Do you know, I almost miss the days when you made a pretense at courtesy. It was inefficient, but charming in its way." He gave a small nod. "I'm calling to discuss two things. One, I now have credible intelligence that Alsea is the target of the latest Voloth activity."

At last, confirmation of what everyone had suspected. "Do you know what they're sending? What is Fleet sending in response?" She would have to rewrite the plan for the next war game to include additional ships.

"Regrettably, none of my sources are embedded that high up. As for the Fleet response, that's already been sent."

"Good. Which ships? When can we expect them?" She pulled the pad from her sleeve, preparing to take notes.

"They're already there."

The pad clattered to the table. "What?"

"Alsea has a battle group permanently assigned to it," he said patiently. "Now, I realize you believe that planet is our only ally of importance, but there are others with vital resources and governments asking why they don't get the same treatment. There's no support in Gov Dome for sending additional assets after the substantial investment we've already made."

"Since when do you allow politics to override Protectorate security?"

"Don't play the ingenue, Captain. It's unworthy of you."

"Then perhaps you could explain to me how something other than politics is preventing a sensible response to an active Voloth threat!"

He spread his hands. "What you call sensible, others call excessive. I have knowledge of a threat. I have no knowledge of its breadth, intent, or date of play. It's not politics; it's a lack of actionable intelligence."

"You can't tell me you don't know the date of play. We all know when they're most likely to come."

"'Likely' is not a word that unlocks a massive allocation of resources." His expression darkened. "I'm giving you a warning, Captain. I strongly advise you to use it."

"For what? You're telling me I'll have no reinforcements. Not to mention that I'm not in command of this battle group." She sat back, hearing her own words. "Why are you talking to me and not Greve?"

"I'm talking to the person in charge of the battle plan."

On paper, Greve was that person. In reality, Ekatya had been driving every bit of it. How Sholokhov had determined that, she did not want to know.

He leaned forward, crossing his hands on his desk. "You destroyed half of the Voloth Empire's Fifth Fleet by yourself. The Alseans destroyed the entire hardware inventory and most of the personnel of the Third Fleet before they had a single functional fighter. Now they have over two hundred. We know for a fact that the Voloth haven't built any new orbital invaders. We also know they've had trouble restocking the Third. We're not seeing movement of invasion groups. What that leaves for an attack doesn't look like a threat you and the Alseans can't handle, especially given the presence of a defensive minefield and two destroyers you didn't have before."

It began to sink in. "That's your warning. That we won't have reinforcements even if you do get actionable intelligence."

"Yes."

She set an elbow on the table and rubbed her forehead. "Lovely."

"You're a victim of your own success, Captain. You and the Alseans. Which brings me to my second topic. I want to leverage your connection with Lancer Tal."

"For what?" she asked absently, still processing the unwelcome news.

"An offer of trade. What price do you think she'd ask for twenty high empaths?"

She was frozen by shock before bursting into laughter. "No price you could pay. She doesn't sell her people."

"I don't want to buy people. I want to trade resources."

"I don't care what phrasing you use, she won't give it two seconds of thought."

"Then perhaps you could convince her to think more carefully."

"Even if I were willing to interfere in her governance, nothing I could say would convince her."

His slight huff of air could hardly be called a laugh, but it was more than he had ever done in her presence. "Really, Captain. 'Interfere in her governance'? You sat on her side of the table during treaty negotiations. She procured the *Phoenix* for you. Then she made it a governmental demand that you stay in command of it after infecting you with an Alsean mental bond. You can't possibly be so blind as to think you have no connection with her policy decisions."

"What she does, she chooses to do." If he was hoping to get a rise out of her with the "infected" comment, she would be happy to disappoint him. "What do you want with twenty high empaths?"

"I want them to work for me," he said in a tone that indicated her idiocy for asking. "High empaths are to my work what the first surf engines were to space travel. They will make things possible that couldn't be done before."

"That's exactly why she won't give them to you."

He examined her as if she were a particularly interesting insect. "Tell me, Captain, why would you not want the Protectorate to have a security advantage?"

She didn't want *him* to have the advantage, but it would not be wise to say so. "I'm a Fleet captain. Keeping the Protectorate and its allies safe is my job. Lancer Tal's primary concern is the safety and future growth of Alsea. Public perception of Alsean empathic power is an inextricable part of that, and she won't risk fueling the fear of her people acting as weapons against us. Or being used as weapons."

"A reasonable concern, given the torture of your bondmate by people fearing exactly that."

His understanding caught her flat-footed, as did his use of *bondmate*. It was a respectful gesture, the same one Greve withheld every day.

"In this, our purposes align," he continued. "There are two types of weapons in my line of work: the kind that are effective as a threat, and the kind that are effective because no one knows they're a threat. Having Alsean high empaths on my side would be effective no matter what. But I could get a great deal more out of them if their existence was unknown."

"A secret trade? You'd have to conduct the entire negotiation outside diplomatic channels."

"Correct. Hence this call to you and not Ambassador Solvassen."

It all fell into place. "That's why you saved my command. You wanted me as your conduit."

He frowned. "Who told you I saved your command?"

"Who do you think? Your pet admiral."

"Greve is a gasbag," he said dismissively. "Useful for a limited purpose, useless beyond that."

It was a sign of how ludicrous her Fleet life had become when she felt solidarity with Sholokhov. "Then why did you put him here?"

"I only deal with the big decisions. Meddling in the minutiae of Fleet personnel choices is not in my bailiwick."

Unless that personnel choice put a spy or an assassin on her ship, she thought.

"Convey my proposal, Captain. We'll see where it goes from there."

"And when she says no? Is that when you take the gloves off Greve?"

"Is he using gloves?" he asked mildly. "My impression was that he hated you enough to piss in your command chair before you sat in it. Lancer Tal won't say no right away. She's too savvy a negotiator, as we all know from the outrageous terms of our treaty. Tell her the Protectorate has more to offer than what she has right now. I'm willing to listen to any reasonable proposal. Call me when you have an update."

His visage blinked out and was replaced by the priority blue emblem. Ekatya stared at it, her thoughts whirling before settling on one revealing point.

Sholokhov knew Admiral Greve was riding on her shoulder. If there were no gloves to take off, then it couldn't get worse.

Which meant Greve had no power over her career unless she gave it to him.

18

SYMBOLISM

Rahel didn't know what to do with herself. She was buzzing with the thrill of the war game, when she and Candini had worked as a perfect team and the lead cog in the intricate machinery of Alsea's fighter fleet. They had danced through space like nightwings, power and grace in a deadly ballet against the backdrop of the space elevator.

Though the shield breakers and missiles were dummies, designed to burn down to their constituent molecules and leave no debris, that hadn't lessened the impact of seeing so many of them hurled through space. The unending streaks of laser cannon fire were even more impressive due to their greater visibility. But most impressive of all was Candini's ability to dodge every danger, flitting through a shifting, lethal maze while chasing down targets. Her call sign, Nightwing, was perfectly chosen. Rahel had never doubted that they would make it through unscathed.

The best part of the battle came at the end, when Candini swung them around the elevator in time to see the *Phoenix* perform the double Serrado Spin. Their war game was based on an optimal scenario, in which a Voloth heavy cruiser and two escort destroyers entered the system only to be immediately whittled down by the defender mines guarding the base space exit point. With its destroyers disabled, the heavy cruiser and the fighters it carried would be at a disadvantage.

Captain Serrado was not supposed to win. When Rahel watched her ship hurl barrage after barrage of weapons, spinning gracefully with each one, she had nearly burst with pride.

Now she was back aboard, floating on that pride and wanting to twirl down the ship's corridors. She wanted to spar against a worthy opponent until she dropped. Most of all, she wanted to speak with someone who understood.

Her feet had brought her here seemingly of their own accord. The clipped response to the entry chime did not dampen her enthusiasm, and when she stepped through the door, she knew she was in the right place.

Dr. Wells looked up from her computer with an impatience that instantly melted to welcome. "There you are! What did you think of your first war game? I heard you killed half of our fighters."

Rahel crossed her office, skirted around the desk, and bent down for a warmron. "It was *fantastic*."

Though startled, Dr. Wells returned the embrace as well as she could from her chair. "I see that," she said with a laugh. "Sit down and tell me."

"I can't sit. I'm still flying." Rahel leaned against the desk, one hand tapping a beat on its surface. "I've heard of this, but it's never happened to me before. The bloodfire. When a warrior finds so much joy in the dance of combat that she doesn't know how to stop dancing."

"That's not limited to warriors. I've come out of emergency surgery still high on the adrenaline rush." Her understanding smile curled into a smirk. "Ordinarily, I'd recommend a vigorous round of sex."

"Helpful, thanks. I know what you'll be doing two ticks after landing on Alsea."

"Give me some credit; it'll be at least five ticks. Getting undressed takes time."

While many Gaians were oddly shy about discussing it, Dr. Wells brought the same matter-of-fact attitude to joining that she did to her work. She also brought the same drive for knowledge, leading to interesting conversations during Rahel's treatments. Based on those, Colonel Micah had to be the happiest man on Alsea.

"Physical activity of any kind can help," she added in a more serious tone. "Even something as simple as walking."

Rahel pounced on the idea. "Come for a walk with me?"

"I'm still collating the results from our simulations. I really should—"

Dr. Wells stopped with a shake of the head. "Stars above, that look. It's like I'd be breaking your heart to say no."

"I'm not that fragile. But there could be bruising."

She glanced at her computer terminal, lips pursed, then reached out to blank the display. "I'm sick of numbers. Let's go."

Instead of walking downstairs to the lobby and its busy entrance, she led them up two flights and through a little-used exit from the medbay's storage areas.

"How did your simulations go?" Rahel asked as they emerged into a main corridor. "Now that I think about it, you never told me exactly what you'd be doing."

"Practicing for battle casualties. We ran simulations of blunt force traumas, sprains and fractures, the kinds of injuries you see when people are thrown around."

"I thought the Pulsar design prevented that?" She had learned about this while studying blueprints of the ship in her early days of training. The battle hull and the sacrificial decks outside of it absorbed the greatest impacts, leaving the majority of the ship relatively unaffected.

"Prevents? Not possible. It reduces. Besides, there will always be some crew caught out on the sacrificial decks, or forced to go there to repair something. Or retrieve someone. We also ran a simulation for fighter crew injuries, which I'll thank you never to incur." Dr. Wells pointed at a tile mosaic they were passing. "That's one of my favorites."

She stopped to examine the bucolic scene. "Why?"

"It reminds me of my home planet. These crops are nebulous enough that I can see my own in them. The ones we used in our crop genetics work."

Rahel absorbed her emotional warmth, increasingly common on the occasions when she spoke of her life before Fleet. "You talk about it more than you used to."

"Do I?" Dr. Wells traced a row of plants in the mosaic before resuming their walk. "Makes sense, I suppose. I'm thinking about it more than I used to. Seeing things in new ways. I'm realizing that I threw out the good with the bad."

Perfect translation capability didn't always mean perfect understanding. Rahel was still puzzling out the meaning when Dr. Wells offered an assist.

"What I mean is, when I left that life behind, I left it all behind. I couldn't think about what I'd lost, so I didn't think about any of it. Do that long enough and it becomes a habit."

"Huh. I couldn't *stop* thinking. That was part of the reason for the drinking."

"We all cope in different ways."

"Now you sound like Lanaril."

"I'll take that as a high compliment. She's a planetary treasure, as far as I'm concerned. I wish we could talk more often."

They turned into the crew services hall, lined on both sides with shops and bars. With most of the crew still engaged in postgame tasks, there was little traffic at the moment.

"Ah, that reminds me." Dr. Wells veered toward a shop with a sign showing scissors and a comb laid across each other. "I need to make an appointment."

A slender man in a white coat descended on them the moment they walked through the door. "Dr. Wells! About time you came in. I thought you'd gone to the competition."

"And let other hands touch my hair? Not a chance. I'm due for a trim, though. Do you have any openings tomorrow night?"

"I have one now."

"Oh, I can't, I'm—"

"Yes, you can," Rahel said. "We can still talk, can't we?"

"Not about anything to do with patients or her personal life," the man said. "But we can gossip about anything else in Fleet. Our lovely chief surgeon has the most acid tongue this side of . . . well, me."

Rahel was intrigued by his lack of nervousness. Most crew members did not react that way to Dr. Wells, who intimidated everyone from her staff right up to Commander Lokomorra.

"I thought you needed to move," Dr. Wells said.

"I did, but I've never seen this." Rahel made a gesture encompassing the room.

"It can't be that different from what Alseans do, can it?"

"Sure it can. For one thing, you do it with your clothes on."

They stared at her, one shocked and intrigued, the other skeptical but unsure. She managed to keep her expression bland until Dr. Wells put her hands on her hips.

"Rahel Sayana. You are kicking the dokshin."

Her use of an Alsean phrase sent Rahel into helpless laughter. Bent over, hands on her thighs, she gasped, "Yes, but your faces!"

"I don't know what you just said, but I like her," the man said. "Why haven't you brought her here before now?"

"Because I always get mine cut on Alsea." Rahel straightened and held out a hand. "First Guard Rahel Sayana."

"As if I'd need an introduction. You're the third most famous person on the ship after the captain and this lady." He shook her hand with a firm grip. "I'm Reynard. Stop wasting your precious leave time getting your trims dirtside. For the love of flight, it's all the same length. I could do that in three minutes. Give me thirty and I'd make you a new woman."

"Good luck with that. She doesn't—"

"What would you do?" Rahel interrupted.

Dr. Wells's eyebrows nearly vanished off her forehead. "Really?"

"I've been thinking about it for a while. Every time we fly, I have to put my hair up like yours to keep it from interfering with the pressure seat." She shrugged. "I'm ready for something different. Easier."

"Something like Candini's?"

"Oh, no!" Reynard held up his hands. "Nope. I've seen First Pilot Candini. Our lovely Alsean here will *not* do spiky hair. That face is not for spikes." He studied her, his chin resting between forefinger and thumb. "Hm. Yes, possibly. Come here." With an authority that brooked no dissent, he steered her by the shoulders and sat her in a chair before a long mirror. In a few deft movements, he had her braid undone and was running strands of hair through his fingers, staring at her reflection and humming thoughtfully.

Dr. Wells sat in the neighboring chair. "If you're not sure, say so now. He's working up to light speed, I can see it."

"Your hair is practically edible," Reynard said. "It's a shame to keep it tied in a braid. Look how thick this is! It wants to be free."

"See what I mean?"

"I'm sure," Rahel said. "It's a traditional warrior braid, but I'm not a traditional warrior anymore." And the bloodfire still humming through her veins approved of a drastic change.

"I like her even more. You want easier? You're lucky. With hair this thick and the right cut, you can step out of the shower, finger comb it, and go. I would cut it to here"—he laid a hand across the back of her neck—"and leave it a little thicker on top. You've got a natural wave that will take care of that. Then a bit in front of the ears to keep it soft." He drew a line to illustrate. "And you'll break hearts."

"I'm not interested in breaking hearts, but go ahead."

Dr. Wells leaned back in her chair, an intrigued smile lighting her face. "This will be fun."

"Watching mere attractiveness transcend to beauty? Yes, it will." Reynard whisked a black cape around her before wheeling a columnar piece of furniture behind her chair. With the tap of a button, the top retracted to reveal a sink. A moment later, she was leaned back with her neck resting on the curved sink edge. He wet down her hair, soaped it up, and began massaging.

She melted instantly. "Fahla," she mumbled. "Dr. Wells, this could count as a treatment."

Amusement brushed her senses. "I should have thought of that back when we were trying the massage therapists. Reynard has a special touch."

"What's this?" Reynard wanted to know.

"Rahel?"

"You can tell him." It was such common knowledge now that she no longer cared. She closed her eyes, sinking into the wondrous scalp massage while Dr. Wells explained how physical touch relieved the emotional pressure from a thousand unshielded minds.

"The massage should have worked," Dr. Wells concluded, "but we tried two therapists and neither could get past the fact that she's not Gaian. They made it worse."

Indignation sparked through the fingers rubbing her scalp. "What kind of massage therapists were they? We're out here to see new things, not cling to old."

"I like him," Rahel said.

"It's mutual," he assured her.

He rinsed her hair, somehow combining a gentle touch with brisk effi-ciency, and Rahel thought she might come here just for this. Then he ran a dehumidifying comb through her hair, just enough to keep it from drip-ping, and set her upright again. A tap closed the sink, and a kick sent it rolling back to its spot along the wall.

"Now," he said, brandishing the scissors. "Watch an artist work."

The first few cuts were shocking. She had expected something more gradual, but within a few seconds, what looked like half her hair was lying on the floor in auburn coils.

"That's quite a difference already," Dr. Wells remarked. "If you're making this radical a change after your first war game, what will you do after the next one? Get a tattoo?"

"I've thought about it," she said honestly. "Since long before this. But I could never decide on a design."

"That's the usual issue. If you do decide, get it done on Alsea or in my medbay. Not on a space station."

Rahel hummed agreement, watching Reynard carefully snip along his comb.

"I mean it, Rahel. I've had to clean up too many messes. Allergic reactions to ink, skin infections, granulomas, keloids, blood-borne diseases from contaminated tools—"

"You make it sound so cheery," Reynard interjected. "I'm glad I only cut hair."

"We always prefer that crew members come to us." Dr. Wells ignored the comment. "And you're at additional risk given your different body chemistry. Promise me."

"I promise that *if* I ever get a tattoo, I won't do it on a space station." It was an easy assurance to make, but she was startled at the relief it engendered.

"Thank you. Three of my nurses are licensed, just so you're aware. So am I, of course."

"You are? How did I not know that?"

Dr. Wells shrugged, a small smile giving away her satisfaction at this surprise. "I enjoy drawing. Skin is just another medium for making art."

"But it's not, is it? You can't make any mistakes."

Reynard chuckled. "She doesn't make mistakes."

"And don't you forget it." Dr. Wells sat back, arms loose on the chair and a broader smile taking over her face. "This is looking good."

Rahel thought so, too. She was fascinated by the process as Reynard measured and cut, measured and cut, always using his fingers to feel the hair as if it were speaking to him. At times, the lopsided results were worrisome, but then he would come around and even things up, following a path only he could see. She had no idea where he was going until suddenly, there it was. He fluffed the hair over her forehead, pulled out the wisps in front of her ears and examined their length critically, then made a few adjustments so tiny that she thought they couldn't possibly matter.

After another rinse, a glorious scalp massage, and a bit of finger combing, he whisked away the cape with palpable pride. "What do you think?"

"My sainted Shippers," Dr. Wells said. "You weren't kidding about beauty. Rahel, you look gorgeous."

She turned her head this way and that, startled by how light it felt without the weight of her braid. And how could something so simple as cutting hair change the shape of her face? Her eyes seemed larger and her cheekbone ridges more pronounced, while her forehead ridges were softened by the hair that curled down. Reynard had been correct; her hair had waves that went their own way. But he had made sure they settled in a pleasing manner.

Experimentally, she ran her fingers through and watched the waves land precisely where they had been before. "Huh. This does look easy."

"Easy." Dr. Wells snorted. "He made you into a recruitment poster for Fleet, and you're thinking about simplicity. You really are a warrior."

"I never pretended to be anything else." She experimented again, grinning as it became apparent that this would indeed be a matter of finger combing and going out the door. "Candini is going to birth a brick."

"So will most of the men and half the women on the crew," Reynard said with satisfaction. "You'll need to set up a waiting list."

"I'm asexual."

"In that case, you might consider putting out a ship-wide memo. It would save time."

Dr. Wells put on a look of wide-eyed interest. "I want a waiting list. Can you do that for me, too?"

"I could, but first you'd have to stop making them terrified of you."

"Hm. No. Better just trim the ends."

19

CONNECTION

Wearily, Ekatya walked through the door of her quarters and straight to her desk, where she removed a small device from the bottom drawer. It activated with a quiet hum, sweeping the vicinity for spy cams. Twenty seconds later, the hum ceased and a steady green light appeared.

Safe for now. The confirmation brought less relief each day, as her anger deepened its roots and sent branches of resentment into every part of her shipboard life.

She replaced the scanner and shut the drawer. "Phoenix, set display to Alsea One."

Across the room, the long wall between the entry and kitchen came awake, transforming from gray nothingness to a vibrant and achingly familiar scene. The Fahlinor River flowed across the foreground while verdant lawns and brilliant landscaping extended from the far bank to the forest beyond. Above the treetops, standing out against a clear blue sky, the colorful domes of Alsea's six largest caste houses ringed the great glassed dome of Blacksun Temple and the imposing height of the State House.

She dropped onto the sofa, lost in the view and a painful longing to be inside it. Lhyn was probably in the State House right now, reading some thousand-year-old book she'd gotten from Lanaril. Andira was with the war council at Blacksun Base, going over today's results in preparation for the second, all-teams analysis tomorrow. And Salomen was at Hol-Opah for the nineday, burying herself in the work she loved. They were well into spring now, prime growing season and a time when Salomen was less the Bondlancer and more the head of Hol-Opah.

All three of them knew who they were and who they should be. She was the only one who didn't.

She slumped back and closed her eyes, too tired to do anything but listen to the Fahlinor's comforting song. She should be changing clothes, eating something, trying to relax enough to connect with Lhyn tonight. But moving off this couch was too great a task to consider at the moment.

"I miss you," she whispered, and fell through the door.

"Fucking stars!" Lhyn jolted upright, nearly tipping out of the wooden deck chair in her surprise.

Beside her, Salomen twitched violently, sloshing spirits from the half-full glass she held. "What? What happened?"

"It's Ekatya." Lhyn scrambled to her feet and set her glass on the top railing of the deck. "You're early. I haven't even centered. How are we connecting?"

Shocked by her sudden displacement, Ekatya turned in place, absorbing the peaceful scenery of Hol-Opah. They were alone on the back deck and had recently finished evenmeal, judging by the activity of Salomen's family visible through the dining room windows. Though it was early afternoon in ship time, Blacksun Basin was shrouded in the shadows of dusk, both moons shining over the eastern mountains. She could see it all because Lhyn had been here a thousand times. The details were imprinted in her mind and available in their connection.

"I don't know," she said. "I'm as surprised as you are."

Salomen's head jerked up from where she had been setting her wet glass on the deck. "Goddess above, I heard her!" Her gaze swept blindly past Ekatya. "I heard you. Where are you?"

Lhyn pointed. "There."

She followed the pointing finger, frowning in concentration, then shook her head. "Ekatya, say something."

"I have no idea how this happened. I was sitting in my quarters, missing you. All of you. Then I was here."

Lhyn glanced at Salomen, whose face was a picture of awe. "You heard that?"

"Fahla, yes. This is incredible."

"It is." Lhyn reached out, her hand brushing through Ekatya's shoulder. They could not touch in this telepathic link, but it never stopped them from trying. "It's getting stronger."

"Exponentially. I wasn't even close to relaxed. I haven't had anything to drink. And I didn't have the sensation of dropping through the tunnel. One piptick I was on the sofa, the next I was through the door into your mind."

"And mine," Salomen said. "It's like you're truly here. I've heard whispers before—"

Lhyn's eyes rounded. "You have? Why didn't you say something?"

"I thought it was wishful thinking. I wanted to hear you, Ekatya. And see you. It was as if I simply didn't know how. But this! I'd swear you're standing next to me."

"I *am* standing next to you." Ekatya looked toward the mountains, savoring their sharp beauty in the light of the moons and wishing she could smell the crisp air. "What a gorgeous evening. Is that why you're here?" she asked, turning back to Lhyn. "I thought you'd be in the State House."

"I was, but Andira's at Blacksun Base and Salomen was here. And you're in orbit. Our quarters were too quiet, so I invited myself over."

"As if you ever have to do that." Salomen brushed her hand against Lhyn's, a gesture of affection that left Ekatya *wanting*. They could touch, but she could not.

She was always removed, always apart.

"I was hoping Andira would be here soon," Salomen added. "But she's stuck in the war council. They didn't expect you to win. She's half frustrated and half proud of you."

It was amazing how good that felt, knowing she had made Andira proud. She basked in the thought, her spirits rising enough that she could laugh at herself for her morose thoughts a moment ago.

Lhyn was watching her thoughtfully. "Are you all right, tyrina?"

"I am now."

"Oh, no." Salomen rested her head against the back of her chair, eyes closed in what Ekatya guessed was an effort to focus on what she could hear inside her mind. "That's not a good enough answer. Something pushed you to a new level in your connection, a level I can reach. You said you missed us. I cannot think that's all of it."

"Does Andira get away with anything when you're around?"

"Only when I allow it."

"Poor woman."

Lhyn laughed. "You realize that being in a six-pointed bond means you're never getting away with anything again. Tell us what's going on."

Ekatya leaned against the railing—a mental construct, but one that felt comfortable nevertheless—and crossed her arms. "I think I'm losing my mind."

Salomen looked alarmed, but Lhyn knew her better. "Be more specific, please."

"I don't know who I am anymore. Today I was a warship captain, a respected leader among other captains. One tick after that, I was a suspected traitor. Now I find I'm a tool Sholokhov kept around just to influence a negotiation."

"What?" Lhyn demanded. "What did he—"

"Lhyn. Let her finish."

Ekatya had to smile at the interaction, so typical of them. Lhyn, rising swiftly to her defense and wanting facts, while Salomen recognized that those facts did not matter as much as the emotional truth.

A well-rubbed memory rose, shiny with frequent use: the afternoon when she had confessed her envy and shame to all three of them, and Salomen had cracked her heart with three words.

We see you.

"I think that's why I'm here," she said. "I needed to be seen. I needed my anchor."

Lhyn's mouth twisted in frustration. "I wish I could touch you."

"Do we ever connect this way and not say that? This is enough. Just being here helps."

"At least we can do that much. I hate the thought of you up there with that asshead grinding you down."

For some reason, hearing Lhyn call Greve an asshead lightened her heart. "Have you taught that word to Salomen?"

"She tried," Salomen said. "It didn't take."

"Because you're too proper," Lhyn grumbled. "You never swear."

"I do when the occasion calls for it."

"Well, what if someone is always an asshead? When does the right occasion come along?"

"When they're enough of an asshead to send Ekatya down here looking for her sense of self." Salomen pronounced the Common word precisely, leaving no doubt as to her own feelings. "I'm sorry, Ekatya. Of the four of us, you and Andira have the most difficult roles. And Andira isn't being subjected to water wheel torture."

Ekatya bristled at the very idea of Andira being treated that way. But then, she wouldn't let it grind her down. She'd either turn the tables on her tormenter or find a way to make him irrelevant.

Irrelevant, she thought. Sholokhov's hint about the gloves had indicated exactly that—Greve was irrelevant. He was depending on his rank to keep her cowed, not a power kept leashed only by Sholokhov's temporary protection.

With a smooth click, a puzzle piece fit into place.

"Don't be sorry," she said. "You're my power. All of you. This bond. As long as I have my anchor, I know who I am."

"Words for Fahla," Salomen said with an approving nod.

Lhyn beamed, her earlier frustration erased. "An extremely high-quality anchor at that. The best model available. Triple redundancy in case of stress fatigue of any single part."

"Scholars." Salomen looked skyward with exaggerated patience. "Always complicating things. We're an anchor with three flukes instead of one."

"Or four instead of two," Lhyn shot back.

Ekatya could easily visualize it, buried in the sandy sea bed. "Would that ever come loose?"

"Not unless you wanted it to," Salomen said.

"Then no. Not ever." She hadn't planned or even imagined such an unorthodox personal life, but now that she had it, no power in this universe could make her give it up. Without a Sharing, without Andira or her own physical presence, her anchor was still powerful enough to neutralize the weary despair that had fueled this connection. Lhyn and Salomen had seen to that in ten minutes flat.

Despite her interrupting them, she realized. The two forgotten spirit glasses loomed large in her vision, evidence that they had set aside their plans in favor of her need.

"I'm having second thoughts about the physical aspects," she said.

"You're ready?" Lhyn asked doubtfully.

"No, but you are. I'm holding you back. I'm sick of being the one holding everyone back."

"For the love of Fahla," Salomen said with a sigh. "If I'm not telling one of you this, I'm telling the other."

"They're not fast learners, are they?" Lhyn asked.

Their expressions spoke of an inside joke Ekatya was not privy to. "Is this a slur on warriors?" she asked.

"Not a slur. An observation based on abundant evidence."

"Ekatya, did you not just agree that we're your anchor?" Salomen asked.

"Yes?"

"What happens when the flukes of an anchor aren't the same size? Does it hold as well?"

She was silent, imagining the result.

"We're all connected. You cannot keep thinking of yourself as a separate piece somehow responsible for the rest. What we do, we all decide to do. Didn't we agree on that after the uprising?"

"That was seven moons ago."

"I didn't know there was a time limit."

Ekatya gestured at the glasses, and though Salomen could not see, Lhyn could. "Lhyn came here because she was lonely and missed you. I'm here because I was lonely and missed all of you. We've acknowledged the bonds; we know where the threads are attached. It's all getting stronger. It's strong enough that I dropped in here without trying! If you don't keep strengthening your part, don't you think *that* will throw it out of balance?"

"What makes you think we're not strengthening it?" Salomen asked reasonably.

While Ekatya stumbled over that, Lhyn said, "Remember when we met? We were in bed together before we knew each other's names."

"That's not true. I knew—" She stopped. "Your first name."

Salomen snickered.

"Right. And I knew your rank and family name. We didn't get around to more detailed conversation until later. We were driven by something we didn't understand then, but we understand it better now."

"My first Sharing with Andira was physical and mental torment." All traces of amusement had vanished from Salomen's expression. "Our early courtship was conducted under pressure and with Andira's government and life in the balance. Our later courtship was as public as it could be."

Ekatya looked from one to the other. "What are you saying? That you want it to be this way?"

"We're enjoying the opportunity to do it differently this time," Lhyn said.

"In private," Salomen added. "With no pressure whatsoever."

"Actually, a kind of reverse pressure. A set of parameters that keeps us focused on everything else. All the things that build a relationship, excluding joining and a two-way Sharing."

"Like transplanting a sapling. You hardly see growth in the first cycle because it's happening underground. The tree is repairing and expanding its roots, preparing them for the next growing season."

"What happens in the next growing season?" Lhyn asked.

"It doubles in size. It bursts into life because the roots can support it."

"Oh, I like that." Her fingers twitched, as if she were looking for her pad to record the thought.

"You and your plant analogies," Ekatya said.

"But you understand it?"

She nodded, then remembered that Salomen couldn't see her. "Yes, I think so."

Lhyn retrieved her glass from the railing. "Stop fretting about holding us back."

"I don't *fret*."

"You have an opportunity to do it differently, too," Salomen said.

Ekatya froze.

For four years, she and Andira had skirted the edges of what they could have, acknowledging the draw while reinforcing each other's resistance to it. When those edges vanished, she was distressed by the loss of her guiding boundaries.

Not once had she considered that she could still have a boundary while giving in.

"What is she doing?" Salomen whispered.

"Looking like you hit her in the chest with a posthead," Lhyn whispered back.

Ekatya leaned back and laughed, a joyous release that loosened her shoulders and made the first stars of the night dance in her vision. When she faced forward again, Salomen was listening with closed eyes and a delighted smile that matched Lhyn's.

"I'm going to leave you to it. Thank you. You have no idea how much you helped."

"Got a date to plan?" Lhyn asked knowingly.

"I have a flight to arrange, weather permitting." She thought for a moment, then gave a satisfied nod. "And it's just the right season for it."

20

LEAD FROM THE FRONT

"Hey, Red." Candini looked at her through the quantum com, her spiky hair more rumpled than usual. "I have a question for y—holy fucking fuck, what happened to your hair?"

Rahel stretched out her legs, comfortable in her off-duty clothing, and focused on the wall display across her living area. "Well met to you, too. I see my lessons on Alsean courtesy aren't sinking in."

"Never mind that, when did this happen? It looks fantastic, by the way." Grinning, she pointed at her own head. "Though you're missing the spikes."

"Yesterday after you dropped me off, and there will be no spikes. Reynard says my face isn't the right shape for them."

"Reynard? Seeders, I'd know he was a hairdresser just from the name. He did good work," she said grudgingly. "Despite having no sense of creativity. Let me come up there with some gel and show you how it would look."

"No."

"Come on—"

"No."

"You're a wet branch on the fire."

"Good usage of an Alsean idiom, but the answer is still no."

"Fine." She swiped a finger horizontally through the air. "Given the wide view, you must have me up on the massive display of yours. Is my head about two meters wide?"

"Yes. Life size."

"Ha, ha," she said dryly.

Rahel laughed. "You set yourself up for that. Don't blame me for accepting the gift. I tried to show you my new cut last night, by the way. Where were you? I thought you'd have called back long before now."

"Er . . ." Candini rubbed her earlobe. "I was visiting an old friend."

"All night and most of the next day? Fahla's farts, it's true what they say about pilots."

"That's a stereotype. Anyway, it's not related to my question." She was suddenly serious. "The captains and the Alsean war council finished their analysis. I just got my orders from Colonel Alportel. I'm supposed to pick out six Serrado flight teams and train them to grapple the space elevator if it gets severed during a battle. To keep the lower part from falling back to Alsea long enough to get a repair team up there."

"Seems like a sound strategy." Though she couldn't sense Candini over the quantum com, she had come to know her well enough to recognize this expression. "What's bothering you about it?"

"Do you realize what that means? Sending fighters to hold that thing up in the middle of a battle? They won't be able to maneuver, their defensive options will be minimal, and they'll be a target. It's a suicide mission." She scrubbed a hand through her hair, rumpling it further. "How do I choose?"

"You choose the ones with the best skills at grappling. This isn't a job for the pilots, it's a job for the gunners."

"Did you hear what I said? It's a *suicide mission.*"

Ah, now she understood. "You've never had to send someone to die before."

"No! It's not usually an issue when you're fighting pirates, and that's all I've done since leaving the *Caphenon.* Before that, I was the ship's pilot. The last time I sent someone to die was in a theoretical exam."

"It might not be an issue now," Rahel pointed out. "These are just war games."

Candini scowled. "You know as well as I do that's not true. They're not saying it, but this is preparation."

She did know. It had been eye-opening to see the sheer volume of weaponry fired during that war game. Even without weapons-grade explosives, that amount of hardware could not be cheap. Someone in Fleet had signed off on an expensive line item, and Rahel knew from her service to Prime Warrior Shantu that such things did not happen without a compelling reason.

"It is," she agreed.

"So how do I choose? How did you?"

"It's not the same thi—"

"You were a leader," Candini interrupted. "Of criminals most of the time, sure, but you still led them. You sent people to do dangerous things. And you told me you liked some of those people, so it wasn't as if you were only choosing the dokkers and the assheads. How did you decide?"

She wasn't asking for advice, Rahel realized. Candini was a trained warrior; she knew what was expected. What she was asking for, in a roundabout way, was absolution.

"I chose the ones whose skills were best suited to the need," she said. "Which is what you will do. The first team you'll put on that list is you and me."

"I'm commanding the orbital fighter fleet," Candini objected. "We can't tie ourselves to the elevator in the middle of a battle!"

"Stop thinking like a Fleeter and think like an Alsean. Warriors respect commanders who lead from the front. Show them that you're willing to do what you're asking them to do. They'll follow you gladly." She swung her legs off the couch and leaned forward, forearms resting on her thighs. "Listen, Nightwing. We don't have to be the ones who do it. But we should be able to do it if no one else can. We should train with them."

"Red . . ."

"If we don't, you'll lose their respect," she warned. "They know who scored the highest in the grappling competition."

Candini scrunched her face and scrubbed her hair as if she were trying to pull it out. "To think I was proud when you did that. Now I'm wishing you were all thumbs."

"It's easier to risk your own life than someone else's, isn't it?"

She nodded miserably. "Especially a friend's."

"When I became a warrior, I swore an oath to protect Alsea. If I go to my Return keeping that elevator from crashing all over Pallea, I'll go happily. That would be a truly honorable death."

She waited through a long silence.

"It's not just words to you, is it?" Candini said at last. "You really mean that."

"On my honor."

She sighed. "We'll start tomorrow."

"All right, eyes front," Candini said loudly, cutting through the conversation. Five pilots and six gunners fell silent, giving her their full attention.

"Thank you. This is Chief Kameha, an old friend of mine. You may know him as the beard behind the space elevator."

"Hey, I'm more than just my beard," Kameha retorted, setting off a wave of chuckles.

Rahel laughed with the others, having seen her share of interviews and images of the famous Chief of Advanced Technology. He was the only *Caphenon* crew member to remain on Alsea after the crash, and had spent the intervening cycles working with the Prime Builder to restore the ship and its fighters, design the space elevator, and help create the sleek new Alsean shuttles. Initially, his face had appeared normal, or at least as normal as a Gaian could be. Then he began growing his facial hair, commenting in interviews that he enjoyed having the only beard on the planet. The increasing numbers of *Phoenix* crew taking shore leave on Alsea had made facial hair slightly less shocking, but Kameha still set the standard with the eye-popping shrubbery draped to his chest.

He turned to the semicircle of Alseans facing him and spread his short arms, indicating the cavernous space and its bustling hordes of builders. "Welcome to my domain. This is where things get built that need a lot of room. We built the space elevator spool booster here."

Rahel craned her neck to view the curved ceiling far above. Candini had flown their fighter straight through the doors with plenty of room to spare.

"Now, I've read the analysis from the war council. I'll be shekking furious if the Voloth manage to break my beautiful elevator. But I'll be devastated if it falls back to Alsea. Does anyone know what that would do?"

"Set us back a couple of cycles," one pilot offered. "And a shipload of cinteks."

"Destroy the port platform," said a gunner.

"Cause a giant wave when it hits the water?" another pilot guessed.

"Yes, yes, and probably not." Kameha pointed to each in turn.

"Rain debris across northern Pallea," Rahel said.

Kameha tilted his head with an approving waggle of his beard. "Because . . . ?"

"It won't fall in one piece. The very bottom part will, and that will be enough to smash our port platform to splinters and kill everyone on it. But there will be a lot of forces acting on the rest. Natural coiling," she began, counting off on her fingers. "Atmospheric drag. Turbulence from high winds in our upper troposphere. The magtran rails aren't as flexible as the cable, so they'll break off in pieces and become projectiles."

"Whoa," said a pilot. "Nasty."

Kameha gave her a pleased nod, encouraging her to continue.

"Some of the debris will burn up on reentry, but not enough. The rest will rain down on the equatorial zone, because while the cable is falling, Alsea is still rotating beneath it, west to east. And it won't all fall at once. Depending on where it's cut, there could be twenty, thirty thousand lengths of cable coming down. That takes time. Whitemoon would probably be hit hard."

"Did Captain Serrado tell you all of that?" Kameha asked.

She shook her head. "I've been fascinated with orbital space since I was seventeen. My tutor gave me a math problem where I had to calculate the amount of fuel I'd need to launch a satellite into low orbit. It took me several hanticks because I started researching the variables and couldn't stop." She shrugged, self-conscious under the expectant stare of Alsea's most celebrated engineer. "I've read everything I could about our space elevator."

"Hmph. Of course Serrado would find an Alsean with her head already in the stars." Fondness wrapped around him. "She always did have a built-in detector for things like that. Sayana is right," he added in a sharper tone. "The cable would break up and fall in pieces all over northern Pallea. It would be impossible to predict the impact coordinates of every piece. Impossible to evacuate people. Impossible to prevent property damage and deaths, unless we prevent it from falling in the first place. That's why you're in my workshop. Now, everyone follow me. I'm going to show you a piece of the elevator cable and why your grapplers won't work on it."

Rahel was riveted by the rest of Kameha's presentation and thrilled when they gathered around a segment of cable to touch it. Despite knowing the dimensions since construction began, she couldn't believe how thin it was. It should have been called a ribbon.

The need for constant tension along its length meant a gradual increase in width from port platform to geosync station, and this segment represented the cable at its widest. Even so, they could have parked their fighter on it and covered most of the width. Kameha was correct, seeing and feeling for oneself was different than reading about it.

As soon as he held the jointed hooks of a fighter's grappler next to the cable with its attached magtran rails, she understood the problem. Their grapplers were designed to close around tow loops built into fighter hulls, enabling a functional fighter to tow a damaged one back to a ship—or soon, the space elevator dock—for repairs or rescue. Magtran rails were much wider than tow loops. Their grapplers weren't nearly large enough to clamp around them.

The builders were already manufacturing new grapplers for the six fighters now parked in the workshop. Kameha demonstrated a prototype, with its longer hooks and stronger joints, then opened the belly of the nearest fighter to show them the attachment point and where it would need to be reinforced to handle the load.

Rahel was still peering into the guts of the fighter, fascinated by details she had never considered, when Candini clapped her hands together.

"Right, now that you all know what Kameha and his miracle workers will be doing today and tonight, it's time for us to get busy. Tomorrow we'll practice in orbit with the real thing, but today we're hitting the simulators."

Kameha held up his prototype. "You may think this won't make much difference in handling, but believe me, it will. You're going to miss the first few times you try."

"I won't," one gunner boasted, prompting laughter and good-natured bets as they followed Candini out.

Another gunner sidled up to Rahel. His call sign was Archer, after the constellation every Alsean learned as a child, and he had scored second in the grappling competition.

"Bet I get it before you," he said.

"Oh? What will you bet?"

"How about one of those sparkly drinks you're always bragging about?"

"I don't brag," she scoffed. "And even if you won, which you won't, by the time I got a Synobian Sparkler down here, it wouldn't be sparkling."

"If I win, which I will, you can take me up there. You always get to go back and I've never even seen the inside. We've all practiced flying into the *Caphenon*'s bays, but it's not the same as being on a ship in orbit."

He was trying for nonchalance, but Rahel read the hope in his expression. In a flash of understanding, she saw herself through his eyes: the privileged one, coming and going at will from a magical place the others could not enter.

A plan unrolled in her mind. She followed the options to their possible ends, nodded in approval, and held out her forearm. "If I win, you buy my rajaltas for our next five trainings."

He clasped it gleefully. "Done! This will be fun."

They all missed the first three attempts, bearing out Kameha's prediction. Rahel clamped her grappler around a magtran rail on the fourth try and smiled at the quiet curse from the simulator pod to her left. Archer had lost his bet.

He succeeded on the fifth attempt, and the other gunners began to catch up. When all of them could successfully operate the new grapplers, Candini upped the difficulty level. The previously static elevator cable was now dropping away from them, bringing the pilots into greater play. When the six teams mastered that, she increased the speed. The step after that added unpredictable motion.

By the end of the training, they were sweaty, tired, and exuberant at their success. Tomorrow, Candini informed them, Kameha would take a segment of cable into orbit and shove it out the back of a shuttle. Attached drones would propel it at different speeds and in different directions, giving them a real-life approximation of the difficulty in catching a falling cable.

"Double or nothing," Archer said.

Rahel had expected no less. "You'll lose that one, too."

"If you believe that, you'll have no trouble betting."

"Done."

When Candini returned her to the *Phoenix*, she wasted no time tracking down Commander Zeppy.

He listened to her request and eventually nodded. "But I'm not the final approval," he cautioned. "The bay doors stay closed without an order from Captain Serrado."

She thanked him and went straight to the captain's office.

"Why do you want to do this?" Serrado asked.

Rahel's spine was so straight that it did not touch the back of her chair. "We're asking them to risk their lives. Shouldn't that be worth something?"

"We're asking every fighter crew, both Fleet and Alsean, to risk their lives. They're by far the most vulnerable component of our battle plan. Why should these get special consideration?"

It was a test, she realized. Serrado liked the idea but wanted a better reason.

"Candini has been drilling her pilots on entering and exiting the *Caphenon*'s bays," she offered, noting Serrado's twinge of melancholy at the mention of her old ship. "But it's not the same as in orbit. This could be a training opportunity. There might be a time when we need Alsean fighters to come into our bays."

"That's a little weak." The corner of Serrado's mouth tilted up. "But I can work with it. Permission granted."

Rahel floated all the way back to her quarters.

The next day's training was ten times more fun. Real flying was always better than a simulator. She never tired of the magnificent view of Alsea beneath them, nor of the stars dancing around their cockpit cover as Candini dove and spiraled. Her piloting skills made Rahel's job easy, and she caught the cable on her first try.

"*Shek!*" Archer grumbled over the open com. "*You're not normal, Red.*"

She grinned. "I never pretended to be."

Candini lined them up with the others to watch while Archer and his pilot took their turn. The cable segment was half as long as a fighter and hurtling through space at the same speed as the real elevator cable. This first test approximated the time just after severing, when the cable still moved at normal speed and was not yet falling toward Alsea.

The fighter approached the cable segment, matched its velocity, and maneuvered until its underside was in grappling range. At this distance, none of them could make out the grappler arm emerging from the fighter's belly, but the ventral cam footage was on the quantum com. They all saw the grappler extend, open its hooks, close on the edge of the magtran rail, and slip off again.

Rahel kept her amusement to herself as the com filled with curses.

"That's why we're out here," Candini said. "To learn while there are no stakes. Don't worry, you'll get it."

"I know I'll get it. But I wanted to get it before that red-headed dokker!"

"Hoi," Rahel said. "Nightwing here has red hair, too."

"It's a gift from the gods," Candini agreed. "Signifying natural skill at everything we do."

That brought a litany of teasing, and the rest of the training went by in a light-hearted blur that obscured the sobering truth: they were perfecting their skills for a task that might be their last.

Rahel still held the highest score at the end, giving her the honor of catching the cable segment one last time to tow it back to the waiting shuttle, where it would be held for the Fleet fighters now on their way. Once they had turned it over, Candini addressed the group.

"Red has an announcement. Give her your full attention."

"Archer bet me that he'd be the first to catch the cable in our simulation," Rahel said. "Then he was stupid enough to bet me double or nothing for today. He owes me ten rajaltas." She paused long enough for Archer to get the teasing he deserved, then spoke again. "But I've decided I'd rather have Synobian Sparklers. Then I thought maybe you'd all like to help him pay off his debt, so I got landing permission from Captain Serrado for six fighters on the *Phoenix*."

A startled silence was followed by raucous cheering, flowery compliments, and one offer to bear her first child.

Laughing, she instructed them to follow her fighter in. They were taking the spaces vacated by the Fleet fighters while they conducted their own training, giving them three hanticks for a tour of the ship and all the Synobian Sparklers they could buy her.

They were halfway back to the ship when Candini spoke. "I don't think I could have managed this. Serrado really has a soft spot for you."

Rahel watched the starboard bay doors open as they approached, the green guidance lights already flashing. "Remember the reasons I gave her for the request? She said the first was why she agreed, but the second was what she would write on the order."

"Makes sense. She's under more scrutiny these days. All her orders have to pass the smell test."

The last phrase was in Common, a rather disgusting idiom for which there was no Alsean equivalent. Rahel wrinkled her nose. "Why is she under more scrutiny?"

"Divine tyree bond," Candini said shortly.

"Still? But she was cleared for duty."

"I can't talk about it. Sorry, she spoke to me in confidence."

Rahel asked no further questions, but her thoughts were churning. Serrado's anger and frustration made sense now. So did the end of their conversation the day before.

"I applaud your intent," Serrado had said. "It's good team building and good leadership. What inspired it?"

"I wanted to share some of the magic."

"Magic." The earlier melancholy resurfaced. "I'm glad you see it that way. In fact, I think I needed a reminder. We do work in a magical place, don't we?"

Rahel had left the office pleased that she could perform a service for her oath holder, but it looked different now. There was only one person aboard the *Phoenix* who could scrutinize Serrado's performance of duty. Surely Admiral Greve had never found anything to complain about.

What was he doing to take away the captain's sense of magic?

21

FLIGHT DATE

Tal came out of the dressing room in time to see Salomen turn away from the small vidcom built into the desk. "Don't tell me there's another emergency," she said, tucking in her shirt. "Anything short of a Voloth invasion, they can take care of it themselves." She had been looking forward to this day off, especially after Salomen's unexpected arrival the previous night.

"It's not, don't worry." Salomen ogled her from top to bottom. "You're so rarely in casual clothing that I've developed an appreciation for this look. Hmm . . ."

"Oh, no." Tal held up her hands. "I'm still sore from last night. I didn't even get to return the favor."

"And you slept very well, didn't you?"

"Like a mountzar in winter. Why do I sense a plot?"

"You're naturally suspicious?"

She crossed her arms with a frown.

"If that's meant to intimidate me, it's not working." Salomen's gaze was glued to her chest. "In truth, it's improving the view."

No frown could withstand that. Tal tightened her arms, shamelessly improving the view further. "Stop avoiding the question."

"What question?" she said absently.

Tal waited. It was a good three pipticks before Salomen finally processed her words and looked up.

"Ah. You needed a decent night's sleep for once. I've been working the fields from dawn to dusk and I'm less tired than you are. If being knocked out was what you required, I was more than happy to oblige." Wiggling her eyebrows, she added, "It was no hardship."

Maintaining a severe look was impossible while laughing. "You've become devious since settling into your title."

"Are you objecting?"

"No, but do I at least get to return the favor today?"

"Perhaps tonight. You have other plans at the moment."

"Do I? They're strangely absent from my calendar. What have you cooked up, tyrina?"

Any answer was forestalled by the strong emotional presence coming down their private corridor—a presence that did not surprise Salomen, despite the fact that Ekatya's leave didn't start until tomorrow.

Salomen tilted her head toward the door. "Are you going to let her in?"

"It's not a plot. It's a conspiracy." Tal strode across the room and yanked open the door.

Ekatya's fist hovered in the air; she had not had the chance to knock. "I hate it when you do that."

"I know. Welcome back." Tal pulled her across the threshold and into a warmron, basking in the familiar scents of her skin, Gaian shampoo, and State House laundry soap. The Alsean clothing meant she and Lhyn had already gone through their coming home ritual. It must have been while Tal was sleeping and couldn't sense it.

Ekatya held on with a happy glow. "Did you miss me that much?"

"She did." Salomen stepped in for her own warmron. "It's good to see you this time."

"Maybe someday it'll be strong enough for both of you to see me."

"I look forward to that." Tal brushed away the sting of envy. After the astonishing connection of four nights ago, they had tried to repeat it while including her. Once again, Salomen could hear Ekatya, but her own mind had been frustratingly silent.

"It will happen," Salomen assured her. "Give it time." She turned her attention to Ekatya, holding her at arm's length. "You're remarkably relaxed. We haven't even Shared."

"I had a rewarding day yesterday. Technically, I'm on duty right now. I told Admiral Greve that I had Protectorate Security business with the Lancer, and if he had issues with it, he could call Director Sholokhov." Triumph spiced the air as she added, "He did. I'm given to understand he didn't enjoy the results of that call."

Her emotional signature held a sharp edge that Tal had not seen in several moons. "You're changing the rules of engagement."

"I'm tired of being used," she said firmly. "And of standing still. You and I are going to have a talk. That'll take about a tentick and satisfy my official reason for being here. Then we'll enjoy the rest of our date."

Tal would have thought she hadn't heard correctly if not for the jittery anticipation. She stared at Ekatya, who tugged down the hem of her jacket and stood straighter.

"I've been doing some cultural research. It seems I've failed to ask you an important question. Andira Shaldone Tal, will you do me the honor of allowing me to court you?"

Her brain went in six directions at once. The ascendant and most disturbing thought was that Salomen's dominance last night, though wildly arousing at the time, now held an unsettling new significance.

Warily, she turned to Salomen. "Is that why you—"

"No! Andira, no."

"You weren't planting your banner? Even unknowingly?"

"If I were, you would sense it now. Do I feel threatened?"

She shook her head. Emotions did not lie, yet the ground felt unsteady.

"You already know my ulterior motive. I wanted you to get some proper rest. I also missed you and yes, I wanted that physical connection, but it had nothing to do with this. Nothing has changed."

"I think something did change," she pointed out.

"Lhyn and Salomen knocked some sense into me, that's what changed." Ekatya's hopeful expression dimmed. "Maybe we should have given you some warning."

"It's not a joining, tyrina. It's not a two-way Sharing. It's just a date."

"How is this so easy for you?" Tal demanded.

"Well, it wasn't always."

That was the understatement of the cycle. The humor hit without warning, evaporating her alarm in a dry chuckle. "Words for Fahla."

"It's easy now because I know who I am in all of our bonds. I'm your divine tyree. Nothing and no one will ever challenge that. But Ekatya is your normal tyree, and you two have been falling out of balance." Salomen held her by the shoulders, her expression the one she wore while instructing field workers. "Now, you will go on your date and *relax*. I'll take Lhyn for a trail walk in the Snowmounts. We'll meet back here at evenmeal and compare our days. Yes?"

She knew when to concede. "Since you made it an order," she said, only half teasing.

With an arch look, Salomen leaned down and spoke in a sultry tone. "You took them so well last night."

Her knees threatened to dissolve. "You're making it difficult to walk away."

"You're not walking away. I'm sending you, knowing you'll come back." Straightening, Salomen added, "I expect a full and detailed report."

It was a perfect reproduction of Tal's crisp tone and phrasing, uttered many a time in her bondmate's hearing. In her unique way, Salomen was making a point. No, last night hadn't been about planting a banner. It had been about establishing her power to state that this was what she wanted. Further doubt or questioning would be an insult, a sign that Tal did not recognize her equality in their bond.

"You'll have it, tyrina. Well played, by the way." She kissed her before facing their visibly worried guest. "Ekatya Lucia Serrado, it would be my honor."

The cloud that had been eclipsing Ekatya's emotions vanished in a blaze of sunshine. "Lovely! Then put on a warmer shirt and bring a jacket."

"Where are we going?"

She made a shooing motion. "Jacket."

"Why are all the women in my life suddenly giving me orders?" Tal complained as she crossed the room. The chuckles behind her lightened her heart.

When she returned to the living area, jacket in hand, Salomen and Ekatya had their heads together and were speaking in low tones.

"Plotting?" she asked.

"Already did that," Ekatya said. "Ready?"

She stood in front of Salomen and watched her, testing their link for anything out of place. Reassured and not a little awed, she pulled her into a warmron. "There is nothing so beautiful as a confident love," she said softly. "You wear it like a goddess."

"That was your gift to me." Salomen squeezed, then pulled back to arm's length. "Let this be mine to you."

There was a world of meaning in those words. Tal nodded and leaned in, unable to resist one more kiss before turning for the door.

"I'm ready."

⌇

"She really does know you," Ekatya said as they walked between the ancient trees flanking the main State House path. "She said she'd need to be here this morning to help you out the door."

"Then you weren't joking about the plotting."

"There was no chance I was doing this on my own. I put the bigger things in motion, but I needed Lhyn and Salomen for the finer details."

"What bigger things?"

"Someone is fishing for clues," Ekatya announced in a sing-song voice. "Do you remember your bonding break, when you woke me at an obscenely early hantick and dragged me out for a flight in a newly rebuilt Serrado fighter?"

"Yes . . . ?"

"Do you remember how I kept asking you to tell me what you had planned, and you refused?"

"So this is revenge."

"And it is sweet!"

She was outrageously pleased with herself, her enjoyment growing with each of Tal's questions or guesses. Not until they neared the landing pad did she finally release a drop of information.

"I've coordinated this with the ADF, Micah and your Guards, Ambassador Solvassen, and a few Alseans in charge of a certain restricted flight zone to get the proper permit."

"Restricted flight zone," Tal repeated. "That would cover our military bases . . ."

"Bad guess."

"But we're leaving Blacksun."

"Yes, which apparently doesn't happen without the involvement of fifty people. Of all the potential dates on Alsea, I had to pick the Lancer."

"Salomen doesn't have this much trouble taking me on a date."

"Only because she tells Micah where she wants to take you, and he deals with the security while Chief Counselor Aldirk deals with the scheduling. It's still fifty people."

Waiting on the landing pad was Tal's first surprise: three Serrado fighters guarded by four uniformed figures. All four snapped into a crisp salute, first to her, then to Ekatya.

"You don't need to salute me, Candini," Ekatya said. "I'm not in the ADF."

"You should be," Candini responded. "Well met, Lancer Tal."

"Well met." Tal's attention was caught by the woman beside her, whose radically altered appearance made her almost unrecognizable. "Well met, First Guard Sayana. Did you lose a bet?"

Rahel ran a hand through her short hair. "No, it was voluntary. I was ready for a change."

"It looks good."

"Not good enough," Candini put in. "She was so close, but then she didn't get the spikes."

"We don't need two of you," Ekatya said. "One is all the galaxy can handle."

"Good morning, Lancer." Head Guardian Gehrain was more formal.

"Gehrain, Vellmar, good morning. I thought you were off duty today?"

"We switched a few shifts around to be sure you had top quality coverage."

"What he means is, we heard where you were going and pulled rank," Vellmar added with a grin.

"Oh? Where are we going?"

Ekatya loudly cleared her throat. "Pay no attention to the cheater trying to use her title to get around my instructions."

"We'll tell if you order us," Vellmar said. "But that would ruin your surprise and disappoint Captain Serrado."

"Disappoint?" Gehrain said. "I think it would make her sad. Very sad, especially after all she's done to organize this."

Tal shook her head at them. "Effective. Obvious, but effective."

"Good." Ekatya pushed her toward the middle fighter. "Then we're leaving."

Laughing, Tal climbed the short ladder. Waiting on her seat was a crash collar, which she clipped around her neck before settling into the seat and fastening her harness. Ekatya slid in beside her, radiating excitement.

They were in the air a few ticks later, doing a slow circuit of the State House while barely gaining altitude. When they reached the level of the fifteenth floor, Ekatya brought them to a hover in front of a familiar set of windows.

Salomen was there, smiling broadly as she waved from their living area. Tal waved back and absorbed the unadulterated happiness in their link. She couldn't imagine loving her tyree more than she did in this moment.

Ekatya waggled their wings, then rose straight up to clear the dome before turning south. She kept their airspeed at the city flight limit until the moment they crossed the boundary, then pointed their nose skyward and looked over with a grin. "Ready?"

"Ready." Tal let out a whoop as she was pressed into the seat. "Yes! Now we're getting somewhere!"

Ekatya's laugh was pure joy. She wove between towering columns of white clouds until the last wisps fell away beneath them, and still they climbed. At an altitude well above the public flight paths, she spoke briefly with Candini and Gehrain and opened up the throttle. They were now traveling at several times the speed of sound, making short work of the distance between Blacksun and the southern edge of the Argolis continent. Brilliant sunlight glinted off the wings and cockpit covers of the two fighters flanking them, and Tal thought that even if Ekatya had nothing else planned, she was already delighted.

"The last time we did this together, you were still using headsets," Ekatya commented.

"It *has* been a while, hasn't it?"

"Too long. Why haven't we flown again until now?"

"Because we're both so tied to our duties that we forget our duty to ourselves."

"That sounds like Salomen."

"True words. I've absorbed some of her wisdom in spite of myself." Tal tried to keep a straight face, but when Ekatya snorted a laugh, she followed suit. "I know. It's fighting into the sun, but she keeps trying."

"We'd call that an uphill battle."

"Even more visual than ours! I may have to start using that."

She watched the wrinkled landscape passing below. From this height, even the most forbidding mountain ranges seemed easily manageable. It was difficult to imagine a time when Blacksun was impervious to attack because no army could pass through the mountains without being decimated by defenders.

"Speaking of duties," Ekatya said, "let's get this part over with. Remember when I told the war council about my call with Sholokhov?"

"Yes?"

"I didn't tell them the other half of it. It turns out that he's the one who tipped the vote to keep me in my command."

"That's a surprise. Perhaps he respects you more than you thought."

"Ha. No, he thought I could convince you to give him twenty high empaths in exchange for . . . something. He didn't specify, just said he'd listen to any reasonable proposal."

"So he finally made a move. I've been wondering how long he'd wait."

Ekatya's head whipped around. "You knew he'd ask?"

"Didn't you? Why else would he have put a kill order on Rahel?"

"To test empaths for future deployment, sure, but he hasn't authorized any new placements. I never thought—why didn't you say something?"

"You have enough to worry about without taking on issues that aren't part of your command. We prepared for this."

"We?"

"Me, the Prime Scholar and Warrior, the heads of the AIF and ADF, and Lanaril and the Prime Producer as our ethics checks."

"You mean you're considering it?" Her voice rose, shock slamming into Tal's senses. "I told him you'd never give him what he wanted. Andira, he thinks of them as *weapons*. You can't let him have them!"

"He'll get them eventually. Once we've completed our orbital infrastructure, we expect some recruitment. The Alseans who sign those contracts won't necessarily be the ones you'd like Sholokhov or other state actors to have. If we negotiate with him now, we can restrict him to high empaths with unquestionable honor."

"Fucking Hades." The shock had dimmed to dismay. "I should have known you'd have this gamed out."

"I'm surprised it took him this long. We thought he'd act earlier, given the limited window of time."

Ekatya scowled, focusing fiercely on her controls. "Because they're a scarce resource now? Right, he wants them before anyone else can get them. He said they were a more potent weapon if no one knew he had them."

"And if he's the only one who has them. I'm afraid the Protectorate hasn't made the best of impressions even with the treaty. No one who lived through the Battle of Alsea will ever forget that we were abandoned to the Voloth. The way both you and Lhyn were treated hardened opinions. We'll have plenty of Alseans wanting to work on the space elevator station, and eventually the space dock and our own ships. But on ships with Protectorate crews? Or worlds where they're the only Alseans around? I think it will be a generation before we start seeing much of that beyond the few truly restless souls."

"And you think Sholokhov has come to the same conclusion?"

"I know Ambassador Solvassen has."

"Which means that's what Sholokhov is working with. That's why he waited until now. He took the time to put a system in place for managing them. By the time anyone else has empaths, he'll already have the best of the best. Agh!" She raised a fist, her jaw clenching, then slowly opened her hand. "Do you have to give him what he wants? I hate the thought of it."

"Oh, no. Not at all." Tal watched her press the now-flat hand on her thigh, fascinated by the way she was physically controlling her frustration. "Nor will we, unless he makes an offer we cannot refuse."

"Such as?"

"We won't have the *Caphenon* ready for service for another cycle or two, depending on the success of our other projects. Even when we raise it, the new hull will limit its capability. It would be nice to have our own warship in the meantime. One that can go into base space."

Ekatya inhaled sharply. "You can't be serious."

"I'm perfectly serious."

"Ha! You've got horns."

"They're a prerequisite for the title."

"No, I mean it." She checked her controls, all traces of anger erased by sparkling mirth and the heat of admiration. "You'll drive a bargain so hard that Sholokhov either gives up or gives you a Pulsar-class concession. Either way, you win. He'll birth a brick when I pass that on."

"Don't pass it on." Tal tried not to look as ridiculously pleased as she felt. "I don't want him to have time to strategize before we speak. Tell him I'm amenable to negotiations and that he needs to call my office directly. Are we done with your duty?"

"Yes."

"Good. May I fly it now?"

"Well, Lancer Tal, I'm not sure," she said with exaggerated care. "Are you current on your certifications?"

"Signed and stamped." Tal pointed toward Candini's fighter. "Does she know I can fly this?"

"Not unless Gehrain or Vellmar told her. I don't think Rahel knows."

"Perfect. Let's scare her hair into a few more spikes."

Ekatya grinned. "I'm in! Finally, I get to be the one who plays instead of the one being played. Same thing you did to me?"

"Why not? It worked so well."

"Take over."

Tal grasped the control stick and tested the feel in all directions. The fighter responded with a wing waggle, a brief climb, and an equally brief drop.

The quantum com blinked on, showing the other two crews on a split screen. "Is anything wrong, Captain?" Candini asked.

"Not a thing. My new pilot was just testing the controls. Look." She held up her hands.

"What are—you're letting her fly?"

Tal didn't need her empathic senses to hear the horror in her voice. "Have a little faith, First Pilot. I've done this before."

Ekatya somehow managed to keep a straight face despite the glee fizzing around her. "She had a hantick with a trainer as a gift."

"A hantick?" Candini's voice was nearly a screech. "We're at top speed! If she makes even a small error, you're one-dimensional!"

"I'm in an Alsean fighter and you think I'm supposed to say no to the Lancer?" Ekatya asked reasonably.

"You're the senior pilot. You outrank her as long as she's in that fighter. Lancer Tal, this is not a good idea. A Serrado fighter is not a transport—"

The com went dark, cutting her off in mid-sentence, and Ekatya looked over with a wicked sparkle in her eyes. "Oops. Must have hit the wrong button."

"To think I called Salomen devious this morning."

"I guess you're attracted to devious women."

"A specific subset of devious women, as Lhyn would say." Tal slowed their groundspeed until she felt safe enough to flip the fighter ninety degrees, then ninety more. With the sky at her feet and the mountainous terrain overhead, she let the fighter go into a lazy dive. "Put a solo call through to Gehrain. Tell him we're about to prank Candini."

Gehrain chuckled as he listened to the news. "I hope Rahel knows basic medic skills for Gaians."

"Poor Rahel," Vellmar said. "She has no idea you're capable of this."

"It's about time she learned, don't you think?" Tal bottomed out her dive and began a gut-crushing climb that grew closer and closer to vertical.

The screen split again, showing Candini's worried face. "Captain," she said in a too-calm voice. "That's too steep an angle of attack."

"I agree. Andira, let me take over."

"No, I know what I'm doing."

"This is not the time for warrior pride." Ekatya made a grab for her control stick. "Shek! What did you do? I'm locked out!"

Tal thought Ekatya deserved an award for her acting as Candini began to fray at the edges. She kept the pressure on, pushing the fighter to a point where its wings were rocking, the airspeed no longer sufficient for lift.

"Shipper shit!" Candini shouted. "Lancer Tal, push it forward!"

Tal did, but with a slight shift that had the fighter falling onto its left wing. They plummeted toward the mountains in what appeared to be a catastrophic stall.

"My control stick is still dead!" Ekatya sounded properly alarmed. "Andira, you have to level it out!"

"She can't! Eject the cockpit pod! You still have time, eject!"

Tal let the fighter fall for a further count of four before smoothly leveling out and beginning a slow climb back to their prior altitude. "Relax, Candini," she said. "I have a little more than one hantick of training."

"What—" Candini stopped, her jaw loose as Ekatya burst into laughter, echoed by Gehrain and Vellmar. "I don't believe it," she muttered, then said something under her breath that sounded like *assheads*.

"First Guard Sayana," Tal said. "I apologize for giving you a dose of pure Gaian panic. I hope you don't have a headache after that."

Rahel looked flummoxed. "Even if I did, it would be worth it. I never imagined . . ." She hesitated.

"That I'm a normal Alsean capable of pranks? I'm bonded with Salomen, if you recall. Do you think I could survive her if I didn't have a sense of humor?"

Her expression smoothed into a smile. "I should have realized."

"Hoi, Rahel. Remember when we were discussing our service history?" Vellmar asked. "And you said you'd never been in the kind of unit where Guards pranked each other?"

"Yes?"

"You are now."

"Um. I don't really think of Lancer Tal as a Guard."

"I used to be," Tal said. "Vellmar is right. Consider yourself properly inducted into the Bondlancer's Guards."

Rahel's delighted grin earned her a punch in the shoulder from Candini.

"Stop being so happy about it, you grainbird. They nailed our asses to the wall! We'll never get back at them for that."

"I wouldn't try if I were you." Ekatya clasped her hands behind her head and affected a pose of studied ease. "I'm going to take a nap. Let me know when we're over the ocean."

"Oh, shut up," Candini grumbled.

22

FALLING WATER

Tal had been keeping a steady eye on the navigation screen. When they passed over the coastline of Argolis, she thought they might begin arcing westward toward Whitemoon. Instead, Ekatya held her heading, continuing south.

They weren't landing anywhere on the Pallea continent, then. Were they going to the port platform anchoring the space elevator? It was a spectacular sight, if not particularly romantic.

No, that didn't feel right. Mahaite Island made more sense. Ekatya had loved her time there, becoming a whole new person as she let go of her tension and fears for Lhyn. But would she choose the location of Tal's bonding break with Salomen for a date?

It seemed she had. Though a solid layer of clouds concealed the ocean below, the nav screen showed the hidden terrain to the west. Ekatya was descending, and there was no other place to land.

They broke through the cloud ceiling at two thousand strides above sea level. The ocean was not the brilliant, sparkling blue she remembered but a dark green, crisscrossed with dashes of white. Turbulence buffeted the fighter.

"Lots of storms over the past few ninedays," Ekatya said. "Another just yesterday. We're lucky, though. No rain predicted today. Have you figured out where we're going?"

Tal squinted out her window. Mahaite Island was the obvious answer, but if Ekatya was asking . . .

The pressure seat flowed up around her head as Ekatya banked steeply to the east. Straight ahead, Pica Mahal's massive bulk reared from the water, its flanks carpeted with tropical forest and its top hidden in the clouds.

"Oh," Tal breathed. "No, I didn't guess it. Oh! The storms!"

A wave of delighted satisfaction filled the fighter. "The storms. We never had a chance to see the waterfalls."

They had come here during the bonding break, on that memorable morning when Tal surprised Ekatya with one of the first Serrado fighters. It had been perfect weather, excellent for flying and views, but with no possibility of seeing the caldera's famous ephemeral waterfalls.

Tal let out a startled laugh as she put it together. "You *told* me where we were going! On the way to the landing pad, when you reminded me of that morning. Great Mother, you're more devious than I gave you credit for."

That brilliant grin was one she had not seen for moons, nor had she sensed this easy, joyous confidence. It made Ekatya more beautiful, striking in a way Tal thought she should always be.

She settled back, enjoying the ride as they flew a rapid circuit of the volcano. Ekatya climbed back into the cloud layer, navigating by instrument until they passed over the rim of the caldera and hovered near its center. Their escorts were barely visible in the gray mist.

Ekatya activated the com. "Ready to drop in?"

"To think I'm being paid for this," Gehrain said.

"No kidding." Candini was glowing. "I even forgive you for that nasty trick earlier. I want to fly laps around this volcano."

"You haven't seen the best yet. Here we go." She initiated a gradual vertical descent.

Tal stared out the front, waiting for the view to clear. They marked off two hundred strides of altitude before the mist began to thin. In another thirty strides, it abruptly vanished, revealing a spectacular scene hidden to all the world but the six of them.

The walls were carpeted with lush vegetation, hundreds of different species crowding together except in the dark band that ran a circuit around the caldera. Only a few plants found footholds in that layer of denser rock, which acted as a barrier to the rain water seeping through the porous substrate above.

The last time she and Ekatya had been here, that trapped water emerged in a single waterfall, the only permanent one in the caldera. But recent storms had dumped great volumes of rain on the volcano, all filtering down to collect above the band and search for the nearest egress.

There were waterfalls everywhere Tal looked. Roaring torrents jetting out to drop straight down, lacy networks many strides wide, smaller trickles going this way and that as they followed the topography—it was a banquet of beauty, so glorious that she felt a sting behind her eyes.

"Incredible," Ekatya murmured. "The vids didn't do it justice." She made an adjustment to the controls, putting the fighter into a slow horizontal rotation as it hovered.

"No, they didn't." Tal watched avidly as the caldera walls slid past, every moment revealing new splendor.

"How many are there?" Candini wanted to know.

"Thirty-two. Enjoy the view, we're headed down."

"We'll be here until you power down." Gehrain was all business. "I contacted the resort on our way in. They're ready for us to take up some space on their landing pad."

"Did you ask if they had some of that special fruit juice?"

A smile cracked his serious demeanor. "No, but now that you mention it, I'd love a glass of that."

"Me too," Vellmar agreed. "While we're laboring at our duties, sitting around in a tropical paradise."

"See you on the bottom." Ekatya tapped off the com and resumed their descent.

The caldera was immense at the top, fully six lengths in diameter, but the walls angled inward, reaching a relatively narrow space at the bottom. Pools of water near the walls restricted that space further, as did the hills of boulders piled up from innumerable small landslides. Still, the available level ground was enough to accommodate a whole squadron of fighters.

"How did you talk Micah into letting us have this to ourselves?" Tal asked.

"I appealed to his sense of practicality. Other than the people involved in planning this trip, no one knows you're here. No other permits were issued today. Orbital trackers will flag any craft approaching without one, so Gehrain and Candini will have plenty of warning if someone tries."

"And that was enough?" Micah wasn't normally so flexible when it came to her security, especially this far from assistance.

"I also pointed out that you've been working too hard and needed a quality rest from your duties. He's been worried about that."

"I'm surprised he'd worry."

"Why would you say that?"

"Never mind." She was already regretting her slip.

"No, that's not how this works. What—wait, hold that thought." Ekatya settled the fighter on its landing gear, waited for the legs to adjust to the variation in terrain, then powered down the engines and activated the com. "We're secure. Go get that fruit juice."

"Lancer Tal?" Gehrain would not leave until he had her affirmation.

"All safe. Thank you for the escort."

"Very well. Enjoy your time, Lancer. Captain," he added in a respectful tone before closing the frequency. Overhead, the two hovering fighters ascended, rapidly vanishing into the mist.

Ekatya disconnected her harness, hung her crash collar over the control stick, and turned in her seat. "Now. What's wrong?"

Tal looked up from hanging her own crash collar. "Nothing is wrong. Isn't this a date? I want to get out there and see this." She reached for the door release, but her other wrist was caught.

"Something is bothering you about Micah. Tell me." Ekatya's fingers slipped down.

Tal watched them tangle with her own, sensed the concern, and knew she would not let this go. "If I tell you, I'll sound like a pre-Rite child."

Ekatya waved her other hand, indicating their surroundings. "Do you see anyone here who would judge you?"

"When you put it that way, no." She hesitated, then gave up. "Micah is distracted."

"With Alejandra." Understanding flowed through their touch.

"It was fine at first. He asked about the possible issues, we discussed it, I gave my blessing."

"Your political blessing, or your personal one?"

Startled, Tal met her eyes. "Political."

"Has he asked for your personal blessing? Would he need to?"

"He's a family elder. Blessings are given from the top down, not the bottom up. He can do whatever he wants." She congratulated herself on keeping the bitterness from her voice.

"But you're a higher rank and he reports to you. In a way, you *are* an elder."

Perhaps she hadn't been as successful as she'd thought. "It's—I hate it," she burst out. "He asked about joining, Ekatya. Not courting. He's in love and I want to be happy for him, but it feels as if he's forgotten me outside his duties. He's spending every free tick with her, or talking to her on the com, or—" She tossed up her free hand in exasperation. "I never see him anymore. Not for leisure time. He turned down my last two invitations for a drink. I can hardly remember what his quarters look like."

"That's why you're working so hard," Ekatya said, realization sparking from her skin. "Salomen is buried in plantings and mostly at Hol-Opah this moon—"

"And she's nurturing her own bond with Lhyn. Which is exactly what I want," she hastened to add. "She needs it, and I cannot be there as often as I'd wish. But when I missed her the most, I'd always go to Micah."

"Oh," Ekatya murmured. She looked around, then gave a brisk nod. "We're getting out of here."

"All right." Startled by the shift and unaccountably disappointed, Tal opened her door.

The silent cocoon of their cockpit gave way to the roar of thirty-two waterfalls, distracting her from gloomy thoughts. She swung her legs out and stood on the top rung of the ladder, staring in wonder.

The caldera walls were even more majestic from here, rising a thousand strides before disappearing in the mist. The waterfalls originated three hundred strides below that, even the smallest ones glorious in their height. The largest were outright breathtaking as they tumbled down the walls. Between them, enormous trees clung to the rocks, waving gracefully in the breeze. Sparks of white, yellow, and at least four shades of blue shone through the greenery, each a flowering tree or shrub making the most of the plentiful moisture.

Tal thought she could faintly sense the collective satisfaction of this lush growth. Feeling better already, she filled her lungs with heavy, fragrant air and felt as if the clouds had sealed them in. They were the only living beings on this entire mountain.

Looking down, she realized that the caldera floor hosted an entirely different set of plants: short, fleshy, and adapted to arid soil. Unable to benefit from the water percolating through the porous walls, they depended solely on the rainfall that reached them.

Ekatya appeared at the bottom of the ladder, a pack slung over one shoulder. "Are you going to stand there all day?"

She tapped the control to seal the door and climbed down. As soon as she stepped off the last rung, Ekatya dropped the pack and pulled her into a warmron.

"This is why I wanted to be outside," she said.

Tal rested their heads together, enjoying the peace and the soothing sound of falling water. "I thought you were done with the conversation."

"I was done with being limited to holding your hand." She tightened her embrace. "I'm used to tucking my face into Lhyn's throat. You and I fit differently. I like it, though."

"Salomen said that was one of the first things that attracted her to Lhyn."

"Different fit?"

"And being able to tuck her face in."

"Not to mention being able to thoroughly understand her."

With a chuckle, Tal pulled back, her palms sliding down Ekatya's arms. They stood a pace apart, hands held loosely between them. "Salomen understands me because we share our emotions. She understands Lhyn because they share a brain."

"Isn't that the truth and a half. But we do, too. You know me better than anyone in the universe."

She took an inordinate pride in that. "Does it feel to you as if this was meant to be? Each of us with a partner we love for their differences, and one we love for the similarities?"

"I'm not one to believe in . . . fate or Fahla, isn't that the phrase? But it's true that there's a ridiculous amount of symmetry in our bonds. Salomen was right about the balance." Ekatya lifted their hands. "This would never have happened if she and Lhyn hadn't found each other."

Tal nodded. It was simply fact. No matter how deep the attraction, no matter that they held an actual tyree bond, they could not have hurt their bondmates.

"I'm sorry about Micah. If it helps, I'm feeling a little abandoned by

Alejandra, too." A flicker of wry humor was quickly pushed aside by empathy. "She's a good friend, and she's healing from a very old wound. I'm happy for her, but I can see how hard this is for you."

Tal let go and stepped away, arms wrapped around her waist as she gazed up at the waterfalls. "It shouldn't be hard for me. I should be as glad for him as you are for Alejandra, but I cannot find that in my heart. What does that make me? An ungrateful, selfish—"

"Perfectly normal Alsean with understandable feelings." Ekatya moved up beside her. "Micah is the one being selfish right now. But he's earned it, don't you think?"

"Yes, of course. He's earned all the happiness in the world! I don't know why—" She blew out a frustrated breath and shook her head.

Ekatya slid a hand across her lower back and settled it on the curve of her hip. She was not judging. She was simply there, providing comfort as they both watched the falling water.

Tal relaxed against her, uncrossing her arms and matching Ekatya's gesture. As warmth spread through her from shoulder to hip, she felt something unwind.

"I might know why," Ekatya offered quietly. "Deep down, does your heart believe he's replacing Realta?"

That had not occurred to her.

"He's had his share of lovers," she said after a long pause. "I never gave any of them a second thought. They were here and gone. But when he brought up Alejandra in our sparring session, I knew she was different. *He* was different. Goddess above, am I truly such a child? To resent him for letting someone take my mother's place?"

Though there was no space between them, Ekatya pulled her closer. "A wise woman once said we can't apologize for our emotions because we can't help what we feel."

"That wise woman isn't feeling up to her usual standards at the moment."

"Good thing she doesn't need to worry about that here." She let go and turned. "Tell me something. Am I taking Salomen's place?"

Tal frowned. "Obviously not."

"Because you love me in a different way," she said with a knowing nod. "And you can't take Lhyn's place because I love you both in different ways. These bonds we're building—they're *additions*, not replacements. Micah can't ever replace your mother. But he can have a different love."

The waterfalls seemed to grow louder as Tal stared at her.

"I'll need time for that to settle," she said at last. "But you've probably hit the target in the red zone."

"Good. Then let's set that aside for now." Ekatya reached for her hands. "You said he's earned all the happiness in the world. You've earned it, too. I think, maybe, so have I." She lifted their hands and stepped forward to hold them against her chest. "Andira, I'm here. Right here."

They were alone at the bottom of a volcano, surrounded by waterfalls that might be gone next nineday. It was a unique moment in a unique place, and Ekatya had arranged it just to stand in front of her and say two words loaded with meaning.

Tal gently detached her hands, sliding them up and over Ekatya's shoulders to meet at the back of her neck. The fabric was Alsean, the skin Gaian—but the heart and soul beneath that? She thought they might be more Alsean than not.

"I never believed you'd be here," she said.

"I've given up trying to predict what will happen with us. Any of us." Ekatya held her by the waist, neither pulling her closer nor pushing her away. She had spoken her truth and was simply waiting.

"I don't know how to do this," Tal confessed. "I don't know how to let go. It's like the first time I sparred with a sword."

This close, she saw the smile in Ekatya's eyes before it reached her lips. "Oh, do tell."

"They set us up in pairs with wooden practice swords. Every move was choreographed. There were four instructors watching us, ready to correct any wrong move we made. I desperately wanted to get through the lesson without being corrected."

The smile grew. "That sounds like you. How old were you?"

"Six."

"Are there images? You must have been adorable."

"I have a few. You could probably see more if you bribed Micah."

"Noted. Go on, I'm enjoying the mental picture."

Her emotional signature was a study in contrasts: heavy desire and expectation, buoyant delight at hearing this childhood story. They seldom spoke of their distant pasts, Tal realized. There were too many pressing things to discuss, too many plans to make, and far too little time. In truth, she knew more of Lhyn's childhood than of Ekatya's, thanks to Salomen relating the tales.

This was what Salomen meant by balance. Not merely the physical, but also the deeper emotional knowing of each other, built up through shared stories and understanding.

She brushed a thumb along the back of Ekatya's neck. "When the lesson ended, I couldn't let go of my sword. I had been holding it so tightly and for so long that my fingers didn't remember how to loosen. One of the instructors had to put his hand over mine and tell me to relax. I was mortified," she added. "All that effort to be perfect, and I needed a correction at the very end."

Ekatya's thumbs were in motion as well, rubbing up and down her waist. "You didn't need a correction. Just encouragement. Andira, you're not doing anything wrong. Salomen planned this with me. She pushed you out the door. Lhyn wants us to catch up with them. We have both permission and consent. Or at least, you have my consent. Do I have yours?"

"Yes," Tal whispered, staring at her mouth. Even now, she couldn't close the distance.

Ekatya did it for her, leaning forward with no hesitation. Their lips brushed together so gently that it barely qualified as a kiss, yet Tal shivered with the power of it.

"Are you cold?"

"Fahla, no. I'm burning up." She slid her hands down Ekatya's back and pulled her closer.

This kiss was more solid. It multiplied, then transformed as they explored each other, taking turns mapping jaws, cheekbones, and throats. When Ekatya tilted her head back to bare her throat, Tal nibbled down its length and closed her teeth on the skin where a throat ridge would be.

At the nudge of a memory, she let go and drew back.

"What is it?" Ekatya was breathing hard, pleasure saturating the air.

"Something Salomen warned me about. Your skin, it's . . . more delicate." Gently, she rubbed the reddened spot. "I'm sorry, I didn't mean to mark you. I know it's different in your culture."

"Mark me all you want." Ekatya shrugged at her surprise. "I've been doing a lot of thinking. I can't keep clinging to rules that applied to an old life. I'm not in that life anymore. Or I'm only half in it. The other half is here." She locked her wrists behind Tal's neck and looked around with a broad smile. "In this beautiful place, with a beautiful woman who grew up in a culture where those marks mean something else. They're not an embarrassment to you."

"But they're—" Tal cleared her throat. "An announcement. Of a sort."

"It's good to know you're not always so articulate."

"Not when there's a blood shortage in my brain. You don't mind the announcement?"

"That I'm wanted? Loved?" She shook her head.

"But you were shocked that Salomen told the divine tyrees about the vase."

"Well, I'm not going to walk around my ship *telling* people why I have a mark. Or who gave it to me. Though Lhyn will love the assumptions they'll make."

"It will do wonders for her reputation, won't it?" Tal still couldn't believe this was real. She had Ekatya in her arms and Salomen in her mind, both radiating happiness: Ekatya's tinged with wonder, Salomen's with the joy of fulfilled hopes.

"Did Lhyn send you off with the same expectations Salomen did?" she asked.

"She's waiting for my report tonight. She'll be disappointed when I tell her I didn't mark you, too." Her shining confidence clouded over. "Is that all right? Do you want—I don't know where the lines are anymore."

Tal slipped her hands under the open jacket and held her at the waist, warm and vital and *here*. "It's all right. I need the same time you do."

Relief loosened Ekatya's restraint. "I think I've loved you since the battle with that first ground pounder. You directed your forces like you'd been fighting the Voloth all your life. Then you turned around and gave Lhyn exactly what she needed. How could I not love the woman who was both warrior and scholar?"

"You couldn't have loved me then. I'd have sensed it."

Her lips drifted down Tal's throat. "Would you sense it if I didn't recognize it?" she murmured. "If I didn't let myself feel it?"

"I—you're making it difficult to think."

"Good." Smiling, she pulled back. "Lhyn has a theory."

"When doesn't she?"

"When she's sleeping," they said in unison, breaking into chuckles.

"She thinks that's why I was so furious when you outmaneuvered me with the *Caphenon*. And when I thought you'd forced her. It wasn't just anger on her behalf or mine. It was also the thought of being betrayed by someone I wanted to love."

Startled, Tal ran through her memories with a new filter in place. "She may be right. That would explain why you trusted me to Share with you after our challenge fight. If you look at that logically, with what you knew about me then . . . you should never have trusted me so soon."

"I had perfectly logical reasons for it. Or so I thought." Ekatya pinned her with a knowing look. "How hard was that Sharing for you? Tell the truth."

"Physically exhausting. Emotionally? That wasn't the worst one. The worst was the first time I connected you and Lhyn. To channel your love and know I could never have it—" She stopped, caught in an odd twist between remembered pain and the impossibility of what she held in her hands.

Ekatya ran her fingertips along a cheekbone ridge. "You gave us such a gift. You're the reason we survived that. I broke Lhyn's heart. I didn't have the tools to repair it. You did. It's the most selfless thing anyone has ever done for me." She looked up, her eyes full of warmth, and Tal could hardly breathe. "How are we both so lucky?"

"I don't know." Tal gathered her close again, needing to feel the reality of her. "Finding Salomen was a gift from Fahla. Being allowed to love you both is—I think I need to go to Blacksun Temple and light every rack in the place."

"I'll want an image of that. Lanaril will be thrilled."

"Salomen will light them with me. Do you know what else she and Lhyn have in common? They both thought they weren't lovable."

"Idiots," Ekatya said affectionately. "But at least Lhyn found some comfort in the fact that she was proven wrong *empirically*."

That made them laugh hard enough that they had to let go of each other. When they recovered, Ekatya scooped up her pack. "I brought food. Let's find a spot for midmeal."

"You can think about food?"

"It's not a date if we don't eat something."

"By whose standards?"

"Mine. We have to give a report to our bondmates, remember? They'll expect a picnic."

"Is there a checklist?" Tal shook her head. "Never mind. If Lhyn had anything to do with it, there is."

She listened to Ekatya's laughter, sensed her rare relaxation, and watched the ease of her movements as they walked side by side. Then she looked up, taking in the curving wall of waterfalls, and realized the wonderful truth.

They needed to savor their limited time here. Such a chance would not soon come again.

But they had all the time in the world to explore their bond.

23

FREE AND HONORABLE

R ahel stopped at the bottom of the imposing steps and looked up to the even more imposing columns framing the tribunal's entrance. She had been here once before, a penitent signing documents that saved her from prison. Grateful as she was, the memory was not a good one. The forms had defined her crimes in dispassionate terms that made her sick. Adding her signature locked them to her caste record. She could work the rest of her life to atone, but those words would never be erased.

"It's all right," Salomen said patiently. "This is a good day."

"I know. I was just remembering."

"You're not the same person you were then."

"No, but signing these forms won't make the last ones disappear."

On her other side, Colonel Micah mounted the first step. "You cannot change the past, First Guard. You can only change the future."

Rahel lifted her chin and rolled her shoulders. "Let's go change it."

With its high ceiling, stone counters, and echoing space, the lobby was every bit as intimidating as she remembered. At least she didn't have to worry about interacting with judgmental clerks. Wearing the dress uniform of a Bondlancer's First Guard did wonders for respect levels, as did the presence of Salomen, Colonel Micah, and three additional Guards. It took mere pipticks for the suddenly efficient clerk to find her record and point toward an archway to the left. "You're in chamber three."

"Thank you."

They passed through the arch and into a long corridor, where the sound of their boot heels on tile flooring was reflected back by stone walls. She remembered that, too.

Inside the otherwise empty judgment chamber, a distinctive form sat in the front row of chairs.

"Captain Serrado!" She hurried down the center aisle. "I didn't know you'd be here."

Serrado stood up, looking crisp and official in her own dress uniform. "I'm your oath holder by proxy. I'm here to speak to your performance."

"I thought Salomen and Colonel Micah were doing that."

"We are." Salomen had caught up. "But we wanted the record to be complete. Ekatya, good morning. I'm glad to see you've recovered from your long night." Offering a double palm touch, she added, "Spending time with one makes you want the other even more, doesn't it? At least, that's what I've found."

"Salomen!" Captain Serrado turned bright red as she pulled her hands away.

Had Rahel embarrassed her that badly, she would have scrambled to apologize. Salomen merely laughed.

"I'll make an Alsean of you yet," she said, waggling her eyebrows.

"You'll never convince me that this is an appropriate place for that kind of conversation." Serrado's gesture took in the judgment room, and the sideways glance seemed to indicate Rahel and Colonel Micah as well.

"Well, not when the adjudicator is present." Salomen held up her hands against the exasperated glare. "I'll stop. Talking, that is. I won't stop being amused."

"You're a pain."

"So I've been told. Many times and by many people."

"And you take pride in that, don't you?"

"As I would in any accomplishment I've worked to achieve."

Serrado shook her head with a grudging smile. "You have more in common with your bondmate than you realize."

The door at the other end of the chamber opened, admitting a Tribunal Guard who strode forward, hands loose and ready as he checked the room. Behind him, the adjudicator entered and turned toward the judgment platform.

Rahel watched the Guard position himself before the bar separating the defense chair from the rest of the court and offered silent thanks that she'd never had to sit there.

"Bondlancer Opah, this is an honor," the adjudicator said as he walked up the two steps to his platform. "Please be seated. As this is not a public hearing, I think we can cover the necessary information from more comfortable positions."

"Thank you, Honored Adjudicator." Salomen motioned for Rahel to sit and took the chair to her left. Captain Serrado resumed her previous seat, now at Salomen's left, while Colonel Micah sat on Rahel's right.

"I've reviewed the records. An extraordinary case, to be sure." The adjudicator's sharp gaze drilled into Rahel. "First Guard Rahel Sayana, one cycle ago you entered into a period of restitution for your involvement in kidnapping and unlawful detainment, assault with an energy weapon, physical assault with stave and sedative, unlawful detonation of a shock bomb, and—" He glanced at his reader card, as if the list was too long to remember every item. "Unlawful detainment and physical assault against Bondlancer Opah."

Her stomach roiled. For thirteen moons, she had lived a life in which those charges were ghosts of her past. Now they filled the room, given new form in the clipped words of an adjudicator who was clearly unimpressed with her punishment.

"Your victims chose not to press charges," he continued. "But the nature of your crimes mandated a response from the state. You were assigned to the Bondlancer's service and that of Captain Serrado as proxy. I ask you now, do you feel that you have completed the terms of your restitution honorably and in full?"

It was difficult to remain seated when her instincts said she should be standing to address him. But he had ordered them to sit, so she sat as straight as she could.

"Yes, Honored Adjudicator. I've served with honor and to the best of my ability. I have undergone therapeutic counseling and continued it via quantum com while in orbit or on patrol. I've done everything asked of me, and more when I could." She didn't know if he wanted to hear more, but was compelled to add, "I know the purpose of this hearing isn't to defend or explain my crimes, but I want to say that I have never stopped regretting that I caused harm to so many. I've never stopped trying to make up for it. I don't think I ever can. But every day, I'm grateful that I've been given the chance to try."

His eyes narrowed as he listened, and she knew he was scanning her. Now he nodded, his expression a fraction more open. "Honestly spoken. Yet it is possible to believe one thing while the truth is somewhat different. For this reason, the tribunal requires corroborative statements. Bondlancer Opah, as the holder of her oath, do you have any such statements to offer?"

"I do." Salomen's back was as straight as Rahel's, but she appeared far more at ease. "It is not a simple thing to serve two oath holders, and for the most part I have stood aside in favor of Captain Serrado. But a day did come when I needed Rahel's service most urgently. When I called, she came without question, despite being in orbit at the time. She is the one who gained the cooperation of the Voloth Empire settlers for the march in Blacksun. She did so by revealing herself as my attacker. They were convinced to follow me because she took public responsibility for her actions."

The adjudicator's brows lowered. "Why did you do that?" he asked Rahel. "Those records were sealed for your protection."

"They wanted proof that she wasn't like the abusive rulers they were used to. In their empire, I'd have been tortured and executed. They asked what happened to me, but Sa—Bondlancer Opah couldn't say anything without breaking the law and putting me at risk. So I told them I was the one. I told them she saved me."

"I see." He had not expected that. "Interesting. Please continue, Bondlancer."

"I would only add that Rahel served flawlessly during the march, and did not limit her service to me. She also protected Prime Producer Arabisar and saved the life of Lead Templar Satran. She put her body between mine and an assassin's disruptor rifle. I felt her in that moment. She knew she might be shot. There was no guarantee that the assassin would not simply remove her as an obstacle to get to me. Yet she did not hesitate. I do not believe that restitution should require the sacrifice of one's life, yet she was willing."

"It seems to me that she swore to do exactly that at the beginning of her term," said the adjudicator.

"Yes, she did, and upheld her oath as any honorable warrior would. If she were still a criminal in need of further rehabilitation, would that not be the failure point?"

He nodded. "I believe it would. Have you any further statements?"

"Not at this time. Captain Serrado has the greater experience with First Guard Sayana's service. I yield to her."

"Very well." He made several notes on his reader card, then looked up with bright eyes. "Captain Serrado, what a pleasure to see you in my judgment chamber. I must say I never imagined such a thing when I was named to this post."

Could adjudicators be star struck? Rahel hadn't thought so, but this one seemed to be.

"Thank you, Honored Adjudicator. I appreciate that you're allowing a Gaian to speak in an Alsean legal matter."

"We do seem to be setting several precedents today. Please, take your time and make your statement."

"First Guard Sayana has been an exemplary officer on my crew," Serrado said. "On her first patrol, she worked hard to learn our culture, made contact with a new sentient species, and displayed admirable control when attacked with lethal intent."

That got the adjudicator's attention. The rest was public record; this was not. "Someone tried to murder her on your ship?"

"A political assassin disguised as a member of my crew. She neutralized him with a nonlethal strike. Her decision, made instantly and in a combat situation, told me what I needed to know about her restraint and judgment."

Rahel stared straight ahead, her ears burning for an excruciating tentick while Captain Serrado spoke in glowing terms of her service. While it was true that she had done everything described, she was well aware of what was being left out: the punishment she had earned in her first eight days, the difficulties she encountered fitting in with some of the security officers, the times she reverted to lifelong habit and charged off without waiting for backup. Commander Cox had frequently called her into his office for a lecture on expectations and procedure.

Although now that she thought about it, she hadn't been subjected to one of those lectures in several moons. And he had been visibly unhappy about having to share her with the weapons section once she began flying with Candini.

Serrado's statement was followed by a much shorter one from Colonel Micah, who also testified to her good faith service. When he finished, the room was silent while the adjudicator made far too many notes on his reader card. Rahel waited nervously, forcing herself not to fidget.

"First Guard Sayana," he said at last, setting the reader card on the desk. "I'm ready to render my judgment. Please stand."

She shot upright, heart in her throat and stomach clenched.

"It is my opinion that what appeared to be a lenient sentence has in fact accomplished its purpose of rehabilitation. You have not merely fulfilled the terms of your restitution; you have gone beyond them. The tribunal considers your case closed. As of today, you are a free member of the warrior caste. You may work where you wish and choose your oath holder at will."

Euphoria poured through her veins, only to evaporate at his next words.

"At this time, your service to Bondlancer Opah is ended."

"What?" she gasped.

"That service was part of your restitution and cannot continue beyond this point."

"No!" She turned, looking for reassurance, but Salomen shook her head.

"I cannot hold your oath as it was. You gave it under duress. You're no longer constrained to my service. You can still serve Captain Serrado—"

"I *want* to serve you. Don't push me out."

"I'm not pushing you." Salomen stood and spoke quietly. "Rahel, you should take some time to think about it. You're free. You've worked hard for this. Don't—"

Rahel pivoted to face the platform. "Honored Adjudicator, didn't you say I can choose any oath holder I want? If that oath holder is willing to accept my service?"

"Of course."

She turned back. "Are you willing?"

"If that's what you want, but you've only been free for two ticks! Stop for a moment and consider your options. Aren't you tired of serving two oath holders? It would be simpler to let Captain Serrado hold your oath directly."

Understanding struck. "You're still looking out for me."

"Shouldn't I be?"

"No. I mean, it's not necessary." She waved a hand down her uniform. "Don't you know how much this means to me? Putting this on was one of the happiest days of my life. I'm *proud* to wear your colors. My oath was under duress only by the legal definition. It was the one thing I wanted most in the world. I still do. You want it too, don't you?"

Salomen hesitated, looking deep into her eyes. Whatever she saw or sensed made her shoulders relax. "I'll always want you in my service."

"Then that's all that matters." She blew out a relieved breath. "Thank Fahla. I thought you were going to kick me out."

"I was trying to do the right thing," Salomen protested. "I didn't want to abuse my position."

"As if you were capable of it. I've never met anyone less likely to use her title for personal gain." She glanced down at her belt, sadly lacking an important accoutrement. "I wasn't expecting to swear an oath today. I don't have my sword."

"Don't worry. We can do it later."

"And have you come up with some other self-sacrificing reason why I shouldn't? I don't think so. This place is full of Tribunal Guards; maybe I can borrow one."

Captain Serrado and Colonel Micah had moved from their chairs and were standing a small distance away, trying to look as if they weren't listening. Now Serrado gave up the ruse.

"Does it have to be a sword? Can you use your stave?"

Rahel looked to Colonel Micah, who would understand how wrong that suggestion was.

"Swords are traditional," he said. "But they're not specifically required. Very little about her service has been traditional." He gazed at Rahel thoughtfully. "I believe it might be uniquely appropriate for you to use your stave. It's your weapon of choice." Stepping closer, he indicated the stave holster attached to her belt. "May I?"

She flipped open the strap and drew out her stave grip.

"It's a fine piece," he said, examining the engravings.

"Thank you. It was a special gift. I've had it since I was sixteen."

"Then it must carry good memories."

"Very good ones. And some that aren't."

He stepped back to give himself room. The stave extended with its familiar song of smoothly sliding metal, and she instinctively clenched her fist. Her hand felt empty.

Colonel Micah turned to the adjudicator, who was watching with great interest. "This stave protected Bondlancer Opah and Prime Producer Arabisar from armed attackers," he said. "It saved the life of Lead Templar Satran. It has saved First Guard Sayana's life twice that we know of." He turned back to Rahel, his gaze intent. "A weapon acquires a reputation from the choices and actions of its owner. You have imbued this weapon with honor."

Rahel could not have moved if her life depended on it. She was weighed down by the sudden significance Colonel Micah had injected into this moment.

"If you swore your oath on a sword used only for ceremonies, how could that be any more binding than one you swear on this? A weapon steeped in history, wearing its honor proudly? This has been your constant companion."

Her stave sang again, retracting back into its grip.

"Swear your oath on a worthy weapon." He held it out.

Silently, her throat too tight for words, Rahel took it from his palm. "Thank you," she whispered.

Salomen was watching with a furrowed brow. "There's just one problem. I don't know how to sheath it. Close it." She made a frustrated gesture. "Whatever you call it!"

The laugh blew apart the restriction in Rahel's throat. "Retract. It's easy; I'll show you." She pulled Salomen to a more open area, away from the others. "The release is here, see? If you hold it like this and make a fist, that depresses the release and extends it. It's the same to retract it." She demonstrated, extending and retracting, then put it in Salomen's hand.

"Like this?"

"Yes. Hold it firmly—more firmly than that—good. Now squeeze."

The stave extended with its metallic song, and Salomen jumped in surprise. Then she grinned. "Nice. And now . . ." It slid back, collapsing into the grip. She practiced twice more, each time growing more confident, and laughed at the final retraction. "This is speedy! Fianna should have taught me with one of these instead of a knife."

"It takes a long time to learn." Rahel accepted her stave once more.

"You get a lot of bruises in the process. I'd teach you if you wanted, but you don't need it."

"Not for self defense. Perhaps for working out my frustrations."

"It's effective for that. Though I have to warn you, the early training will only add to your frustrations."

A familiar mischief sparkled in her eyes. "But then you'll let me hit you, yes? As part of your service to me." She took a step back, effortlessly shifting into her Bondlancer persona, and spoke in a louder voice. "First Guard Sayana. You have reached the end of a difficult road, and stand before me a free and honorable warrior. I am in need of a warrior such as you. But my need is for more than security. I require a warrior I can trust, who would no more betray me than our two moons would fall from the sky. I need a friend who knows me as more than my title. Will you be that warrior for me?"

Still stunned by the phrase "free and honorable," Rahel scrambled to catch up. She looked around the room, noting the banners on the walls, the Shield of Alsea over the adjudicator's platform, the empty seats, and their tiny audience of Captain Serrado, Colonel Micah, the adjudicator, and the Tribunal Guard.

"Bondlancer Opah," she said, "I have sworn just two oaths in my life. The first was a lifelong dream. I stood on Dock One, at the edge of Wildwind Bay at sunset, and believed nothing could match it. But I was twenty cycles old and thought only of what it would gain me. I didn't understand what I gave up."

Salomen nodded, her dark eyes warm with understanding.

"My second oath was even more of a dream. I stood on the deck at the center of Blacksun Temple, with the sun shining on the molwyn tree, and believed nothing could match it. But my honor was stained, and I was not free."

She felt as tall as the temple dome, strong and confident and bursting with pride.

"My third oath is the greatest dream of all. I give it with full honor, gaining everything while losing nothing. I am finally free to choose my oath holder. My heart chooses you. I am your friend, and I will be the warrior you need."

Though Salomen's eyes shone with tears, her smile was brilliant. "I know you will."

Despite the import of the moment, Rahel could not stop her own smile. "I stand before you with a clear heart and an honorable name," she said, beginning the traditional wording. "I wish to serve you in any capacity I am able. I place my strength between you and harm, my—my stave between you and your enemies, and my last breath between you and death. This I swear in Fahla's name. I am Rahel Periso Sayana, and I ask this gift of you: Will you accept my service?"

The stave sang once more as she extended it. Then she realized that her hold precluded Salomen from easily taking and retracting it. There would be an unavoidable shuffle to arrange handholds.

She couldn't bear the thought. Without hesitation, she tossed it upward, dropped to one knee, and bowed her head with her hands outstretched. Her stave fell obediently into place, one hand on either side of the grip.

It was gently pulled away, and she heard it retract.

"Please stand, Rahel Periso Sayana."

She rose, her heart pounding with the import of the moment. Fahla willing, this would be her last oath.

Salomen pressed the grip into her palm. "You offer me a worthy weapon extended, and I return it to you sheathed. I accept the gift of your service with a glad heart, and trust that you will stand between me and harm. Should your last breath be expended in my defense, I swear to you that your name will be honored to the utmost of my ability, and the flames from your pyre will reach the stars themselves."

She released Rahel's wrist. "Captain Serrado?"

Serrado stepped forward. "I'm here."

"Once again, I name you my proxy in holding the oath of Rahel Periso Sayana, this time for the length of her service in Fleet—"

"No," Serrado interrupted, her emotions darkening. "For the length of her service *with me* in Fleet. I will not have her bound to Fleet. This is an Alsean oath."

Though surprised, Salomen did not hesitate. "For the length of her service with you in Fleet. Do you understand your responsibilities as an oath holder?"

"Better than I did a cycle ago. I accept my responsibilities."

"Do you agree that service is a gift to be earned, not an obligation to be abused?"

"I do."

"Then First Guard Sayana remains in your service." She met Rahel's eyes with a radiant smile. "And in mine. That was a fancy move, by the way."

Rahel grinned. "Not really."

Salomen bumped her shoulder. "Show-off."

Her grin grew wider.

She was not the only one who had changed in the last cycle. Salomen was more open with her affections, more confident in her title, and less prone to withdraw inside her intimidating shell.

Perhaps, she thought, they had both earned their freedom.

24

A LIVING SHIP

In his long career, Micah had lived through more than his share of extraordinary experiences. One of the most powerful had been his first trip into orbit, a moment he thought would never be surpassed.

Now he walked through the corridors of a far larger ship, not as security for Tal but as Alejandra's guest. He had flown up in one shuttle with Ekatya and would return in another ferrying the latest batch of Gaians taking their leave on Alsea. It was easily arranged and perfectly normal, which made it truly extraordinary.

So much had changed in a few short cycles.

Striding beside him was another symbol of that change. Rahel Sayana had returned with them and was taking him to the medbay via the "scenic route," having volunteered when Alejandra was delayed by a minor emergency.

She had been a Bondlancer's Guard for a full cycle and an officer on this ship for nearly as long. Eight moons before that, he had done his best to kill her and she had, in turn, damn near killed him. Yet here they were, on the same side and improbably connected through both Salomen and Alejandra.

Fahla had a quirky sense of humor.

"Do you ever think about the odds against us being here?" he asked as they passed a tailor's shop.

"Us meaning Alseans, or us meaning you and me?"

"You and me. Former opponents."

"Yes," she said thoughtfully, "but that's not the most unlikely thing that's happened to me. Being sworn to Salomen tops the list."

"Even more than being the first Alsean space explorer?"

"Much more. It's all related. I wouldn't be here if Salomen hadn't arranged it. And she couldn't have done that if you hadn't withdrawn your charges. I still don't understand why you did."

After a short internal debate, he said, "Because I found your record at the Kynea healing center."

She stopped walking.

He turned to face her, ignoring the crew members streaming past in the broad corridor. "Salomen thought I should know. She didn't give details, just said I did injure you. I couldn't leave it at that. I had the date and a likely geographic range to work with, but it still took me four days. Posing as a crafter was clever. I was impressed that you thought up a story like that when you were a tentick away from bleeding out."

"Practice."

The dismissive answer did not reflect what he saw in her eyes. "Until Salomen told me and I tracked down that record, I thought you left me for dead and danced away without a scratch. I had no idea you were so badly injured."

"That's why you withdrew the charges? Because we were even?"

"We weren't even. I was flown to the best specialist in central Pallea for surgery. My warriors, my friends, Tal and Salomen, even Chief Counselor Aldirk all Shared with me to try to bring me out of my coma. I had the best of care and visitors almost every hantick. You dragged yourself to a healing center, bleeding and alone. You gave a false name and had no visitors. Had you Returned, your loved ones would never have known where you were."

She looked away. "I had no choice."

"You had no chance," he corrected. "Your oath holder should have taken care of you. As mine took care of me."

"Your oath holder was on the right side," she said quietly.

"That doesn't matter. Shantu had a responsibility for you. He did not fulfill it." It was a vast understatement, but he would not speak badly of the man. Not when Rahel still viewed him as her father.

"He wasn't in a position to help. I never expected it."

Micah looked down the corridor with its colorful shops. "If you're injured here or in Salomen's service, will you expect help?"

"Yes," she said without hesitation. "Of course."

He nodded, pleased at the answer. Of the many lessons she had learned in the past cycle, this was one of the most important.

"That's the way it should be. That's why I withdrew my charges. I touched your palm and knew you were honorable. You deserved a chance to serve properly."

She swallowed, then held a fist to her chest and bowed her head. "Thank you, Colonel."

"No thanks are necessary. You earned that chance. You even impressed the adjudicator, and he was looking for a reason to dislike you."

"Salomen and Captain Serrado impressed him." Amusement lit her face. "Especially the captain. I'm surprised he didn't ask for her autograph."

"You noticed that too, eh? If Captain Serrado ever needs a favor from an adjudicator, she'll know where to go." He didn't need stronger empathic senses to know she did not want to talk about her hearing. Resuming their walk, he looked around with unfeigned interest. "Didn't Lhyn say there's a bar here?"

"Her favorite one," she confirmed. "The Blue Rocket. It's up ahead. Would you like to go inside? I can recommend the Synobian Sparkler. You'd never guess it has no spirits."

"Not right now. No offense meant, but if I take a date to Lhyn's favorite bar, it will be someone from medical."

She grinned broadly, her posture changing with the topic. "Someone? Medbay has a large staff. There's a lot to choose from. Do you have any preferences?"

"Someone who challenges me," he said, pretending to think. "Someone who fights for what she believes in and loves like she fights. Someone who will never take me for granted and never let me forget how special she is."

"Huh. You don't want much. Still, I think I know one person who might fit all those requirements. Let me introduce you."

~

"Someone who loves like she fights, hm?"

Micah turned around from his inspection of Alejandra's office. She was leaning against the doorway, sleek in her dark green and silver uniform, and he could not take his eyes off her.

Then he processed her words. "She told you?"

With a smirk, she pushed off and sauntered into the office, the door whispering shut behind her. "Rahel can keep a secret, but you have to tell her that's what it is. Otherwise, she and I don't keep much from each other." She set her hands on his chest and leaned up for a soft kiss. "I like the way you think of me."

"I never stop thinking of you."

"You have to sleep sometime."

"Doesn't count. That's not thinking."

"It's subconscious processing. That still counts."

"Are you going to argue with me before we even say well met?"

The smirk reappeared. "If you think this is an argument, I have bad news for you."

He brushed his thumbs along her cheekbones. They were the most Alsean part of her, and he wasn't sure if he loved them for that or simply because they lent her face such sharp beauty. "Let me guess. You fight like you love?"

"Let's just say I've had more practice at one than the other."

"I'd like to help you with that."

"Fighting?"

"Impossible woman," he murmured, and kissed her properly.

When they broke apart, she turned him by the waist and nudged him to the large window overlooking the lobby. "I'm sorry I couldn't give you the tour, but Rahel knows what she's talking about. What do you think of my domain?"

"It's impressive," he said honestly, gazing out at the two-story lobby with its profusion of hanging gardens and potted trees. "I didn't realize it was this grand."

The minor emergency had turned into a moderate one, delaying her longer than expected. Rahel had conducted the tour in her place, showing him the medbay from the top down. It spanned parts of four decks, with one level for surgery bays and another for treatment rooms. Having some of the offices overlook the lobby and treatment rooms was a useful design, he thought. Alejandra's office was directly across from the main doors, giving her the best view of any activity below.

"You didn't realize? It's a twin to the medbay on the *Caphenon*."

"This one has people."

"Hm. I know what you mean. I spent a day in there with the healers, doing inventory and explaining the equipment they hadn't figured out. It was eerie. A ghost ship. A ghost medbay."

Two crew members arrived in the lobby below, a third limping between them with his arms over their shoulders. One of the nurses at the central desk walked out to meet them, pad in hand.

"Recreational injury," Alejandra said. "Ten to one he's due for a rotation off the ship. They get restless when the clock counts down."

"I've only been here a short time, but I've already seen six people come through those doors." Micah watched the nurse lead them to a treatment room. "Your medbay is alive. This whole ship is alive. I was in the *Caphenon* right after it crashed, when it was still tilted forward on its nose. It felt wounded, but not dead. As if it were waiting for its people to come back. Now it's clean and repaired and all it needs is the rebuilt hull, but it feels empty." He turned to face her. "After walking through this ship, I understand why Ekatya only returned to the *Caphenon* once."

"I remember that. I had to pour half a bottle of iceflame down her throat when she came back." She held out a hand. "Come on, I'll buy you a Synobian Sparkler."

The Blue Rocket, he soon learned, was named not for a space vehicle but for a plant species. Its walls were hidden behind vines with blue, tube-shaped flowers, while large displays showing outdoor scenes added to a planetside feel.

Alejandra placed their order on the small pad embedded in the table and leaned back. "They show different themes at different times of day," she said, nodding toward a display. "And coordinate it with drinks and food from cultures where the programs were recorded."

"No wonder Lhyn loves it."

"She dragged Rahel in here often enough to hit every theme. We teased her about calling it cultural immersion when she really wanted a drink, but Rahel said it did help."

"Is there anything on the menu that would represent your culture?"

"Yes, in about three—Phoenix, convert three hours to hanticks?" She listened to her internal com, then refocused. "In two point one six hanticks, they'll serve spicy foods similar to what I grew up with. Foods that might blow off the top of your head, if what I've had in Blacksun is any indication."

"That sounds like a challenge," he observed.

She shrugged, but the smile gave her away. "If you're a wise elder, you won't take it."

That also sounded like a challenge. He was enjoying this view of her too much to answer.

"I miss the food," she said. "And the smell of the research fields first thing in the morning, before the dew burned off. I miss walking through the forest and knowing every single medicinal plant."

He wished the table were not between them. "I cannot imagine knowing a place as well as you knew Xhaline and leaving it forever."

"When I left, I didn't think it would be forever. It hurt too much to stay, but I thought someday it wouldn't."

"And now?"

"I don't think it would hurt. It also wouldn't be home."

They had discussed the idea of home one night, twined together with sated bodies and languid minds. He had been surprised that a scholar shared his experience of duty first, home second. But then, she had surprised him from the beginning.

"What brought that expression?" she asked.

"I was remembering the day we met. You weren't what I thought you'd be."

She snickered. "You expected me to be some sort of medical assassin."

"I didn't *expect* it—"

"You made me swear I meant no harm. With skin contact for proof."

"I was doing my duty," he defended. "I also noticed that you had very soft hands."

Now she laughed outright. "Was that part of your duty, too?"

"I'm reasonably certain that assassins don't have soft hands."

"That is the biggest pile of—" She stopped as a silver-haired server slid their drinks on the table. "Thank you, Makena," she said in Common.

Micah's new wristcom translated her words, as well as Makena's "you're welcome," delivering the results via his earcuff in the voice of Lhyn Rivers.

"That's disconcerting," he said, tapping his ear. "Hearing Lhyn in my head."

"How is it working?"

"Perfectly. I'm impressed by how well it filters out background voices. There's only one voice I want to hear." He raised his glass.

"We're not twenty," she grumbled, fighting back a smile. "Let's not act like it."

"Romance is not reserved for the young." He took an experimental sip of the violet drink, pleasantly startled when it fizzed on his tongue and tickled his throat. Only when it was gone did he notice the crisp taste. "Delicious. Rahel was right."

"She knows her spirit-free drinks." Alejandra's first taste was accompanied by a happy hum. "Did you know she brought five Alsean fighter crews here a few days ago? Quite a raucous party, from what I heard."

"She mentioned it on our flight up. How are you feeling about her new assignment?"

Her glass clicked back to the table. "How am I feeling about a likely death sentence? Wonderful, why do you ask?"

She had so much in common with Realta that it was no surprise he had fallen for her. Their great hearts and love of learning surely came from the same source, despite their different species. At times like this, however, he marveled at the contrasts. Realta had spoken easily of her emotions, but Alejandra could guard hers as if they were treasures under siege. She veered between two extremes, one moment sharing herself with a thoughtless touch as no Alsean would, the next withdrawing behind walls of stone.

"Candini is the best pilot on Alsea," he said. "Rahel is the best at grappling. She said their strategy is to let go of the cable if they need to dodge weapons fire, then catch it again when they can. They'll have eleven other fighters helping. They won't be a sitting target."

She stared at him in silence, then reached into the bag she had brought from her office.

He propped his head on a fist while she pulled out a sketch pad and pencil, flipped the pad to a clean page, and began to draw. A few quick strokes later, she turned the pad to face him. Though the sketch was the merest outline, he easily recognized a rail gun shooting a projectile that had separated into five components.

She tapped the outer parts with her pencil. "When one of these is fired, the sabot falls away in four pieces while the projectile keeps going."

"Very similar to our design," he said with a nod.

"What happens to your sabot components?"

"They fall to the gr—oh."

She nodded. "In a long battle, or one between multiple ships, there might be thousands of these rocketing around."

He could see where this was leading.

"Now add the projectiles that missed their target or bounced off a ship's shield. Then the shield breakers and missiles that didn't fully atomize on impact, or didn't impact at all. We call it battle trash. Fighters are small; their shields can only handle a finite number of these impacts. That's why they leave a battle the moment their shields are compromised. At that point, weapons fire isn't the biggest threat. Weapons can be seen and tracked by the fighter's systems. Battle trash comes out of nowhere. And where will most of it be concentrated? Right around that damned elevator. If it hits a fighter without shields . . ." She paused.

"A quick and painless death?" He winced; those words had sounded better in his head.

The skin around her eyes tightened. "Only if it breaches the fusion core. If it penetrates both the outer and inner hulls, that's a slower and nastier death. They can't eject the cockpit pod then. Unless the hole is small enough to seal, they'll die in vacuum. That's assuming they're not impaled, shredded, or dismembered by shrapnel. We've been doing simulations of those sorts of injuries. I already told Rahel she'd better not put our skills to the test. Two days later, I found out she was a thousand times more likely to need them. If this battle happens, her best chance of survival is for us to keep that elevator in one piece." She dropped the sketch to the table, tossed the pencil atop it, and scowled at her drink. "I need something with a little more kick."

While she tapped a new order into the embedded pad, he cast about for a means of defusing the tension.

"There is one advantage of battle trash," he said.

She looked up, her head tilted to one side.

"It's what we used for the space elevator counterweight. After Ekatya destroyed an entire Voloth invasion group."

As he had hoped, the reminder of Ekatya's past victory lightened her expression. "I remember hearing about that when the cleaner ships were sent out. It was an ingenious use of the high-mass pieces left from those ships."

"That reminds me. Rahel said the dummy missiles and shield breakers are designed to atomize on impact. I forgot to ask her what happens if they don't. Do you send out crews to collect them, too? Or do they self-destruct?"

She tore the page out of her sketch pad, held it up, and ripped it down the center. Then she put the two pieces together and tore them in half. After four repetitions, she opened her hands and let the confetti flutter to the table.

He folded his arms. "You could have said yes."

"I could have, but that felt better."

She wasn't entirely joking. Over the next few ticks, she displayed an ability to compartmentalize fears that was worthy of a warrior.

Realta had been all scholar, he thought as she illustrated a medbay story with graceful hand gestures. He would never have discussed weaponry or battle tactics with her. Alejandra was a fascinating mix of scholar and warrior, more one than the other depending on the need of the moment.

Her hands came to rest on the table when Makena arrived to exchange their empty glasses. The new drinks were a brilliant orange with swirls of deeper red.

Micah eyed his doubtfully. "What is it?"

"A Neutron Star. The name should give you a clue." She took a sip and licked her lips. "Mm."

He knew a challenge when he saw one.

The drink seared off his throat lining on the way down, stronger than his preferred grain spirits at home, and his tongue needed several pipticks to recover from the shock. First he thought he'd lost his taste buds. Then the flavors hit, hot and peppery.

He wiped his eyes. "Invigorating."

She made an odd choking noise, then gave up and laughed uproariously. He grinned, delighted at this result. Alejandra loose and happy was one of his favorite sights.

Still chuckling, she took a much larger drink and swallowed with visible relish. "I should warn you, in case you're getting ideas that involve warrior pride. Don't try to keep up with me when it comes to drinking."

"You're half my size!"

"But my liver is *very* experienced."

The Neutron Star smoothed out considerably after the first few sips. Halfway down the glass, Micah was beginning to appreciate it. By the end, he concluded that it was one of the finest drinks he'd ever had.

"Stars above, I think you're tipsy off one glass," Alejandra said as she steered him into the lift.

"Impossible."

"Possible, given the potency of the spirits and the fact that our systems are slightly different. Alsean spirits affected me more than I exp—whoa."

He had pinned her to the back of the lift and bent to kiss the elegant column of her neck. "You always smell delicious here."

"Just there?" Amusement rose through her skin.

"Everywhere, but particularly here."

"Micah."

"Mm?"

"You need to stop."

"Why?"

"Because we're here and Commander Lokomorra is curious."

He straightened and turned to the lift doors he hadn't heard open. "Commander, well met," he said, before remembering that few crew members spoke High Alsean.

The commander's forked beard and eye tattoos gave him a ferocious look that was entirely belied by his grin. "Well met, Colonel."

"You have an Alsean language chip?"

"I'm the executive officer of the warship assigned to Alsea. If I didn't have this chip, I wouldn't get much done. And you've just solved a mystery for me. I was wondering why so many medbay staff were talking about Dr. Wells's good mood today."

"I'd appreciate it if you wouldn't spread this around," Alejandra said.

"That you have an Alsean lover, or that I caught you in the lift?"

"I've already advertised my Alsean lover," she said archly.

Micah frowned. When had she done that?

"But I'd like to maintain my professional reputation, if you don't mind." She led him past the commander.

"Dr. Wells, what you do off duty is your own affair." Lokomorra snickered as he entered the lift. She was still glaring at him when the doors shut.

"Why was he laughing?" Micah followed her down the quiet corridor.

"Because he thinks bad puns qualify as humor. Oh, stars, not you too," she groaned when he chuckled. "It took you that long to put it together? You really are intoxicated." She tapped the pad next to a door and walked through, stopping just on the other side. "Welcome to my home."

Fascinated, he began to prowl.

Across from the door, a high stool was tucked under a long table crowded with paintbrushes of various sizes, colorfully stained rags, and racks holding small pots. He knew she used painting as a means of stress relief, but holding one of her brushes brought a new level of meaning. This was not her telling him what she loved. This was him being given access to her truth.

Niches in the wall held plants unlike any he had seen before. Larger plants dotted the living area, tucked next to chairs and filling corners. It felt like the home of a producer.

"You should show these to Salomen," he said.

When she didn't reply, he looked around to find her in the small kitchen at the other end of the living area. Focused on a device atop the counter, she hadn't heard him.

He scanned the remainder of the room. There was a desk just outside the kitchen, a dining table nearly as cluttered as the painting area, comfortable reading chairs, and an oddly bare wall taking up the length of the room from kitchen to entry. A doorway to his left led to what must be her bedroom.

"Phoenix, set display to Allendohan Firefall and play Xhaline atmo collection."

He twitched as the bare wall came to life, transforming to a window that overlooked a breathtaking alpine valley. In the foreground, a field of blue and yellow wildflowers provided colorful contrast to the rugged, sheer cliff dominating the scene. A few determined trees clung to its barren surface, but what drew his eye was the magnificent waterfall, glowing such a bright orange that it appeared to be an endless stream of fire. Music floated out from an unseen source, gentle and relaxing, a type of wind instrument accompanied by strings and soft percussion.

Alejandra appeared next to him, holding up the Gaian version of a skinspray. "Let me take care of those excess spirits."

A tiny sting hissed at his throat.

"Impressive," he said as the fog receded. "I didn't realize I was that drunk."

"You were cute, though."

"Please refrain from using that term. Vallcat kittens are cute. Fully grown, battle-proven warriors are—"

"Adorable?"

His scowl only amused her more.

"The waterfall is from Lhyn's home world," she said, waving him toward one of the reading chairs. "The music is from mine. I need to discuss something with you."

"Is this about the test?" He sank into the chair and watched her take the other in her usual way: sideways, with knees drawn up.

"The test? No, that doesn't need discussion." She set the skinspray device on the table between them. "I've been offered a job on Alsea."

"Prime Scholar Yaserka," he guessed, remembering the bouquet in her State House suite.

"He wants me to establish a new healing center with hybrid treatments and equipment. We'd combine the best of Protectorate and Alsean medicine." Her expression made him yearn to touch her, to *feel* the excitement he could see. "It's the opportunity of a lifetime. But I can't build a new healing center in a cycle or two and go back to Fleet. It would be a career change. I'd leave this behind forever. I don't know if I'm ready to do that."

"Where would you be based?"

"Blacksun."

His mind flooded with fantasies, each more enticing than the last: meeting her for midmeal at a moment's notice, taking walks in the State Park, showing her the most beautiful parts of Alsea . . .

Living with her.

He forced the images away. "Would this be a challenge for you?"

"Shippers, yes. A challenge and a learning experience." Her gaze drifted to the waterfall behind him. "And a chance to do something that will outlive me."

"Are you challenged here?"

"Honestly? I'm at the top of my field. The only place to go from here is heading up a department at Fleet Medical. I can't think of anything I'd hate more. Politics," she added shortly. "But Alsea would be an endless challenge. And there's the other benefit. Being closer to you."

He was afraid his elation was showing. "I didn't want to assume I'd factor into your considerations."

Her eyebrows rose. "After what we've said to each other?"

"That doesn't necessarily have weight in career decisions," he said carefully. "Not this early. I'd consider it a gift from Fahla to have you so close, but you would be far from others you care for."

"That's the sticking point," she said with a sigh. "Leaving Rahel would be difficult enough. Leaving Ekatya . . . I don't know if I can. She's in a hard place."

"She is," he agreed. "And she treasures you. But I can guess what she'd say if you told her what you're telling me."

Distractedly, she slid the wooden sticks from her hair, letting it tumble around her shoulders. One stick landed with a clatter on the side table; the other began dancing between her fingers. "She'd tell me to go, I know. But I can't stand the thought of her dealing with Admiral Asshead alone." She smiled at his expression. "That's what Lhyn calls him. It's all right, you can laugh. Shippers know that's the only thing we *can* laugh at when it comes to him. He's a political plant. Incompetent as a battle group commander but damned good at making people miserable."

"I hope he hasn't hidden spy cams in your quarters, too. That comment might be enough to get you in trouble."

"No, we're safe. I checked while you were admiring my worktable."

His stomach dropped. "I was joking!"

"I don't check every day. Not like Ekatya," she said, as if that should be reassuring. "If he did plant any, she scared him enough to pull them out. But I'm probably a close second behind her on the least-favorite-officer list."

"Because of . . . ?" He gestured between them.

"He can't possibly know about us yet. I did a genetic project for your government," she reminded him. "Greve was furious when I told him I turned over my data and kept no copies. In his world, that's called misplaced loyalties. It doesn't matter that I did that on my own time."

"Shouldn't we be more discreet, then? You told Commander Lokomorra you advertised me."

Confusion creased her brow. "Oh, that. I've never taken a man to the Blue Rocket before. Well," she amended, "I have, but they were all in Fleet Medical uniforms and talking about work. Makena, our server? He was grinning at us every time I glanced over."

"And how many people will he tell?"

"Eventually? Everyone. I'm not going to hide you."

"You can refuse to hide without actively telling. Alejandra—" He paused, looking for the right words. "Is it possible that you're unconsciously sabotaging yourself? To force a decision?"

She stared at him, the endlessly twirling stick coming to a halt between her fingers. "I don't know. I don't think so. I've never been one to let people tell me what I can do."

"Words for Fahla." He checked his wristcom. "Which does make you a good choice for the projection, loathe as I am to admit it. It's almost time. Are you absolutely sure you want to do this?"

The stick resumed its motion. "I'm absolutely sure I'm the only one who can. Ekatya can't risk asking anyone else."

He had hit the farthest moon when Tal told him. The divine tyrees had done as much as they could with Rahel. Once Salomen learned to reach her even in orbit, they needed to switch to a Gaian mind—and to real empathic force.

This was a dress rehearsal, a projection to force obedience on a resistant target.

"I'm glad you came," Alejandra said softly. "I really do appreciate it."

"Of course I came. You asked." He watched the stick increase its speed and could no longer tolerate the distance.

She looked up as he left the chair, then dropped the stick when he bent to slide his arms around her. "Thank you," she murmured, resting her head against his chest.

He was still holding her when Ekatya arrived five ticks later.

25

ORBITAL TEST

They gathered in an open meadow on the State House grounds, having long since learned that line of sight made a difference. Not a large one, but given what they were attempting today, every bit of power might be necessary.

Salomen stood apart from the divine tyrees, taking her usual time to prepare. By now, she knew these people nearly as well as her field workers, an intimacy that worked both ways. They understood her need to be alone before becoming the head of their collective force.

She pressed her hands against a sallgreen tree at the edge of the meadow, letting the rough bark bite into her skin as she leaned in. These orbital jumps stretched her thinner than she had ever been, but loading her senses with textures and scents helped. The physical memory of rough bark, fuzzy hairgrass, or the prickly twigs of sallgreen; the invigorating scent of winterbloom and the soothing comfort of a crumbled cinnoralis leaf—these sensations grounded her when she flung her spirit self into the stars and aided her reintegration when she returned.

Leaning more heavily onto the trunk, she turned her head toward the path that wound past her and into the shadows of the ancient trees. She wished she could step onto it and walk away.

In a few ticks, she would be committing assault. Legal, approved assault, authorized and consented to, but assault nevertheless.

Her hands dragged down the bark as she straightened, leaving small bits stuck to her palms. She dusted them off, focusing on the change in texture from rough, rolling debris to smooth skin, then reached up to snap off a small twig. From this she plucked a needlelike leaf, rubbed it between her fingers, and held it to her nose. The brisk scent brought to mind deep forest and winter cold, a vibrant contrast to the sunny meadow behind her.

Still holding the twig in one hand, she retrieved her earcuff from her pocket and slid it into place.

"Activate," she said. "Are we ready?"

"Ready, tyrina. Micah is with Alejandra, and Ekatya just called. Linking you now."

Andira had the Gaian pad that had been modified to accept communications from their earcuffs. It would allow Salomen to speak with Ekatya from here while mindwalking in orbit, a necessity if they were to adapt the test on the fly. Andira would remain on the channel and be joined by Gehrain, who was overseeing their security today.

Ekatya's voice sounded in her ear. *"Salomen? We're all here. Alejandra's on the call."*

She closed her hand around the spiky twig and stared at the path beneath the trees. "Alejandra, how are you?"

"Nervous," came the crisp reply. *"Wanting to be done with it."*

No more delays, then. Turning her back on temptation, she faced a meadow full of people. "I must ask you one more time. Do you consent?"

"I consent."

"All right. I'm going into the center now."

Her boots swished through grass bearing the tiny yellow flowers of late spring. The grounds were ringing with birdsong, the air was laden with the delicious fragrance that only appeared when the soil warmed, and she was about to harm Corozen's lover and a potential friend.

That potential might be gone a tentick from now.

The divine tyrees were in position, arranged in a geometric pattern around the center where Andira waited for her. Salomen walked between them and knew without looking that they were closing ranks behind her.

Andira reached for her as soon as she could, pulling their bodies close. "What is it today?" she asked.

Salomen showed her the sallgreen twig, then crushed another leaf and held it up.

"Early morning runs in the Snowmounts," Andira said, and inhaled a second time. "On a cold autumn day with a cloudless sky."

"Winter for me. Deep in the woods by Blacksun Base." She rolled the crushed leaf between her fingers, releasing more of the scent, and filled her lungs. After two more breaths, she dropped the used leaf and held out the twig.

Andira carefully stored it in her jacket pocket, then slid one hand along Salomen's jaw and the other behind her neck. "Initiating."

Salomen matched her hand positions and rested their foreheads together.

The surge of power no longer jolted them. They were long used to it and welcomed it as an extension of themselves, holding it close and ready.

Two hands came down on the back of her neck, warm and familiar: Pilannon and Savisi. Behind Andira, Jorsil and his bondmate were making the same connection. They initiated their own Sharing, completing the circuit and sending a new surge of power.

Others added to it, couple by couple, in a smooth flow they had perfected over moons of training. Salomen had watched hologram play-backs and seen how it looked from the outside: a series of silent explosions of light, enveloping each couple until the whole group seemed to be in a shifting sphere of flame.

Once she separated, that power would flow inward, lighting her and Andira until the brightness of the playback became difficult to watch. She often wished she could see it in real time.

"I don't feel anything," Alejandra observed.

"She hasn't made the jump yet," said Ekatya. *"I'll tell you when we're ready."*

"That's a damn slow weapon, then."

"It's time to isolate you. Phoenix, remove Dr. Wells from this call."

Reassured by Alejandra's crankiness, Salomen reached inside herself and released the lock. Her empathic senses unfurled, bringing the joyous rush of freedom.

Her first separation, at the age of ten, had been so incomprehensible to her young mind that she decided it hadn't happened. Her second, just fifteen moons ago, had been uncontrolled and traumatic for everyone.

She had full control over it now. The power she once feared she now embraced, glorying in its strength and the places it could take her.

Somewhere overhead, the *Phoenix* orbited with more than one thousand and two hundred minds aboard. It was easier to locate than Rahel and Ekatya in a shuttle. Two minds were a mere speck of emotional output in the vastness of near orbit, but Ekatya's crew created a beacon that drew her in.

She gathered her strength and leaped.

The shift was instantaneous, the power of thirty-one divine tyrees added to her own and driving her at the speed of thought.

"This isn't where I thought I'd land." She turned in place, taking in the rows of high racks bursting with alien plants. A vine laden with black-and-red flowers dangled in the space her shoulder occupied, and she traced it to a tree branch overhead. The tree itself soared upward, its top brushing the ceiling four decks above.

"Where are you?" Andira's voice was soft, speaking to the physical body she had left far behind.

"Hydroponics."

"It makes sense, in truth. It's the part of the ship where you're most comfortable."

"Not very useful for a Voloth ship, though, is it?"

"Try to locate the bridge," Andira urged. "Look for a concentration of minds that are—"

"Like Andira," said Ekatya. *"Look for the ones that feel like her."*

Salomen closed her eyes and focused. There were so many minds here, a roar of emotion pouring past in a torrent. She listened to the flow, waiting for something that felt right.

There. A bright point, confidence and power and fierce focus on the task at hand, all leavened by concern. She reached for it and leaped again.

With a startled laugh, she said, "I'm not on the bridge."

Ekatya spun around, eyes wide with the shock that blasted her senses. "Salomen?"

"You can see me?" Salomen blurted. Dazzled by the dual voices, she reduced the volume of her earcuff. More sparks of surprise hit as Corozen and Alejandra stood up from their chairs, looking first at Ekatya and then around the room.

"No, but I can hear you. From two different sources. Phoenix, reduce my com volume by eighty percent. Salomen, say something."

"Tell Alejandra that I'd like a tour of her indoor garden."

"Shekking Mother," Ekatya gasped. "I really can hear you. How is that possible when Lhyn's not in the link?"

"Because Salomen is separated?" Andira guessed. "It does augment her powers by a considerable degree. Or it could be the combined power we're feeding her."

"We'll have to experiment," Salomen said. "Find out whether it's me or the thirty-one divine tyrees behind me."

Ekatya nodded, still dazed. "Right. We will. Great galaxies, this is unbelievable. You're *here*."

"That was the point, wasn't it?"

"Yes, but—" She shook her head and took control with an effort that rippled across Salomen's senses. "Let's do this. Alejandra, I need to speak with Micah privately before we start. May we use your bedroom? Or you can go in the bedroom and we'll stay here."

"Go." Alejandra waved a hand.

Though visibly uncomfortable, Corozen straightened his shoulders and followed Ekatya.

Left alone in the room, Alejandra fidgeted, wrapping her arms around her torso and beating out a rhythm with her fingers. Giving up on that, she picked up a thin stick from the table between the chairs and flipped it through her fingers with the ease of long practice.

"I have to say, the idea of you being here and not being able to see or hear you is discomfiting." Her gaze was fixed on the spinning bit of wood.

"I understand." Salomen was compelled to answer. "I think I should take you out for evenmeal. We can speak the way we haven't had a chance to yet."

"I'd like to get to know you better," Alejandra continued. "You and Tal are so important to Micah, and he's . . . becoming very important to me." The stick changed directions. "Sainted Shippers, I don't recognize my life anymore. For all I know, I'm talking to myself." She cast a quick look around the room and refocused on her stick. "About making a future with a man who isn't of my species. That's crazy enough, but my other option is that I'm talking to an apparition who used an incomprehensible power to send her mind into orbit. To think my biggest concern three years ago was whether or not I should stay in Fleet."

Salomen didn't know how many cycles three years came out to, but she could guess.

"*Salomen,*" Ekatya said on her earcuff. "*We're ready. Is she?*"

"Just a moment." She watched Alejandra, still spinning the stick, and reminded herself that she had consent. "I'm sorry," she whispered, and reached into her unshielded mind.

It was easy, too easy. Much simpler than projecting on Rahel, who had the built-in shielding of all Alseans. "She's ready."

Alejandra's head snapped up as the bedroom door opened. She relaxed her arm—but still held the stick, Salomen noted—and turned to face Ekatya as she emerged.

"We've had a little accident. I was prepping Micah and, well . . ." Ekatya gestured at Corozen, who stepped out holding a blood-soaked cloth wrapped around his wrist.

"What did you do?" Horrified, Alejandra dropped the stick and started forward.

"Stop," Ekatya said.

She stopped instantly, compelled to obey with Salomen's projection in her mind. But she still had her voice. "Ekatya, I need to treat him. It's his wrist, for the love of flight, that's too much blood. It looks like you nicked a vein!"

Ekatya shook her head. "It doesn't matter. You can't treat him."

"I can't—" Her mouth moved silently. "I can't treat him."

She was resisting, but it was the helpless wriggling of a mouse trapped in the talons of a great bird of prey. Salomen almost let go, sickened by the tiny beating of a will against her own.

"Hold on," Andira whispered. "Just a tick or two longer."

The will in her grip beat more weakly. A few steps away, Alejandra looked at Corozen with agony written on her face. "I'm sorry. I'm so sorry. Please, you have to go to medbay. Right now."

"No." Ekatya's voice was steady, belying her own turmoil. "We can't treat Alseans who aren't serving in Fleet. It's a new order; I only got it yesterday. He'll have to go back to Alsea."

The will surged, finding strength from a source beyond Salomen's grip. "With that much blood? Shek that order and take him to my medbay!"

"I can't disobey my orders. Neither can you. Tell Micah he'll have to go to Blacksun for treatment."

Obey, Salomen thought. She desperately did not want to go deeper than this.

Despair saturated the room as Alejandra clenched her trembling hands. "Micah, we can't treat you here. You have to go to Blacksun. Wrap that as tightly as you can, keep pressure on it, and hold it above your heart. If you compress the vein enough, you'll stop or at least slow the bleeding until someone else can help you."

"Fucking Hades." Ekatya closed her eyes. "Salomen, stop. We're done."

Salomen released her and sagged with relief. "She's free."

"You're—done? That was the test?" Alejandra crossed the room in a whirl of fury. "Let me see your wrist."

"It's artificial blood," Corozen said.

"Let me see your wrist!"

Hurriedly, he unwound the cloth and held out his arm. She seized it in a none-too-gentle hold, ran her fingers over the inside of his wrist, and let go with a growl.

"That was *low*. I thought you'd order me to do something embarrassing. Or stupid. I can't believe you'd force me to go against—dammit!" She turned away, anger collapsing into anguish.

"Alejandra," Ekatya began.

"Don't you even speak to me," she snarled. "Either of you!"

They looked at each other in distress and did not see her wipe her eyes.

Salomen's heart was breaking. "Put her back on the call. Then I want everyone else off. This is between me and her."

After a reluctant pause, Ekatya conceded. "Phoenix, transfer this call to Dr. Wells."

Alejandra shook her head and stalked toward the kitchen.

"Alejandra," Salomen said.

"I don't want to talk to you, either."

"Dr. Wells," Andira said formally. "Please accept our apologies and our deepest gratitude. We will speak later."

In the kitchen, Alejandra pulled a square bottle from a cupboard.

"You and Corozen need to go," Salomen said.

Ekatya nodded miserably. "Come on," she said, tugging Corozen by the arm. He went unwillingly, never taking his eyes off Alejandra until he was through the door.

She kept her back to him.

"It's just us," Salomen assured her.

"Did you not hear me say I don't want to talk to you?"

"I heard. I also heard what you said earlier, about getting to know me."

With a snort, Alejandra scooped up the short glass she had just filled and turned to lean against the counter. "You could hardly have picked a worse time."

"I'm so sorry about the test. Will you let me explain why we chose that?"

"To tear my heart in half?"

"Because if I have to do that for real, I'll be forcing a Voloth captain to disobey orders. You know what happens to Voloth soldiers who disobey."

Alejandra silently sipped her drink, but she was listening.

"I may even have to force them to act against deeply held beliefs. Making you do something foolish or embarrassing would not have been enough."

"I understand the logic. I still don't want to talk to you."

It was a lie. She was wounded and covering it with anger that might have deceived a Gaian, but it did not deceive Salomen. Alejandra had chosen not to end this call.

"Would you mind if I talked to you, then?"

Silently, she waved a hand.

"I'd like to get to know you better, too. So would Andira. You're important to Corozen, and he's precious to us."

"Corozen," she scoffed. "Don't you know he prefers Micah?"

"I'm the only one who calls him that. Me and my family. We're producers; the warrior family name tradition doesn't come naturally to us. He made an allowance for us, and I didn't realize until later how great an allowance that was. But he didn't have to do that for you. You're a scholar who understands warriors."

"I'm not understanding them at the moment. I asked him here to *support* me. Not take part in that—" With a jerky movement, she lifted her glass and took a gulp.

"We had planned to use Rahel. Corozen told us that would be worse for you."

She paused, then set her glass on the counter and crossed her arms. "He was right about that, at least."

"Please believe me when I say I'm sorry. I've been dreading this test for a nineday."

That held her attention. "Why?"

"Because I had to act against some deeply held beliefs."

Alejandra tilted her head, comprehension expanding through the room.

"Until now, it was all distance testing and making Rahel happy. This is the first time I had to do something . . . damaging. I wanted it to be Commander Lokomorra. Someone I wouldn't have to look in the eye afterward."

Her stiff posture crumbled as she dropped her face in her hands. "What a sewage sump. I'm hurt, you're hurt, Ekatya hated to ask me, Micah—damn."

"I know. But it had to be done. We cannot be learning how this works during a Voloth attack. I couldn't even find the bridge today."

"Is that where you were trying to go?"

"At the start. I landed in hydroponics first."

Alejandra's lips thinned as a faint glimmer of humor showed through. "Not the best tactical option."

"Ekatya told me to look for minds that felt like Andira. That brought me straight here."

"To her." A tiny smile lifted one side of her mouth. "Only Ekatya would think that was useful advice, because only she would think she's not unique on this ship. You want to find the bridge on a Voloth ship? Look for the highest concentration of arrogance. The minds that don't care how much harm they do, because it's their prerogative."

"That's . . . good advice," Salomen said slowly.

They were silent then, and she wondered if she should break the link. Alejandra was feeling better, the razor edges of her pain blunted by under-standing. Surely Ekatya and Corozen would be better options now?

"Salomen."

"Yes?"

"That moment when Ekatya told me to stop—" She cleared her throat. "I couldn't move. It didn't even occur to me that it was possible. Is that what happened to Rahel? When she was seventeen?"

"Yes," Salomen whispered. "He froze her in place, and then he hurt her."

Alejandra retrieved her glass and drank off a sizable amount. "He deserved to die."

There was no good response to that.

"If she hadn't killed him, if he was caught, what would have happened?"

"It's the worst crime possible. He would have been buried underground in the fifth level of the Pit for the rest of his miserable life."

"Good." She tipped back the remainder of her glass, slapped it on the counter, and crossed her arms again. "You asked for my consent three times. And apologized I don't know how many times in the past five ticks. You're not like him."

"No. But I still hurt you."

She acknowledged that with a nod. "You have powers that defy medical understanding. They're fearsome in a way I never comprehended before now. I'm glad you're on our side."

"I'm glad you are, too." Salomen spoke automatically, the diplomatic words covering her dawning realization: Alejandra was not afraid. Despite the pain that still radiated from her, she did not fear its cause.

She had offered absolution.

Gratitude made Salomen's voice catch. "Thank you. Andira will say it on behalf of Alsea, but I'm speaking for myself. Thank you for not—for understanding."

Alejandra dropped her head back and took a deep breath. "I'd say you're welcome, but nothing about that was welcome. Thank you for staying. It did help. You already know that, don't you?"

"I'm . . . happy to sense that you're feeling better."

"Less likely to take the heads off those two, at least. Isn't this using an enormous amount of power? Go home. We can keep talking the old-fashioned way."

"You're not ending the call?"

"I'm not ready to talk to them yet. But this is the first chance I've had to really talk to you. Unless you have other plans?"

"I have no other plans. Give me a moment, I'm going now."

She remembered a time when returning to her body had been an effort. Now it was an anchor, calling her back. As soon as she thought of it, standing in a sunny meadow with the State House domes towering behind, she landed with a jarring impact.

Her senses collapsed in a tangled confusion, no longer fitting this unresponsive receptacle. She barely managed to drag her eyes open.

Andira broke the Sharing at the same moment and pulled the sall-green twig from her pocket. Moving swiftly, she yanked off several leaves and clamped them between her teeth, then lifted Salomen's hand and closed it around the twig.

The pointy, prickly twig jolted her physical body out of its stasis. While she instinctively clenched her hand, increasing the pressure and the sensory input, Andira retrieved the leaves, crushed them, and held them beneath her nose.

Winter in deep forest, hiking a trail with Fianna.

Autumn in the Snowmounts, watching Andira run beneath a cloudless sky.

Home. She was home, in her true body, its physical senses waking and working together once more. Her spirit self was no longer adrift, sucking all of her physical energy with it.

She lifted a heavy hand to close her fingers around Andira's wrist. "I'm all right. I'm here."

Andira dropped the leaves and wrapped her in a warmron. "Welcome back. You did an extraordinary job, tyrina. I'm sorry it was so hard for you."

Salomen's arms dangled; she had no strength to hold her. "Will you take care of them? I need some time."

"I'll take care of them after I take care of you. You're still wobbly."

"We're fine," Jorsil assured them. "Ready to stampede over to the food table. We don't need you for that."

"Thank you," Andira said gratefully. "I'll be there in a few ticks."

Jorsil moved off with his bondmate, calling to the others and leading them away. Only Pilannon and Savisi remained.

"She sounds like a special person," Pilannon said. "Tell her we're all sorry."

"We didn't mean to overhear," Savisi hastened to add. "It's impossible when we're right behind you. What she did took a lot of courage. What you did took just as much." She rested a hand on Salomen's shoulder, a gesture few Alseans would dare to make. "I've been afraid of this test since the beginning. I'm not anymore. You'll never use us badly."

The warmth from her hand spread along Salomen's spine, adding a small amount of light and energy to the river pouring in from Andira. It was enough to tip the balance, awakening her muscles.

She patted Savisi's hand clumsily, still getting used to her physical self. "Thank you. I'll tell her."

Savisi let Pilannon tug her away. They hadn't gotten two steps before Salomen wrapped her arms around Andira. "Thank Fahla I have you to come back to."

"You always will." Andira's relief brightened their link. "Is Alejandra all right?"

"She's recovering. I think we need to recover together." Salomen kissed her and stepped back, taking a sniff of the sallgreen twig she still held. "This truly helped. Food would help more."

"I'll bring it to you."

"I'll be over there." She pointed to the tree line.

"Five ticks," Andira promised, and jogged toward the food table.

Salomen began walking, each step easier than the one before. "Alejandra. Are you still there?"

"Still here. Working on my second drink."

"Do spirits put you in a better mood or a worse one?"

"In this case, there was nowhere to go but up. That sounded like you had a rough landing."

Once a healer, always a healer, she thought. "The worst yet, but now I know what to expect."

"Sensory disorientation and loss of proprioception?"

"How do you know that from what you heard?"

"It's what I didn't hear, along with several deep breaths that weren't about respiration. They were about inhaling. I'm guessing you used sensory intervention. Something sharp-smelling?"

"It's no mystery why Ekatya thinks so highly of you. Yes, it was sallgreen leaves this time. But how did you know about the loss of proprioception?"

"Educated guess. You were in orbit one piptick and on the ground the next. I can't imagine your body processing a shift that massive without a few hiccups along the way." Her tone grew admonishing. *"I assume you have a qualified healer on site."*

"Healer Wellernal has been consulting from the beginning."

"Then where the shek was he just now?"

She was glad Alejandra couldn't see her smile. "Over by the food and supplies. Once Andira knew what to do, we found that I recover faster if she's the one helping me. No matter how confused my body might be, it always recognizes her."

"Astonishing. And sweet," Alejandra added a beat later.

Salomen passed beneath the branches of the first tree, a thousand times lighter than when she had walked out.

"Tell me about meeting Tal. How did you know she was the one for you?"

"I didn't. I detested her on sight."

Alejandra laughed for the first time. *"That sounds like a story."*

Settling on a bench beside the path, Salomen said, "Then let me tell you."

26

CHECK-IN 2

E katya stepped into the lift and hesitated. She was almost certain Commander Lokomorra had been joking when he said the ship's computer was now accepting an alternative designation for Admiral Greve.

Almost.

"Admiral Asshead's office," she said.

The lift hummed into action, its lights shifting to the blue cast that meant she was in motion.

"For the love of flight." She had to laugh. If Greve checked this security footage, he was going to be incandescent.

The doors opened, revealing a location that was decidedly not Greve's office.

She leaned against the wall of the lift, roaring with laughter until her ribs hurt and she was gasping. "That's rich. That is *inspired*. Serrado to Commander Przepyszny!"

"Yes, Captain." Her operations section chief was prompt as always.

"I've just learned of an appalling act of disrespect toward our battle group commander. It seems the ship's computer has been reprogrammed. If you ask the lift to take you to, er, Admiral Asshead's office—"

"Admiral who?"

"Don't make me say it again, Zeppy."

"I think I can piece it together."

"Sure you can. I just tested it and I'm standing in front of, ah hah hah hah . . ." Her head thumped back against the wall as an uncontrollable burst of laughter seized her diaphragm. "Waste reclamation," she managed in a tiny voice before doubling over.

"What?" Zeppy began to chortle, which only made her laugh harder. *"I assure you, Captain, I had no idea."*

"It doesn't seem your style." She wiped a tear and inhaled, only to let out a guffaw that actually hurt her nose. "I'm not laughing. I'm absolutely furious at this behavior."

"Yes, I can hear your fury."

"Good. Then you know I want this fixed."

"I'll get right on it. It'll be done by next week at the latest."

"Zeppy . . ."

"We have a backlog of repair issues, Captain. This is minor."

"It'll be major if Greve hears about it." She envisioned his face and laughed again. "Well, Commander, I've done my duty by informing you. Time for my daily check-in."

"Might be two weeks," Zeppy grumbled.

"I didn't hear that." She cut the call and put a hand to her aching stomach.

The last few days had taken her so high and so low that it was a wonder she wasn't getting motion sickness. She'd had a sublime date with Andira, followed by the joy of watching Rahel walk free—and returned yesterday to inflict deliberate, sickening cruelty on Alejandra. She didn't think she would ever forget that anguished expression, or the fury mere seconds later.

Poor Micah had never seen Alejandra under full sail, much less had it directed at him. He had been devastated and sick with worry. She had taken him to her quarters, where they spoke with Andira first, then with Salomen more than an hour later. Her advice was to let Alejandra come to them.

It had been a long wait. Alejandra finally appeared after midnight, no longer angry but not her normal self, either. She accepted Ekatya's apology, even hugged her, but had little to say except that she understood and it was all right.

It didn't feel all right. Which probably explained why Ekatya was here now, still chuckling over a juvenile prank. She had to get control of herself in time to face Greve.

"Right," she said aloud. "Admiral Greve's office."

Sadly, that command worked. Even more sadly, his adjutant was playing no games today and showed her in without delay.

"Ah, Captain, right on time." Greve was in a jovial mood. "I've decided that if both of us have to go through this ridiculous charade, we might as well enjoy it. Drink?" He pulled a copper flask from his desk drawer and held it up. "Naalian tonic, the real stuff. Not from a matter printer."

She hesitated. Drinking on duty was actionable, but refusing an invitation from an admiral was also problematic. "Thank you," she said politely. "I'm afraid I never developed a taste for it."

"Then you've never had the good stuff. Please, I insist." He produced matching cups and poured a measure in each. "Sit, sit."

After months of open hostility, this was unnerving. "You'll be wasting that on me," she said, settling into a guest chair.

"Educating a palate is never a waste." The cup flashed in the light as he held it out.

She accepted reluctantly but made no move to drink.

He lifted his cup and inhaled. "Ahh. Smell that? The hint of citrus? Matter printers never get that right."

Cautiously, she raised hers to her nose. "I can't say I ever noticed."

"What do you expect, getting your drinks from bars on ships and space stations? Some officers lose touch with what they're protecting. They spend too much time in space and not enough time dirtside, getting real sun and eating real food. This took years to make, not seconds. Go on, see the difference." He waited, his gaze sharp and his own drink untouched.

She held out her cup. "To the things we protect."

"To the things we protect." The cups made a muted *ting* as their rims touched, and his eyes never left hers as he sipped.

She moved more slowly, waiting until she saw him swallow before she allowed the liquid in her mouth to go down. It wasn't a drink she would ever ask for, but he was right about one thing: it was better than any Naalian tonic she'd had before.

"Interesting," she said, setting the cup on the desk. "Orange in the nose, lime on the tongue."

"You see? You'll never taste that in the Blue Rocket." His smile hardened. "I'm surprised you noticed, considering how focused you were on whether or not I was poisoning you."

It was useless to deny it, so she said nothing at all.

"It's a sad statement when Fleet officers can't trust one another, isn't it? I was thinking about this farce we play every day, where you lie and I have to accept it, and I thought, let's try something new. I'll offer a gesture of trust. If she accepts, I'll take her at her word." He held up his cup in a mocking toast, then tilted it back and swallowed. With a gusty exhale, he added, "You were right, Captain. It was wasted on you."

"Trust isn't built with a single gesture." She gestured at the two cups on the desk, one empty and the other nearly full. "And by your own admission, this was just another game."

"But a useful one. Let's play another, shall we? Commander Jonquart, is she here? Good, send her in."

The door opened, revealing the last person Ekatya expected.

"First Guard Sayana." He beckoned her in. "Have a seat."

Rahel's walk was confident, but Ekatya had worked with her long enough to see caution in the way she sat, spine straight and hands gripping the armrests for an instant launch into action.

Nothing she could say would prevent what was about to happen. Ekatya met her eyes, hoping she could sense the silent plea.

Rahel gave no indication as she faced forward.

"First Guard, do you understand the chain of command in Fleet?"

"I do."

"Then you know that I outrank Captain Serrado, and if I give you an order that countermands one of hers, mine is the one you must obey."

"I'm a warrior," Rahel said. "I've spent my life observing the chain of command."

"Have you ever disobeyed an order?"

"Never."

"Not even when obeying made you a criminal and an outcaste."

Rahel's outward calm faltered as she looked at Ekatya.

That fucking torquat. "I'm sorry. He has the security clearance to access the locked part of your file."

"Fascinating reading," Greve said. "I respect your integrity, First

230

Guard. In fact, I think you could teach Captain Serrado a few things in that department."

Rahel was silent, but the air around her crackled with tension.

"To that end, I have a job for you. I know you can tell when Gaians are lying. I'm about to ask Captain Serrado a series of questions. You will listen to her answers, and you will tell me if she's being truthful."

In her peripheral vision, Ekatya saw Rahel's knuckles whiten.

"I understand."

"Very good." Greve picked up his pad and made a show of accessing the file. "Captain Serrado, have you received instructions from Lancer Tal or any member of the Alsean government?"

Rahel stared at her in open shock.

"I have not." Ekatya kept her eyes on Greve and her expression calm, but she was seething. This was intentional humiliation, meant to damage her authority.

"First Guard?"

"True," Rahel said, still watching her.

Greve tapped his pad. "Has your command been mentally or emotionally influenced through your tyree bond?"

"It has not."

Rahel didn't confirm right away. Ekatya found herself compelled to meet her gaze as she waited.

"True."

"Interesting." Greve tapped again. "If you receive an order in conflict with anything you've promised Lancer Tal or your wife, how will you respond?"

"I will uphold my oath to the Protectorate."

This time, the pause was longer. "True," Rahel said at last.

Ekatya forced herself not to react.

"True today," Greve said with another tap to the pad. He looked over its edge to Ekatya. "But will it be true tomorrow?"

"Ask me then," Ekatya snapped.

"I will, of course. First Guard, thank you. You're both dismissed."

Rahel was silent as they walked down the corridor to the nearest lift. Once the doors shut, Ekatya said, "I apologize. You should never have been put in that position."

"Neither should you." Rahel's bearing was stiff. "Captain, I found some old *Resilere* damage in one of the chases that you should see. Do you have time?"

Anything amiss in a chase would be reported to Zeppy, not her. Rahel was speaking in code, but Ekatya didn't know what it meant.

"Show me," she said.

"Deck twenty-six, chase three-F."

They stood in silence until the doors reopened.

"This way."

Ekatya followed her down the corridor, through the limited access door, and into the noisy confines of the chase. Rahel negotiated the ramps over conduits with loose-jointed ease as she turned left, right, then left again before stopping beneath an overhead pipe. The air thrummed with rhythmic swooshes as water moved through.

"It's a dead spot," she said, indicating a circle on the deck two meters in diameter. "The nearest security cams don't reach this point, and the water noise means they won't pick up our voices."

"Should I be worried that you know this?"

"It's a hard habit to break. Captain, he hates you."

"I know." She rolled her shoulders, trying to loosen the painful knot between them. "Thank you for not telling him. I'm truly sorry you had to make that choice."

"That's no choice," Rahel said contemptuously. "He reads my private file and thinks he knows me? He knows nothing about me or my chain of command."

"I hesitate to ask," Ekatya said. "But if your chain of command doesn't mean Fleet, and it doesn't mean Alsean, what does it mean?"

"It *is* Alsean. Just adapted to Fleet in the best way I can. I obey orders from my superior officers, but you're my oath holder."

The matter-of-fact statement rocked her.

She had never been comfortable with the reality of a warrior sworn to her service. Her acute awareness of the potential for abuse made her cautious about the orders she gave and how she framed them.

She had thought Fleet's system far superior: a system built on loyalty to rank, not individuals. Loyalty that was quickly transferable, enabling a structure that could span vast distances and innumerable cultures. It was self-policing, with higher ranks being limited to those demonstrating the qualities required to hold that authority.

In theory, it was ideal. In practice, Greve was living proof of its flaws. The system she had spent her life serving was now being used against her. Today, it would have ended her career.

But Rahel had lied.

Months of discomfort gave way to overwhelming gratitude. Greve could pull rank until this sun went nova, but he would never turn Rahel.

"Thank you," she said again, her voice rough with emotion. "I can't tell you what it means to me that you made that choice. But I know you can feel it."

Rahel nodded, offering the courtesy of silence.

She pulled the clip from her hair and pocketed it, then ran her fingers through the loosened strands. "It worries me, though. How do Alseans deal with the temptation? Would you do anything I ordered you to?"

"Yes, unless it was illegal or—" Rahel frowned. "You're thinking of Shantu."

"I know it's not a fair comparison. The circumstances were unique and terrible. But you've given me a loyalty I didn't earn, and I—" She stopped at the incredulous look. "What?"

"It's just surprising that you can be so wrong."

"There goes my worry that you have too much respect for me," Ekatya said dryly. "Although after what Greve did, that probably wasn't an issue."

"Shekking blindworm," Rahel growled. "If he were an Alsean warrior, I'd report him to the nearest caste house. You could, too. Trying to humiliate you in front of your sworn warrior? And making me the tool for doing it?" She let loose a string of words that baffled Ekatya's language chip.

"Do I want to know what you just said?"

"No. On Alsea, our report would go on his permanent record. He'd be fined, and you could withdraw your oath of service with full caste approval. That would go on his record, too. Service is a gift, not an obligation. He's abusing yours."

Ekatya stared at her as the clouds parted. In all her worries about taking advantage, she had forgotten the built-in failsafe: Rahel had agency.

Rahel seemed to have come to an equally brilliant understanding.

"I had months of training in your system," she said. "Didn't anyone train you in mine?"

"Andira did. I know the basics. But she's hardly representative, is she? The leader of your entire caste."

"I refused her order once."

Ekatya put a hand on the overhead pipe, needing the support. "You can't be serious. You disobeyed your Lancer?"

"It was the day of the uprising. Salomen had no Guards, because we couldn't trust them after Demerah's betrayal. She burned herself out finding that sniper, and then she slept the rest of the day in a ground-floor salon. The security situation was a nightmare. Vellmar and I guarded her door until Lancer Tal called in reinforcements from her own Guard unit. She said we should get some rest. I told her she wasn't my oath holder."

Unbelievable. "What did she say?"

"That Salomen was fortunate to have me. And that she was better served by an alert, rested warrior than a stubborn one."

The laugh bubbled out of her throat. She pictured the scene, heard Andira's exasperated tones, and laughed again. "You are something else. No wonder she likes you."

"She does?" Rahel's eyes rounded. "Did she tell you that?"

"Not in so many words, but I know her."

She flicked a hand in a dismissive motion. "She tolerates me because of Salomen."

"She did in the beginning, yes. But she's come to appreciate you on her own terms. How many times has she given you advice?"

"Um. Quite a few."

"Andira Tal doesn't advise warriors she doesn't like. Didn't you realize she's mentoring you?"

"No!" Now it was Rahel reaching for the overhead pipe. "Fahla's farts and fantasies. I never even *imagined* that."

"It seems to be the day for it." She had never imagined her personal warrior saving her from her own superior officer, either.

"Shekking Mother on a burning boat," Rahel croaked.

Ekatya had never seen her so visibly overwhelmed. It was her turn to offer the courtesy of silence as Rahel hung her head and wiped her eyes with her free hand.

"Thank you for telling me." She did not look up. "It, um, it means a lot."

"You're welcome. Was that the last piece of your redemption?"

Something that was not quite a laugh shook her upper body. "It doesn't work that way, does it? Even if everyone else forgives, there's one person who never will." She rested a palm against her chest in illustration. "But Lancer Tal, of all people. Maybe it really is just me now."

She pulled herself together with remarkable speed, straightening and crossing her arms in a familiar stance. "May I tell you something, Captain? About my system?"

"Go ahead."

"You earned my loyalty the moment you accepted my oath even knowing what I'd done. You've earned it every day since then. It's in the way you lead this crew. You're so honorable that you worry about giving me orders. Honor is what counts for us, much more than rank. I would never serve someone like Greve. But I'm proud to serve you."

Ekatya stood beneath a gurgling pipe, in a security-blind spot that wasn't supposed to exist on her ship, and wondered why the most extraordinary moments of her life always happened in the strangest places.

Because she knew now. She had been fighting it for years, trying to hold on to an identity that once meant everything. Eventually she had accepted a hybridized role, a Fleet captain whose responsibilities included an alien culture in addition to her own.

That culture was alien no longer. It was hers.

Silently, she held up a palm. When Rahel met it, she interlaced their fingers.

Alseans could be so efficient. A single gesture to say so much: that their relationship was not solely professional, that they had helped each other and could expect more of each other than simple crew mates.

"I accept the gift of your service with a glad heart," she said in High Alsean.

Rahel inhaled sharply, then offered a breathtaking smile.

It was part of the oath of acceptance—the oath Salomen had spoken, and Ekatya had taken by proxy. But she had never said the words herself, because she had never considered herself a true oath holder.

Until now.

27

NEGOTIATION

With the last file sent on its way, Tal rolled up her reader card and shut down her office. Today had been a short one, with the afternoon reserved for the party at Hol-Opah. It had been Salomen's idea to host it as a way of rewarding the divine tyrees for their hard work. The success of yesterday's test meant it was now a victory party as well.

But first she had an errand to run. Blacksun Base was holding a special package for her, and while she hadn't personally arranged this surprise, she planned to take full advantage of it.

She had nearly made it out of her antechamber when her aide paused a call and said, "I think you'll want to accept this."

Her shoulders slumped. "Who is it?"

"Director Sholokhov of Protectorate Security."

"Oh, I do," she said, wheeling around. "Is he using an Alsean translator, or is he playing power games?"

"Power games."

"Naturally."

Back at her desk, she activated her Gaian pad, briefly considered engaging Sholokhov in his ridiculous power play, then dismissed the thought as being both unproductive and beneath her.

She pulled up the Common translator and accepted the transfer. "Director Sholokhov," she said. "You've made an interesting request."

The images Ekatya had shown her were accurate, but they didn't capture the intensity of his stare. "Right to business. I appreciate that. I'm sure your time is just as limited as mine."

His mouth movements did not match the words, a dissonance that came with translation and made her itch.

"It is. I'm sure you can understand my disinclination to consider your request, given your attempt to murder First Guard Rahel Sayana."

"Hardly that." He waved a dismissive hand. "You wouldn't have sent an incapable warrior as your first envoy to Fleet. Sayana was in no danger."

"If you were so certain, why bother with your little test?"

"Expectation is one thing. Proof is another. Politicians always want the latter, particularly when reviewing a request for funding."

He was cool and unruffled, discussing an attempted assassination as if it were nothing more than supporting documentation for a budgetary request.

"Whatever funding you received will not be enough to induce me to reconsider," she said.

"You might be surprised. Let's not waste each other's time, Lancer Tal. Tell me what you have in mind and I'll tell you whether I have the funding."

"First I'll tell you that you won't get twenty high empaths. What you're looking for requires a very specific skill set and long cycles of training. Those empaths are in perennially short supply and tend to have multiple employers hoping to procure their services. Finding twenty we can spare would be difficult enough. Finding twenty willing to work for the government that sold us to the Voloth?" She shook her head. "I could possibly find ten, if I looked under every rock."

He seemed neither surprised nor disappointed, confirming her guess that he had opened with a high ask and expected to be bargained down.

"I suppose I'll have to accept that explanation, given the impossibility of confirming it. What would ten high empaths cost me?"

"One Pulsar-class warship."

Ekatya had been startled by her audacity. Sholokhov merely raised his eyebrows. "I knew you'd ask something outrageous. I have to admit, this is more excessive than I imagined. Surely you realize it's not possible."

"Surely you realize it's a bargain. Our treaty requires the commitment of a warship to our protection on a permanent basis. It's already here, staffed by your people, maintained by your space docks and stations, paid for by your government. In the long term, the Protectorate will save money by turning the staffing and maintenance over to us."

"The *very* long term. Do you have any idea how much it costs to build a Pulsar-class warship?"

"Do you have any idea how much it costs to raise and fully train ten high empaths?"

His eyes narrowed. "That is a false comparison."

"If you truly believe that, then you don't know the value of what you're asking for. I'd be surprised if that were the case. You want a resource that's unavailable anywhere else in the galaxy. The resource I want isn't nearly so rare." She looked at her wristcom. "You caught me as I was leaving for an unbreakable appointment. Unless you have something better to offer than denials, this conversation is over."

"I believe we can reach an agreement with a more nuanced discussion of what you're prepared to accept. Your initial ask is too high, but it does give me an idea of what you're looking for. There are other ways to provide the protection you want. An orbital weapon installation, perhaps, in—"

"No."

"In combination with putting Captain Serrado in command of your battle group," he finished. "With a promotion to rear admiral and a guarantee that she will remain in that command until retirement. We both know that's what she wants."

The wave of fury made her voice clipped. "I will not allow you to use her career as a bargaining chip."

"I already have. You accepted my call."

If only she could reach through the com to wipe that smug expression off his face.

Shutting down all outward emotion, she said, "I will accept a Pulsar-class warship in exchange for the services of ten high empaths. They will serve on a rotating basis of no longer than two of your years, for a total of ten of your years. If you want a more nuanced discussion of that proposal, I'll listen. Otherwise, you needn't call again."

She ended the call before he could respond.

28

CARETAKERS

The chime startled Ekatya, who had just turned out her living room lights in preparation for going to bed. Grumbling to herself, she changed direction. If someone wanted a signature, they would get an eyeful of her in loose trousers and a sleeveless sleep shirt.

It was not a duty officer but a tired-looking Alejandra on the other side of her door.

"Sorry, I know it's late," she said. "Can I come in?"

"Of course. Phoenix, resume prior light setting."

Alejandra entered and stood uncertainly, arms crossed and head down.

"I was about to make a cup of bluethread tea," Ekatya said, crossing to the kitchen. "Would you like some?"

"Bluethread?"

"Alsean flower. Salomen turned me on to it. It has actual flavor, as opposed to every other bedtime tea I've tried."

"That sounds good, thank you." Alejandra followed her. "You made an appointment for me with Lanaril."

Ekatya pulled two cups from behind the wooden rib that kept them secure on their shelf against ship movement. "I knew that test would be difficult. I didn't want to leave you alone with the aftermath." She opened the center drawer, popped the lid off the tin Salomen had given her, and removed two tea packs.

"How long ago did you make it?"

"The day you agreed." The packs went into the cups, followed by steaming water from her dispenser. A fragrant cloud arose, redolent of sun-warmed berries. Cradling a cup between her hands, she leaned against the counter. "Did it help?"

"Immensely. I've been thinking about what she said. About caretakers." Alejandra braced herself against the opposite counter and looked into her mug. "How long does it need to steep?"

"Phoenix, timer for three minutes." She plucked two spoons from another drawer and set them out. "What about caretakers?"

"That's what we are. You and me. Credit where it's due; you chose the perfect test for the purpose. I've been a caretaker all my life. My first instinct is always to provide aid. Do you know why I was so upset?"

"We took away your free will. I'd have been more worried if you weren't upset."

She shook her head. "Because you made me helpless. You forced me to stand there and watch someone I love be hurt. Without any way to change the outcome. Without any *ability* to change the outcome."

Ekatya frowned. "I know. That was the design of the test."

"It's happened before. A long time ago. Lanaril knew right away why I was so devastated, because I've been working with her on the cause."

When the understanding hit, Ekatya barely managed to set down her mug without spilling it. "Josue. Fucking Hades, I never made that connection." She clutched her stomach, sick with the knowledge. "I didn't —it wasn't supposed to—I'm so sorry."

"I know you didn't do it on purpose."

"I would *never* hurt you that way on purpose. We should have used Lokomorra."

"Then you'd worry yourself sick over risking his career instead of worrying yourself sick about me. Who counseled you?"

She could not meet her eyes, too ashamed that she hadn't foreseen what that test would bring up. "I've been so happy for you, finally coming to terms with his loss, and then I put you—"

"Ekatya, stop. Look at me."

Reluctantly, she looked up.

Alejandra sighed and set her own cup aside. "I had Micah last night. Physical assurance that it wasn't real. It's a phantom wound. You made sure Lanaril would be there for me today, and now I know exactly why it went so deep. That makes it easier to process. Who have you talked to?"

"I talked to Andira and Salomen last night—"

"About me, right?"

"We were all worried about you."

"Have you talked to Lhyn?"

"Not about that. Not yet."

"So you took care of me, but not yourself."

A soft chime rang through her quarters.

"That's our tea." Ekatya picked up a spoon and fished out her pack. "I'm not the one who was hurt."

"I don't think that's true. Do you know what one of my worst experiences as a new mother was?" Alejandra tossed her own pack in the organics recycler. "Taking Josue for his first vaccinations. They can't use injectors at that age. The tissues are too delicate; a needle is actually less damaging. But it hurts, and there's no way to explain to an infant that the pain is necessary. I held him while a doctor hurt him, and I swear it hurt me just as much. More, in some ways."

Ekatya sipped her tea, needing the bracing heat and the excuse to keep silent.

"We all did what was necessary. We were all hurt. I had Micah and Lanaril, Salomen had Tal, and you were here alone last night, not telling Lhyn about it. So I came by to make sure the caretaker was given proper care." Alejandra took the mug from her hand, set it on the counter, and pulled her into an embrace. "I'm sorry you had to do that."

"I'm sorry I hurt you." Ekatya held her tightly. "Thank you for coming. I knew you weren't all right last night."

"I'm much better tonight. And I did get the benefit of a good talk with Salomen. She's an interesting person."

"That's what you say when you don't like someone but you're being tactful."

"Yes, because I'm known for my tact."

That made her laugh. "Why interesting?" she asked as they separated.

"She's the closest I'll ever come to meeting a genuine goddess, and what does she do with her days? Spends them tending to plants. I respect that." Alejandra tried her tea and made a face. "Not sure about her taste in teas, though."

"Keep drinking. It'll grow on you. It's a learned taste, like alcohol."

"Oh, speaking of that. Did you know you can take down a grown Alsean warrior with a little Gaian alcohol? We should probably keep that data away from Sholokhov."

"Is that why Lokomorra caught you acting like hormonal teenagers in the lift?"

"He wasn't supposed to spread it around!"

"Telling his captain isn't spreading it around. It's sharing important personnel information."

"Dokshin."

Ekatya studied her over the rim of her cup. She still looked tired, but the uncertainty had lifted, making her looser and more herself than she had been since the test.

Because she had been able to change an outcome, Ekatya realized. To be a caretaker instead of the one needing care.

"I'm so glad you're here," she said.

"Me too." Alejandra relaxed against the counter, took another sip, and wrinkled her nose. "It still tastes like dried twigs and fermented berries."

"Focus on the fermented part." Ekatya watched her smile and felt a load slide off her shoulders.

They would be all right.

29

SURPRISE PACKAGE

Tal rarely had occasion to visit the detention center on Blacksun Base. Those occasions were invariably unpleasant, but today she trod the corridors buoyed by happy expectation. Her destination was not a cell but a small, unguarded waiting area, occupied by a single person whose attention was on the room's vidscreen.

"I had no idea you liked *Merchant of the Mountain*," she said.

His head snapped around, surprise blasting her senses as he hurriedly stood. "Lancer Tal!"

"I thought we discussed this. I'm your bondsister. You can call me Andira."

Herot Opah shook his head. "Not in here, I don't think." Suspicion colored the air. "Are you the reason—"

"No. You asked me not to interfere and I respected that." She held up both hands. "Your sentence was reduced because you earned it. Congratulations, Herot."

He met her palms, sensed her sincerity, and relaxed with a wide grin. "Thank you. I'm still shocked. You could have knocked me over with a horten leaf when the administrator came this morning and told me to pack my things. Five moons early!"

"I was surprised, too. It's not only the prisoners they don't tell when they're considering early release."

"It makes sense, though. They don't tell us because it would be cruel to raise our hopes and then kill them if it doesn't happen. Family and friends would suffer just the same."

That he considered the well-being of others was a clear indicator of his growth. The Herot she had first known thought only of himself.

"But I was sure they'd have told you," he continued. "You're the Lancer."

"I did get the first notification. And, ah, I didn't tell your family."

"Why not?"

She indicated the bag next to his chair. "Is that everything?"

"It's more than I came in with." He shouldered it and patted the side. "Twenty-one moons of my life, right here. Why didn't you tell them?"

"Come on, we'll talk on the way," she said, leading him out the door. "Salomen has been working herself into the ground, both at Hol-Opah and with the divine tyrees. We're hosting a party this afternoon to celebrate how much the tyrees have accomplished in their training."

"Let me guess. She decided she had to organize that, too."

"You know her well. At least I convinced her to accept State House kitchen staff. Had I told her you were free, she would have insisted on coming here to get you. So would Shikal, Nikin, and Jaros. It would have been a frantic scramble before the party. I chose to eliminate that stress and replace it with a wonderful surprise and time to enjoy it."

They passed into the lobby, where Herot's emotional signature glowed with anticipation at the sight of the double doors. "It's nice to think I could be a wonderful surprise."

"You've been surprising us all along." She stood aside. "Go ahead."

He grasped the nearest handle, a smile spreading across his face. "I've dreamed of this moment."

The door opened with a mechanical sigh. He stepped through and stopped, turning his face up to the sun. A small breeze ruffled his hair, bringing with it the distant calls and clacking sounds of a group stave practice.

"Thank you, Fahla," he breathed.

Tal absorbed his elation and worried that she had made the wrong choice. But the Opahs would have spent eighty ticks in transit at the worst possible time. This way, they could relax with Herot before the guests arrived.

And they would be there when he set foot on Opah land for the first time in twenty-one moons. That, she thought, would mean far more to him than walking out of the detention center he had occupied for a hantick. Herot had spent his morning packing up, taking leave of friends made in prison, and being transported here for the tedious process of formal release. This was merely one more step on the path.

Her guess was confirmed when he turned to her, eyes sparkling. "I'm ready to go home."

It was a quiet flight. Herot was absorbed in the scenery, and Tal found peace in flying her transport, isolated from the myriad voices needing something from her. Herot needed nothing, not even conversation.

A tentick out from Hol-Opah, she called Vellmar, who was already at the holding with her Guards.

"I'm bringing a surprise for the Opahs. Will you ask them to meet me? Tell them I'll need all their help to unload it."

"Of course," Vellmar said. *"Time to arrival?"*

"We're almost to the Silverrun. Less than ten ticks."

"We?"

"Shek." Tal laughed at herself. "Don't tell them that part."

"What are you plotting, Lancer Tal?"

"Something that will make them very happy. Go round them up." She ended the call and activated the privacy glass. "There. They won't know it's you until you step out."

Herot grinned at her. "This is the best day ever. I can't wait to see their faces."

His joy filled the transport when they crossed the Silverrun River, so abundant that Tal's skin tingled with it.

"There they are!" He stabbed a finger toward the round house atop the hill. From this distance, the figures on the back deck were barely more than specks, but Herot's breath was short. "Fahla, Goddess above," he whispered.

Tal brought the transport to a hover over the grassy yard behind the house and began her descent. Jaros was already running down the wooden steps, eager to help, while Salomen descended at a more sedate pace. Nikin and Shikal followed.

Jaros danced from foot to foot, waiting anxiously for the transport to land and the engines to power down. He had been subjected to too many lectures about approaching an active transport to risk another, but the delay never grew easier. Behind him, Salomen rested a hand on his shoulder and watched with rising curiosity.

Tal opened her door and called, "It's on the passenger side." She stepped onto the soft turf as Jaros ran around the nose of her transport.

"Andira, what is going on? You're blocking our view for a reason." Salomen stopped in her tracks when Jaros let out a screech.

"Herot!"

Herot barely had time to exit the transport before his arms were full. "Jaros! Oh, I've missed you!" He twirled them around, laughing.

Shocked to her core, Salomen simply stared at them. "Is he . . . ?"

"He's home."

"Home! My son!" Shikal hurried past, Nikin at his heels.

Rooted to the ground, Salomen looked from Tal to her brother and back again. "Did you do this?"

She shook her head. "I had nothing to do with it. He earned an early release."

The tears came then, along with an explosion of euphoria as Salomen allowed herself to believe. She raced around the transport to join the laughing, crying group and met Herot in a double palm touch as soon as he turned. "Welcome home!"

"Thank you. I can't tell you how great this feels." He leaned in and kissed her cheek. "You look good. Tired, but good."

"You look *wonderful*. And I'm not tired at all." She beamed at him, her happiness so blinding that Tal's senses were dazzled.

Vellmar appeared next to her, grinning as she watched the scene. "Nice surprise," she said. "I hope you don't mind being relegated to the shadows at this party."

"I don't mind." Tal could not take her eyes off Salomen, luminous in her joy. "Great Mother, look at her."

"Her family is whole again," Vellmar said quietly. "She's been missing a piece of it for as long as I've known her."

Tal nodded. "She once said she could never forgive him. Half a cycle ago, she said she would forgive him someday."

"And now?"

"She forgave him the moment she realized he was home."

The creak of wood woke Salomen from a dreamless sleep.

She rolled onto her back, listening for the out-of-place sound. It was hanticks before dawn, and Hol-Opah was silent but for the leafthrum singing from a nearby tree. Its buzzing call rang out every few pipticks, advertising its readiness to mate. After the third call, she heard the creak again.

Someone was walking on the back deck and trying to be quiet about it. She reached out with her senses, confident in what she would find.

She was no longer intimately familiar with Herot's emotional signature. He had matured in prison, and his signature had changed with him. The presence she brushed against on the deck bore only a tangential resemblance to the Herot whose resentful anger was always just under the surface, waiting for an excuse to boil out.

Before he committed the act that nearly destroyed their family, she had avoided sensing him when she could. In her untrained days, she had little control over how deeply a skim impacted her. Touching his emotions had rubbed her raw, like clenching her fist around a sallgreen branch with its stiff, spiky leaves.

Now she brushed against him and felt the peace and wonder she had sensed in him all day. He still could not believe he was home.

She glanced at Andira sleeping beside her and slipped from the bed.

Two ticks later, she was settling a shawl around her shoulders while tiptoeing down the back stairs. As the dining room windows came into view, she saw Herot by the railing, gazing at the moonlit mountains.

The sound of the opening door brought his head around. "Why are you awake?" he asked when she reached him.

She rested her forearms on the top railing and set one foot on the bottom, her habitual stance. "I heard you. Then I sensed you."

"And that brought you out of bed?"

"I hate lying awake in bed. Coming out here seemed a better option than waking Andira. Why are you awake?"

"It won't stop whirling." He tapped the side of his head before turning back to the view. "I forgot how beautiful they are."

His prison had been in the foothills southeast of Blacksun Base.

Salomen had found its forested environment surprisingly pleasant, but there were no views of the mountains.

"Do you remember the day you and Father came to see me in the Blacksun Base detention center?" he asked.

"That would be difficult to forget."

"Remember how tiny that cell was?"

She nodded.

"That's what I thought prison would be like. We all know about the Pit, and there I was in that little cell, thinking I was doomed to cycles of that. It was miserable. When they processed me out to Lakefall after my hearing, I nearly fainted with relief. I had a room with a window. There were caste houses and a library, and trails to walk on. It wasn't what I thought prison would be. Except everywhere I walked, I'd eventually hit a fence. And I never saw the mountains."

"I don't recall you spending much time looking at them before," she said.

"I took a lot of things for granted. This view. Family meals. Driving a skimmer. You."

"Me?"

"Fahla, look at the moons. I could only see them when they were overhead." He inhaled with visible satisfaction. "And the air never smelled right."

"I like the forest scent," she said. "But I understand. It's not Hol-Opah."

"Nothing is Hol-Opah."

"On that, we can devoutly agree."

His lips twitched. "I'm sorry I couldn't stay for your party."

"Herot, no one expected you to walk out of prison and straight into a party with thirty people you didn't know. I was surprised you came at all. In your place, I'd have been roaming all over our land, reacquainting myself."

"That's what I'm doing tomorrow." He hugged himself, grinning at the thought. "A whole day of going where I want, when I want. Unbelievable."

"Where will you go first?"

"First? Mornmeal with my family. I can't tell you how long I've looked forward to that. And then . . ." He shrugged. "I think I might go to the Silverrun and sit on the bank for a few hanticks."

"That sounds delightful."

"You could come with me."

"I—" She had been about to say she couldn't; there was too much to do. But this was her brother, newly returned from prison. "I could use a break, come to think of it. It's been a hard few ninedays."

"So I've heard." He turned to face her, one arm braced on the railing. "I also heard you accepted Rahel Sayana's oath a few days ago. For real this time."

"I did," she said warily.

"She's the reason I got an early release."

"What did she have to do with that?"

He looked down, rubbing his other hand along his thigh. "I want to tell you something, but you have to promise not to get angry."

"Herot—" She stopped at his pleading look, though he would not say the words. "I cannot promise that. But I promise to listen."

"And not interrupt?"

"When do I interrupt? It's ill-bred."

His emotional signature swelled with affection. "I even missed your righteousness."

"That should last about a day."

"No," he said solemnly. "Much longer than that. There was so much I didn't value. So much I didn't know how to value until it was gone. The way you tried to parent me after we lost Mother—I hated it. Then you weren't there to parent me anymore, and I missed it. I missed you."

"We missed you, too. You left a hole in this family." She plucked a bit of bark from his shoulder and crumbled it between her fingers, catching an unmistakable scent. "Where have you been that you have cinnoralis bark on your shirt?"

"Out walking."

He was smiling at her with quiet delight, and she dusted off her hands in sudden awareness of her unconscious gesture. "What did you want to tell me?"

The smile slipped, replaced by a surge of determination. "Remember when you came to talk to me about Rahel? And asked me not to file charges?"

"Of course."

"I said yes, but after you left and I was alone again, I got angry." He held up a hand. "You promised not to interrupt."

She pressed her lips together and nodded, dreading where this would lead.

"It hurt. I was in prison, and it felt like you left me there while you were trying to help her. She kidnapped me. Sure, she never raised a hand to me, but she also didn't step in and stop the others. And you wanted to *save* her. All I could think was, why weren't you saving me? Goddess above, I was jealous of her."

He turned again, setting both arms on the railing and watching the thin wisps of moonlit clouds drift over the mountaintops. "But then I realized. You did try to save me. You tried for moons, and I never listened. I was angry with you for trying. I ruined everything and almost got you killed."

In twenty-one moons, Herot had never spoken openly of that terrible time. Salomen kept silent, listening with what she hoped was a nonjudgmental expression.

"You can't stop yourself, can you? You saw someone else in trouble, and you couldn't walk away. The way you talked about her—I wished you'd talk about me that way. But I lost my chance. And I thought maybe I could fix it, somehow, by giving you what you asked for. So when those forms came, I signed them."

"Herot," she murmured.

"Let me finish."

Silently, she rested her hand atop his wrist. Though he did not look, his hand covered hers.

"I told my counselor about it. How it was so unfair that I was in prison and she was going to walk away free. He said, if it was that unfair, why did I enable it? I said because you asked me to. He told me to look deeper. I spent a nineday thinking about it, and when I went back for my next session, I had an answer."

His grip tightened, affection pouring through their skin contact.

"I told him I couldn't let you fail a second time. You failed with me, and you were trying again with her. You needed to save her."

She leaned her head against his shoulder. There was no longer any danger of interrupting; she was speechless at this revelation.

"Yesterday, when the administrator told me I was being released, she gave me a letter. It's in my bag right now. It's a recommendation for early release from my counselor. He listed that session as the moment when I was put on the release track. He said I had committed a selfless act, that I was learning to empathize and think beyond my own interests. There were a number of other events along the way, but that was the start."

Salomen listened to the leafthrum call twice before speaking. "I'm not interrupting now, am I?"

"No."

She turned her head and waited until he met her eyes. "You said Rahel was the reason you were given an early release. That's not true. You did it, Herot. She was only an agent of change. You made the choice."

"It was the right choice, wasn't it?" He smiled, happy and hopeful, and she blinked away her tears.

"It was. I'm proud of you. Why did you think I'd be angry?"

"I never told you the real reason I signed. Or that I was such a dokker's ass at first. Seven moons in prison by then, and I still hadn't learned a damn thing."

"I disagree. You just proved how much you had learned. You simply didn't know how to recognize it then."

He craned his neck, looking up at the stars. "I'm still jealous of her. Just not for the same reasons. You tried to help me, and I turned my back and made a miserable mess of my life. She was so much smarter. She took your help, and look where she is now. Up there, doing extraordinary things. And you love her."

"She's easy to love." Salomen would not apologize for the most hard-earned friendship of her life.

"I'm not," he said without a trace of self-pity. "But I'm hoping you still do."

"You know I do."

He stared at their hands, the truth of skin contact making her statement incontrovertible. "You'll come with me to the Silverrun tomorrow?"

"With a picnic," she agreed. "We have a pile of leftovers in our cooling unit."

"We'll have to pack some of the mallowfish. Those were fabulous. And a bottle of the spirits you were serving. I wish it were high summer," he added wistfully. "I'd love to go swimming at the waterfall."

She scoffed. "Did prison make you soft? Who cares if the water is cold? It only hurts until you can breathe again. I'm going swimming."

He grinned, a flash of the old Herot showing through. "I bet you can't go in without shrieking."

"I bet I go in faster than you."

"Are your Guards going to shoot me if I push you in?"

"Yes. Because I'll tell them to."

With a laugh, he said, "I believe you."

30

FACT FINDING

At the end of her duty shift, Rahel took the lift back to security and walked straight through the outer office, past the observation room with its wraparound wall displays, and to the door of Commander Cox's office. He was reclined in the control chair that operated the sophisticated data system, working through security footage.

"Commander? May I speak with you?"

He paused the playback. "Anything I should know about?"

"I'm not sure," she said, stepping in and closing the door behind her. "There's something I need to ask. It's private."

"Ah." He pushed himself upright and crossed to his desk, pointing at the guest chair as he went.

One of the things she appreciated about Cox was his disdain for unnecessary speech. He didn't waste time on what most considered proper social courtesies, a trait often interpreted as ego. Rahel found it restful. With Cox, she never had to worry about saying the right thing.

Today she said nothing at all, merely placing her pad in front of him.

He read the short message with no outward reaction and a bright flare of intrigue. "I see," he said, pushing the pad back. "One moment."

She deleted the text while he reached into a drawer, shuffled through its contents, and closed it again.

"We're clear. How did you know I can disable the voice recordings in this office?" he inquired.

"I'd be surprised if you couldn't. There must be conversations in here that you don't want recorded."

"Rarely." He crossed his hands atop the desk.

"The hardest thing I've had to learn on this ship is trust in my team," she said. "As you know."

One side of his mouth quirked up. "I have a passing acquaintance with the issue. Why?"

"Something happened yesterday that made me wonder. Who is on Captain Serrado's team?"

"All of us. This crew is her team."

"But it's not, is it? If Admiral Greve orders any of us to act against her, she has no backup."

His eyes narrowed, dark suspicion thickening the air. "What did he order you to do?"

"I can't say without compromising the captain's privacy. Unless you have a passing acquaintance with this issue, too."

Suspicion solidified into certainty, but he still took the time to weigh his options. "I can guess," he said at last. "Did it have to do with questioning her loyalty?"

She nodded. "It wasn't the first time for either of them. She expected the questions."

"What a—" He bit off the exclamation. "That was an inappropriate use of your skills. You shouldn't be involved in this."

"It was a reprehensible use of my skills," she corrected. "Which is why I'm asking you. Who is on her team?"

The anger clouding the office was poisoned by helplessness. "We're doing everything we can. The fact remains that he's an admiral and the commander of this battle group. Don't put yourself in opposition. It won't work out well for either of you."

She stared at him in silence, struggling with her disappointment in an officer she admired. "Then she has no backup."

"Sayana—"

"Am I wrong?"

"Captain Serrado made her choice. Keeping this command came with a price, and she accepted that. I know you hate it, but we can't pick and choose which orders we obey." He paused. "Or have you done that already?"

"If I'd disobeyed his order, would I still be on this ship?" She stood up, her back stiff with discomfort. Until this moment, she'd never had to watch her words with him. "Thank you for your time, Commander. May I be dismissed?"

His emotions roiled, oil and water mixing yet never blending into a coherent whole. He wanted too many things, all of them incompatible.

With a sigh, he waved her out.

The view never grew any less amazing, Rahel thought as she sat on the empty bench. The top of Bridge Hill was the highest location on Deck Zero, giving her the perfect vantage point to see the paths twisting and turning through the landscaped park. As much as she loved flying over this deck in the shuttle, she loved being on it more. An actual park in space was something even her most fantastical childhood stories hadn't envisioned.

Only one thing kept it from being perfect. They were traveling through base space, where the vastly higher radiation levels required hull-skin protection. The transparent hull was covered, presenting a featureless ceiling in place of the spectacular window to the stars.

It felt odd to be here without Lhyn. Deck Zero was Lhyn's favorite place on the ship, giving her the space and visual freedom she needed, and this bench was her favorite spot in the park. Rahel once joked that the ship's computer had a malfunction because every time she asked for her location, it gave the same answer.

Lhyn hadn't come on this patrol, an out-and-back trip with a six-day stay at Tlahana Station. Since her safety could not be guaranteed on a Protectorate space station, she would not be able to leave the ship, and most of their travel time would be in base space when Deck Zero offered no view.

Rahel always missed her when she stayed behind. Today, worrying about who she could trust, she missed her more than usual.

She scanned the paths, dotted with off-duty crew members strolling in singles and pairs and groups, and found one man with a familiar, purposeful stride. Katsuro Lokomorra looked up, spotted her on the bench, and waved before entering a small copse of trees.

For several minutes, she followed his progress as he wound through the park. The shrubs he was walking past now, with their bell-shaped orange flowers, smelled like the aromatherapy room back in her Whitesun pleasure house. The low blue flowers planted along the path had no scent but served as both visual contrast and tactile treat: their leaves were coated with soft hairs that begged to be petted. Rahel had learned from the chief of botanics that the plants enjoyed it, lengthening each leaf being petted as if reaching for more.

In the herb section, the path gave way to intermittent paving stones set in a thick ground cover. Katsuro hopped from stone to stone, carefully avoiding the tiny plants. It wasn't out of consideration for the herbs, which had a polarizing effect on crew members depending on which form of a gene they carried. Those with the dominant gene stepped happily on the ground cover, delighting in the crisp scent that arose. Katsuro, who had the recessive gene, said it stank like stale urine. He normally avoided this section, but it was the shortest route to her location.

When he vanished behind the hill, she leaned back and waited. The path stitched back and forth up the opposite side; he wouldn't be visible again until he was nearly here.

She sensed him before she could hear his footsteps. He was concerned and determined, an odd combination for what was supposed to be a social occasion.

He came around the curve and called a greeting before climbing the rest of the way to drop onto the bench. "Got your message," he said unnecessarily. "Why the change of scenery? I was looking forward to a Neutron Star tonight."

"I'm feeling some pressure." She tapped her head. "Too many people in the Blue Rocket."

He stroked his forked beard, the beads at the ends clacking together. "Huh. I think this is the first time you've lied to me. At least, I hope it is." A reluctant smile tugged his lips as he saw her surprise. "No, I didn't suddenly become empathic. Cox called me."

Her stomach dropped. Had she miscalculated that badly?

"You don't want to go to the Blue Rocket because we could be overheard there. You chose the top of Bridge Hill because you can see anyone approaching before they're in hearing distance." With a wave indicating the distant ceiling, he added, "And the security cams can't pick up voices. It's a good choice. Hydroponics is good, too, if you need another option."

She stared, all of her planned tactics abruptly upended. "Did Cox tell you that?"

"Didn't need to." He rested one arm along the back of the bench, an image of ease at odds with the worry coating his skin. "He thinks you're about to get yourself in big trouble. I'm hoping I can talk you out of it."

"That depends on the trouble," she said warily.

"See, the problem is that Cox has a limited view of you. He only sees you on duty, so he thought he could warn you off without giving any real information. I know better."

Hope flared through her chest. "What do you know?"

"I know you've got a bone between your teeth and you won't let go just because your supervisor told you to. You'll need better reasons. Here's a reason: Captain Serrado isn't alone in this. Several of us are doing what we can for her. But she won't let us do much, and she definitely didn't want you involved. That's why Cox tried to warn you off."

Rahel scoffed. "I'm already involved. Greve saw to that."

"What did he do? Cox didn't give me details."

"I didn't give him many." It was such a relief to be able to speak openly to her friend. His emotional signature bore no whiff of deception; he was on Serrado's side. "Greve called me into his office yesterday afternoon. Captain Serrado was already there."

His expression turned to stone. "Fuck a rock. He ordered you to scan her during her check-in? Oh, that—" He clapped both hands against his face and dragged them down. "Fuck! What did you do?"

"Check-in?" she repeated incredulously. "That's what he calls it?"

"This is Fleet. We specialize in innocuous euphemisms."

She needed a moment to fight down her anger at the trivialization of what she had witnessed. "That wasn't a check-in. That was the ritual humiliation of a war hero. He wanted to make her so small that I'd lose my respect for her. She's not the one I lost respect for."

Katsuro's dimples appeared. "I guess I know what you did, then."

"I told him what he didn't want to hear, and he had to let her go. Katsuro, he wants to destroy her. Why isn't anyone helping? All Cox would say was that Captain Serrado made her choice. I don't know what that means."

He sighed. "It means that after the Fleet brass found out she was a divine tyree, they wanted to take this command away from her. They would have put her on some third-rate exploration ship where she couldn't do any damage. But somebody pointed out that if they did that, she'd quit, and then they'd have to explain why their decorated hero was leaving Fleet. Much as some of them hate her, she's still a golden egg for the public relations and recruitment offices. Not to mention that the Alseans would have made a galactic stink about it. So they let her keep her command, but it came with conditions."

"The price," Rahel said, remembering Cox's words.

"A babysitter in command of the battle group, daily check-ins reaffirming her loyalty, weekly security reports on her movements—"

"You are joking," she spat. "Cox gives that up?"

"He has to. Refusing would be disobeying orders all the way from the top. He doesn't have a choice."

"Everyone has a choice." Cox had been viewing security footage when she entered his office. Had he been compiling a report for Greve then? The thought made her sick to her stomach.

"That's not true," Katsuro said reasonably. "This isn't the sort of disobedience that gets you a punishment of shoveling shit in waste reclamation. It's the kind that gets you a demotion. Or a boot straight out of Fleet. Not everyone is willing or able to give up a career they've spent a lifetime working for. Some people are supporting families or older parents. There are plenty of reasons why people can't take a stand that might mean losing everything. And the higher they are, the more they have to lose."

"She spent her life working for her career, too! Is that suddenly worthless because Fahla blessed her with a divine tyree bond?"

"The Fleet brass don't consider it a blessing."

"They need a high-velocity enema," she snapped.

To her consternation, Katsuro laughed. "You've been hanging around Dr. Wells too long."

"It's not a laughing matter!"

He sobered. "No, it's not. It's just—I heard her voice when you said that."

"I suppose I did get that from her," she admitted. "Do *you* have a choice?"

"Up to a point." He held up a calming hand. "It's not only me. Even if I were ready to throw away any chance at a captaincy, Serrado wouldn't allow it. She's keeping me farther on the fringes than anyone else. But I promise you, I'm doing what she'll let me do."

He was telling the truth. And Serrado had already proved that she was the kind of oath holder who would protect her people at any cost.

"Who's involved besides you?" she asked.

"You're not supposed to know any of this. You're definitely not supposed to be wading even deeper. Rahel, you wouldn't just be risking yourself. You'd be risking the entire program. You think the Fleet brass would accept any more Alsean officers if the first one gets caught acting against a battle group commander? That's why Serrado wanted you kept out of it."

Rahel thought back to her hearing, when Captain Serrado had made a very specific change to the wording of her proxy oath. "She knows."

"What?"

"She knows I won't want to be here if Greve succeeds. Maybe she thought differently when this started, but she knows me better now. And the program isn't tied to Fleet. It's tied to her." She would call Salomen and ask if she could speak with Lancer Tal about it. The political maneuverings were far over her head, but she didn't think the Lancer would want to place more warriors in a system where people like Greve could abuse the gift of service without repercussions.

Katsuro studied her, his emotions coalescing into a point of decision. "Do you promise you won't reveal this to anyone other than the names I give?"

She held a fist over her heart. "I swear on my honor as a warrior."

"That's a lot of honor," he said gravely.

The rush of affection warmed her from the inside out. "Thank Fahla you're supporting her. I couldn't bear it if I lost my respect for you, too."

"Don't lose your respect for Cox. He's on the inside."

"He said we can't pick and choose the orders we obey."

"He was trying to keep you safe. He's the one who suspected Greve was using illegal spy cams in the captain's quarters. He and Commander

Kenji went shopping in the black market at Tlahana Station and came back with a scanner so she could detect them."

Shocked, she slumped back against the bench. Crew quarters were sacrosanct; no security cams were allowed inside. The only other protected places on a ship were the toilets. "She found some?"

He grimaced. "Yes. But she hasn't found any since then. I think she scared Greve. He broke the law having those installed. Of course, she can't prove it was him."

"That would be too easy," she grumbled. Then it hit her. "Cox did that?"

"Yeah, and he's scrubbing the security reports of any problematic data. Such as the fact that operations was temporarily missing a tool the captain needed to cause an electrical short."

"In the shuttle." Rahel remembered the flash of light and Captain Serrado's triumph. "Then Commander Zeppy is in, too." As chief of operations, he'd have to be in order to make that sabotage look like a maintenance issue. And Commander Kenji was the chief of data systems, so if he was in, he could be taking care of problematic communications.

"All the senior staff are. Serrado didn't ask, but they offered. So far, she's only taken up the offer from me, Cox, Zeppy, and Kenji."

And Dr. Wells, Rahel added silently. But if Katsuro didn't know that, she didn't think she should share.

Captain Serrado had more support than she'd realized, but there were too many limitations. She wouldn't allow her officers to risk their careers, even if they were inclined to put everything on the line. They were all playing a delicate game of balance.

A life in the shadows had taught Rahel a great deal about these kinds of games. One rule always held: the more delicate the balance, the more likely its eventual failure.

Greve was pushing hard. Dragging her in was an escalation, and Serrado's team was restricted by rules.

What the captain needed was someone who was not afraid to break them.

31

THE RIGHT SIDE

The next evening was Rahel's first scheduled treatment since returning to the *Phoenix*. She waited anxiously in her quarters, unable to remain seated for long, and ran for the door when the familiar emotional signature brushed her senses.

Dr. Wells was still two doors away. "You're eager," she said as she closed the distance. "Are you feeling all right?"

"Just tense." Rahel stepped aside and watched her walk in. She felt better already. "Would you like something to drink?"

"No, thank you. I'd rather relieve your tension first." Dr. Wells stripped off her jacket and tossed it onto the short leg of the L-shaped couch. "I can't relax if I know you need treatment."

"I don't need it that badly. I can get you a drink."

She scooped up the small pillow from beside her jacket and settled into the corner of the couch. "Lie down."

The time had long passed when they concerned themselves with physical boundaries and professional distance. Dr. Wells enjoyed this as much as she did, and Rahel was not one to refuse an order like that. She went down immediately, her feet at one end of the couch and her head on the pillow in Dr. Wells's lap.

The first touch of practiced fingers on her scalp loosened every muscle in her body. She couldn't hold back the appreciative groan.

"You shouldn't be this tense so soon. Are you getting unusual emotional exposure?" The air prickled with realization. "Is this because of me?"

"Partly," Rahel said truthfully. "But you feel much calmer now."

"I am." She offered nothing else.

After a minute of silence, Rahel stopped waiting and let herself sink into the physical relief of her treatment.

"Thank you for not asking. In the medbay."

"You didn't want me to." Her voice was slow and soft, fading along with the rest of her body.

A gentle touch drifted over her forehead ridges, lightly rubbing each one from her hairline to the bridge of her nose. "You Alseans are impossible to be around sometimes. I can't keep a damn thought in my head without you seeing. And then there are times like this, when you make it so easy."

"We can't sense thoughts."

"You might as well. But I appreciate that you didn't push me. I couldn't talk about it then."

It had been three days since the test. The morning after, Rahel had dropped by the medbay and been horrified by the state of her friend's emotional signature. If she was still that bad after a night of recovery with Colonel Micah, it must have been truly terrible.

"I'm sorry it was so hard for you," she said.

"Hard. That's a word for it. I don't ever want to experience that again. But it did give me more insight into you."

Her eyes flew open. Dr. Wells was watching the scenic program on the wall display while her fingers moved with the sureness of long practice.

"Salomen didn't—she couldn't have—"

"No." She looked down then, her brows furrowed in surprise. "Sainted Shippers, you just turned into a plank of wood. Relax. Salomen didn't hurt me intentionally." She slipped a hand beneath Rahel's neck and began a gentle massage. "I only meant that a few seconds of having my will taken away gave me a new understanding of your experience. Although there's one aspect I don't understand at all. I have no idea how you broke free."

"He was arrogant," Rahel said. "He forced me to stay, but he didn't think to force me not to fight. He never saw me as a threat."

"That explains. Salomen forced obedience. When Ekatya told me to stop, I couldn't have moved if my life depended on it." Her fingers shifted higher. "I do like your short hair. It makes this easier."

"It makes everything easier. Dr. Wells, it took a lot of courage to do what you did. I hope you know that."

"Is it courage if it's rooted in ignorance? I'm not sure I'd have agreed if I'd fully understood."

"You would have," she said with assurance. "Because Captain Serrado asked you."

"Hm. What does that say about me?"

"It says you know Greve is watching her. You know how few options she has."

The massage stopped. "How do you know about that?"

"He called me into his office two days ago and ordered me to scan her during that travesty he calls a check-in. To tell him if she was lying."

Through their skin contact, she felt the full brunt of the anger that blew through the room. Dr. Wells growled a curse in her own language, and Rahel had been friends with her long enough to recognize a scatological reference that would make a dockworker blush.

The explosion abruptly reversed direction, condensing to a vibrating point of suspicion.

"Wait a minute. When did you say that happened?"

"Two days ago, why?"

She let her head fall back with an exasperated groan. "That woman! And she never said a word. Caretaker, ha."

"Um. Should I ask?"

"No." She resumed the massage, lips compressed in a tight line. "Greve's a bigger fool than I thought if he believed you'd obey that order."

Rahel smiled up at her.

"What?" Dr. Wells asked.

"Cox and Lokomorra had to ask what I did. You knew."

"I know you," she said simply. "And I see you're already sniffing out the senior officers who have gotten involved. Serrado doesn't want you wading in this sewage."

"I keep hearing that. But I've seen this before."

"When?"

"Shantu trapped Lancer Tal by invoking an ancient law. She had to meet him in that challenge or forfeit her title. Greve is doing the same thing, using your legal system to cage Captain Serrado." She paused while Dr. Wells shifted to a scalp massage. "I've spent a lot of time thinking about it. I could have prevented it all. I knew those orders were wrong. Everything about it was wrong. But I shoved down my doubts because he was my oath holder."

"And your father."

She nodded. "All it would have taken was a trip to the nearest AIF office. If I'd told them the Prime Warrior ordered a kidnapping, it would have ended before Lancer Tal was put in danger. Sometimes—" She tilted her head, giving better access. "Sometimes I think that's why I fell so far. Because Fahla gave me a choice, and I made the wrong one. I won't do that again."

"Rahel." Dr. Wells stilled her massage. "I'm only beginning to under-stand Fahla's teachings, but I don't think she punishes people for making the wrong choice. What does happen is that choices have consequences."

"Maybe," Rahel conceded. "I still won't do it again. Lokomorra said some people can't do the right thing because they have too much to lose. For me, it was the opposite. I lost everything because I didn't do the right thing. I know Captain Serrado doesn't want me involved, but it was too late for that the moment Greve gave me that order."

Dr. Wells heaved a great sigh, resignation flowing from her fingertips as they renewed their motion. "What will you do?"

"I don't know," she said in frustration. "With Shantu, I had the power to stop it. I don't have any power here. Greve has all the rules on his side. Lokomorra told me who's involved, and I can't do any of the things they're doing. I think I might have to be the last resort."

"I don't like the sound of that."

Rahel readied herself. "If I had to physically incapacitate Greve, what would be the best way to do it without causing damage?"

"For the love of flight!" Dr. Wells pulled away, eyes wide with the shock that reverberated off her skin. "Are you insane? I'm not kidding, have you gone completely out the airlock? You can't assault an admiral! You'd be shipped back to Command Dome for general court-martial and imprisonment!"

"I'm not in Fleet. And there's no extradition agreement in our treaty."

She clapped a hand to her face. "You looked it up. Wonderful."

With her treatment clearly ended, Rahel sat upright. "If I acted in defense of Captain Serrado, Lancer Tal would never let them take me."

"Serrado would be obligated to throw you in the brig. An extradition battle might feel different if you're already trapped on the wrong side."

"Then I'd need to figure out a way off the ship."

"Rahel." Her voice cracked; she was truly frightened. "I don't think you realize the kind of power that would be coming after you for a stunt like that."

"It might not be necessary." It hurt, sensing the distress she was causing, but she had to push forward. "But if it *is* necessary, who else would do it?"

"Stars above, I'm surrounded by noble idiots." Dr. Wells glanced upward, her jaw tightening. "I'm not telling you a damned thing. I won't enable your self-destruction."

"I'm not eager to destroy myself, either. Not after everything it's taken to recover my honor. I promise it would only be as a last resort." She captured Dr. Wells's hand and held it tight, wishing she could share her emotions and convey how critically important this was. "When I was in Greve's office, I sensed more than distrust and dislike. He *hates* her. This is war to him, and she's the enemy. I think there may come a time when she'll be in real danger. If that happens, I can't sit on my hands like a merchant with no wares. I won't let her be helpless."

Something shifted in their skin contact, a flare of deep, instinctive comprehension.

"Helpless," Dr. Wells murmured. "Without any ability to change the outcome."

She nodded, afraid to speak aloud.

Dr. Wells blew out a long breath. "I know what you need."

32

STRESS RELIEF

Vellmar looked up at the sound of the back door opening. Lancer Tal emerged, now dressed in her running clothes, and trotted down the wooden steps. Swishing toward them through lush grass in need of cutting, she offered a broad smile. "Ready?"

"We're ready."

After more than a cycle and a half, Vellmar had this routine down to a science. Lancer Tal used running as both stress relief and a way to work through thorny problems. She expected all of her Guards to be ready to run on short notice, and woe betide any who failed to keep up: despite her small stature, she was fast and tireless. Vellmar had underestimated her on their first run together. She had never repeated the mistake.

With a hand motion, she sent two of her warriors to the front and two to the back. They would keep a respectful distance, close enough for protection but far enough for privacy, while she ran beside the Lancer. It was her duty as Lead Guard—and a cherished opportunity.

Since the memorable day when Lancer Tal apologized to her, their relationship had changed to something approaching friendship. It showed in all of their interactions but never more so than on their runs, when Lancer Tal became more approachable, was quicker to laugh, and frequently revealed personal depths that were otherwise kept hidden.

They moved as one, swinging out in an easy jog. Runs normally started at a slow pace to warm up their legs, but here at Hol-Opah it was a necessity. The house was situated atop a steep-sided hill; descending that slope at full speed was never advisable. Lancer Tal had done it once after a sharp argument with Salomen, boiling off the hilltop and tripping twice as she pelted down the slope. Vellmar's heart had been in her mouth as she followed, terrified that the Lancer would break a leg or worse on her watch.

Today's descent was leisurely and a good deal safer. Lancer Tal was in a bright mood, having flown out from Blacksun to join the Opahs in their day off. After Salomen's swim party with Herot yesterday, Shikal had decreed today a family holiday and left the holding in the hands of their field workers. All five Opahs were at the waterfall, picnicking, sunbathing, and swimming.

They reached the bottom of the hill and picked up speed, now on a grassy access road between a field of grain on the left and horten on the right. Though the horten wasn't yet knee high, it already had the distinctive scent that made Vellmar think of fine meals and candlelit evenings.

"You could have flown straight there," she said.

"I could have. But then I'd have missed a good run."

"They're swimming. It's not as if you'd miss out on exercise."

Lancer Tal gave a dismissive huff. "It takes all of fifteen strokes to cross that plunge pool. I'd be swimming laps from now until sundown to get a decent workout."

"You're assuming they'd let you swim unimpeded. Jaros is there," she pointed out. "I've got fifty cinteks that says he'll be on your back before you make it halfway through the first lap."

She savored the easy laugh. These days, she took the Lancer's relaxation as seriously as her safety. Hearing a laugh like that meant her oath holder had already let go of the day's stress.

"No bet. How is Lanaril doing? I haven't seen her in a couple of days."

"She's working too hard. Sometimes I want to slam the temple doors closed and tell people to solve their own damned problems."

"If you try that and it works, come to my office and slam those doors shut, too."

Vellmar pictured irate Councilors lining the corridor outside the Lancer's office, shouting and waving their reader cards. It might be worth an attempt just to see it.

"She'd never allow it. But her retreat starts next nineday. A whole nineday for her to be nothing more than a worshiper, in a temple that's not her own. I think I'm looking forward to it as much as she is."

Lancer Tal cast a startled look in her direction. "Great Mother, I forgot you were leaving."

"I've put everything in place. Senshalon is taking over as acting Lead Guard. You won't even miss me."

"Don't sell yourself for a bargain price. I'll miss you. I know when I'm outranked, though." She paused before adding, "Lanaril said she's never taken anyone with her on a retreat before now."

"Not even her ex-bondmate," Vellmar acknowledged. "She needed the time away from him, but she doesn't need it from me. The benefit of working different schedules."

"Did you say that to her?"

"No, but it's obvious. We don't spend enough time together to get tired of each other."

"Selling yourself for a bargain price right after I told you not to? It's about the quality of time, not the quantity. Her bondmate added to her burdens rather than taking them away. You give her what she needs."

"That's the part I'll never understand. All she needs is a little comfort and care after she's spent a day caring for others. It's not an effort." She was perennially mystified by a man she had never met, who had held Lanaril's love and lost it through sheer negligence. "The retreat sounds ideal for us. I'll have mornings to do what I want while she's in prayers and meditation, and we'll have afternoons and evenings together. Has she shown you images of the view from our room?"

"From your room, from the refectory, from the observation platform on the Ridgeline Trail . . ."

Laughing, they rounded the edge of the horten field and headed south toward the Silverrun River. Ahead was the linear forest that followed the river all the way through Blacksun Basin.

"What did you learn from the settlers today?" Lancer Tal asked.

"Not a great deal more. I think they've taught us all they can. I wish there was just one officer among them."

"It would be helpful, but we cannot wish for what we don't have. Rax and the others don't need to be officers to know a ship's layout—"

"Most of it," Vellmar interrupted, something she would only do on a run. "There are areas they couldn't go. Such as the bridge."

"That's an important one," Lancer Tal conceded. "But if all goes well, Salomen will be there long before you. I can tell you what to expect."

They reached the trees and turned east to follow the trail along the riverbank, passing from one world to another. Behind them lay open, sun-drenched fields; ahead was a narrow, shady trail winding through leaf litter beneath ancient trees. The air was abruptly and profoundly different, trading pungent horten and dry soil for damp loam, decaying leaves, and the rich scents of a wild river.

"I've been wondering," Vellmar ventured. "You said Captain Serrado confirmed that the Voloth are coming, but not when. Yet our preparations have felt more . . . urgent. Do you know something?"

"Not for certain. It's guesswork, but Captain Serrado agrees with it. So does the Director of Protectorate Security." She paused while they jogged up a short but steep set of steps cut into the slope. Once the trail leveled out, she continued, "Put yourself into the mind of your opponent. You threw an entire invasion fleet at a backward race and lost every asset except your ships. You came expecting to exterminate and enslave and were slaughtered instead. The defeat toppled your government and cost your treasury untold amounts."

Vellmar focused on delicate footwork as they traversed a section of trail rumpled and riven by tree roots. "I'm shocked by the loss," she said. "We've been set back several cycles. Once the shock wears off, I'm angry."

"Good. Now you're in the new government that took power. Your economy is suffering, your people are demoralized by the worst defeat they can remember, and you need to prove that your government is better than the one you replaced. What would be the easiest way to do that?"

"A successful strike against the enemy that defeated the last government," she said promptly. "But why now? Why not a cycle from now, when they've had more time to replace their assets?"

"Because winning isn't enough. Remember, you were defeated by a technologically backward race. It shouldn't have been possible. You were *embarrassed.*"

"Revenge, then." She leaped over an old, decaying log, while Lancer Tal's shorter legs meant she had to jump to its top and off the other side.

"Exactly. Now extrapolate that."

"I want revenge," Vellmar mused. "I want to win, but that's not enough. So I want . . . I want to punish the people who embarrassed me. Humiliate them."

"You're on the right path. Keep going."

"I can't invade again, it's too high risk. It has to be something I can do from orbit. Which means the space elevator, but we already knew that. So what changed?" She nearly tripped over a tree root as the answer came. "They're waiting for us to finish it, aren't they? Like the school bully waiting for a child to put the last block on her tower before knocking it all down."

"Well done. Maximum demoralization, maximum loss of investment, and maximum time lost before we can reach the same point again. Not to mention a bloody nose for the Protectorate."

"But that's hardly more than a moon from now!"

"We'll be ready. The war council and the builder caste were prepared to delay completion of the space elevator, but it hasn't been necessary. Salomen's test was successful. Our shuttles have passed every test with all flags flying. You and Ronlin have reached the point of diminishing returns with the settlers. Candini has learned the capabilities of our pilots and how we can work with Fleet pilots. We're not the naive target we were three cycles ago."

"Shekking Mother," Vellmar groaned. "I'll have to tell Lanaril."

Lancer Tal looked over with raised brows. "You haven't mentioned your role?"

"No. Not yet," she amended.

The brows rose further.

"There was never a good time! I want to relax her, not terrify her."

"Take it from one who learned the hard way. The longer you wait, the worse it will be." Lancer Tal sped up, leaving her to stew in her own juices.

In her preoccupation, the remainder of their run flew by. They were soon at the western entrance of the waterfall canyon, where she left their four Guards to join the two already posted there. She and Lancer Tal walked on, picking their way through jumbled rocks as the walls rose higher above them. Up ahead, two massive boulders created a pinch point, sending the placid river into a whitewater froth as it squeezed through and plunged to the pool below.

At the base of the boulder on their side of the river, Lancer Tal moved to the first handhold and rapidly climbed its steep face to stand atop, hands on her hips as she surveyed the scene.

Vellmar checked her wristcom and called Senshalon. "I'm handing over."

"Handover received," came the prompt answer. *"You certainly timed that one well."*

"Nothing like ending a shift with a good run. Hope it's a quiet one for you."

"With Jaros screaming down there? It hasn't been quiet since I arrived."

On cue, a high-pitched shriek rose from the pool below. Vellmar ended the call and scrambled up the boulder.

During the autumn rains or spring snowmelt, the waterfall was a roaring torrent that no one would dare put a toe into. Now it was relatively tame, a gentle drop that even Jaros could safely go over in a floater ring.

He had done just that, judging by his giggling presence in the pool. Still in the floater ring, he was frantically kicking toward the sand bar on the southern bank while Salomen made a great show of chasing him. Shikal, Nikin, and Herot relaxed on low chairs in the sun, surrounded by drinks, towels, and various articles of clothing. Nikin was still nude, a sign that he had only recently emerged from the water, while Shikal and Herot were dry enough to be dressed.

"Faster, Jaros, faster!" Lancer Tal called. "She's right behind you!"

The exhortation failed as Jaros stopped kicking and spun in place to look up. "Lancer Tal! When did—agh!"

Salomen had taken advantage, diving underwater to yank him down by the legs. Jaros vanished from sight, reappearing a moment later with much sputtering and a shriek of "Not fair!"

Salomen surfaced halfway across the pool, smiling up at them as she treaded water. "Why are you standing up there? Come on down, the water's practically tepid."

Over on the bank, Nikin let out a snort. "Sure, if by tepid you mean cold enough to freeze a fanten's teats."

"Just jump," Herot called. "It's easier if you go in all at once."

"I'm still dressed," Lancer Tal pointed out.

Vellmar thought that was an unwise comment, especially given the expression on Salomen's face before she dove again.

From their vantage point, they had a perfect view of her sleek shape slicing toward them. She surfaced beside the waterfall and slicked back her hair with both hands, then pulled herself out and began climbing.

"Mother of us all," Lancer Tal murmured. "She looks like a river goddess."

Even given the Lancer's obvious bias, Vellmar had to agree. Water streamed off Salomen's nude body as she moved from one handhold to another. A lifetime of physical labor had made her as strong as any trained warrior, and the climb showed her lean musculature to perfection.

She reached the base of their boulder and disappeared around the side. Soon her dark head came into view, bent down while she focused on the footholds, and in a flash of muscles and tanned skin she stood before them, water still dripping from her hair to slide down her chest ridges and between her breasts.

"That is a very complimentary feeling," she said with a broad smile. "It's good to know I can still strike you mute after a cycle and a half of bonding."

"Mute and stunned. You look—Salomen!" Lancer Tal cried, finding herself wrapped in a warmron. "Gah! You're wet and freezing!"

"So? You're sweaty. Get those clothes off and come in with me."

"I'm still cooling down. Do you want me to die of cardiac arrest?"

Salomen stepped back. "Fianna, in your professional opinion as her Lead Guard, is she likely to go into cardiac arrest if I throw her in?"

"No. She's had enough time to cool down."

Lancer Tal swung around, eyes wide with disbelief. "You're supposed to be protecting me!"

She tapped her wristcom. "I went off duty right before we climbed up here. You want protection, call Senshalon."

"Traitor."

Salomen's grin was wicked. "Get those clothes off or I'm taking them off you."

"I'll hold them for you," Vellmar said helpfully.

"Such a relief," Lancer Tal grumbled. "Thank you for your considera-tion." With exaggerated care, she unsealed her light running jacket and handed it over. After toeing off her shoes, she shimmied out of her shorts and held those out as well.

Salomen took over then, pulling the shirt over her head and blindly thrusting it toward Vellmar while kissing her bondmate with enough passion to earn hoots and commentary from the audience below.

"Yuck!" Jaros complained. "Do that somewhere else!"

They broke apart laughing, and Salomen took her hands. "Ready?"

"Do I get another kiss if I survive?"

"You get two."

"Then I'm ready."

Salomen nodded once, twice—and they leaped off together, twin shrieks of glee ringing through the canyon before they hit the water and vanished.

Lancer Tal surfaced first, her head barely clearing the water before she let loose with a vehement string of words not meant for Jaros's ears. Salomen caught the tail end of it when she came up and was already laughing as she swam over. They met and embraced, Lancer Tal still gasping while Salomen said something Vellmar could not hear over the sound of the waterfall.

A sense of resolve settled in her bones as she watched the scene below. Tonight she would speak to Lanaril. If the next moon brought Lancer Tal's prediction to life, then she would fight with every weapon at her disposal. And she would remember this moment, these people, as an image of what she fought to preserve.

33

ICE BOX

T hey were still three days out from Tlahana Station when the distress
call came in.

"It's automated," reported the comm officer. "Not even a voice
recording attached. The *Blue Arctic*, TC-125738. I think it's an ejected
beacon."

"Coordinates?" asked the navigation officer. He waited for the data,
then tapped his console. "I'll have it up in one moment, Captain."

In her chair atop the central dais, Ekatya waited.

All around them, from the deck upward, the hemispherical upper display
was showing a real-time view of the base space they were traveling through.
Though some found it difficult to adapt to the eerie red mists, which always
seemed to be shifting in one's peripheral vision, she had never liked being here
without at least one of the two displays active. As far as she was concerned, the
bridge officers were fortunate she didn't have the lower display on as well.

"Here it is."

The red mists vanished, replaced by a navigational grid showing their
location, the network of base space relays around them, and the coordinates of the distress beacon. A green line marked their route to the relay
nearest the coordinates.

"Eight hours out," Ekatya noted. They were already traveling at just under the speed of light and could go no faster. Breaking the L1 barrier in base space was a death sentence. "Is there anyone closer?"

"No, Captain. We're the only Fleet ship in the area."

She straightened. "Helm, alter course for the Zekari relay. Comms, notify Fleet that we're responding."

"Captain." Down on the first level, Lieutenant Kitt's fingers were dancing over her data analysis console. "I have a visual on that ident."

"Let's see it."

The navigational grid shrank and shifted to one-half of the upper display, while the other half was taken up by a long, rectangular ship. Beneath the image, columns of data listed its name, dimensions, flight plan, and crew.

"An icebox?" In the second ring, Commander Lokomorra tilted his head to the side, puzzlement painting his features. "I've never heard of an icebox getting into trouble before. They're cooling units with engines attached. Not much to go wrong."

Next to him, Lieutenant Scarp finalized their new course and gave his full attention to the display. "Could be pirates."

"Because enormous blocks of ice are so easy to unload on the black market," Lokomorra said dryly.

"Maybe they aren't carrying ice. Maybe they're just pretending to."

"Maybe we should refrain from conjecture until we know more," Ekatya suggested.

Lokomorra spun his chair to look up at her. "It's always good to go into a situation with possibilities in mind," he said, his twin dimples showing. "You taught me that."

"Are you entertaining the possibility of pirates, then?"

"Not for a flat second."

"If you'd wait a few minutes," Kitt said, "I'll have the traffic records and then you won't have to guess."

Unfortunately, base space relays could not record ship traffic that passed them. Such data was impossible to collect due to the compressed nature of base space and its abnormal physics. The same did not apply to their paired marker buoys in normal space, however. Within twenty minutes, Lieutenant Kitt had downloaded the most recent data and scanned through it.

"You're not going to believe it," she said as the upper display switched to her recording. "This happened two hours ago."

Ekatya watched the buoy float in empty space for three seconds before a flare of light appeared next to it. A brilliant hole was torn in the layer between normal and base space, spilling baleful red mists while a small, triangular ship snapped through the opening as if shot from a catapult. It came to an abrupt halt upon hitting normal space, its crew no doubt fighting nausea as they adjusted to the physiological trauma of exit transition.

Another flare appeared, disgorging a ship that was a twin to the first. Then another, and a fourth and fifth.

"Lieutenant Scarp," Lokomorra said, "you jinxed us."

"I was joking!"

"Since when do pirates hit ice boxes?" Ekatya thought Kitt had been right: she could hardly believe her eyes.

"Since today, apparently." Lokomorra looked grim. "Unless they're waiting for us with tea and toast, we won't be able to do a damned thing. It'll be long over by the time we get there."

The five ships accelerated away from the buoy, vanishing off the recording in seconds.

"They're better trained than some Fleet crews," Ekatya said. "That was an impressive recovery time. They can't be over the nausea yet, but they're not only operational, they're flying in formation."

"They haven't come back," Kitt reported. "That's the most recent activity."

"The icebox is too far from the buoy. These pirate ships are built for maneuverability, not speed. Keep an eye on the data, Lieutenant. Let me know when you see them again."

As Lokomorra predicted, it was over before they were halfway to the base space relay. The five ships reappeared, now accompanied by the *Blue Arctic*. The cargo ship seemed unharmed, but its identity transmitter had been disabled.

One by one, the ships opened a portal and slipped into base space. The *Blue Arctic* went last, indicating that it was piloted by a pirate or a crew member working with them.

And they were now untraceable.

"Nothing to do now but gather evidence," Ekatya said.

"If there is any," Lokomorra grumbled.

～

Once back in normal space, the *Phoenix's* enormous surf engines made short work of the distance from the exit point to the distress beacon. They arrived in less than half an hour, a speed that would have made Ekatya proud had it accomplished anything.

Both upper and lower displays were now active, giving the impression that the bridge was hovering in space. To the port side, an orange gas giant dominated the scene, the only planet in this system. One of its many moons moved silently overhead, its icy surface ghostly white in the shadow of the planet. To starboard, a dozen smaller moons swung through a brilliant carpet of stars.

And just ahead, tumbling together in an irregular dance, were hundreds of straight-edged blocks of ice, each the size of a small shuttle.

Ice boxes were named for their long, boxy shape and their lumbering speed. They were low cost and low tech, a cooling unit with engines attached, as Lokomorra had so aptly put it. Their ice cargo had little intrinsic value, but was worth a great deal due to the effort of mining and transporting it to buyers who needed large, easily storable sources of water. Orbital industries, space stations, shipping bases, asteroid mining operations—all required water and had no easy way to procure it.

To hijack an icebox and dump the cargo into space defied explanation. These pirates had taken the ice *after* it had been mined from the moon above, after it had acquired the invested value, and tossed it out like so much trash.

"They must have wanted the ship," Lokomorra said, breaking the silence.

"For what?" Ekatya asked. "Ice boxes can barely make L1 on a good day. They're not suited to move anything other than ice. Wherever those pirates are going can't be far from a base space exit point, or it'll take them half a lifetime to get there."

"Mobile storage?" Lieutenant Kitt offered. "There's a lot of room inside an icebox. They can hold even the bulkiest cargo. Or small ships, even."

Lokomorra snapped his fingers and pointed at her. "Good thinking. They may be setting up a new base of operations. Or a depot."

"That makes sense, except for one thing," Ekatya said. "Pirates don't set up housekeeping close to base space exit points. Even the most remote exit points still get enough traffic to elevate the risk of discovery. They rely on secrecy and mobility. A stolen icebox gets them neither."

Kitt's face fell. "I should have thought of that."

"We're brainstorming," Lokomorra said before Ekatya could utter a word. "No idea is a bad one. Keep firing those neurons of yours and we'll sort out the possibilities after."

He would make an excellent captain someday, the kind who inspired his crew. She thought she could take some credit for that, having seen his potential when other captains did not. It was another reason she was keeping him as far as she could from Greve.

"Maybe we're thinking in the wrong direction," she said. "Could it be a case of ransom? Holding the ship and its crew for a payout?"

Lokomorra hummed thoughtfully. "That would explain taking such a slow ship. They'd want to be near an exit point then. Get the payment, leave the ship, dive into base space long before the closest authorities could get there."

Kitt tapped out a quick command. "Let's have another look at the crew manifest. Maybe one of them is related to a big shareholder in the company."

The data readout appeared on the upper display, superimposed against the starry background: names, length of service, previous employers. Ekatya read through it, noting that the captain was a thirty-year veteran who had worked his way from an entry-level mining job to the highest position he could achieve without giving up space for corporate headquarters. It was an admirable history, but one that made him an unlikely target for a ransom demand. Scions of wealth did not normally start at the bottom.

She had worked through three more names when the scene in front of them transformed.

They were keeping pace with the distress beacon and ejected cargo, swinging through space along with everything else caught in the gas giant's gravity well, and had just moved out from the planet's shadow.

Light from the system's star poured past them, turning the ghostly blocks of ice into mini-stars reflecting so brightly that the display brought up a filter to shield their eyes.

But not before Ekatya saw a tiny, distinctive silhouette.

She pulled up the display controls on her console and magnified a grid cell.

"Crap," Lokomorra muttered as he stared up at the new view. "Probably not ransom."

Even at this magnification, they could see few details against the brilliant reflection. It didn't matter. The two arms, two legs, and small round head were enough.

"Lieutenant Kitt," Ekatya said quietly, "scan the debris for matching silhouettes."

The bridge was silent as they waited.

"Scan complete." Kitt shifted the display, zooming back out to show the whole field. Red markers outlined fourteen dead crew in total, slowly tumbling along with their ice.

Ekatya glanced at the crew list still superimposed on the starboard side of the display.

Fourteen names.

"Serrado to Commander Przepyszny," she said. "Check your bridge display feed. This is now a retrieval mission."

34

RETRIEVAL

Body retrieval was a grim, hands-on duty. Using the ship's tractor beam would be easier, but theirs was designed for moving shuttles and other objects with significant mass. It would tear apart the tiny, delicate bits of tissue that made up a Gaian body.

Zeppy oversaw the operation, sending out teams in five shuttles. His choice meant no team had to collect more than three bodies, reducing the likelihood of traumatic reactions. No matter how inured Fleet crew became to the hardships and risks of space travel, grappling corpses left a mark.

Alejandra put her psychology staff on standby, ready to assist any of the retrieval crew upon their return. Her medical teams geared up and began the long process of autopsies as the first bodies arrived.

They were nearing the end of a double shift when Alejandra delivered her report to Ekatya's office. The pirates had been oddly restrained: with one exception, none of the crew were assaulted, physically or sexually. They had simply been flung out the nearest airlocks. One young man had a blood alcohol level indicating that he had drunk heavily after finishing his prior shift; Alejandra theorized that he had slept through the intruder alarm and was caught in bed. He had been tossed into space in nothing but sleep shorts.

The exception was the captain. His body bore signs of a hard fight, the broken knuckles showing that at least some of those pirates paid for their attack. In the end, it hadn't mattered. Thirty years of clawing his way up from low-paid miner to captain of a ship was ended with the push of a button.

Perhaps it was the sympathy of one captain for another, regardless of the size or purpose of their ships, but Ekatya felt this loss keenly. She hoped the captain had stared down those pirates in the last few seconds before they decompressed the airlock and shot him into space.

In the end, sometimes the best you could hope for was to die with dignity.

"I know it's probably useless," Alejandra said, "but would you like to speak with one of my staff?"

"No."

"No, of course not." She rubbed her eyes. "Well, I'm calling it a day. A long, thoroughly unpleasant day. I'm looking forward to a hot shower, a glass of wine, and a nice talk with someone who understands."

"It *is* nice to have someone who understands, isn't it?"

"Fahla, yes."

Despite her own weariness, Ekatya chuckled. "Your swearing has changed."

"Might as well swear on something I believe in."

"Do you?"

Alejandra glanced toward the security cam in the corner. "Shall I make it for the record?"

"Hold that thought. I need to call this in."

Though confused, Alejandra crossed her arms and waited.

Ekatya placed a call, tapped a key on her deskpad, and relished the momentary ease. "A priority blue call to myself. You can speak freely."

It was a measure of Alejandra's exhaustion that she needed several seconds to figure it out. Then her shoulders dropped and her neck loosened, tilting her head to one side. "The security data is encrypted until you end the call. Ingenious. Who does it look like you're calling?"

"It varies," Ekatya said vaguely. Even with the encryption, she would not risk exposing her methods or the officers who assisted with them. "I've had it with the lack of privacy. This office should be as sacrosanct as my quarters. More so, given the kinds of conversations I have with my officers and the rights they should be able to expect. I refuse to drag them to my quarters just so they can speak off the record, not to mention that the act of walking into my quarters puts a target on their backs. Now, you were about to say something?"

Alejandra stretched, ending slumped in her chair with her legs extended straight out and hands draped over the armrests. "I was about to say yes. I do."

"That's wonderful! I'm happy for you."

"Even though you don't?"

"I don't have to believe in Fahla to understand what your faith means to you. I can't think of a greater gift than for you to recover something so critical to your sense of self."

"That's a good way of putting it," Alejandra mused. "Critical to my sense of self. It feels like I'm bigger on the inside."

Ekatya thought of a six-pointed bond and relationships that might have conflicted but instead strengthened one another. "You are. It doesn't matter what anyone else thinks, or what your past experiences tell you to believe. You know your truth. Accepting it frees you from self-imposed constraints. You're more now. Full of potential. Just . . . more."

"I must be tired. That actually made sense."

"Good. Don't expect me to repeat it tomorrow."

Alejandra's laugh turned into a yawn. "Thanks for the little bit of privacy. Next time, don't waste it on something I'd be glad to tell Greve to his obnoxious face."

"Giving us a chance to have a real conversation outside our quarters isn't a waste. I miss being able to talk to you."

"Me too." She pulled in her legs and straightened. "I'm off to make a quantum com call and have a real conversation with Micah. I know you're in Captain Invulnerable mode, but you should do the same with Lhyn."

"I will. Just not by quantum com."

"You're spoiled. Give her my regards."

"First I'm Captain Invulnerable, then I'm spoiled? Make up your mind."

Alejandra smiled, tapped her temple, and walked out.

35

INVISIBLE

The first thing Ekatya told Lhyn when she connected that night was that she was following doctor's orders.

"That's a first." Lhyn was stretched out on the floor of their suite, propped up on an elbow and surrounded by open books. "So the secret to getting you to take care of yourself is to prescribe what you already want to do."

"Don't I get any more credit than that?"

"No. Why would Alejandra tell you to talk to me? What happened?"

Ekatya looked down at her, safe and happy in her nest of research, and changed her mind. She would not bring the day's death into this peaceful place.

"Just a reminder that bad things happen to good people. And I can't always be there to prevent it."

In a graceful movement, Lhyn crossed her long legs and sat upright. "Any of your good people?"

"No, thank the stars. The crew of an icebox."

"The whole crew? How did that happen? Catastrophic environmental failure?"

She should have known better. Incomplete information never satisfied Lhyn's curiosity; quite the contrary.

"They were spaced by pirates," she admitted.

The look of horror made her feel worse. Lhyn had seen a spaced corpse once, when one of her researchers sold Alsea's location to the Voloth and was promptly murdered. It still haunted her.

But the expression faded into something closer to assurance. "This isn't a me conversation, is it? It's an Andira conversation."

"I needed to see you," Ekatya said truthfully. "But I don't want to talk to you about today."

"So much for doctor's orders, eh?" Lhyn rose and stepped over the books. "Fortunately for you, there's a medical substitute right over there."

Following her pointing finger, Ekatya turned in place and was startled to find Andira and Salomen asleep on the sofa.

Sharing minds meant she only saw what was in Lhyn's thoughts. In a familiar place such as this suite or Hol-Opah, the views were extensive, built from detailed memories. People were not included unless they were in Lhyn's field of view or had a strong presence in her thoughts.

Of the latter, the two strongest were right here.

"Why didn't I see them?" she asked, moving closer.

"I wondered that when you appeared. It might be a combination of factors. They're asleep, which enabled me to set aside my awareness of them, and I've been down a research hole, which means—"

"—the Blacksun Symphony could play in here and you wouldn't notice."

"I'm not *that* bad."

"Yes, you are. Remember when I walked through the room naked to get your attention?"

"Remember? You won't let me forget. I was in the middle of a difficult translation!"

"My ego has never recovered."

"Your ego was in perfect condition the last time I checked." Lhyn looked her up and down with a smirk before turning back to the sleeping women. "They're adorable, aren't they?"

Salomen had somehow managed to fall asleep sitting upright, her head resting against the back of the sofa and her mouth slightly open. Andira was lying on her side, knees tucked up and head pillowed on Salomen's thigh. She still wore State House clothing, though her jacket was thrown over the back of a nearby chair and her polished boots were lined up neatly at its base.

Lhyn reached down and extracted a book that had slipped from Salomen's lap to wedge itself between her leg and the side of the sofa. "Andira has been in meetings all day," she said, straightening a bent page and setting the book on the side table. "Salomen came back from Hol-Opah and asked if she could wait for her here. So she read and I researched, and then Andira came stumbling in, dead on her feet. She hardly said three words before curling up there."

It was easy to picture the rest: Salomen idly stroking Andira's hair as she read, sending her bondmate to sleep and following shortly after. "You realize that Andira would hate being called adorable."

"You'll notice I didn't do it while she was awake."

Ekatya laughed, secure in the knowledge that it wouldn't disturb the sleeping pair. But when Lhyn joined in, they began to stir.

Andira rolled onto her back, bare feet on the sofa and knees bent. Rubbing her eyes, she mumbled, "What are you laughing at?"

"Nothing I can tell you without getting in trouble. Welcome back to the land of the living."

"I'm not entirely back." Her arms fell to the sides, eyes still closed.

Salomen rested a hand on her chest. "Stay put. I like you here." She brushed back her hair with her free hand and smiled up at Lhyn. "I did promise that I wouldn't disturb you."

"You were quiet as an empty temple. Andira, are you awake enough for a visitor? There's someone here to see the Lancer."

"For the love of Fahla." Andira let out a heartfelt groan as she rolled over and thumped her feet to the floor. With her back bent, forearms on her thighs, and head hanging, she was the picture of exhaustion. "Have they no sense of self-preservation? I'll throttle whoever chased me down here. Just as soon as I can call up the energy."

"Fleet captains aren't known for their sense of self-preservation," Ekatya said.

Her head snapped up. "Ekatya? When did—oh. Oh! Goddess above, I can *hear* you!" A joyous laugh bubbled out, chasing away the lines of fatigue from her face. "This is brilliant! Speedier than speedy."

"As Jaros would say." Smiling broadly, Salomen pulled her into a side embrace and kissed her cheek. "She sounds good, doesn't she?"

"She sounds—" Her breath shuddered. "Like something I've been hoping to hear."

"I can hear you, too," Ekatya said, tactfully ignoring the emotional overload. "Did you know that you snore?"

"Nice try. I do not."

"I can vouch for that," Lhyn offered. "Given that you've been sleeping here for the last half hantick."

"Yes, don't you have your own quarters in this enormous place? You have to clutter up ours?"

"Don't forget who arranged for you to have these quarters. I remember a time when you were grateful." Andira brushed a thumb under one eye and laughed again. "Thank you. This is just what I needed today. I was, ah, a little concerned that it might not work for me."

"You rebalanced," Salomen said. "You strengthened the connection."

Lhyn cocked her head. "Do you think it wouldn't have worked if they hadn't gone on their date?"

"The first time I heard a faint whisper of Ekatya was the night before the uprising, after you and I spent three days forging a deeper connection. It makes sense, does it not? The closer one of us gets to one of you, the easier it is to slip into your link."

"That does makes sense. Huh. I wonder—what if the energy frequencies of our bonds are almost identical? Right next to each other on the spectrum, so if we shift one frequency ever so slightly, they overlap?"

"Like radio channels." Ekatya could easily visualize it. "Even if you don't have the frequency perfectly dialed in, you can still hear some of the data. It just isn't clear or complete."

"You're clear. It's as if you're standing right in front of us," Andira said.

"I am."

"Don't bother," Salomen advised as Andira focused. "You'll only confuse your brain. I find it easier to close my eyes."

"I suppose it's Alsean nature to be given a gift and want even more. You're right, Ekatya. It's not complete."

"Not yet," Lhyn said. "I don't think we should assume this is the end point. We're learning as we go."

That sent them on a happy discussion of possibilities, with three of them doing most of the talking while Salomen listened with her eyes closed and a soft smile on her face. Andira didn't seem able to limit herself that way, instead glancing out the windows, at Lhyn, or at the approximate area she thought Ekatya might be.

As they wound down, Lhyn brought up the original purpose of Ekatya's visit and announced that "an Andira conversation" needed to happen.

"I don't think that's necessary," Ekatya objected. "I'm in a much better mood. Just being here with the three of you is a tonic."

"I've no doubt." Andira was leaning against Salomen, their hands tangled together and resting on her thigh. "I also have no doubt that if I tried that with Salomen, she wouldn't allow it."

"Not without a good reason. Lhyn, wasn't it you who said Ekatya would never get away with anything again?"

"That was me." Lhyn crossed her arms and looked expectant.

"What happened, Ekatya?"

Though Andira was merely repeating Lhyn's earlier question, Ekatya found it easier to tell her the story of a difficult day.

"My official involvement ended when I sent the report to Fleet," she concluded. "But I can't get that captain out of my mind. He fought so hard, and all for nothing. He never had a chance."

"No," Andira agreed. "But that wasn't the point of fighting, was it?"

Ekatya shook her head, briefly forgetting her invisibility. "I went down to the morgue to see him. I needed to do something, if only to bear witness. To tell the universe that another captain knew he went down swinging. He deserved that respect."

In the silence that fell, Andira looked at a spot to the right of Ekatya's waist—and then straight into her eyes.

"That will not happen to you," she said.

Ekatya froze. Could she—?

"If you go down swinging, it will not be for nothing, and it will not be in anonymity. You've already earned a hero's memorial on Alsea. No matter what happens, you won't be alone in a morgue, depending on the recognition of a fellow captain who never knew you."

She opened her mouth, prepared to deny it as a concern, but the words would not come. Andira had brought a hard truth to the surface.

She was losing her place in Fleet, still a hero in some corners but increasingly viewed as a dangerous renegade. They had put her on a short leash and given the other end to Admiral Greve. He had isolated her, forcing her to push others away to protect them. Talking with Alejandra in her office had been a painful reminder that what she once took for granted was now an illicit act.

She had taken dignity and respect for granted as well, trusting that she had earned them with a lifetime of service. Having conducted her share of official memorials, she was secure in the knowledge that if her luck ran out, Fleet would repay her sacrifice with honor.

That security had been chipped away, day by day. She hadn't paid attention until it was already gone, taking her last bit of faith with it.

"How did you know?" she asked.

"You're a warrior. You gave that captain the respect he deserved because you were afraid no one else would."

"And you extrapolated from that to—are you sure you're not sensing my emotions?"

"She doesn't need to," Salomen answered. "She knows you."

Andira nodded. "You once gave me your captain's bars and an oath of service. You took back the bars but not the oath. Even if I didn't have a personal stake, I would still have an oath holder's responsibility to honor you."

"Stars and Shippers, I forgot! I never got around to canceling it." The memories poured out of a box she had sealed and shoved to the back of her mind—that interminable month when she hung in limbo, trapped on Alsea while Fleet decided her fate. "You never said anything. Greve would blow an aneurysm if he knew I really am serving two governments."

"You're not. You're serving one while being the best ally you can to another. That oath was rendered moot the day you returned to Fleet. That said, until you formally rescind it, my responsibility remains."

"That's not fair to you. I should—"

"Furthermore," Andira said firmly, "we both know the day will come when you'll swear a new oath, this time to Fahla and Alsea. I will gladly transfer my responsibility to the state then." In a gentler tone, she added, "Since the day you put your captain's bars in my hand, there has never been a time when you could Return unrecognized. There never will be."

The words hit with the weight of truth. Her inexplicable grief for the *Blue Arctic*'s captain was in fact a mourning of her own loss—yet a far stronger safety net still hung beneath her.

"Thank you," she managed. "I've seen how you honor your heroes. I know you'd do the same for me."

"I would inscribe your name in the stars, Ekatya. But I do ask that you delay that event for a long, long while."

"I'll do my best."

Movement in her peripheral vision caught her attention, and she glanced down in time to see Lhyn's arm dropping away.

It had been curled around her waist, she realized. Lhyn was giving the others a visual cue, and Andira had used it to create an illusion.

Then again, was it really an illusion? Andira did see her. Based solely on Lhyn's cue, she had known exactly where her eyes would be. It was careful attention to detail, a knowledge that made her feel more seen than if her body had actually been standing there.

We see you, Salomen had said all those ninedays ago.

She had to appreciate the irony.

36

TLAHANA STATION

Given the increasing ease of their connections, Ekatya was barely surprised when Lhyn suddenly appeared next to her command chair while they were docking at Tlahana Station.

"I always wanted to see this," she said happily. "Stupid Fleet rules about civilians on the bridge during operations. Wow, your display is *spectacular*."

A quick smile was all Ekatya could offer in response, mindful of the twelve officers within easy hearing distance in the two lower rings.

"I didn't realize the station was this big," Lhyn continued as they neared their assigned dock at the end of a pylon. "Then again, I didn't see much the last time I was here."

The unwelcome reminder was a splash of cold, oily water. Lhyn had been brought to Tlahana Medical unconscious and badly injured, her body struggling with the damage from torture and too many contraindicated drugs. She had departed in far better condition but still confined to a gurney, never once seeing the majesty of the immense station.

"It's good to come back this way, don't you think? Both of us here, together. I wonder if we would have figured out how to control our link if you hadn't been forced into such creative thinking?"

She risked a short nod.

"Eventually, maybe. But I doubt we'd have managed it yet. Alejandra would never have accepted the risk to you if my life weren't hanging in the balance. The healers on Alsea still don't know enough about Gaian brains to manage something that delicate. Without the chemical intervention, we wouldn't have known what was possible. Maybe Kane Muir did us a favor in the long term." She winced at Ekatya's glare. "I didn't say we should thank him. But I'd rather find things to appreciate than wallow in the shit I can't change."

"Well done, Lieutenant Scarp," Ekatya said crisply. "I think you beat your record for closest approach. Fire mooring cables."

The bridge erupted into the flurry of activity that accompanied every docking. They needed to monitor the cable attachment and tensioning, hook up the umbilicals, test the seals—the checklist was long, and Ekatya wasn't needed for any of it. Instead, she watched Lhyn find immense pleasure in an operation she had long since taken for granted.

"You're right," she murmured once the docking was completed and her officers were moving from their stations. "It would have taken much longer. You might not know how to be here now, and I'm glad you are."

Lhyn's bright smile made the risk of speaking worthwhile.

At the request of the station commander, who wanted more details on the pirated icebox, Ekatya was the first off the ship. The familiar corridors of Tlahana Station acquired a new feel with Lhyn gliding beside her, entertaining herself with her invisibility.

They were in one of the smaller spokes that led to the central hub when a large group of station workers came toward them, filling the corridor from one side to the other. Though Ekatya's uniform gave her right of way, she had never been one of those officers who would force others to step aside. A few steps took her to the wall, where she paused by a large viewport and only then realized she was alone.

Lhyn was still out in the middle of the corridor, watching the group approach.

The workers closed the gap, an older man walking straight through her as she whooped in delight. Soon she was surrounded, a head higher than the people streaming past. She pinched her nose shut, waved one hand over her head, and dropped to vanish from view. Then she surged back up and began an exaggerated breast stroke.

Ekatya could not stop herself from grinning like an idiot. Several of the passing workers responded in kind, enjoying her good humor despite having no idea of its source.

Lhyn continued to swim.

By the time the last straggler went by, Ekatya's grin threatened to blind unsuspecting victims and Lhyn was laughing.

"I've wanted to do that since I was fifteen! My favorite book was about a scientist who made herself invisible and became her world's greatest thief."

"Do I need to worry about you carrying contraband off the station?"

Lhyn passed her hand through the bulkhead as they resumed their walk. "If only I could interact with physical matter. Still, this is literally a dream come true. It was the invisibility I loved, not the thieving part."

"Let me guess. You fantasized about being able to observe new cultures without being seen."

"You know me so well."

"This is my dream come true, too." Ekatya nodded at a passing ensign who saluted the uniform and then looked shocked at who was wearing it. "I always wanted to bring you back to see Tlahana the right way. But it was never safe for you."

"See? Invisibility. That scientist had the right idea."

"Stealing?"

"Right idea, wrong application."

"That could probably sum up ninety percent of Protectorate politics."

"Captain Serrado?"

Stifling her groan, Ekatya stopped and turned. "Ensign."

The young woman jogged up. "I'm sorry to disturb you, but, um—" She scratched the back of her neck. "I wanted to say that you're my hero."

Startled, Ekatya could only stare.

"Greve doesn't represent all of Fleet," Lhyn said quietly. "He only makes you think he does."

"I'm sorry, Ensign . . ." Ekatya glanced at her name tag. "Bokamoso. You've caught me by surprise."

"I know, you're probably on your way to a meeting where you decide the fate of the galaxy." Folding her hands together, she gave a self-conscious laugh. "And I know you don't have time for someone like me, but I've—Seeders, I've dreamed of meeting you. When I tell my club, they'll go nova." Her hands fluttered to her hips, then behind her back. She was like a young Lieutenant Kitt, all tight curls and restless energy.

"Your club? Do I want to know?"

It was all the encouragement the ensign needed. "Oh! There are five of us. We formed a study group as cadets and now—we just never stopped, I guess. They teased me about my crush when you were reassigned to Director Sholokhov, but I had the last laugh when you got the *Phoenix*. I knew you'd come out on top."

Lhyn folded her arms with a smirk. "A crush! How adorable."

Ensign Bokamoso seemed to have heard her own words at the same time. A small squeak escaped as she covered her mouth.

"It's all right, Ensign. I take it as a compliment." Ekatya found it impossible not to smile at this earnest young woman. "And I appreciate your faith in me."

"Of course I have faith, you're the greatest captain in Fleet! The Serrado Spin? I can only dream of having a battle tactic named after me. You had one of the best records in Fleet *before* you took out a Voloth invasion group single-handedly. You saved an entire planet! My stars and asteroids, you're the reason the Alseans are free. Well, you and your bondmate." She beamed. "Ha! Yang is going to be so jealous. He has a crush on Dr. Rivers. He's in xenobiology, but he swears if he'd read her book earlier, he would have chosen anthropology instead."

"I like this club," Lhyn announced. "Bright young minds and impeccable taste in role models."

"Dr. Rivers will be proud to know she inspired someone in the next generation of scientists," Ekatya said. "Insufferably proud, I'm sure."

"Hoi. That was uncalled for."

Ensign Bokamoso looked as if she'd been given a promotion. "You said 'will be.' You're going to tell her? Yang will *die*."

"But at least he'll die happy," Lhyn said. "Get his com code, will you? Let's make these kids' year."

Ekatya pulled her pad from its sleeve pocket. "I'll make you a deal, Ensign. Give me your com code and your friend's, and Lhyn and I will send something. If your club is full of scientists and skeptical ensigns, they'll need proof before they go nova."

"Oh my stars! Thank you!" She ripped the pad from Ekatya's hand as if afraid the offer would be rescinded and entered the codes in a rapid blur. Handing it back, she grinned so widely that the corridor illumination might have increased. "This is phenomenal! I'm so glad I talked myself into saying something. I wasn't going to, because you deserve your privacy, but—" She gulped. "But I'll shut up now and let you be on your way."

"I'm glad you talked yourself into it, too." Ekatya pocketed the pad. "It's made my day to have a reminder that not everyone disagrees with my decision at Alsea."

Her eyes widened. "Everyone I know backs you. I mean, we hear about the ossified admirals who don't, but they're two generations out of touch. Fleet shouldn't punish a captain who did the right thing. Yang and I, we're planning to make admiral someday. When we do, look out."

"I believe you." Ekatya held out a hand. "It was good to meet you, Ensign."

The corridor brightened. "It was a *dream* to meet you, Captain."

"You realize she'll never wash that hand again," Lhyn said, watching the ensign practically dance down the corridor.

Ekatya chuckled. "What are you planning to send your admirer?"

"I don't know yet. But it'll be fun to think about while I wait for you to come home."

They passed out of the spoke and into the great central hub, where floor-to-ceiling viewports offered spectacular views of the station's pylons stretching into space. Ekatya stopped at one that overlooked the *Phoenix*'s pylon and tried to take in every detail for Lhyn's benefit.

"My stars and asteroids," Lhyn said. "I'm adopting that phrase, by the way. But what a scene! Why are you all the way out at the end?"

"Tlahana was built before Pulsar-class ships were a twinkle in a ship designer's eye. It's why docking here is such a hassle. All that activity you saw on the bridge? That wouldn't happen at a place like Quinton Shipyards. We'd glide in and everything would snap into place. Here, we have to get creative with attachments that are made for smaller ships. And the only place we fit is out there at the end."

"But you make it work."

"We always do."

"That could be your motto," Lhyn mused. "Make it work."

"Make it work *right*," Ekatya corrected.

"I thought that went without saying."

They took a lift up several decks, then passed through a corridor of service shops and into the administrative area. This was a restricted part of the station, with narrower corridors and lower ceilings, and everyone wore Fleet uniforms.

"I see why you feel at home here," Lhyn said, dodging a lieutenant who had snapped to attention as Ekatya passed. "The rest of the station is like a floating city. Big, open spaces full of civilians. This is more like a ship."

"Does that make me hopelessly Fleet? Sometimes I wonder if I've lived so long in this culture that I don't know how to be normal."

Lhyn snorted. "Normal? You're in a six-pointed bond with two aliens. You're talking to me mind to mind over a distance of half the quadrant. The leader of an entire planet is trusting you to protect her people. Nothing about your life is normal."

"That wasn't exactly the answer I was hoping for."

"Every culture defines its own version. Do you know how to be normal on Gaia? I'd say yes. When we go back to visit your grandparents, you fit right in."

"For a while." She couldn't imagine living there again. It was wonderful to visit, but . . .

"And you're learning how to fit in on Alsea. Which has a dramatically different definition of normal than any culture I've studied."

"That's the truth and a half. Maybe that's why I'm so comfortable there, even when I feel like an outsider."

"You won't always feel that way. It's simple exposure, tyrina. You're only there a few days at a time, like a parent who sees her children twice a week and wonders why they keep surprising her. It's not you. It's your schedule. When that changes, so will the rest of it."

"I'm ready for that schedule to change," Ekatya admitted. "I hate being away from you. From all of you. It feels wrong."

"It *is* wrong. You're a tyree; you're supposed to be here. What you're doing, no tyree has ever done. Andira says it shouldn't even be possible. I told her you don't tend to listen when you're warned something is impossible. And thank the stars for that, or I wouldn't be alive."

"Maybe we should thank Fahla for it," she said, only half joking.

They had arrived at the station commander's office, where Lhyn remained silent as Ekatya presented herself and waited. The normally loquacious aide was oddly reserved today, offering formal greetings and none of the usual questions about where she had been and what she had done.

Ekatya understood why the moment she entered the office and found the station commander absent.

"It was worth staying the extra day just for that look on your face," Director Sholokhov said genially. He gestured toward the two guest chairs across the desk. "Have a seat, Captain Serrado."

"Fucking stars." Lhyn sat next to her. "You weren't kidding. He's scary."

Ekatya flicked her hand to the side and hoped the message was clear. Taking on Sholokhov would require all of her attention; she couldn't afford to be distracted.

"I hadn't heard about your demotion," she said.

He smiled. "I'll admit one thing. You were right when you said I might appreciate your honesty. There's not another person in the Protectorate who would use an insult as an opening gambit with me."

"Actually, that was a joke, but I wouldn't expect you to recognize one."

"Now *that* is an insult. You're coming in with all weapons loaded, I see. There's no need. I merely wanted to ask you about the icebox."

"Don't tell me you came all the way here from Gov Dome for that."

"I had other business in the sector. But I did stay to speak with you."

"Why?"

"Because this is the third icebox in a month." He crossed his hands atop the desk. "You called the pirates 'restrained' in their actions. Why would you say that? They spaced the entire crew."

Ekatya ticked off the points on her fingers. "No rapes, no assaults, no physical injuries other than bruises and abrasions from restraining them. Except for the captain, but his wounds were from a fight. He wasn't held down and beaten. Those pirates had a purpose, and it wasn't to steal ice or amuse themselves. They didn't dally. It was an efficient operation, designed to neutralize the crew, dump the cargo, and get that ship back into base space before anyone could respond."

"And? Anything else out of the ordinary?"

She hesitated.

"Go on. I know you don't put everything into your reports. You're focused on facts." He leaned forward. "But my job is to assemble the pieces, and for that, I need all the details. Not just the ones you can prove."

It was an odd thing, she mused. She was facing her most dangerous antagonist, yet she felt better talking to him than to Greve. At least Sholokhov respected her abilities, even while he strove to put her down.

"I'm not convinced they were pirates," she said.

"I'm not either. What's your reasoning?"

"They were too good at transition recovery. They came out of base space and were operational faster than some Fleet crews. That requires a significant investment in training. But the part that's been sticking in my mind is that they flew off in formation. On a covert mission, in an area where there were no other ships within an eight-hour radius. There was no reason for it except that it's what they're used to. That means they have a military background."

"Pirates are always recruiting ex-military."

"For an entire squadron?"

He steepled his fingers. "Valid point. I recognize that this is conjecture, but sometimes that's exactly what we need. It's not only Fleet that depends on the experience of its officers. Protectorate Security does as well. You should have included this in your report."

"My current supervisor does not encourage conjecture," she said flatly.

"Your current supervisor is an inflated gasbag who is underperforming already low expectations. That's why I proposed replacing him with you. Along with your promotion to rear admiral, of course." His lips twitched. "I do enjoy striking you speechless."

She was certainly stunned. Sholokhov didn't propose things; he made them happen and announced it after the fact.

"I thought you didn't meddle in Fleet personnel choices."

"I told you I don't meddle in the minutiae. This would be a major personnel choice, impacting the security of the Protectorate."

"Why wasn't Greve's placement just as major?"

"Because that was about controlling you. This would be about freeing you. I trust you understand the strategic difference."

She had not expected him to baldly confirm what everyone in Fleet refused to admit. "I know I'm in a cage," she said. "It's refreshing to hear someone finally say it."

"If you thought Fleet would let you go merrily on your way with an alien influence embedded in your brain, you're even more naive than I gave you credit for. Of course you're in a cage. You're an unknown risk. I had a way to mitigate that risk, free you, and get what I wanted, all in one easy move. Your patron put a stop to it."

"You offered my career in exchange for high empaths." She shook her head. "Is that why you stayed here? To throw this in my face? I know it wasn't about the icebox; you could have called me for that."

"It was about both, and I'm merely informing you that Lancer Tal isn't the friend you think she is. I offered her a good deal. A very good deal, where everyone walked away happy. She turned me down. I thought it was a negotiating tactic, so I gave her time to think about it. My second offer was received with the same disdain as the first." He sat back with a scowl. "That means I was working with faulty intelligence. I believed you had a special value to her. You don't. You're useful to her, just as you are to me. When the price was too high, she threw you off the deck."

"What a Seeder-sucking asshead." Lhyn couldn't keep silent. "And I thought he was *smart*."

Ekatya held back a smile, both at Lhyn's ire and Sholokhov's error. He was judging Andira by his own measure. It would never occur to him that her refusal was based on anything other than political calculation.

"She's a world leader who already negotiated an advantageous treaty with the Protectorate. You may think I'm naive, but you can't possibly think she is. Even if she did value my career at such a stratospheric level, the Council wouldn't. Whatever she said she'd trade for, she meant it."

"A Pulsar-class ship," he said scornfully. "Ridiculous."

"Why? The *Phoenix* is already out there."

"Under Protectorate ownership and control! We don't hand over billion-credit assets."

"But that number includes costs that don't apply, doesn't it? Research and development, for a ship you can replace without any further investment in design. Repairs and maintenance that you won't be performing. Weaponry and supplies you won't have to stock. Strip it down to what you're actually trading, and that number loses a zero or two. Besides," she added, "you know they're working on raising the *Caphenon*. Once they get that in orbit, you won't have anything to offer. They'll have their very own Pulsar-class ship."

"The *Caphenon* will have the same hull plating as their fighters. It won't be able to enter base space."

"Why would they care if it goes into base space? They're not the Voloth, searching for new territory and resources. They're not even us, trying to expand our influence. All they want is to protect themselves. They don't need to leave their system to do that."

He stared at her.

"Did that not occur to you?" she asked.

"How long until they raise that ship? Best estimate."

Great galaxies, it really hadn't. How could he overlook something so obvious?

Then again, perhaps it shouldn't be a surprise. If there was one thing Sholokhov would not expect, it was an adversary who didn't seek power.

"Two years. Three at the outside."

He drummed his fingers on the armrests, staring at an invisible point over her shoulder. "Faulty intelligence," he murmured.

Though soft, his tone was so menacing that Ekatya suppressed a shiver. Someone would surely be punished for this failure.

His unsettling light eyes refocused on her. "Thank you for your input, Captain. I need to get back to Gov Dome. But first, I agree with your conjecture about the pirates. They're not pirates at all."

"What do you think they are?"

"Ex-military mercenaries if we're lucky. Active military if we're not. My strong suspicion is the Voloth. They're planning something; I just can't think what they'd do with iceboxes. You've received the latest update on their movements?"

"Increasing activity, nothing that can be traced to a specific intent," she said. "No invasion groups."

"No, they learned their lesson with that. You won't have to deal with orbital invaders." Though he did not move a muscle, he suddenly seemed sharper. "I have more recent intel. A heavy cruiser is taking on supplies and preparing to leave Voloth space in three weeks."

Which would put it in Alsean space in six weeks, right on schedule. "I don't suppose this new intel will result in reinforcements."

"A single heavy cruiser is not cause for alarm, given your presence."

"And if it brings friends? You know the Voloth won't send just one. They'll want to outgun us."

"My intel is of one heavy cruiser and its accompanying destroyers," he repeated. "That is the data informing deployment decisions. That and your reputation. I did tell you that you and the Alseans were victims of your own success."

"I think he tried to get reinforcements," Lhyn said. "But he hit the wall of political idiocy."

And he would never admit that he didn't fully control the situation. This was his version of friendly advice.

"If I were you, I'd keep my eyes open," Sholokhov added, confirming her guess. "Alsea is almost finished with that space elevator, isn't it?"

37

PEACE IN WAR

I t was a paradox, Micah thought, that the moon in which Alsea prepared for battle was one of the best moons of his life.

Fahla did love her ironies.

Ekatya brought the *Phoenix* back from Tlahana Station fully restocked with dummy missiles and shield breakers, enabling a new and more serious round of war games. The initial game had shown them what did and didn't work; now they relentlessly practiced strategies and honed their skills.

During this final push, the *Phoenix* never left orbit. For a glorious moon, Micah saw Alejandra nearly every day. Candini flew to the ship three days out of four with an empty seat in her Serrado fighter that she graciously lent him. The nature of her duties meant she was not there long, making it simple for Alejandra to schedule her work breaks in conjunction with Micah's presence on the ship. When he couldn't go there, Alejandra would fly down in a shuttle for a precious day of leave.

The very air of the State House was tense, the staff scurrying around as if slowing to a walk might endanger the battle's outcome. Tal worked from dawn to dusk in her office, at Blacksun Base, or out in the park, practicing with the divine tyrees. Salomen became adept at finding the bridge of any ship in the battle group.

Micah rarely had time for more than a passing word with either of them. He and Gehrain were setting up protection for the divine tyrees, who would be dangerously exposed should the Voloth send modified fighters to Blacksun. When Gehrain had that sufficiently in hand, Micah left him to the smaller details and lent his expertise to the emergency shelter plan.

Citywide evacuations were not planned. They should not be necessary, due to their much improved defenses and the improbability of another invasion. In addition, past experience had shown that such large-scale evacuations caused an entirely different set of issues, including fatalities. If the worst occurred, the temple bells would ring to alert residents to seek shelter.

Micah's task lay in a different type of evacuation. Wanting to prepare for any eventuality, Tal had ordered a plan to shelter a small population from orbital bombardment. It was a war crime to devastate cities from orbit, one Ekatya said the Voloth had never committed.

Neither Tal nor Micah found that of any great comfort.

In the event of the unthinkable, they would need to protect their government and a cross section of Alseans chosen for their ability to reestablish Alsean civilization. The *Caphenon* was their largest shelter, shielded and equipped to feed more than a thousand. Even more secure was the war room level of Blacksun Base, their original hardened shelter before the *Caphenon* crashed. Other bunkers and shelters abounded within the cities.

Those selected for the plan called Alsea Ascendant would be escorted when the time came. Even as a hypothetical exercise, the decisions of who would live and who would be left to die wore down his soul.

All around him were the stresses of impending warfare. Their tactics were risky, their strategies based largely on conjecture and Tal's instincts, and the consequences of failure could shatter Alsea.

None of it mattered when he held Alejandra in his arms.

For most of his life, he had been faithful to the memory of Realta. Casual joinings never touched his heart, and working with Tal made it impossible to forget. She would smile a certain way, or raise an eyebrow, or speak in a particular tone of voice, and he would see Realta shining through her daughter. It wasn't that he couldn't move past his ancient loss. It was that he had no wish to.

When he and Alejandra conducted their Rite of Knowing, his heart opened wide in a single night. Every hantick they spent together anchored the truth more firmly: Fahla had given him a second love as great as the first. Yet it was different, and the differences were glorious.

Realta had never been free to openly love him. Alejandra had no such restrictions. She did indeed love like she fought, with a passion and intensity that left him breathless, and she had made it immediately clear that she did not intend to hide him. On their first visit to Blacksun Temple, he had kept his distance, old habit making him cautious. She had allowed that only for the length of time it took to light the oil bowls. When she slipped her arm around his waist, openly advertising their relationship, he felt as if the light streaming through the roof was solely for them.

What surprised him most was the ease of it. His relationship with Realta had been tumultuous, stressed by their youth and the fact that her bondmate was his best friend. She had a great heart and a bottomless depth of love to give, yet remained a scholar who did not fully comprehend or value the warrior way of thinking. He had never realized what a barrier that created until Alejandra slipped into his life with no barrier at all. She was a different sort of scholar, one who understood warriors and worked in a warrior world. It made their communication nearly effortless.

He thought of that one day after mornmeal, when Alejandra sat at the dining table in her State House suite with a drawing pad in one hand, a pencil in the other, and a cup of shannel at her elbow. It was a peaceful moment of a well-earned day off, and had it been Realta sitting there, he would never have spoken what was on his mind.

"Do you think it's enough?"

She looked up. "Do I think what is enough?"

"Everything. Our preparations. Ekatya's preparations. Yours. You've battled the Voloth before. In space, I mean. Will it be enough?"

"All I saw of those battles were the bodies that came into my medbay. Are my preparations enough? Yes. But that's not what you're asking."

She set down her pencil and turned the pad to face him. Using fine lines and shading, she had drawn what she saw: the window of the dining area, looking onto a sweeping view of the State Park and Blacksun's skyline beyond. In the foreground, drawn with more detail than the rest, was the bud vase on the sill with its tiny bouquet of flowers.

"This is what we're all fighting for," she said. "Keeping this from harm. I fight on the individual scale, one body at a time. You and Tal and

Ekatya, you're all fighting on a global scale. You've told me what Tal did during the Battle of Alsea. I've read Ekatya's service record. You want my opinion? I think the Voloth are fools to come back and get their heads handed to them a third time."

No, she was not Realta, he thought as she rose from her chair and slipped around the table. With a dancer's grace, she straddled his lap and crossed her wrists behind his neck.

"I want to draw you," she said.

"Which part of me?"

"Well . . ." Her eyebrows lifted suggestively. "Your face, of course."

"Oh. I was hoping I'd need to be naked."

"It's best if you are."

"For your creative urges?"

"For the urges that come after those."

Laughing, he tried to kiss her but couldn't keep his lips in the right shape. "You'd get kissed more often if you didn't keep making me smile."

"That's not an incentive to stop. I love your smile." Hers dimmed, though, and he sensed a serious conversation approaching.

"What is it?" he asked.

"I've decided to accept the job."

In the moon and a half since telling him of Prime Scholar Yaserka's offer, she had not mentioned it again. He had been afraid to ask, fearing disappointment. Now his heart soared.

"That cannot have been an easy decision," he said.

She gave him a look of gratitude. "No, but these simulations have tipped me over the edge. I'm done with this part of my life. I'll get through this battle, and that will give Ekatya a good long time to find my replacement before she'll need another war-ready chief surgeon. I hate to leave her there, but you were right. She wouldn't want me to stay just for her."

"And Rahel?"

Her lips thinned. "Rahel is . . . making plans for her own future. We've talked about it, and we're supporting each other in the paths we've chosen."

While the truth of that was in their skin contact, a world of unspoken meaning ran beneath her words.

He did not press her. When she wanted him to know, she would tell him.

"I'll be living in Blacksun by next moon, if all goes well." She leaned against the table, her hands at his waist. "I don't want you to feel pressured by this. Nothing has to change. I plan to find a house somewhere close, so I can walk over and see you."

"That must be a fine salary Yaserka is offering. Houses close to the State Park are handsomely priced."

"It's a very fine salary." A disbelieving smile crossed her face. "I don't think I'll be budgeting for my next set of paintbrushes."

Her happiness, even as cautious as it was, released his own elation. "Yaserka is an arrogant ass, but he's also a skilled politician. He knows what you're worth. You'll be a credit to his caste and a gift to Alsea." He tucked a lock of hair behind her shoulder. "I don't feel pressured. I feel blessed. Do you think one rack of oil bowls will be enough to thank Fahla? Perhaps I should light two."

She caught his hand and kissed it. "Light as many as you want. I'll help. This is all my dreams but one, and I've made my peace with that one."

"Josue."

She nodded.

"I know that you would never, *could* never replace him," he said carefully. "But if you're leaving Fleet and setting up a new life on Alsea . . . is there any reason you couldn't include a family in that life?"

"Well, I was hoping for a family of two at some point." She squeezed his hand.

"As do I. But I'm referring to a child."

Shock jolted through her touch. "What?"

"Being a mother is as much a part of your heart as being a healer. If you had the opportunity, is that something you would consider?"

"I don't—are you talking about adoption?"

"I'm talking about us. Having our own child."

"I can't. You know that. Even if I still had a uterus, I'd be past the age of child bearing."

"But I'm not."

She scrambled off his lap with none of her earlier grace. "You're

Alsean," she blurted. "My sainted Shippers, I never—" A vehement string of foreign words followed.

"I'm Alsean," he agreed.

"Micah, you're my age."

What did that matter? "It's true that most of us bear children earlier, but I couldn't with Realta, and there was no one else until you. I'm still capable. You didn't know that?"

"I'm not studying for obstetrics! Or pediatrics! Making peace with that loss doesn't mean I want to *torture* myself with—no. No, no, you can't say that like it's—you can't—" She bent her head, clasping it with both hands, then whirled and marched to the window.

Quietly, he collected their dishes and carried them to the kitchen. He poured out the now-cool shannel and scraped the plates, stacked everything on the cart, pushed it into the corridor, and activated the call signal. State House staff would pick it up within five ticks.

When he rejoined her, Alejandra had not moved. She stared out the window, radiating such tension that the walls were virtually visible around her body. His touch, and the emotional disclosure it enabled, would not be welcome.

"I'm sorry if I hurt you," he said. "It was never my intention."

"Hurt me?" She let out a harsh laugh. "Hurt me. More like shred my heart. Why would you bring that up?"

"You said you had all your dreams but one. I thought—"

"We're not compatible," she snapped. "Your healers tested it when it became a potential issue with the Voloth settlers. Even if implantation were possible, the gametes won't combine. I'm happy for you that you can still have children. By all means, go out and have them. But it won't be with me."

"I don't want to do it without you."

"Then I'm sorry."

He caught her wrist as she turned away and winced at the searing pain beneath her skin. "Alejandra."

"Let me go."

"Please listen."

She pulled with all her strength. "Let me go or so help me, I will—"

"Alseans use a surrogate."

Her arm went slack. She didn't speak or look at him, but she wasn't trying to run.

He let his hand slide past her limp fingers. "When one bondmate is not capable, the couple choose a surrogate and begin the creation ceremony together. All three of them work to create life. They're *all* involved."

Her only response was to wrap her arms around her waist and stare at the floor.

"You grieve because you had only one opportunity," he said softly. "That's no longer true. I wanted you to know that you have a choice."

Without turning her head, she gave a single nod.

Then she went straight out the door.

38

BATTLE PREP

R ahel suspected she shouldn't enjoy this as much as she did. There was so much at stake, both for Alsea and the Fleet battle group assigned to protect it. The intelligence regarding a Voloth attack was now plentiful and incontrovertible, according to Captain Serrado. They were on their way. The only questions remaining were how many ships would come and when they would arrive. People on all sides would die, possibly thousands of them. She herself would be at great risk.

Yet she had never felt so alive.

It wasn't until they returned from Tlahana Station that she realized how profoundly the ship's spirit had been affected by Serrado's mood. Something had happened on that station, or perhaps Serrado was simply done tolerating the malevolent machinations of Admiral Greve. Or perhaps, as Dr. Wells suggested, she had thrown herself so far into battle prep that she had no time to waste on walking sewage.

Whatever the cause, she had transformed. She was everywhere at once, answering questions, suggesting improvements to plans and tactics, running drills, and encouraging any crew member who needed it. Under her unflagging guidance, the crew coalesced into an efficient, deadly fighting force.

Rahel was fiercely proud to be part of it.

She basked in the sense of purpose that permeated the corridors.

Small rivalries or petty grievances gave way to a shared identity, and the level of fear was bafflingly low. One cycle ago, the death of a single crew member eaten by starving aliens had instigated such terror that she had crumpled under the emotional bombardment. Now, facing a far greater risk, she sensed determination more than anything else.

"It's because this is an external foe, not one hidden in the ship," Lokomorra explained one evening. "It's not an unknown terror. The crew know the Voloth. They know Captain Serrado has beaten them before, and they know they're safer inside this ship than anywhere else."

"But Captain Serrado isn't in charge of the battle group," Rahel pointed out. "Admiral Greve is."

"In name only," he said wryly. "Every time the captains and execs meet for a strategy session, Greve tries to throw his weight around. We listen politely, and then we agree with whatever Serrado says is best. He puts his boot down just to soothe his ego, but he can't countermand everything because even he has to see that she knows what she's doing. He has the rank, but she has the respect. He's been seething over it."

That was worrisome. If Greve felt threatened by the woman he viewed as an enemy, then Serrado was in more danger than ever.

After that, Rahel found ways to be near the captain as often as possible. In a stroke of genius, she asked permission to shadow her. After all, part of her job description was to learn about Fleet methods so she could take the knowledge back to Alsea. What better time to learn than during the preparations for a battle?

Serrado had gladly approved. From that moment forward, Rahel was constantly at her side, leaving only to fly drills.

Greve noticed, of course. He dragged Rahel into another of those infuriating check-ins, this time eyeing her with distrust and asking pointed questions before they began. But she had spent most of her career deflecting suspicious mid empaths and even an occasional high empath. Greve was no challenge at all.

"Lancer Tal ordered me to shadow her," she said. "She believes Captain Serrado is the best choice to teach us battle tactics in this kind of warfare. I did mention that you command the battle group, but . . ." She gave a tiny shrug. "I obey my orders."

Gratification rolled over her senses. "At least someone does."

Serrado didn't bother to hide her contempt during the check-in, giving Rahel the perfect opportunity to offer a contrast. She kept it subtle, simply bobbing her head in a respectful nod as they rose to leave.

A day later, she passed him in a corridor on her way to the shuttle bay. "Admiral," she said, touching her fist to her chest.

She had gone two more steps when he stopped her.

"Was that a salute, First Guard?"

"Yes, Admiral."

"You've never saluted me before."

"Captain Serrado says there's a time and a place for formal observation of protocol. She dislikes it most of the time, but since you asked for my assistance, I paid closer attention to how you observe it. Was I wrong to think you prefer proper observation of rank?"

"You're not wrong." He gave a brisk nod. "Carry on."

"Thank you, Admiral."

The next time he demanded her "assistance" for a check-in, his suspicion was reserved for the captain. At the end, she saluted him again before following Serrado out the door.

After that, her presence at the check-ins became a daily requirement. Greve took great satisfaction in her respectful demeanor, frequently using it to jab Serrado. Rahel despised him more each time.

At long last, the day came when the Alsean government released an announcement through Ambassador Solvassen: the grand opening of the space elevator would take place in a nineday.

The date was a misdirection. The elevator was ready now, but Lancer Tal was setting out bait. According to the announcement, all six caste Primes would be passengers for the inaugural trip—an irresistible target if the Voloth wanted to devastate their government.

Even if Rahel hadn't known the truth through Captain Serrado, she wouldn't have believed Lancer Tal would allow such a risk. But the Primes played it up, releasing their own statements about the historic moment when Alseans would step into the stars.

Five days before the grand opening, the battle group moved into position. The *Victory* and *Thea* patrolled just outside the minefield surrounding the base space exit marker, while the *Phoenix* remained at a point between the minefield and Alsea.

In their best-case scenarios, the mines would neutralize at least one and possibly two Voloth ships while damaging another two to three. In the less optimal but more likely scenario, the first ships out would not be fully neutralized but would incur sufficient damage to enable a swift and decisive attack. As long as the mines knocked out Voloth shielding, the *Victory* and *Thea* had the advantage. Once the mines were used up, the strategy changed. At that point, the Fleet destroyers would fall back toward the *Phoenix*, which would move up to support them.

In their first war games, the *Phoenix* had begun in the same position as the *Thea*, with the *Victory* playing the role of a Voloth heavy cruiser. Their assumption had been that with the entire battle group on offense, they could cause more damage during the precious seconds when the mines did their jobs and the Voloth were recovering from exit transition nausea. Then they would fight in a fallback pattern, always keeping a defensive line between the Voloth and Alsea.

That attempt had revealed a significant weakness: the defending ships could not shoot down all of the missiles the Voloth were likely to launch toward Alsea. As Captain Serrado pointed out, the goal of the attack was not to defeat Protectorate ships but to demolish the space elevator. As soon as that was accomplished, the Voloth would probably retreat. If they could succeed without ever moving past the exit point, so much the better, making it likely that they would fire missiles as soon as they could.

With its greater size and larger number of launch tubes, the *Phoenix* was the best choice for defending against those missiles. It had taken several war games to determine the optimal placement: far enough back for the best chance of shooting them down, close enough to run up to the *Thea* and *Victory* when it became necessary.

When the ships took their final positions, Candini moved aboard. She would eat and sleep on the *Phoenix* until the battle began, enabling her to launch in space rather than from the planet's surface. Captain Serrado endorsed the strategy, agreeing that she would have a commanding view of the initial battle and be better able to direct her fighters when they arrived.

Rahel was overjoyed that it had worked out this way. Since her arrival, Candini had flown with a number of Alsean gunners, both to train them and to find an alternate. For her part, Rahel had trained with several *Phoenix* pilots as a backup gunner. Both agreed that they worked better together than with their second choices. They simply clicked.

For four days, the crew of the *Phoenix* held its collective breath. Other than regular sorties flown into base space—a tactic Serrado admitted was nearly useless but which kept part of the crew busy and the fighter pilots sharp—it was now a waiting game. She also rotated pairs of fighters through tedious scouting shifts, a job Rahel was glad not to be doing. The scouts had to sit on their hands, engines spun down and quantum coms deactivated, while they hid next to the base space relay. Not until the Voloth ships reached the relay would the scouts be able to detect them, making their warning of little use in terms of preparation time. But time wasn't the issue, Serrado said. What she wanted to know was how many and what types of ships they were facing before they came out of base space.

"Have you ever considered that this was all a misdirection and they're attacking some other planet?" Rahel asked on the afternoon of the fourth day. She was in the captain's office, a location she had seen more in the past month than the previous six combined.

"Yes, of course. That's the best of all possibilities for us. And the worst." Captain Serrado leaned back in her chair with a quiet groan. "Stars and Shippers, I'm tired of waiting."

"Why the worst?"

She pulled the clip from her hair and tossed it on her desk, then ran her fingers through the loosened strands. "Because if they don't come, I won't know what to expect. We've based everything on a strategy that makes sense. To me, to Lancer Tal, to Fleet. If we're wrong, we have to rethink everything. I don't believe for one moment that the Voloth are ready to leave Alsea alone. But if they do come, we're prepared. Right down to the hour of attack. Well," she amended, "one of two hours."

This was new. "How do you know that?"

"Physics. The space elevator swings with Alsea's rotation. There are two points in every rotation when it presents the greatest profile as viewed from the base space exit point. The rest of the time, it's partly or wholly shielded by the planet, or barely visible in front of it."

"You *do* have it all figured out."

"Hades, I hope so." She rose from her chair and stretched, then shook out her arms. "The inactivity is killing me. I'm afraid to do anything that might reduce my readiness, in case they don't do what I expect."

"Does that include showers?" Rahel joked.

"Didn't you get the ship-wide memo? No one is taking showers. They were forbidden as of two days ago."

"You're lying."

"It's no fun trying to fool an Alsean. Come on, I'm ready for a cup of shannel."

That was another benefit of spending so much time with the captain. Every day, she brought a thermal flask of shannel to her office, taken from the dispenser Lancer Tal had given her. And every day, she shared it.

Rahel followed her across the office to the small table and waited behind a chair. "I've realized something," she said, watching her open a cupboard. "This isn't merely shannel. It's an honor. It's like me letting Salomen hold my stave. I wouldn't give it to just anyone."

Serrado turned, thermal flask in hand. "You're right. I've only—"

"Captain Serrado." Commander Lokomorra's voice came over the office com. *"We've got pikamet radiation."*

"Fucking Hades!" She slammed the flask back into the cupboard and ran for the door. "They're a day early!"

39

SAVING THE SAVIOR

Ekatya raced onto the bridge, Rahel at her heels. Lokomorra left her command chair and stood aside as she jogged up the ramp past the first and second rings. "Our scouts?" she asked. They weren't due back for two hours yet.

He shook his head grimly. "No communication. And the radiation signature is too large for a fighter."

They looked at each other in silent acknowledgement. Their scouts were dead.

It was always a gamble. Of course the Voloth would send their own scouts, but hers had the advantage of being in gray mode. They should have remained undetected until they powered up their engines.

"Either their scouts found ours immediately," Lokomorra said, "and shot them down before they could get off a message—"

"Or they've developed jamming tech that works in base space."

"Hard as it is to say, I prefer the first option."

"I hate them both. How many exit points?"

She followed his pointing finger to the bow section of the upper display, where the marker buoy was outlined in bright green. Next to it, a red circle indicated the source of radiation.

"Only one? Something's wrong. What are they doing?"

"I don't know. This isn't any Voloth tactic I've heard of."

"I don't suppose it's a cruise ship that lost its way," she grumbled. "Comms, notify the Alsean war council. Phoenix, sound General Quarters."

As the General Quarters alarm rang out, the lift disgorged the last person she wanted to see. Admiral Greve made his way across the bridge, seeming to tread through space. For a savage moment, she wished the lower display had a trapdoor connecting straight to an airlock. She could drop him through it and watch with a smile as he pinwheeled in vacuum.

"Status report," he demanded, stopping beside Rahel at the bottom of the dais.

As if he had the right. As if he were captaining this ship.

"One pikamet radiation signature, unknown source." Lokomorra spoke for her, saving her the loss of face.

"Captain, the Alsean war council is standing by for further information. I'm linking in with the *Victory* and *Thea* now." Her comm officer tapped his control panel.

The two captains appeared next to the green marker buoy.

"Anybody have a clue?" Kabbai asked.

"It's big," Captain Teriyong said. "A destroyer would be coming through by now. This is a heavy cruiser or bigger." She was breathless and out of uniform, her short, gray hair darkened with sweat and sticking up in all directions.

Ekatya sympathized. She hadn't dared indulge in a good workout for two days, afraid of being caught with her pants down. Teriyong had taken a chance and was paying for it.

Kabbai scratched his beard. "I don't like it. They know something. They're early, they're opening the battle with a single ship, this isn't—"

"Interspace portal opening!"

Ekatya barely heard the announcement. She was too focused on the flare of light and the long, boxy shape sliding through.

"What in all the galaxies—that's not a Voloth ship," Teriyong said.

"Oh, no," Ekatya breathed as she recognized the silhouette. "Lieutenant Scarp, prepare to take us to the minefield. All fighters—"

"Belay that order!" Admiral Greve glared up at her. "Stick to the battle plan, Captain!"

She pointed at the display. "That is an icebox! Don't you see what they're doing? They're taking the minefield out of the equation!"

Greve scowled. "Explain."

"Three iceboxes taken before we went to Tlahana Station. One more after. It wasn't pirates or even mercenaries, it was the Voloth military. They're going to send four iceboxes through and let every one of our mines explode against empty, sacrificial ships. Our battle plan is useless."

It was simple, low-tech, and ingenious. They had turned stolen ships into minesweepers. Attracted by the pikamet radiation, the mines would swarm each ship as it came through. Iceboxes presented an enormous surface area; four of them would attract enough mines to render the field functionally inert. The few mines that remained unexploded would present no danger to the Voloth ships when they emerged.

Already the first explosions were starting, tiny bursts of light against the ship's shields.

"We could send the safe code," Teriyong suggested. "Fool the mines into thinking the iceboxes are ours. Then reactivate them before the Voloth come through."

"That won't work," Lokomorra said. "The mines won't accept the code from us. It has to be from the ship they're targeting."

"And I guarantee you that ship is rigged to detect any transmissions from us and send them straight back to their fleet in base space," Ekatya added. "If we try to disable the mines, we'll be giving them the key to our front door."

"Blow up the iceboxes before the mines can?" Kabbai offered. "That would preserve the field."

"No, it wouldn't." Teriyong distractedly passed a hand through her disheveled hair, making it worse. "Whether the mines take out those ships or we do, the result is the same. Four fusion core explosions will clear the space."

"She's right," Ekatya said. "We're better off letting the mines do the work. At least that will buy us a little time." She strode down the ramp and stopped in front of Greve. "We can't use our battle plan," she said in a low voice. "Everything was predicated on the mines as a first defense. The *Phoenix* needs to stand with the *Victory* and the *Thea*, or they may be hopelessly outgunned once the real battle begins."

"We spent almost two months gaming this out, Captain. We will not change our tactics at the last second on your say-so."

She could not believe he would carry his vendetta this far. "This isn't about me or whatever traitorous scheme you think I'm hatching. This is about not leaving those ships to fight alone!"

"May I remind you that I am in charge of this battle group," he snarled. "Not you! And I say we stick to the plan that has the greatest chance of success."

She glanced up at the display. The icebox was fully engaged now, its shields outlined by explosions.

"We have seconds to decide," she said. "You need—"

"*You* need to shut up and stop questioning me."

Her temper snapped. "I refuse to watch two loyal crews go up in flames because you can't handle being *irrelevant*. You don't know what you're doing and I won't let you put lives at risk just to inflate your ego!"

Straightening, he crossed his hands behind his back and lifted his chin, a dignified stance at odds with his red face. "Captain Serrado," he said loudly. "Hold your position and engage the enemy when they have cleared the minefield. We will proceed according to the established battle plan. That is an order."

And there it was. She had known all along, hadn't she? Sholokhov had said it, if not in so many words: Greve had no power over her unless she gave it to him. Disobeying his direct order, in front of the entire bridge and two watching captains, would give him all the power he could want.

Her next words would end her career in Fleet.

"Admiral Greve—"

"I'm sorry to interrupt," Rahel said, stepping between them. "Admiral, there's something you should know about Captain Serrado."

His furious glare turned expectant. "Your timing could be better, First Guard. What is it?"

She moved so quickly that Ekatya could never recall the exact sequence of events. One moment Rahel was standing there, the next she had him in a chokehold with an injector pressed to his throat.

"She's my oath holder," she growled.

The injector hissed.

He tried to speak, but managed no more than a groan before slumping in her arms. With startling care, she lowered him to a supine position, even making sure his head didn't impact. Then she straightened and held her arms away from her body.

"It's an Alsean sedative," she called out, opening her hand. The injector clattered to the deck in the shocked silence. "He's unharmed, but you have no counteragent aboard. Captain Serrado is in charge of this battle group."

Ekatya stood dumbfounded, unable to believe what she had just witnessed.

On the display, the icebox's shields failed. New explosions began to tear its hull apart.

"Uh. Captain?" Lieutenant Kitt ventured. "We're getting a second pikamet reading."

"Understood." The automatic response unlocked her brain. "Do you realize what you've done?"

Rahel unclipped the stave holster from her belt and offered it on an open palm. "I submit myself to your authority, Captain. I ask only that you understand the law I'm obeying. My oath is to Alsea first. We need you to lead this battle."

She accepted the weapon. It was heavier than she expected, a weight that recalled Rahel's words from bare minutes ago.

I wouldn't give it to just anyone.

Rahel had sensed her intent. She had known Ekatya was about to disobey orders. By stepping in to prevent it, she had traded away her own career in Fleet.

Ekatya could almost admire the poetic tragedy of it. Her disobedience was years in the making, a long journey that had prepared her for the inevitable outcome. It was time. She was ready to leave the institution that had never stopped punishing her for making the right choice—and for the choice she had not made. Though she hadn't asked for a tyree bond, Fleet acted as if its mere existence was treachery.

Rahel was on a very different journey. How many times had she called this her dream? Yet Ekatya had no option but to confine her. She needed to follow every rule now to have any chance of saving her later.

Unless . . .

Her hand tightened around the stave as an idea struck. "Serrado to Dr. Wells, send a gurney to the bridge. Admiral Greve has been dosed with an Alsean sedative."

"Acknowledged."

She caught the eye of the lieutenant at the security station. "I assume you've informed Commander Cox?"

"Yes, Captain. He's on his . . . way," he finished as the lift doors opened and Cox stepped out.

Ekatya waved him over. "Lieutenant Scarp, prepare to take us to the minefield. Line us up with the *Victory* and the *Thea* in a delta-prime formation."

"Acknowledged." The stars moved around them as the *Phoenix* began to turn.

"Weapons, launch all fighters. Tell them to hold position for now."

"Launching fighters, aye, Captain."

Tuning out the sound of barked orders, she faced the astonished captains on the display. "Captain Kabbai, Captain Teriyong, your primary objective is unchanged. Fire first and fire hard. I expect two more iceboxes after this one, then the true assault. My weapons teams and fighters will do their best to take down missiles fired toward Alsea, but we have to prioritize the ships."

They responded with a crisp acknowledgment that told everyone watching who was in command. The mood of the bridge settled, a low hum resuming as officers made their preparations.

Cox straightened after checking Greve's pulse. "Your orders, Captain?"

"First Guard Sayana has sedated the admiral in accordance with a higher oath than the one she swore to me. Given that she has chosen to observe Alsean law above Fleet regulations, her Fleet rights and duties are hereby suspended. Get her off my bridge. I want her deported to Alsea at the first opportunity."

His eyes narrowed. "Yes, Captain. First Guard, please come with me."

Crossing her arms, Ekatya held the stave against her chest.

It would look like a disapproving stance on the security record, but Rahel received the message. She dipped her head in a faint nod and followed Cox off the bridge.

Ekatya walked back up the ramp to her command chair, secured the stave in the compartment beneath her console, and hit the all-call.

"This is Captain Serrado. Our situation has changed."

Read the conclusion of this story in…

ALSEA RISING
THE SEVENTH STAR

GLOSSARY

UNITS OF TIME

piptick: one hundredth of a tick (about half a second).

tick: about a minute (50 seconds).

tentick: ten ticks.

hantick: ten tenticks, just shy of 1.5 hours (83.33 minutes). One Alsean day is twenty hanticks (27.7 hours) or 1.15 days.

moon: a basic unit of Alsean time, similar to our month but 36 days long. Each moon is divided into four parts called **ninedays**. One Alsean moon equals 41.55 stellar (Earth) days.

cycle: the length of time it takes the Alsean planet to revolve around their sun (thirteen moons or approximately seventeen stellar months).

Alsean days are divided into quarters, each five hanticks long, which reset at the end of the eve quarter. The quarters are: **night, morn, mid, and**

eve. A specific hantick can be expressed in one of two ways: its place in the quarter or its exact number. Thus morn-three would be three hanticks into the morning quarter, which can also be expressed as hantick eight (the five hanticks of the night quarter plus three of the morning). In the summer, the long days result in sunrise around morn-one (hantick six), lunch or midmeal at mid-one (hantick eleven), dinner or evenmeal at eve-one (hantick sixteen), and sunset around eve-five (hantick twenty).

UNITS OF MEASUREMENT

pace: half a stride.

stride: the distance of a normal adult's stride at a fast walk (about a meter).

length: a standard of distance equaling one thousand strides (about a kilometer).

GENERAL TERMS

ADF: Alsean Defense Force.

AIF: Alsean Investigative Force.

bana: an endearment between lovers or bondmates.

block: the emotional equivalent of fingers in the ears; a mental protection that prevents one from sensing another's emotions.

bondmate: a life partner.

cinnoralis: a tree valued for its aromatic leaves (which are dried and burned for relaxation purposes) and the rich, brown color of its wood, used in woodworking and carpentry.

cintek: the Alsean monetary unit.

crateskate: a motorized platform for easily moving large crates or heavy equipment.

dartfly: a small, bloodsucking fly known for its speed and agility.

deme: honorific for a secular scholar.

dokker: a farm animal similar to a cow. Slow moving and rather stupid, but with a hell of a kick when it's angry or frightened.

dokshin: vulgar term for dokker feces.

empath (low, mid, high): the three measured levels of Alsean empathic sensitivity. Low empaths normally detect emotions only through skin contact. Mid empaths can detect emotions without touch, but only at short distances. High empaths can sense emotions at significant distances and are also capable of projecting emotions onto others.

evenmeal: dinner.

Fahla: the goddess of the Alseans, also called Mother.

fairy fly: a pollinating insect famous for its camouflaging ability and gossamer wings.

fanten: a farm animal similar to a pig, used for meat.

front: a mental protection that prevents one's emotions from being sensed by another. Selective emotions can be fronted; a "perfect front" refers to a protection so solid that no emotions can be sensed at all.

gender-locked: an Alsean who is unable to temporarily shift genders for the purposes of reproduction. Considered a grave handicap, denying the individual the full blessing of Fahla.

grainbird: a small, black-and-red bird common in agricultural fields. It is known for singing even at night, leading to an old perception of the birds as lacking in intelligence—hence *grainbird* is also a slang term for an idiot.

grainstem powder: powder derived from the crushed stems of a particular grain, which yields a sweet taste. Commonly used in cooking; also used to sprinkle over fresh bread.

hairgrass: a tall grass covered with soft, silky hairs.

hangers: the middle echelon in the Voloth Empire, higher than slaves but much lower than citizens.

holcat: a small, domesticated feline.

hornstalk: a thorny, fast-growing weed.

horten: an Alsean delicacy, often used in soup. It comes from a plant that, once harvested, stays fresh for a very short time and must be processed immediately.

hyacot: a tree whose twigs, when snapped, provide a pleasant and long-lasting scent. Used in fine restaurants and as a room freshener.

joining: sexual relations. Joining is considered less significant than Sharing between lovers. The two acts can take place simultaneously, though this would only occur in a serious relationship.

leafthrum: a large, arboreal insect known for its nocturnal mating calls, which can be heard at great distances.

losslyn: the Alsean male reproductive organ, which takes five days to produce a sperm packet. The name means "hidden seed," referring to the fact that a losslyn is rarely visible except during a creation ceremony.

magtran: a form of public transport consisting of a chain of cylindrical passenger carriers accelerated by magnetic fields through transparent tubes.

marmello: a sweet, orange fruit.

midmeal: lunch.

molwine: the curved apex of the pelvic ridges on both male and female Alseans. A very sensitive sexual organ.

molwyn: Fahla's sacred tree. It has a black trunk and leaves with silver undersides. A molwyn grows at the center of every temple of decent size.

moonbird: a bird with brilliant courtship feathers that it spreads to impress a mate. Also engages in a graceful courtship dance.

mornmeal: breakfast.

mountzar: a large, carnivorous animal that lives at high elevations and hibernates during the winter.

palm touch: the standard greeting among Alseans in which two people touch their hands together, palm to palm, at eye level. The skin contact allows an exchange of emotions regardless of empathic sensitivity. It is impossible to lie during a palm touch. A **double palm touch** is done only among very close friends or family.

panfruit: a common breakfast or dessert fruit, with an orange skin and blood-red pulp.

Pit (the): Alsea's highest security prison, consisting of five underground levels. It is reserved for empathic offenders; the underground location prevents outside contact and weak points. The worst, most violent offenders are housed in the fifth level.

posthead: heavy wooden mallet used for driving stakes without splintering them.

probe: to push beyond the front and read emotions that are not available for a surface skim. Probing without permission is a violation of Alsean law.

rajalta: a spicy drink made by adding toasted seeds to shannel. A famous Whitesun specialty.

reader card: a portable computing device composed of a flexible material that rolls into a cylinder and tucks into a pouch worn at the belt. Reader cards unroll and stiffen into a sheet for use, then relax and roll back up for storage.

Return: the passage after death, in which an Alsean returns to Fahla and embarks on the next plane of existence.

Rite of Ascension: the formal ceremony in which a child becomes a legal and social adult. The Rite takes place at twenty cycles, after which one's choice of caste cannot be changed.

sallgreen: a tree with prickly, needlelike leaves that have a pungent fragrance when crushed.

sansara: asexual.

shannel: a traditional hot drink, used for energy and freshening one's breath. Made from the dried leaves (and sometimes flowers) of the shannel plant.

skim: to sense any emotions that an Alsean is not specifically holding behind her or his front.

Sharing: the act of physically connecting the emotional centers between two or more Alseans, resulting in unshielded emotions that can be fully accessed by anyone in the Sharing link. It is most frequently done between lovers or bondmates but is also part of a bonding ceremony (in which all guests take part in a one-time Sharing with the two new bondmates). It can also be done between friends and family, or for medical purposes.

shek: vulgar slang for penetrative sex. Usually used as a profanity.

sonsales: one who is empathically blind.

Termegon Fields: the home of the Seeders, according to Voloth belief.

tintinatalus: a tree with silver wood used in woodworking.

torquat: a slimy, swamp-dwelling mammal that has expanded to numerous worlds in the Protectorate due to its ability to thrive in sewer systems. Often used as a pejorative.

tyrees: Alseans whose empathic centers share a rare compatibility, which has physiological consequences. Tyrees can sense each other's emotions at greater distances than normal, have difficulty being physically apart, and are ferociously protective of each other. Tyrees are always bonded, usually for life.

vallcat: a large, solitary feline species, striped for camouflage in the open grasslands they inhabit. Vallcats are known for their strength and ferocity, though they do not attack Alseans unless provoked.

warmron: an embrace. Warmrons are shared only between lovers, or parents and children—and then just until the child reaches the Rite of Ascension. A warmron is too close to a Sharing for it to be used at any other time.

winden: a large six-toed mammal, adapted to an alpine environment. It is wary, able to climb nearly sheer walls, and the fastest animal on Alsea. Winden travel in herds and are rarely seen.

winterbloom: a small, low-growing plant that flowers in the cold seasons. Its leaves have a fresh, invigorating scent.

wristcom: a wrist-mounted communication device, often used in conjunction with an earcuff.

zalren: a venomous snake.

Published by Heartsome Publishing
Staffordshire
United Kingdom

ISBN: 978-1-912684-85-4
First Heartsome edition: July 2020

Book cover design by ebooklaunch.com
Molwyn tree illustration by João T. Tavares/GOBIUS

ABOUT THE AUTHOR

Fletcher DeLancey is an Oregon expatriate who left her beloved state when she met a Portuguese woman and had to choose between home and heart. She chose heart. Now she lives in the beautiful, sunny Algarve and is retraining her green thumb from wet Oregon gardening to survive-a-Mediterranean-summer gardening (and thinks about writing a new book: *How I Learned to Love Succulents*).

She is best known for her science fiction/fantasy series Chronicles of Alsea, which has so far collected an Independent Publisher's Award, a Golden Crown Literary Society Award, a Rainbow Award, and been shortlisted twice for the Lambda Literary Award. She has also been awarded the Alice B. Medal in recognition of career achievement.

Fletcher believes that women need far more representation in science fiction and fantasy, and takes great pleasure in writing complex stories with women heading up the action. Her day is made every time another reader says, "I didn't think I liked science fiction, but then I read yours."

All about Alsea: alseaworld.com

facebook.com/fletcherdelanceyauthor

twitter.com/AlseaAuthor

goodreads.com/FletcherD

amazon.com/author/fletcher

ALSO BY FLETCHER DELANCEY

Made in the USA
Monee, IL
23 August 2020